The Lands of Forever

Ruth Anne Meredith

Illustrated by Dian M. Bagent

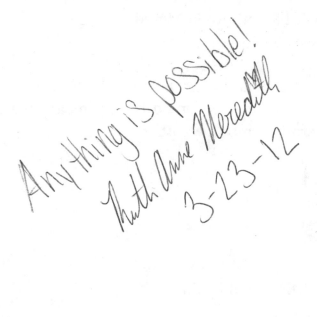

Anything is possible!

Ruth Anne Meredith

3-23-12

ISBN 978-1-61225-088-5

Published by Mirror Publishing
Milwaukee, WI 53214
www.pagesofwonder.com

Printed in the USA

To my beautiful mother, Mary Meredith, who taught me that "fantasies are always free."

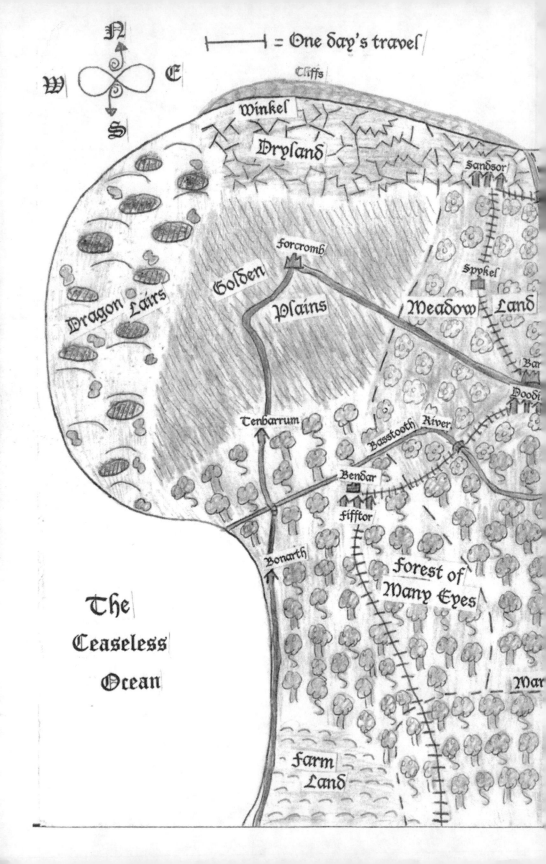

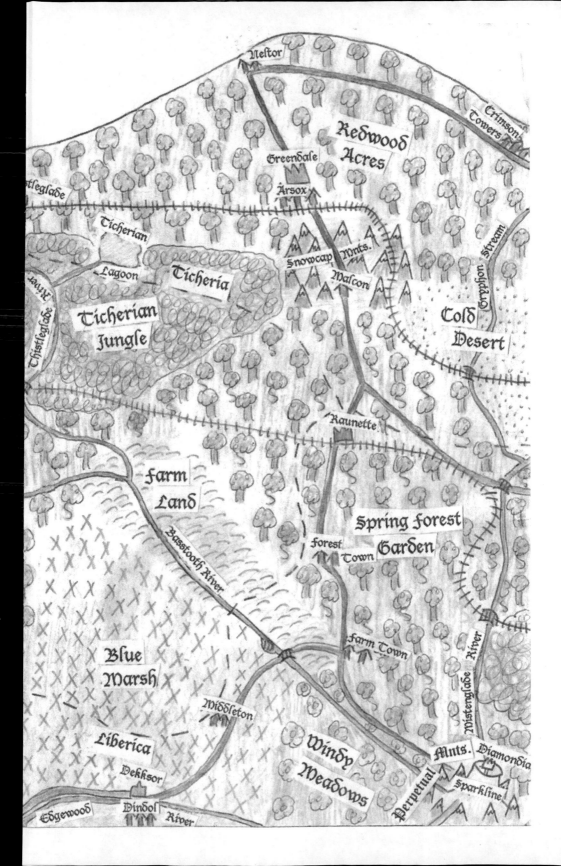

Table of Contents

The Map..4-5

Author's Note..8

Prologue..13

Part One: At Home..21

Chapter One: The Diary..21

Chapter Two: Clever Girl..27

Chapter Three: The Team..33

Chapter Four: Bonding Moments...40

Chapter Five: Anchors Aweigh..45

Chapter Six: The Wavequeen..50

Chapter Seven: Getting There is Half the Fun...58

Chapter Eight: The Lost Continent...67

Chapter Nine: Humble Beginnings...73

Part Two: The Lands of Forever...79

Chapter Ten: Dragon Eggs...79

Chapter Eleven: The Dragons' Lairs and the Hippogryph.....................................88

Chapter Twelve: The Halfbreed and the Frogstorm...97

Chapter Thirteen: The Lands of Forever...104

Chapter Fourteen: Thunder Giants...113

Chapter Fifteen: The Golden Plains...120

Chapter Sixteen: Mosslyn...131

Chapter Seventeen: CatEagles and Unicorns..139

Chapter Eighteen: Follow the Rainbow..146

Chapter Nineteen: Well-earned Rewards..158

Chapter Twenty: As Bombs Burst..167

Chapter Twenty-One: Chains..176

Chapter Twenty-Two: Dawn..188

Chapter Twenty-Three: Escape..198

Chapter Twenty-Four: Over the River and Through the Woods............................206

Part Three: The Heart of Forever...214

Chapter Twenty-Five: The Grandiloquent Prince...214

Chapter Twenty-Six: Fort Bendar..223

Chapter Twenty-Seven: Departure...228

Chapter Twenty-Eight: The Forest of Many Eyes..237

Chapter Twenty-Nine: The Boulder Tribe Campgrounds....................................246

Chapter Thirty: Forest Traveling...253
Chapter Thirty-One: The Sirrush's Den......................................264
Chapter Thirty-Two: Secrets...272
Chapter Thirty-Three: Eht Eulb Hsram......................................279
Chapter Thirty-Four: Marsh Troubles...287
Chapter Thirty-Five: Haunted Spirits...293
Chapter Thirty-Six: Lonvirc's Chamber.......................................302
Chapter Thirty-Seven: The Legend of the Blue Marsh......................311
Chapter Thirty-Eight: Life Goes On...316
Chapter Thirty-Nine: An Old Friend Returns.................................323
Chapter Forty: Melabon of Middleton...329
Chapter Forty-One: Magic...337
Chapter Forty-Two: Turtleback Travel..342
Chapter Forty-Three: The Windy Meadows...................................349
Chapter Forty-Four: Little Angels...355
Chapter Forty-Five: Nothing is Impossible in Forever.......................361
Chapter Forty-Six: The Mountains..366
Chapter Forty-Seven: To the Peak..372
Chapter Forty-Eight: Suspicions..378
Chapter Forty-Nine: On Pegasus' Wings......................................383
Chapter Fifty: Forever Forever..391
Chapter Fifty-One: The Heir to the Throne...................................398
Chapter Fifty-Two: The Heart of Forever.....................................406
Chapter Fifty-Three: Home...414
Epilogue...419
Acknowledgements..423
The Lands of Forever Trivia..424
The Lands of Forever Trivia Answers 426

When I was 16 years old, I was a nerd.

There's really no other way to explain my position better.

Yes, I was a nerd. I read all the time, hardly talked to anybody, was the winner of a few spelling bees, wore my tanglesome blonde hair in a scrunchy and looked at people through circular glasses that I'm sure magnified my blue eyes by at least 25 percent. I must have looked hideous.

But at 16, I wasn't really concerned about looks, like all the other girls. I was a little different. I had discovered my talent.

All Creatures have a talent.

Some can sing, some can dance, some are ingeniously smart, and some are skilled at making things with their hands.

The talent of writing is one that the penman (or woman, in this case) must love. After all, when the ideas come to you when you're preoccupied with another important duty, such as driving, you learn to appreciate the talent. This book is the proof of it. When I turned 16 (and I was more than a little preoccupied with schoolwork), I decided to write a series of children's fantasy novels. But first, I needed my own Land.

I know, the word "Land" isn't supposed to be capitalized because it's a common noun. And it isn't a typo – I meant to capitalize the word, because that is my writing style. Please don't be alarmed at other words you may find capitalized in the following text; I have chosen to do this on purpose to differentiate these things as being specifically Foreveran, not belonging to another World.

There I was, 16 years old, skinny as a pole with jungle-like curls, wide, nerdy glasses and a blue Paper-Mate pen. Aspiring to write a great novel, I was absolutely clueless as to where I should begin.

So where does one start when looking for a good idea?

Nowhere, that's where. Because when that sparking little idea comes, it wants to make sure you are not ready for it.

Then the idea came to me, like God Himself had whispered the name into my ear on that dark and chilly spring evening on a rickety old school bus coming home from a track meet, where not a single shredded scrap of paper or a single pen was available to my tingling, cold fingers.

Forever!

The word forever is a magical term to the race of man. We like the way it sounds, and what it means. Forever is neverending, perpetual, everlasting, infinite, and ceaseless. Forever has always been here, and it always will.

The Lands of Forever is a Magical World. She consists of one main Continent with nine known IsLands. Respectively, their names are: the Serpent's Isle, Blacktail IsLand, Eedarnis IsLand, Morning IsLand, Skeletos Isle, Carnivore IsLand, Evening IsLand, Jarnis IsLand, and the Mysterious Isle. The latter of the nine is an IsLand that changes its Landscape and its shape daily, spins slowly, and completely encircles the inLand Continent once a year.

It is in a great Ocean that the main Continent of Forever and all of her splendid little IsLands reside. The Ocean is called the Ocean Ceaseless, and it is surrounded thickly by great, fluorescent Mists. These Mists are known as the Endless Mists. Every 100 years, Forever descends down from her place in the Sky (for she is the North Star) and lands in the Atlantic Ocean. The Endless Mists are selectively permeable, which means that they choose which travelers may enter the Lands of Forever while they are on Earth, and which may not. Those who may will enter a great Storm with electric blue Lightning, and pass a large bubble called the Shield. Those who cannot will simply pass into the Mists and be transported to the other side, without even knowing what happened.

All Rivers in Forever run backwards – inLand that is – and in the very middle of the mainLand is a great Mountain range (dubbed the Perpetual Mountains) that cradle one vast, gargantuan Mountain made completely of Jewels and precious Stones. It is up the sides of this hollow Mountain (which is called Sparkline Mountain) that all the Rivers of Forever melt together, defying the law of gravity to pour into the enormous pit that is carved from out of the very center of the Mountain. The Water, in its descent up the Mountainside, also collects small Jewels (called the Jewels of Infinity) from the Mountain itself, and carries them up over the sides to create a great circular Waterfall. This Waterfall is called the Neverending Falls. Inside the hollow Mountain, far, far below the Mist forms a massive Lake, which has never been seen because of the thick, dense Mists that shroud it out of sight. Thus, the Lake is named the Misty Lake.

It is up through the middle of these Mists that a long, thick stem grows and flattens at the top into a platform. On this platform is carved the largest, most beautiful Castle that noCreature, alive or dead, has ever imagined.

9

The stem, platform, and Castle itself are all made of pure, smooth Diamond, making the place completely translucent. The Castle is named the Diamondia Castle, and on its tallest tower there is perched a great Diamond, the size of a Dragon's egg (about two feet tall and one foot wide). This Diamond, called the Eternal Diamond, is the source of all Magic in Forever. The whole Castle also spins very slowly, and is the largest structure in Forever. The Diamondia Castle is where the Mother of Forever – the ruler of all of Forever and her Lands – resides.

But the long stem that grows up out of the Mist is special for another reason (other than bearing the magnificent Diamondia Castle). It, like the Sparkline Mountain, is also hollow, and it's through the hollow center that, for a second time, the Waters of the Misty Lake defy gravity and carry themselves, as well as the Magical Jewels of the Mountain, up into Diamondia Castle. Inside the Castle, in the largest, most grand chamber in the whole place, is the Fountain of Youth.

Ponce De Leon, in his travels, claims to have found the legendary Fountain of Youth, which he did, *when he was in Forever*. But, when he decided he wanted to leave Forever, the Mists were too smart to let him tell of the existence of their forgotten Continent, and promptly ripped out every memory he gained while in the Lands of Forever before he left. But, there was one thing they forgot to erase - the name of the Magical Fountain: The Fountain of Youth.

The Fountain of Youth is a great Diamond Fountain, the most beautiful Spring in all of Forever. Its Waters (called Spring Water) are sweet and clear, and can turn ordinary dirt into Jewels. Many have tried to steal Jewels from it, and, in fact, many have succeeded, only to find that once they are beyond the point where the Rivers defy gravity their Jewels have crumpled into useless dirt. This is how the Magical Jewels stay within their origin.

The Spring Water can also heal any and every type of sickness or wound, and can reduce age in an instant. It's the main reason that the Lands are named Forever - because it's very possible that, if a Creature were to drink of its Spring Water every 10 or 20 years to reduce age, that he or she could live forever. Yet, it is a hassle for most Foreverans to climb the Mountains that surround the Sparkline Mountain, to board a Pegasus and fly to the Diamondia Castle. There are many dangers lurking in the Perpetual Mountains, waiting to prey upon helpless travelers. However, most Foreverans do sojourn to the Fountain of Youth at least once in their life.

The inhabitants of these Lands come in all shapes and sizes; there are Elves, Brownies, Dwarves, Gnomes, Nymphs, Pixies, Colored Humans (separated into groups of red Fire Humans, white Sun Humans, black Earth Humans, yellow Gold Humans, orange Sand Humans, green Spring Humans, and violet Night Humans), Dragons, Unicorns, MerMaids, Fauns, etc. There lives a vast array of every kind of Creature imaginable on this hidden Continent, even Dinosaurs, - although none of the Carnivores live anywhere else other than on Carnivore IsLand.

Most Creatures in the Lands of Forever believe in a God called the Creator. Their religion is more transcendental and less structured since they don't have a holy scripture or tales of prophets and Jesus in the history of Forever. But, like all Creatures, they feel very much a part of something bigger than themselves and the nature of Forever.

Depending on the culture of a Creature, they may humble themselves to the Creator through worship services in cathedrals, celebrations, or solitary walks in the Woods. Those who are most diligent pray often to the Creator in a fashion much similar to Christianity. The personality of Forever is the Creator, which created all Creatures. Their philosophical proof of a higher, supernatural and all-powerful being is the concept of Magic in Forever.

The Creatures of Forever may also possess a hereditary gift of Magic. There are five levels of Magical Creatures in Forever: FiveStar, FourStar, ThreeStar, TwoStar, and OneStar Magical Creatures. FiveStars are generally only those Creatures who are extremely Powerful, such as Sorcerers, some Witches and Warlocks, and the Mother of Forever. FourStars are Creatures with less Magical ability, usually Brownies and Elves. ThreeStars are Creatures with lesser Magical abilities than FourStars. TwoStars are Creatures who barely have any kind of hereditary Magic, such as the ability to speak in thought. OneStar Magical Creatures can be anyCreature who wields something instrumental when performing Magic, such as using a bottled Charm, Alicorns from Unicorns or Pixie Powder to fly. Creatures that have no hereditary Magical talent are called Starless Magical Creatures.

Languages and dialects vary across the Lands in Forever, just as they do on Earth. All Foreverans know at least part of the English language - though some speak with an accent (usually British), - because they regularly need a universal language to communicate between different species. Certain species have their own languages, and some written languages exist that are based off the English alphabet.

Forever has Mountains and Meadows, Prairies and Forests, Lakes, Deserts, and Jungles, just as our World has toDay. Some of her primary features include the backwards-running Rivers, the tall Redwood Trees, the Magical Banyan Trees (which grow every type of fruit, berry and nut known to the Foreverans all in the same Tree), the invincible Spirits (SeaLores, MountLores, TreeLores, CaveLores, and SkyLores), spinning Castles, singing Trees, flying ships, a Land where noCreature ever grows any older, and the great Diamondia Castle itself.

The inLand Continent of Forever has 12 separate Realms. Their names are Zorna Realm, Bartle Realm, Thunderia Realm, Youngland Realm, Aquaria Realm, Mistendale Realm, Foxwood Realm, Winkel Realm, Ticheria Realm, Liberica Realm, Belkor Realm, and Marlo Realm. Each Realm has its own special characteristics.

And, no matter how straightforward it may appear, Forever is most certainly *not* your regular fantasy wonderLand. Strange and sometimes dangerous Creatures roam the Forests. Legends of lost treasures and love are passed from family to family. *In Forever, anything is possible.*

I hope you enjoy reading this book as much as I had fun composing it.

Sincerely,

A nerdy but successful author,

Ruth Anne Meredith

Prologue

Twist, over, under, through. Spin and pull. Spin and pull. Twist, over, under, through…

Teresa Gordon, a young British girl on the good ship Cloudsail, sat on the second deck crocheting a blanket for her mother. The year was 1802, and she was quite excited about her quest to America at the young age of 16. She sat up straight as she smelled dawn approaching, closed her eyes and savored the aroma of morning mist and sea. The shady inside of the stuffy second deck was watched with brown eyes sparkling with pride. It was still dark – the air itself seemed to carry the color gray as she made out the dark figures of the thirty-some exhausted people who had accompanied her and her family (her father, her mother, and her) on their voyage. Somewhere along the deck, a baby turned over restlessly and gave two little hiccups of warning before crecendoing into a cry. The mother of the child awoke and took the baby in her arms. The ship creaked and grunted, swaying on the ocean from side to side like the young mother slowly rocking her newborn child. An icy breeze drifted down the stairs from the top deck. Teresa smiled at the crisp, cool air, loving every bit of it.

The poor girl hadn't been able to sleep with all of the creaking timbers (for the Cloudsail was indeed quite old), and the endless snoring and sounds of people deep in slumber. Thus she had crept over to a specific wall of the second deck, where she had discovered for herself her very own porthole, and begun to weave together her yarns for her mother's birthday present. She

13

liked the sound of rolling ocean waves, and the sweet, cool breeze that wafted through the porthole. Her lantern was turned down low and partially covered with fabric, so as not to disturb the slumberers. From the graying glow that seeped through the thin material, Teresa worked on until dawn, never once suspecting what would become of her.

Late morning brought dull, gray clouds and no sun. The winds had begun to pick up speed, and everywhere on the ship sailors strived to batten down hatches and tie up the sails - for they knew a good storm when it was brewing.

Teresa stood, her light, brown curls bouncing beside her rosy cheeks.

"What's happening above this deck, Mother?" she inquired, approaching a woman cladden in a wrinkled, crimson-red dress.

Mrs. Gordon lit a lantern and held it up next to her daughter's face, for the light below deck was still dim in the late morning clouds.

"A storm is coming," Mr. Gordon answered calmly, stepping down the last of the few stairs that led to the top deck. "And a dreadfully large one at that. Funny, somehow I have never seen such an odd storm in my life!"

He stroked his bristling brown mustache and sat beside his daughter and wife on a wooden box. Teresa watched her mother's pale complexion from under the flickering lantern light. A small rumble of conversation was growing among the travelers. Teresa watched as a little boy ran crying into his father's arms, and an older group of boys gathered to peek outside through the stairway opening. Mrs. Gordon straightened, folding up her sleeping blanket and tucking it into her travel bag.

"Oh? How is that so?" she wondered aloud. All around Teresa could hear the people on the ship talking about this strange storm.

"Lightning, my dears," he said in a drastically awing voice. He put his palms before him, staring strangely at the backs of his hands in a very surprised manner. "I've seen it in the distance, flashing before my eyes. Lightning striking the sea. 'Tis almost *spectral* it is so odd!" he exclaimed. He let his hands fall to his lap as he leaned forward and looked his family square in the eye. "There is *never* lightning on the sea unless it strikes a ship, and there are no other ships about as far as Captain Blain knows." he whispered.

Hearing the name of nature in her father's quote, Teresa brightened considerably; her features lit up in delight and she asked,

"Oh, Father! May I go up on deck and see it? Please? May I?"

Mr. Gordon did not miss a beat.

"Of course not, you foolish girl! 'Tis dangerous weather up there – it's only best that you keep down here!"

Teresa frowned, but nevertheless obeyed her father's order.

"Yes, Father." she mumbled and strode off to her abandoned blanket by the wall as her mother and her father began to speak again. But she was no longer interested in their conversation. She seated herself next to the porthole once more, and with a sigh, glanced dismally out of the little opening for an instant. She turned to a clay jug that she had brought with her belongings, and pulled from its open mouth a little canvas diary, a quill and two tiny bottles of ink.

From under the flickering fire light inside her glowing lantern, Teresa opened her diary to one of her last few blank pages, and described the awesome scene that she witnessed through the porthole.

Dear Diary,

Blue lightning, 'tis! There is a tremendous storm outside right now, and I can see from my porthole the delicate strands of metallic blue lightning flashing before my very eyes! The wind is no longer the gentle, misty breeze that wandered through this same porthole earlier this morning. Now it is colder, harsher, and the once-peaceful sea is rising against us in rolling foam-crested tongues. The ship itself is tilting back and forth frantically, maddened by the efforts of the raging wind and sky. It is difficult to write as the ship is moving.

But so calm and beautiful it all was just this morning! I went up on deck before I came down to crochet my mother's birthday gift. It was still dark out when I reached the top deck. When I looked over the railing, I could see nothing but the cream-colored morning mist. I could hear the waves lapping tenderly against the side of the ship, but could not see them.

Jacob Wisten could not sleep either. I wondered as the boy approached me whether he had noticed the several sidelong glances I will often send him when I see him and his friends talking close by. Oh, I do dearly wish he would talk to me!

But of course, he did talk to me up on deck. He said to me,

"Do you see the stars?"

"Yes, they are beautiful, aren't they?" I replied. He leaned lightly

on the railing and flicked a pebble into the ocean. A distant "plunk!" told me that the waters were still there, hiding under their fluffy cotton-white coat of mist.

I hugged my arms, for it was indeed quite chilly in the morning.

"Of course they are. Tell me, Teresa, have you ever star-gazed before?"

Surprised that he even knew my name, I answered,

"Yes, Jacob. But I really do not know any of their names. I don't suppose you would know any of them, would you?"

Flashing me a rather charming smile, Jacob drew me near to him and stood in back of me. Then, with one hand on my shoulder, he leaned forward a bit and pointed at the sky.

So beautiful was that sky, with all its twinkling diamonds knitted into its purest velvety blackness!

Yet again, so beautiful was the voice of Jacob behind me, naming off countless clusters of stars; so many I cannot possibly name them all off again. There were the zodiacs, and the big and little dippers, and so many Roman and Greek constellations! After awhile he stopped and rested his hand on my other shoulder. I looked at him out of the corner of my eye as he went dangerously silent.

"What's the matter?" I whispered as he looked at me.

"That's odd," he puzzled, scratching the top of his black-haired head "I can't seem to find the North Star."

I looked back at the placid sky.

"There aren't any clouds out tonight, either. Why do you suppose 'tisn't out there?" I wondered aloud.

"Oh, I know it's still out there," he said, staring faithfully into the inky blackness. "It's probably just hiding from us at the moment."

And so we went on to tell each other of our families and why we were traveling to America. It turns out that he is a sailor, looking for a career in the U.S. army. I chided him about the funny-looking uniforms they had to wear, but he got me right back by stating that I wouldn't fit into one if I tried, I was so short. We giggled and jabbed each other in the ribs a little more before I turned to leave, because I was getting quite cold up on the deck. The wind was beginning to pick up a little, and the ship was tilting ever so slightly more from side to side.

But he stopped me, and wrapped his large, heavy cloak around *me.*

> *"Thank you!" I whispered, and he beckoned me to stay. I needed no second bidding. The moonlight shone off his smooth, black hair, as dark and calming as the night itself. His large, brown eyes were star lit and dreamy looking. He stood and smiled at me, noticing my admiration of him. I looked away blushing.*

> *His finger curled under my chin and he lifted my face to look at him. He brought his own beam-bathed face very close to mine, and said,*

> *"Do you want to know a secret?"*

> *I didn't need anyone to tell me that my face was a brighter red than a fresh-picked strawberry. I nodded slowly. He leaned closer, hesitantly, and he ki*

> *What has happened just now? The ship gave a horrible jerk, forcing my back against the wall and knocking the air from my lungs! Oh, dear, here comes Jacob, and he looks rather urgent! I must go.*

> *~Teresa Gordon~*

Teresa carefully closed her diary and held it to her chest protectively as she soaked in the information that Jacob was revealing to her. She gasped aloud, despite her shortness of air, at the newfound news.

Teresa slipped a pointed hand over her mouth, her large brown eyes opened wide with fright.

"Are you sure?" she asked, unable to control the quivering in her voice. Jacob nodded, looking about nervously. People from the top deck were darting down to the second deck, rushing about and frantically gathering their families to them. Screams and shrieks of dismay were heard all around.

"No!"

"It cannot be!"

"We shall all perish!"

"Curse this old ship!"

Jacob turned back to Teresa, who stood glassy-eyed and pale.

"Yes, the ship is damaged fatally. I'm afraid we've nothing more to do than to go down with the faithful Cloudsail. Unless…"

He looked at a jutting board further along the wall. He pushed it outward, and, after some consistent yanking, the board snapped, and Jacob held in his hand a splintery plank of wood.

"A raft!" he crowed. Teresa looked up from her diary, which she had opened once more to hurriedly scribble her last message.

"A raft?" she exclaimed. The plan dawned on her like a bucket of bricks had fallen on her head. "Of course, a raft! Oh, Jacob, you're a genius! You must tell our families the idea; my father can help you piece one together!"

"Yes!" he panted. He grabbed the girl and kissed her, and then was gone through the howling crowds. Teresa's father and mother found her.

"Pack your things, Teresa!" said her mother in a frightened voice.

"No – 'twon't do any good, now. Best to dress warmly, Mother – Jacob has a plan!"

"*Jacob*? Jacob who?" gruffed her father, bustling with packing food items in his duffel bag.

"*My* Jacob!" said a nearby father, and Teresa's parents flooded over to where Jacob was ripping floorboards and boards off of boxes with help from his parents and friends.

Teresa overcame the sudden shock she had endured, and bustled about tying up her diary with hair ribbons. She enveloped it in a small velvet bag, mummifying it in the last of her boot strings and then trussing it up into a tight, waterproof bundle. She reverently placed it into a wide-mouthed, thick-walled clay jug, and took a cork, pounding it down fast as though she wished for it to never be removed again.

Teresa stayed very calm, ignoring as best she could the thundering of her heart. The next few moments seemed to fly by in slow motion: the lightning illuminating the scene, screams and cries filling the air, and over all, her heart pounding in her ears. She clutched the jug to her chest as she sloshed through the ankle-deep water that was quickly rising. As she approached the steps, the ship gave another lurch, forcing her back. Like lightning, she leapt up the stairs, barely catching herself as the ship tipped back to sink stern first into the deep blue foam of the raging ocean. People on both sides of her scampered about in chaos, wailing, praying, and flooding to the top deck to say their last good-byes to their loved ones.

On the top deck, Teresa spotted Jacob scrabbling about with loosening a board, and next to him were her own father and a few others doing the same.

In revered silence, she walked to the prow of the vessel and whispered,

"God be with you!" to the jug, then flung the object dramatically into the tumbling sea with a cry of departed dismay.

Teresa stood, the rain splattering on her face, the winds making her skirts and her curls fly about frantically, as though trying to join the wind itself in its journey over the roaring seas. She stood on the stem of the Cloudsail, willing her last prayers that the jug would make it safely to the land of America - even if it meant that she herself would not be able to go along. She opened her eyes skyward and looked up at the angry storm clouds that frowned down upon her. Her rosy cheeks were becoming wind burned, as were her nose and forehead. She grasped a bejeweled cross necklace about her neck and closed her eyes, praying with all her might.

Then something extremely odd happened - a strand of blue lightning tore through the blackness and struck her hand. Immediately, her eyes opened in shock, and her hand leaped away from the pendant as though the lightning itself had picked it up and thrust it off. The tip of the lightning then struck the cross pendant, and Teresa was forced to look away from the blinding light. She expected at any moment to be electrocuted, but when nothing happened, she opened her eyes and forced herself to look back at her necklace. One thin tendril of lightning remained, flickering down from the heavens to touch the pendant of her necklace, which was rapidly changing. First, the cross widened and changed from gold to a transparent jewel. Then, it shaped itself into a smooth shape, but was shining so bright that Teresa again had to turn her face away. When she drew up her courage and looked again, she saw that it was a sideways eight sort of character, made out of diamond and held on the chain at the very center. The metallic thread of lightning shrunk into the necklace to flicker forever and more, full of life, and then it withdrew from the sky quickly with an ear-piercing sound that Teresa had never heard before.

~*~*~*~*~

Teresa turned around and found every eye of the floundering immigrants watching her in awestruck wonder. Chaos resumed, and Jacob paddled over to her on his new (and old) craft.

"Are you alright?" he asked immediately. Teresa nodded, still speechless from the strange situation she had been presented with.

"Yes…" she breathed finally, clutching the new necklace that encircled her neck. Jacob removed her hand from the jewel, and gasped when he saw that it had changed.

"Wasn't this the jeweled cross your aunt gave you for your birthday?"

"Yes…" was her stunned reply as she stared deeply into the heart of the beautiful thing. "Yes, it was," she whispered, gingerly stroking the smooth diamond. Teresa smiled at the strange but beautiful object and set it down gently on her chest.

Just as the water began to lap about her toes, Jacob snatched her up and gingerly lowered her onto the floating cluster of boards he had hastily snapped together, and then paddled off with her to join the other survivors of the tragic wreck.

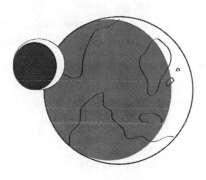

Part One: At Home
Chapter One: The Diary

Obese American Bertha Blackhour pranced the attic of her little house in Springfield, Illinois, muttering dire threats under her breath. Something in the shadows moved, catlike and hardly noticeable. But Bertha was a born hunter, and turned her head slowly to where the something had moved. Hiding a triumphant smirk, she slowly turned on her heel and tip-toed towards the pile of boxes stacked in a corner. Sliding in between two box towers, she pushed aside a curtain and grinned down at her sunbathing feline accomplice, Beauty, with crooked yellowed teeth.

Bertha Blackhour had found the starved black kitten with sunken yellow-green eyes and bent whiskers a pitiful sight on her front doorstep. That pity magnified when the girl that she was rearing found the cat and immediately insisted that they bring her in. So, with what sympathy she could muster up, she allowed the young girl to bring the bedraggled kit inside to warm and feed her by the fire. Now Beauty, as the cat was ever so inappropriately named, was just as fat and evil as Bertha herself, and the two became somewhat attached.

The cat smiled up at her owner with wicked yellow eyes, her happy purr sounding much more like a threatening growl. Bertha didn't need to ask what she wanted of her; Beauty already knew. With a heavy "THUMP!" she landed on the ground from her perch on a box and lumbered into a slow trot. Bertha followed her, a victorious smile hovering on her warty features.

Beauty climbed over a box with a loud cat grunt and leaped onto a heap of blankets that seemed to be flapping in the wind. Bertha looked at the window – it was sealed tight.

The flapping stopped as something beneath the heap of blankets seemed to find a comfortable spot.

Bertha stomped her foot and crossed her arms, putting on her best lecturing frown for special effects.

"Serena!" she thundered. Beauty leaped down from the pile and blithely began to bathe her fat paw. Bertha tapped her foot impatiently as the blankets prepared to erupt.

Suddenly, the head of a pretty blonde-haired girl sprouted from beneath the blankets. She yawned widely and looked sleepily at Bertha.

"I should have known you would be in your bed," snapped Bertha, "sleeping lazily while there's work to be done!"

The skinny 16-year-old-girl, whose name was Serena, shrugged, staring at the ground sadly.

"What didn't I do? I cleaned the kitchen and the bathrooms, vacuumed the basement, dusted the china cabinets, and mowed the front lawn… I got all of my chores done early today, and you said that if I did, I could have a nap."

"I said you *might* earn yourself a nap," growled Bertha, looking the young girl straight in the face with breath that would put a dead skunk to shame. "But I'm not going to get into that now. I came up here to drag you over to some scientist's lab in Chicago."

"Why?" Serena wanted to know. She emerged from her sadly made bed, an attractive young girl dressed in a powder blue T-shirt and bell-bottomed jeans.

Bertha grabbed the girl's wrist and pulled her over to the door.

"Some scientist guy said he found a diary… a 200-year-old diary, mind you, and it was the writer's wishes that the closest of her relatives receive it. They did this little DNA thing with some hair they found of hers, and apparently, you're the only relative she has left. You're related to her uncle's cousin… or something like that."

Serena Gordon almost tripped as Bertha yanked her down the stairs.

"Wow," she mused, catching her balance and trying to fall in step with the short, scuffy steps of her guardian. "What am I going to do with it? Donate it to a museum?"

Bertha stopped abruptly and whirled around in a fly of wispy, course brown hair.

"You'll give it to ME - that's what you'll do with it!" She pointed her blunt, cracked finger at Serena and punctuated each word with an unpleasant poke on the nose. "That diary is worth thousands of dollars – the scientist told me so. Can't you imagine the money we could get out of this? It would be like winning the lottery!" she bellowed dreamily. "We would live in luxury!"

"You mean you would live in luxury," mumbled Serena, slitting her shimmering blue eyes. "And haven't you thought of the sentimental value? Just because I never knew this person doesn't mean I don't care about her! She's the closest I'll ever have to a sister! I want to keep her-"

"You will give it to ME!" seethed Bertha through clenched yellow teeth. Serena almost choked on her foul breath. "...OR ELSE!"

Serena patiently sat in the waiting area. Bertha sat beside her, grunting and leafing through a magazine.

Serena's parents had sadly both died in a car crash on the way home from a party. At the time, little Serena was only 18 months old, and had been left with a babysitter. She had been taken into foster care until she was assigned a legal guardian – the fat, dark woman who called herself Bertha Blackhour. Serena sighed. This horrible woman was her only family. She had no close friends, for she was home-schooled. At the time her parents died, Serena was an only child, as were both of her parents. All of her grandparents had by that time passed away also, leaving only the little blue-eyed baby girl to carry on the family name. She was the last of the Gordon line.

She was a pretty girl with long golden-blonde ringlets and a soft complexion. She had a round, little face and large, almond-shaped blue eyes, with long lashes. A small nose and chin, full lips and youthful cheeks added to the envy of the woman who claimed to be her legal guardian.

Serena bobbed the end of her foot up and down and played with one of her vibrant blonde curls. She pulled the end of it slowly in front of her sky blue eyes, watching it stretch to its full length. Then she let it go, and it bounced back into place, shimmering golden under the light.

She dropped the curl as a man in a white coat and a clipboard appeared in the doorway. He lifted his lab safety goggles, which wasn't hard, for they were far too large and forever falling down his long, beak-like nose.

"Ah, Miss Bertha Blackhour, you are here with young Serena?" he groveled, stopping the goggles from falling over his eyes.

It took about five minutes, it seemed, for Bertha to pry her generous form from the waiting room chair, and a further two to gain her balance and waddle heavily over to the man in the white coat.

Serena sat in the chair and began to play with her curls again, seeing this was a private conversation between guardian and scientist.

A young boy across the room was sitting with his mother, and made it perfectly plain that he had never seen a girl like Serena before. He was about to get up and go talk to her when his mother nudged him.

"Don't stare, Luke," she whispered, "it's rude."

He sulked and allowed his eyes to follow Serena as she got up and strode over to the beckoning scientist.

"Well, now," said the smiling, beak-nosed man, "I hope you understand the value of the diary I am about to present to you."

Serena nodded and smiled politely.

"Yes, sir, I do," she said. She glanced at Bertha and expected her to be beaming with pride at the thought of money, but instead found her scowling as though she had swallowed a raw frog. Serena looked back to the scientist.

"Good." he smirked. "Now, if you'll come with me, I'll show you the diary. And also, I have a surprise for you."

Serena couldn't help but smile giddily at Bertha as she followed the scientist down the hallway. Bertha grunted disapproval and turned to sit down. She was not allowed to follow the scientist and Serena. (She probably wouldn't make it down the thin corridor without becoming stuck anyway.)

She spotted the boy leaning over and staring at the tail-end of Serena's light blonde curls like something resembling a petrified owl. She frowned horribly at him at the same time his mother poked him again, and he looked over at the angry fat woman. He smiled guiltily as a blush arose to his cheeks.

Bertha sighed as she sat down heavily. The chair creaked in protest.

Serena traced the bootlaces and ribbons that lined a spot on the observation table next to the rustic-colored canvas diary. Sitting next to the diary on the table was a rather aged-looking cork broken into several pieces, and a whole clay jug that was very thick and had small, faint, but elegantly painted designs on the side which had been washed and faded from the ocean waters.

"This diary dates back to the 1800's," began the scientist (whose name was Dr. Birkwood) as he pushed his goggles back up onto his nose. "A man that lived on the coast of Florida found the jug with the cork still in it washed up on the beach. He didn't know what was inside, and mistakenly broke the cork taking it out. He found this diary, which was written by a young British girl on her way to America. Her name was Teresa Gordon, and she was about your age, perhaps a bit older, when she wrote it.

"On the inside of the front cover she wrote that should this diary be found, it should be passed down to her closest relative. Well, research from taking a DNA sample from one of her hairs has been done, and you, Serena, are the only descendant in her family line."

Serena felt sentimentally touched. She sighed slowly in wonder as she carefully touched the front of the old diary. Suddenly, a warm feeling of mystery and love sparked up within her. Making to pick it up, she looked at Dr. Birkwood.

"May I?"

"Of course. It is yours, after all," he replied. Serena picked it up gingerly and felt its weight. The cover was made from real canvas, and the inside pages were cut from actual nineteenth century parchment, bound to the cover by a thick, hide-like material. Serena opened the diary, looking at yellowed page after yellowed page of neat cursive writing.

"It's priceless," she whispered, more to herself than to Dr. Birkwood.

"Well, not entirely," said Birkwood. "The diary had been such a discovery that the gift shop downstairs is selling artificial ones. They do look quite authentic, if I do say so myself."

"That's a good idea," Serena smiled. "Who designed them to sell?"

Dr. Birkwood looked genuinely flattered.

"Why, I did, thank you, Miss Gordon!" he said. Serena smiled, looking back at the real diary.

"Excuse me," said a lady scientist at the door, "Miss Gordon, your guardian has gone down to wait in the parking lot. Whenever you're ready, she said you may go down and meet her at the car."

Serena nodded and said thank you, then turned back to Dr. Birkwood.

Sounds just like Bertha to be impatient, she thought.

"Ahem, about the surprise…" said Dr. Birkwood. "We have made arrangements to have you go with a team of explorers to the site where Teresa's ship, called the Cloudsail, wrecked. Our team captain will also be your personal bodyguard, and believes that you and the diary may be important." The scientist stopped to clear his throat, and Serena could tell from the positioning of his body that he was rather nervous - or scared.

"You see, we have recently had two ships completely disappear from the face of the earth at that same spot – vanished without a trace. This has led us to believe that there may be an entirely different continent… an *immortal* continent, perhaps, that is out there and is… swallowing them up…"

Serena stood rooted to the spot. How could two ships simply vanish into thin air and leave behind not a trace of their very existence? Wanting to know more, Serena lowered her eyelids inquisitively and took a step closer, hugging the diary to her chest in the same way her ancestor did 200 years ago.

"Tell me more about this… strange continent…" she said.

Serena's lustrous curls bounced up and down as she walked toward the first floor. She was quite pleased at the praise she had received upon her decision to donate most of the ribbons, all of the boot laces, the broken up cork, and the old jug to scientific study. She kept two ribbons, one a faint pink and the other a worn blue, to tie up the diary like an old schoolbook. She was very excited about the trip she would soon be taking. Thanks to the persuasive words of Dr. Birkwood and Bertha's lifelong will to be rid of the girl, she had been given permission to accompany a discovery team to the Bahamas and then to the spot where the ships had disappeared. He had warned her that the trip would be extremely dangerous should she consent, but Serena saw no reason why she should not strive to discover that which could explain the tragic disappearances of the ships. She smiled. For the first time in her life, she was actually going somewhere without Bertha other than the grocery store.

She skipped down to the first floor and began a sprightly walk to the front door. She stopped stock-still as something caught the corner of her eye. She turned her head slowly as her hand slipped down to the $10 tip the scientist insisted she take for donating the precious items. She smiled at the entrance of the gift area.

Bertha sat snoring loudly in the driver's seat, pausing to cough and snort every now and then.

Tap! *Tap*!

Serena knocked on the window to the passenger's side of Bertha's old junker car.

"Snick! Snuck! HACK! HACK! Huh?" Bertha grumbled, stirring somewhat.

"Bertha! It's me, Serena! Unlock the car!"

Mumbling dark words under her breath, Bertha reached out and unlocked the door. Serena got in with a gift shop bag and the diary hugged tight to her chest.

"I didn't say you could go to the gift shop! Where'd you get the money?" the fat, warty-faced woman demanded. Serena put her seatbelt on as Bertha started the car.

"Dr. Birkwood gave me $10 for donating the ribbons and the jug that the diary was in to scientific study," she explained.

"Oh," the coarse-haired lady grunted. She started the car and sped out of the parking lot, cutting off a green car at the intersection.

Silence.

Then,

"So, I suppose you're excited about getting to go to the Bahamas?" snarled Bertha.

Serena thought, *And the possibility of never having to listen to your selfish demands again…*

"Yes," she said. "Dr. Birkwood said that it was somewhere near there that the boats sank."

Bertha grunted noncommittally.

It was a silent trip home.

Serena's mind was spinning. She had only two days to pack her things and get ready for the big trip. She would take United Air flight 42 from Chicago all the way to the Bahamas. Dr. Birkwood estimated that that particular trip would take about six hours. She was to meet the exploring team in Chicago at a specific hotel, spend the night there and then take a cab to the airport early that morning. Serena could hardly wait.

Bertha screeched to a halt in the driveway of her house. She sat for a moment, watching the hot summer breeze rustle through the prosperous oak tree in her front yard. Then, she turned to Serena.

"Alright, Serena." she growled. "Hand it over." Her quotation was not a question, but a given command.

"H-hand what over?" Serena asked, hugging the diary to her chest and smiling innocently. Her eyes started to grow large and watery as they stared at the ugly woman who had her fat hand held out in expectancy.

"The diary, you brat! Give it here!"

Serena only hugged the diary tighter, all the while willing her eyes to grow larger and her lips to drop from the smile. Her bottom lip quivered as though crestfallen.

"You wouldn't separate a girl and her diary, would-" she squeaked.

"It's not even yours! Give it to me now or I'll call the scientist back right now and deny your permission to go on your little trip!"

"But Bertha, I *need* the diary for the exped-"

"Liar! I would ground you if you weren't already leaving!"

Serena's heart plummeted.

"I'm already grounded," she remarked in a dark tone. At this, Bertha growled and grabbed Serena's long ponytail, pulling it hard.

Tears brimmed in the young girl's eyes as she reluctantly held out the ribbon-tied diary.

Bertha snatched it and released her hair.

And the moment she did, Serena ripped her seatbelt off, gathered up her things and rushed into the house. Through the kitchen, past the living room, up the stairs and into the attic she ran, stopping only when she could throw her gift shop bag down and flop onto her stomach on her bed.

Slowly Bertha made her way up the stairs, the precious diary held as a high prize in one hand.

Serena sobbed as she threw her hands over her face and moaned pitifully. Bertha stopped in the doorway.

"There, there, now. That wasn't so bad, now, was it? You'll feel better when we buy us a nice Jacuzzi," she chirped, then patted the diary like a loving friend.

Serena's back trembled heartbrokenly as the obese woman left, closing the door behind her.

But little did Bertha know that Serena was not stifling sobs – but giggles!

Dr. Birkwood didn't know how long Serena and the exploring team would be investigating the case of the missing ships, and simply encouraged her to pack for a two or three week trip. As a final result, she packed for two and a half. She had two duffel bags full of clothes and other necessities, and a large survival backpack that Dr. Birkwood had sent her through the mail. (He forgot to give it to her while she was at the institution. He was, after all, very excited about her decision to donate the cork, jug, and ribbons to scientific observation.) This she filled with bug spray, a flashlight, some rope, a plastic poncho, a small wallet of money, an extra set of clothing, a warm blanket, and an abundance of food, all of which she swathed in plastic zip-lock baggies.

She sat now in the same waiting room as before with Bertha. Either side of her was a fat duffel bag, and she sat nervously with her large, water-proof knapsack on her lap, waiting for the scientist to come out and assign her to a hotel. Bertha lectured her about the diary shamelessly.

"Now, don't you worry about Tamantha's, or what's her name's, diary – it will be safe with me," she glowered.

"Oh, I'm sure it will," Serena drawled, hiding a snicker with a cough.

"Ahem. Er, Miss Gordon?" said Dr. Birkwood from the door. He pushed his goggles up on his nose again. Serena stood up with her knapsack and walked over to the scientist.

"I'm ready, sir," she said with a pretty smile.

"Ah, if you'll come with me to the back room, I would like to give you a few tools and instructions. Follow me, please."

The skinny, beak-nosed scientist led Serena to a little room at the end of the hallway, where a few select items were laid out on a small table. Dr. Birkwood pushed up his goggles again as he reached for a small square metal object. Those goggles were starting to bother Serena.

"This is a pager. We'll probably page you every once in awhile to check up on your progress."

Serena took the pager and slipped it into the front pocket of her knapsack.

He moved over to a flat-looking black box. He opened the front of the strange box, and revealed several small test tubes. He lifted the bottom of the inside of the box to reveal a little compartment with small canisters, plastic baggies, and little metal tools that looked like miniature spoons, forks, and knives.

"This is a sample kit. If you find any certain dark sand or other substance that is odd or strange-looking, put a little bit of it into these containers so that you can give it back to us when you get back."

He stopped to push his goggles back up again. Then he went on to give her a cell phone, a first aid kit, a flashlight, emergency fireworks, a lighter and some matches for making a campfire, and finally, a small notebook and a ball-point pen.

"If you find something especially interesting or odd, write it down in this notebook. I'll collect it when you return, and perhaps it will help us solve the mystery as to why these ships keep disappearing." He pushed his goggles up for the millionth time and crossed his arms in conclusion. "You'll take a cab to the Peace Night Hotel here in Chicago and go to room 127 on the top floor. The women explorers are expecting you. You'll probably meet the men tomorrow morning if you don't tonight in the lobby. You'll order dinner through room service, I'm sure. All transportation, hotel and food expenses are paid by the scientific institution. I do hope you realize what you're getting into, Miss Gordon."

Serena smiled and nodded quickly, eager to be away from Bertha and her other life. She couldn't wait to board the cab.

"Thank you, Dr. Birkwood." she said, and turned to leave.

"Good luck, Serena!" said the scientist, and his goggles slipped down his nose again. Serena had had enough.

"May I?" she inquired, pointing to the goggles. Shrugging, he took them off and handed them to her. Irritated, she adjusted them and then held them up to the surprised scientist.

"Why, thank you, Miss Gordon," he grinned as he put them on.

"You're welcome."

The flap of the excess rubber band holding the goggles to his face flapped over his eye obnoxiously. Serena nearly shuddered. She was about to help him cut the excess off with a pair of scissors when she looked at her watch.

She handed the scissors to him with a helpful smile.

"Goodbye!" she sang politely, and hurried to catch her cab.

Dr. Birkwood was left standing, inspecting the red-handled scissors. He blew the rubber off of the goggle eye out of the corner of his mouth.

"Now I wonder what she gave me these for?" he mused aloud.

The rubber excess flapped over his eye again.

Bertha stood, both fat feet rooted to the cement slab on the sidewalk. She squinted hard, trying to see just what it was that Serena was waving at her tauntingly from the back window of the cab. Perhaps it was just something of little importance to Bertha, and Serena was goading her with it. The fat woman shrugged carelessly and took her time getting back to her car. That little brat had never meant much to her but trouble anyway.

But what a clever little brat she was! thought Bertha as she started up her car and headed to an antique shop that had offered her a promising reward for giving them the diary.

She remembered when the girl was hardly four years old – she had then gone to a preschool and made several friends while she attended. Then, miraculously, the very day before the girl would start real school, Bertha found her curled up in a corner, sounding out words and reading to herself.

There was no doubt about it; Serena had been a very smart child, and with her electric personality, Bertha had envied every aspect of the pretty girl. Serena had won the heart of all her preschool teachers.

But there was no heart in the fat, dark woman that was her assigned guardian that could be won over. Inspired by this sudden discovery of natural knowledge in the girl, Bertha decided to home school her. Therefore, the child merely taught herself, and it wasfor that same reason she was a very clever girl to that day.

Bertha pulled in to the small parking lot with her signature parking style – right on the line that separated two spaces. Still cackling at her trademark for being evil, Bertha locked the car and grasped the diary to her side.

She sauntered in to the shop, beaming with pride as she approached the front desk.

"Excuse me," she said.

A thin, fine-dressed man with little spectacles perched on his long, slender nose turned and greeted her.

"Good day, ma'am. May I help you?" he asked. His voice trembled in anticipation as he spotted the diary cradled in her arms. He stared shamelessly. "Ah, yes. You must be Miss Bertha Blackhour, with the… the 200 year old diary…" he spoke of the diary in a whisper, almost reverently. He rubbed his hands together, wishing that he could close his fingers around the precious antique.

"Yes. Could you please tell me how much something like this is worth?" Bertha smiled, thinking to herself that this was the first time she had caught herself being polite in years.

The man's fingers quivered uncontrollably as he reached out and accepted the frail-looking item. He did a complete look over of the thing, rustling through the pages, examining the front cover and observing the faded ribbons. But he stopped, staring strangely at the inside of the back cover. He lifted his half-moon spectacles and squinted, then looked up at the awaiting Bertha, who was smiling so much that her fat brown eyes could hardly be seen from underneath her plump dimples. She swayed her big bulk from side to side, expecting some high remark of praise.

But the man furrowed his brow and took off his little spectacles. Tapping furiously at the inside of the back cover with them, he frowned up at Bertha and demanded in a dissatisfied tone,

"Just what kind of game are you trying to play, Miss Blackhour?"

"What?" she replied, outraged. She drew herself to her full height, bristling. "I demand to know how much that diary is worth!"

The man closed the diary and shoved it moodily into Bertha's crossed arms.

"Seven dollars and ninety-nine cents! Get out of my shop!" he growled.

Bertha snorted rudely and opened the diary to the inside of the back cover.

And there was the golden brand, shimmering flawlessly under the dim shop lights. The diary was a fake.

"Why, that clever little brat…" she grumbled under her breath.

Chapter Three: The Team

Serena giggled to herself in the back of the cab. She knew that by now Bertha had figured out that it was the real diary she had waved at her from the cab as it strolled away gallantly.

Now she fell guiltlessly silent, and drew her knees to her chest. She touched the diary and studied it in awe. Then, after revered observation, she opened it and began reading.

It appeared that her ancestor, Teresa, was 16 years old when she wrote the diary, just as Serena was now, and that she was quite excited about her trip to America. Teresa's parents had heard wonderful stories about the prosperous Land of the Free. She was an only child, since the only other sibling she had ever known had suddenly died at four months of age. The poor girl tried hard not to relive those memories, but written deep in the folds of her yellowed parchment laid secrets she had confessed - that every night she would have a terrible dream of waking to find her baby brother dead. She would awake under a drenching cold sweat.

When the time came for the family to board the Cloudsail, Teresa was incredibly eager to get away from her old life and to start anew in America. Many people on her ship had started their own diaries to record their adventures on the sea, but Teresa felt very proud that she had already started a diary for her own, and only had to continue on the saga of her journey.

She told of the blanket she was crocheting for her mother, hoping that she would finish it before her mother's next birthday. Life on the ship was hard for her. The air was musty, boxes and suitcases and traveling bags laid everywhere, and the second deck stunk of salt, rotting food and unwashed bodies. Babies were born on the ship, elders died, storms rocked the ship about on the waves, and bright, sunny days were beauteous and cherished from the top deck. Teresa told of her attraction to the sailor boy, Jacob, and confided in her diary to keep the secret.

Then Serena came to the very last few pages, and read how Teresa met her devastating, unwarned end.

Serena yawned and gathered her things as the cab halted in front of the Peace Night Hotel. Glancing first at the price, she paid the cab driver, who wished her well. Then she turned and looked up at the hotel before her. With a smile of anticipation, she gathered her bags and entered the front door.

Inside, she encountered a carpeted front room with many large fern plants and a homey apple blossom scent. A woman at the front desk greeted her with a smile.

"Ah, yes, Serena Gordon. We've been expecting you," said the lady when Serena told her her name. She gave the girl a room number on the top floor and another wide, toothy smile, and then sent her on her way.

Serena glanced at the number on the piece of paper as she reached the top floor by elevator. Picking up her two duffels, she quickly found room 127 and gave the door a polite knock.

A silent moment passed before the door opened.

Serena came face-to-face with a brown-haired, blue-gray-eyed boy who looked to be in his early 20's. He smiled.

"Well, hello," he said. "You must be Serena."

Serena nodded, trying to look over his shoulder.

"Er, I thought this was my room." she said. He studied her before responding - this was not the bratty, little city kid they had been expecting!

"No, we switched because they liked our room better. By the way, I'm Jerry Johnson, your team captain and body-guard. You'll meet the other guys in the morning. Where are you from again?"

"Springfield."

"Cool – I have family there. You know, you're a lot older than I thought you were. I thought we were in for a babysitting job when the scientist told me I was bodyguarding a minor. If you don't mind my asking – how old are you?"

Serena flushed lightly.

"I'm 16," she said, "and I'm glad to have some form of protection on this discovery mission we're going on – it sounds dangerous."

A beat of silence stole over the air and a hoot from one of the men behind Jerry bounced out into the hallway – it appeared they were watching a movie. Jerry was thinking that maybe this mission was not going to be so bad after all! He watched the girl as she checked something written on the piece of paper she was holding. He knew it would be a dangerous mission for such a young person to endure.

"Are you scared, Serena?"

"What?"

The girl had been taken by surprise – she was wondering which room the girls were in and she was about to ask him when he spoke.

"I said, are you scared?"

"About what?"

The boy shrugged politely.

"About this mission."

Serena stopped to think about that. Was she?

"Kind of," she decided. "But I'm more excited than I am scared right now. I don't travel very much. Hey – do you think you could point me in the direction of the girl's hotel room?"

"Sure," Jerry said, and leaned to one side to knock on the door directly next to his room. Then he shook Serena's hand and told her,

"Nice to meet you, Miss. See you later."

The door to room 126 opened carefully, and this time Serena was left facing a black-haired, dull-eyed girl who looked to be around Jerry's age.

"Um, hi. I'm Serena," Serena introduced herself, holding out her hand. The girl reluctantly took it and shook, then opened the door wider.

"A pleasure, I'm sure. Come on in." she offered, though to Serena it sounded much more like a command.

Another girl was sorting through clothes on one of the beds. After a brief introduction, dinner was ordered and served.

Serena studied the girls as they ate. The black-haired girl she had met at the door was Kate Pentol, the navigator and language decoder for the team. She had a longish sort of face, a round, little nose and chin, and lightly tanned skin. Kate was shorter than the other girl, but not quite as skinny. Serena could tell that Kate didn't like her at all from the very start, although she had tried to be nice to her. Kate was 25 years old, and Serena thought she sensed a bit of a foul temper behind Kate's dark brown, sullen eyes.

But the other girl, Lindsey Bellows, was almost the complete opposite of Kate. She was 26, tall and thin, and sported short, curly brown hair and twinkling gray eyes. Her face was heart-shaped and cheery with large cheeks and lips and tiny eyes and a tiny chin. Her shoulder-length hair framed her face prettily. Serena thought she was one of the nicest, sweetest people she had ever met in her life. (But of course, she reflected, anybody would seem nice and sweet compared to the woman she had previously lived with.) She became instantly attached to the girl, while Kate glared suspiciously at the two girls from across the table.

"Dr. Birkwood said the reason he's sending us out is because there's been a report of two ships mysteriously disappearing in the same month. The weird thing is they disappeared in the *exact same place*. After scientists figured out the math, they discovered that it's the same place where,… oh, what's her name," Lindsey scratched her head, "… that girl with the diary's ship sank, right on the dot where the other two boats went down. It's crazy, really, because the radar can't even detect the ships; they seemed to have vanished without a trace," Lindsey explained.

Serena, intrigued by this mystery, reflected on what Dr. Birkwood had told her before sending her off.

"He told me that he thinks there might be an undiscovered continent out there that is … swallowing them up …" she said, not particularly liking the phrase the scientist had used.

"But don't you think the satellites would show it?" Kate piped up. Serena, half surprised to hear her speak, turned to face her.

"Yes, but Dr. Birkwood also told me that they don't think this continent is … normal. It's abnormal and that's why it doesn't show up."

Lindsey fidgeted with her fork.

"Then how are we supposed to find it?" Kate wanted to know. She had an edgy tone to her voice, as if she were trying to taunt the blue-eyed girl.

Lindsey looked up as she put her fork down.

"You're the navigator, Kate, not me," Serena said.

Serena sat in the small, but comfortable, seat of the airplane and pulled out Teresa's diary from her knapsack, which she had promptly plopped in front of her when she sat down. It was early the next morning, and the six explorers were very eager to get going on their adventure. Serena had spent a fitful night in the hotel, not being able to sleep what with Kate's terrible snoring and the sounds of the laughing and joking boys next door. Another thing kept her up as well – the excitement of the whole trip. She thought to herself as she lay on her side, eyes wide open, about what they would find when they reached the spot where the ships had sunk. They would be taking a submarine, of course, and would surface as soon as they found the exact spot. Serena allowed her active imagination to drift and wonder: what would they find? A sunken ship? An unmapped island? Or, as the scientist had predicted, an immortal, forgotten continent? Soon her dreams turned to thoughts of slumber, and she wished that she could get to sleep. But with the many outcomes she had thought up as to what's waiting for them in the days to come swirling around her mind, she drifted off into a peaceful doze without even trying.

"United Air flight 43, last call!" a lady speaker boomed over the intercom. Serena's thoughts shattered and she awoke to find she had fallen into a short snooze. She blinked to rid the sleep from her eyes and popped her golden head up over the seats to see if she could wave down Lindsey to sit next to her. Since they had boarded the plane very early, Jerry and the other two boys, along with Lindsey and Kate had left to call the fellow who would lend them a submarine. It was voted among them (in high humor) that Serena had to stay and watch the seats, since she was the youngest.

Soon the five team members came trudging down the aisle with jackets and tickets. Serena waved vigorously at Lindsey, but before the girl could make her way over to the empty seat next to Serena, Jerry plunked down next to her, a wide, cheesy grin plastered on his freckled face. Looking half crestfallen, half furious at the boy, Lindsey sat in one of the other two seats across from them. Kate rooted herself next to Lindsey, looking absolutely smug for cutting off the chance of conversation between Lindsey and Serena.

Serena leaned forward, trying to get even a glimpse of her new friend, but Kate leaned forward and back, obviously trying to anger her for obstructing her view. Admitting defeat, Serena leaned back and looked out the window as the plane began to take off. She found herself muttering to herself.

"That girl really does like to be a pain in everyone's side, doesn't she?" Serena mumbled, more to herself than to Jerry.

"Yeah, she does! What was your first clue?" Jerry said sarcastically, tearing up his ticket into tiny pieces. The stewardess began a short speech on using the seats for flotation devices at the front of the plane. Serena giggled.

"Maybe when she first looked at me …" she chortled honestly. She tightened her buckle and glanced out the window. "So, you know her better than I do? I pity you."

Jerry almost choked on the small bottle of water he had brought as he chuckled.

"Thanks for your deepest sympathies, Serena, *cough*, but I think you had better save them for yourself," he said. He coughed again, closed his water bottle and then added, "For being the same gender as she is."

Serena narrowed her eyes at him, forgetting about her rivalry with Kate.

"Well, at least I'm not afraid of her being attracted to me."

Jerry chuckled. No, this trip was not going to be bad at all. This girl was not only pretty, but entertaining!

And so the insult contest continued back and forth, each one having their own prides and discouragements until they both grew very tired of it and switched over to a regular conversation –e ach, of course, throwing in an extra insult or two just for good measure.

Serena learned that Jerry had just graduated from college, and this was his third expedition since then. His first was a journey to find a certain type of endangered snake in the Amazon so that zoos could breed them to save the species. Aside from being bit in the ankle, he did get the snake and was taken by helicopter to a hospital and saved just in the nick of time.

His second mission was to explore a certain old temple somewhere in Colorado, where an ancient people once lived. He was there with a team that time, appointed captain for the bravery of his first expedition alone. He and his team found writing on the walls, and copied it cleverly by taking a piece of paper and rubbing burnt charcoal over it. The indentations showed clearly on the paper, so they numbered them in the order they had copied them and presented them back to the research center. Jerry and his team were praised highly for this, bumping him up to an even higher position than that of the captain. Now he was not only the captain, but also the body guard for Serena, being the keeper of the evidence (which was Teresa's diary).

Serena told him of her own history, which she felt was really nothing compared to his. Yet, he seemed interested, and so she kept going up to the present. Finally, after what seemed like hours of talking, Serena couldn't hold back her fervent yawning any longer and promptly fell asleep in her seat, making up for the sleep she had lost the night before.

In her sleep, Serena shivered. They did, after all, keep the temperature somewhat cool on the plane. Jerry, noticing this, carefully pulled a jacket out of his own survival knapsack and covered her with it. Then he slumped back into the seat and fell asleep too.

~*~*~*~*~

The first thing Serena noticed when she woke up was snoring - loud, irritable snoring.

The second thing she noticed was that she was covered in a jacket that smelled faintly of nice cologne.

And the third thing she noticed, when she opened her eyes, was that she was lying with her back against the hard wall of the airplane, with a snoring, half-drooling face slumped across the armrest between them. She sat up and shook off the jacket as she looked over at Kate and Lindsey, who were both asleep as well. Then she looked at Jerry and smirked. She swung his jacket over him.

"Errrr …" he groaned, licked his lips, smacked them and sniffed. Slowly he opened his eyes.

"Good morning, sleeping beauty!" Serena greeted him. She patted one of his cheeks playfully. "Wake up and smell the roses, I think we're almost there!"

"Ehhhhh …" moaned Jerry, closing his eyes again. Further tampering with his cheeks forced him to awake fully.

"Yes ma'am, Serena! I'll get up right now and get ready to get off the plane so we can go to another hotel!" Serena mocked in a hilariously low voice, pinching his cheeks to make it look like his mouth was moving.

"Awright, awright!" grumbled the voice of the real Jerry. His eyes snapped open just as Serena withdrew her hands, filling his immediate vision with a pearly-white, innocent smile. "I'm getting up."

And with a heave, he was. He flattened his hair to his head and packed up his bags, all the while sending drowsy-yet-still-sarcastic glances over at Serena.

Later, the team reached the Brevada Inn after a fast-food dinner. They sat in the lounge in a circle, discussing their plans for the next morning.

"We'll be taking a submarine to the spot where the ships disappeared. Our estimated time is six hours, because it's 423 miles, which means we'll be traveling 37.5 knots – and for those of you who don't understand the knots system, we'll be going about 70.5 miles an hour underwater," Kate reported, flipping some pages in her notebook.

Serena felt utterly clueless for once, but straightened her back, determined not to let the team know that she hardly had any idea at what Kate had just said. She smiled all the same.

"Alright, enough of the math lessons, Professor Kate, we need to get down to business." Jerry said. He blinked his large, gray-blue eyes and leaned forward with his hands clasped patiently. "Tomorrow we'll take off early – say around 6:30, and we'll meet our sub guy, Mr. Woodlen, at the decks around 7:00. Right, like Kate said, 6 hours under the ocean, and when we reach the point where the ships sank, we'll surface and have a look around. Tell me immediately if you see anything down there – we can't afford to miss out on finding that ship or anything else."

Heads nodding in unison, Serena watched the team sleepily as Jerry went on to explain the importance of the trip. She allowed her mind to wander, already having been lectured by Dr. Birkwood back at the science institution in Chicago. She had met the other two members of their continent-exploring crew that morning during breakfast. Mike Blacksmith, a 29-year-old man fresh from college, was the wildlife expert and survival master for the team. Serena smiled as she remembered his bright, brown eyes, which seemed to hide behind his chubby dimples and small glasses. He wasn't quite an overweight sort, but then he wasn't skinny at all. He reminded Serena of a short, stocky football player. His hair was sleek and black, which he almost always hid under his hat.

The other man was Bob O'Riley, who was, on the other hand, almost the complete opposite of Mike. He was sort of shy, and was tall and skinny with black-brown hair that was tied into a bobbing little ponytail on the back of his head. He was 32, and had large, glistening, dark blue eyes. He was dubbed the electronic technician for the group.

Serena's thoughts drifted away from her and she blinked, looking around the circle of explorers who were now tossing popcorn (laid out on a coffee table within easy reach) into the air and attempting to catch it in their mouths. Serena joined in the fun, and only when they ran out of popcorn did the crew stop and walk up to their rooms.

Seeing that they had a few hours before the group needed to go to bed, Serena suggested they take a trip down to the pool room.

"Why?" Kate wanted to know. "Hasn't this trip been exciting enough for you yet?"

"It's not that," Serena called from within the closed bathroom. "I just want to rest up a bit and have some fun before we take off on this important mission."

The door opened, and Serena gave Kate an extra bathing suit.

"Besides, you'll want to get used to the water. We'll be seeing an awful lot of it tomorrow."

Kate scowled contemptuously, hearing Lindsey, who was wrapped tightly in a towel and lying on a bed watching the television, giggle. With a glare of pure daggers, Kate reluctantly snatched the bathing suit from Serena's waiting hands and slammed the bathroom door behind her.

Lindsey and Serena sat soaking themselves in a bubbling, frothy Jacuzzi in the corner of the pool room.

Serena could not remember when she had last felt so relaxed, so tension-free. Her skin tingled with the pleasurable warmth of the boiling hot pool, and she sunk lower, releasing a sigh that also seemed to release all of her stress to the popping, frizzling bubbles.

"You know, maybe getting ourselves lost trying to find an immortal continent won't be so bad after all," Lindsey moaned in pleasure, stretching luxuriously and resting with her hands behind her head. Mirth bubbled inside Serena's throat like one of the white bubbles surrounding her.

"Getting ourselves lost?" she giggled. "So you're saying we're sailing out in search of something only to end up with those sunken ships?"

Lindsey laughed, her short, damp brown curls bouncing on her shoulders as she shook her head.

41

"No, no, I'm not saying that at all!" she chortled, pushing some of her shoulder-length hair behind her ear.

"Saying what?"

Kate slid into the hot pool next to Serena with this remark, seeming in a much better mood than before. Serena was glad she had lightened up. She felt a little prick against her left hip, but, figuring it only to be an abnormal, absurd bubble, leaned back and promptly forgot about it.

"That we're going to die on this mission," Lindsey explained. She reached across to touch Serena's hair, gazing longingly at its shimmering golden hues.

"Huh! And return alive? Fat chance!" snorted Kate, sensing a better seat on the other side of the pool.

"Hey, are those for us?" Serena asked, gesturing towards a table on the other side of the room. It sat in a tiled area that was somewhat separated from the pool area and held a platter of lemonade and a pitcher, clearly cold, fresh, and tempting.

"I think so." Kate said, her dull black-brown eyes boring holes into Serena's own cool blue ones. "Why don't you go get some? Can you bring one back for me?"

Serena thought she sounded almost sarcastic.

"Sure," she said, and hesitantly arose to retrieve the fresh drinks. It was no sooner than she had left the pool that she heard Kate begin to snicker.

Then, four things happened all at once. One, Lindsey leaned closer to the snickering Kate and demanded in a hushed tone,

"Why did you do that to her?"

Two, Kate pointed to the loosened strings on the left side of Serena's bikini bottom while Serena herself looked down to find them dangling, but not falling. She almost laughed.

I'm not that stupid, she thought with a grin, *I like to double-tie.*

Three, as she reached down to tie the strings, a dreadful noise was conjured from behind the double door on the left side of the room. The doors burst open as Serena looked up.

The color seemed to drain from her face.

And four, when the poor girl was hardly halfway between the hot tub and the corner of the deep end of the large pool, Jerry and the other two boys collided with her and all four were thrown floundering into the cool water from the impact.

Serena's skin awoke to the coldness of the water and tingled as she felt

42

the pressure on her ears. Chlorinated blue water filled her senses. Her nose, her closed eyes, her ears - everything. She opened her eyes to see three distant figures plunging deeper into the depths of the pool. Her hair flowed behind her like a long, blonde ribbon as gravity released its hold on her and she was raised to the surface.

Serena, being the lightest of the four, was the first to come up spluttering. She felt a sound that resembled both a gasp and a groan escape her throat as she bobbed up and down. Her drenched hair hung in front of her, covering her whole face. She stifled the urge to make a rude remark upon hearing Kate's outrageous laughter fill the air.

Mike and Bob, emerging almost together, took one look at Serena and her hilarious hair and began to laugh.

"Hey, look! It's Cousin It!" Mike guffawed.

"Are you okay, Serena?" Bob chuckled, swimming over to her.

Jerry popped up next to her and chuckled. He thought he detected a muffled giggle from under the glittering ringlets.

Delicately, Serena parted her hair as a curtain and glared out at Jerry, as though she were preparing to scold him. Bob laughed even more and ducked off after Mike as he was splashed by the offending black-haired boy.

Then, not being able to help the hilarity of the situation, Serena began to smile. Her smile widened into a chuckle, which finally erupted into a bell-like laughter that rang off of the walls of the pool room. She splashed Jerry in the face, and promptly earned herself one in response.

"Better get used to the water, Serena!" Kate shrieked mockingly from the hot tub. "You'll be seeing an awful lot of it tomorrow!"

Lindsey, finally grown tired of the mean jokes Kate had hatched in her scheming head, lifted herself out of the hot tub and scurried over to join in the fun.

"Oh, don't worry! I am!" Serena cried happily, dealing Bob a white splash of water to the top of his black-brown head.

Lindsey dove into the pool beside Serena, splashing her all the more.

And Serena's melodious giggles echoed along with the laughter of Mike, Bob, Jerry, and Lindsey, mingling together in a chorus of merriment.

~*~*~*~*~

Serena stared dismally at the digital clock from her bed side. For some odd reason, this morning she awoke five minutes before the team was supposed to be up. She hadn't wanted to disturb the other two girls, although she had had second thoughts about waking up Kate.

No, she thought with a yawn, *that would only give her another excuse to complain.*

She gave a weak smile as the clock changed to 6:26 a.m. Serena turned over onto her back and stared at the silent darkness. She wondered what they would find later that day - a bunch of sunken ships - an undiscovered island - a new coral reef?

Serena stopped, thinking hard about the latter.

Could it, in fact, be a coral reef?

No, she decided, *the radar would have picked it up if it had been a reef. Then again …*

Serena reached over to the bedside dresser and fetched Teresa's diary from her open knapsack. She flipped to the very last page and held it up almost reverently next to the light of the digital clock.

She read Teresa's last entry and found a small, hastily scribbled message after the last signature.

He says the ship is caught stiff in a reef.

A reef! Serena thought.

> *There are holes in the sides and water is pouring in below us. I can hear its hurried rushing, like that of a mystic waterfall, beneath our very feet! The ship creaks and groans in protest. The poor Cloud-sail! People are flooding to the top deck. Jacob plans to escape on a raft. I must go now. God be with you. I pray you make it to America, although I myself will not be able to go with you. Farewell.*
> *~Teresa Gordon~*

Serena jumped as the alarm on the clock buzzed loudly, startling both Lindsey and Kate.

Chapter Five: Anchors Aweigh

Mr. Woodlen reminded Serena of an over-grown toad.

In a pair of denim overalls, a red and green flannel shirt, and an old fishing hat with every lure known to man perched or hanging from the rim, the gray-bearded old man cut a comical figure.

"Mornin' young 'uns." he rumbled in a deep bass, spitting tobacco off the dock into the cool, deep waters of the ocean.

"Uhm, good morning, Mr. Woodlen," Jerry coughed, hiding a rather rude snicker. Serena dropped her duffel bags in unison with the others and studied the dock. It looked rather unsteady, but she was soon reassured when she watched the grumpy-looking old man waddle out onto the very end of the dock. Hesitantly looking Lindsey in the eye, she followed.

"Sub's 'iss way," grumbled Mr. Woodlen.

Jerry smirked and was the first out on the dock after him.

Serena didn't like the feel of the shifty, rotten-looking planks under her feet, and even less did she like knowing she had the added weight of both duffels and her knapsack on her back. Soon the small group approached a little barred metal circle protruding from the water. Mr. Woodlen grunted and spat again as he reached down and unchained the top of the submarine, casting the chains aside noisily on the dock.

"Looks like the inside of a little airplane," Mike couldn't help but notice as he dragged his bag into the little hole. Mr. Woodlen belched loudly, then remarked,

"Well, it's far from it." He scratched his bristling mustache distractedly.

Quietly, as though they were afraid of the old man, the crew entered the submarine. Serena waited, feeling something deep inside her that protested going into the submarine. She gulped and looked over at the chubby old man with his hands jammed into his pockets, staring – no - glaring at her. She smiled, hoping to put him in a lighter mood. He belched again, spat, and said nothing. Serena's smile slid off her face as she gathered her things and slipped into the submarine entrance. Kate immediately found her seat next to Bob, who would be driving the submarine.

"I have to admit, it's a lot more comfortable than I thought it would be." said Lindsey, bouncing a little in her seat. Jerry stood and pulled an envelope out of his pocket. A withered, dry hand appeared at the entrance of the sub and snatched it from Jerry, then, with another despicable belch, the lid to the submarine snapped shut.

Lights flickered on with an electric buzz as Serena took a seat. Jerry sat down next to her long enough to scoot his duffels under the seat. He then stood up again and hailed attention.

"Alright, we've made it this far, so we have got to keep it up. By this I mean – keep your eyes open. If you see anything out of place or strange out there through those glass portholes, let me know as soon as possible. Now, I know a couple of us haven't been in a submarine before, but don't worry, we'll get used to it.

"Serena told me this morning that Teresa's ship sank because of a reef, so if you see any dark spots out there that might possibly be a coral reef, let someone know. Okay - weather's fine, right? We're not expecting any storms?" He turned to Mike.

"Yep. Checked the weather last night and this morning, too. It'll be bright and sunny all day long!" Mike grinned.

~*~*~*~*~

CRAAAAAAAAAAAAAAAAAAAAAAAAAAAAAAAAAAAAAAAAAAAAACK!

The sound reverberated underwater like an enormous bass drum had been placed over the submarine, now dubbed the Wavequeen, and pounded itself into the team's ears for all it was worth.

"Bright and sunny all day, huh, Mike?" Kate sniffed, looking anxiously out the circular window.

Mike shrugged, chomping down on another chip from his food supply.

"You can't *always* trust the weather-man."

The discovery team had slipped through the ocean like a bar of soap for five and a half hours, and only now were they slightly slowing because of an encounter with a furious storm that had risen from nowhere.

Serena could have sworn the storm had come from *somewhere*. As she sat in her comfortable little seat, staring dismally out the porthole into the flashing sea, she remembered how she herself had always loved storms. Yet deep inside she felt a peculiar passion for this certain one. It was much more fascinating from underwater than on land. The sound of the thunder, the boiling ocean around them, the blue lightning…

46

"Wait a minute…" she said in a dangerously suspicious tone, lifting her chin from her hand. Realization had snapped inside her mind like a flash of one of the bright electric bolts themselves. "Blue lightning!" she exclaimed.

Everyone except Bob, who was driving, turned silent and expecting at her outburst.

"What about it?" Mike mused, the sound of his crunching down on another chip breaking the silence. Serena swooped up Teresa's diary and, in a flash, found the second to last passage. The lighting illuminated the scene eerily.

"Blue lightning, 'tis! - Metallic blue lightning!" she whispered, the beams of the flickering lights stuttering over her face as her hair swayed about in front of her. She looked up, eyes larger and bluer than any lake known.

Every heart stopped.

"Do you know what this means?" she hissed in a tone that sounded more like a scared whimper.

"We're-"

"No!"

"It can't be!"

"But it is!" Serena cried, blowing out of the corner of her mouth to straighten a stray curl that hung over her face. "It says so right here! We're entering the same type of storm that took Teresa's ship, the Cloudsail, down!"

Kate gulped, turning around from her navigator's seat in the front. Mike, Jerry, and Lindsey crowded around the diary, reading for themselves the writings of Teresa Gordon. Kate's wooden brown eyes studied Serena seriously for a moment or so, and then, as if giving in, she gulped again.

"M-maybe we should turn around … Go back …" she squeaked.

"NO!" exclaimed Jerry forcefully, balling his hand into a fist as he looked up at Kate, his tan colored hair flopping about on his forehead. "No way are we going back! Not now … we're half an hour away from the spot!"

"Thirty-five miles to destination," Bob droned from the front. "At the speed we're going now, it should only take us about 30 minutes."

"Exactly!" Jerry exclaimed. "If we can just hang on for 30 minutes – and I'm very sure we can – we'll be able to make it."

Groans passed around the disheartened crew. Serena knew she had to say something to encourage them all, as well as herself.

"And besides, turning around now would be like running away! We can't run away now, not when we're *so close* … and we weren't sent out here to run away either!"

There was a long silence in which Serena felt her words had touched the hearts of the discouraged explorers. Finally, Mike spoke.

"She's got a point." he said, shrugging to Lindsey.

"Oh my-" squeaked Kate from the front, sounding terrified.

Bob gasped aloud, eyes wide.

In less than a heartbeat, the entire team flooded to the front of the Wavequeen.

And there, in front of them, stood what looked like the wall to an enormous underwater bubble. Electricity licked over the surface of the transparent wall, flickering in many spectral colors. The wall also gave out a distinct buzzing sound that snapped at the ears of the crew as though the bubble itself was alive. The sight alone was enough to drain the color from anyone's face, yet it was also most beautiful to the discovery team, even now in their time of anxiety and panic.

"Whoa – will ya look at that!"

"I've never seen anything like it!"

"I wonder what it is …"

"It's amazing – it's *beautiful*!" gasped the bewildered onlookers.

Quite certain that Bob was about to turn the wheel aside so that they did not collide and electrocute themselves with the great wondrous shield, Serena watched and waited.

And waited.

And waited.

All the while the Wavequeen drew dangerously closer to the lightning-bathed surface of the bubble-skinned wall.

And closer.

And closer.

Finally, after a wait that felt like hours, Serena and the frozen, shocked team seemed to come alive all at once.

"We're not…"

"Turn AROUND!"

"AHHHHHH!"

"I CAN'T!" shouted Bob, gripping the wheel. A droplet of sweat oozed down his red face as he squinted his owlish eyes and turned with all of his strength. Stopping momentarily, he looked up at the other two boys, - "It's stuck!"

Mike and Jerry rushed to help, but even with their combined strength, the wheel refused to budge.

Serena stared at the bubble-like wall. Little tendrils of electricity glided and played about on the surface, so close now to the front window that Serena could almost feel their sharp stings gripping her heart. The buzzing and zapping sound grew nearer, and nearer, until it blocked out every other sound in Serena's ears and grew to a deafening roar. She took a step back. Her vision was now completely obstructed by the electric wall - its colors shining in her eyes as the Wavequeen came nose to nose with it as if in confrontation.

"We're going to-"

"Look out!"

"Grab onto something! Quick!"

"Oh, no!"

The screams of the crew members sounded only faint to Serena against the dominant buzzing of the wall. Then, another sound thundered above that of the buzzing and the screaming, and Serena's own screams which she could not hear.

SSSSSSSSSSSSOOOOOOOOOOOOOOOOOOOOOOOOOOOOOOCK!

Like something out of a fiction story, the Wavequeen was sucked through the electric Shield. Serena's ears popped from the pressure, and the sound that was made as they passed was incredulous.

Serena lay curled in a ball on the floor, her eyes closed tightly and her hands slapped firmly over her ears.

Any moment now, I and the rest of the team will become electrocuted, and fail our mission to find the immortal Continent, she thought. She felt Kate huddled on the ground next to her in a similar position of terror, shivering uncontrollably.

But soon the sound of the buzzing electricity ceased, and the ship gave an odd shudder, followed by a hesitant lurch. And Serena knew, somehow, that all the power on the Wavequeen had been stripped from the submarine and sucked into the Shield of electricity.

Slowly, the petrified discoverers began to awake as though from a Nightmare and stand from their horrified positions on the floor.

As Serena herself stood, a strange, yet desirable, feeling of humbleness flooded through her. The feeling was almost indescribable, something like love and mystery mixed. She reached up and laid a hand over her tingling heart. She felt…

At home? she thought. Shaking the thought from her head in a flurry of light blonde curls, she turned to Bob.

"H-how far now, Bob?" she stuttered.

"I don't know." he replied, leaning back in defeat from trying fervently to revive his precious ship. His brownish-black hair bobbed in its ponytail as he shook his head. "Last time I checked we were 30 miles away."

Jerry sighed a heavy sigh that seemed to heave upon all the hearts of the crew.

"Well, let's not sit around and wait for something to happen," he groaned. "Let's get into the scuba suits and grab our backpacks. Can we surface, Bob?"

Bob shook his head as though the deadness of the Wavequeen had made him cross.

"Can't do anything now except to wait for the ship to drift to the surface or wash up on a Beach somewhere."

Kate sighed loudly, making it quite obvious that she was rather stressed out. Jerry looked at Serena and shrugged.

"Well, let's put on those scuba suits anyway, just in case something happens and we have to make a quick escape."

There was complete silence as the discovery team put on their emergency scuba suits over their clothes. Serena fingered through her knapsack to make sure everything she had in it was sealed tight in a plastic bag, even though it was Waterproof. The others did the same in almost complete darkness.

"Wait!" said Lindsey suddenly. She rummaged in her knapsack and grinned in satisfaction as she pulled out a flashlight.

"Alright!"

"Dude, I forgot we had these!"

"I hope they work!"

"They'd better!"

"Count of three!" said Jerry. Rustling was heard and then all six of the team members pulled out their own flashlight. They stood in an almost complete circle, ready to switch on their escape from the darkness. Serena had a funny feeling that they weren't going to work, but shook the feeling off immediately.

"One ... two ... three!" the explorers chanted, and switched on their flashlights at the exact same time.

Silence.

Nothing happened.

The Wavequeen was still as dark as she had been before they brought the flashlights out. They shook the offending flashlights, and, finally, with several groans of displeasure, they gave up. Serena threw her useless item into a corner with the rest, figuring that the electric Shield had taken away every drop of Power in the ship. She sighed.

Suddenly, an enormous figure loomed past the front window. What little shadow that could be cast down in the darkness of the ship trickled over Serena like a Nightmare, and she crouched low to the ground.

The others did the same.

Mike gulped.

"Wh-what was that?" Kate's voice cracked from behind Serena.

"I don't know," she replied in a soft whisper, edging closer yet to the glass window. "It looked like some type of big Fish ..."

As though on cue, a tremendous yellow and orange eye rose to the glass and stared Serena straight in the eye.

"Don't … move…" she breathed, her lips hardly moving. Very slowly, she began to sink her head lower to the control panel, until only her scared blue eyes showed. The eye flicked around madly, the pupil dilating and growing as it studied the inside of the vessel. The large Fish, whatever it was, reluctantly moved away - its vicious green and black scales glittering as it slunk away through the dark, wet Ocean.

"What was that?!" Jerry enthused, his blue-gray eyes wide.

"It looked like some sort of mutant bass!" said Bob, rolling up the sleeves on his scuba suit.

"Whatever it was, its eyesight wasn't very good. I figured it hunts by movement and smell," Mike reported. Then, seeing the confused expression on Kate's face, he added, "Anything that moves is dead."

Kate let out a low moan and a shiver, and collapsed to a sit on the floor.

"I think I'm going to be sick…" she whined piteously, brushing her limp black hair away from her face.

Lindsey sat down next to her.

"Not in this ship, you're not!" Bob commanded, offended at this remark.

"Shhhhhh, settle down! We're just going to have to wait until the submarine surfaces before we can – *holy beans!*" Jerry exclaimed, seating himself but then leaping up again in surprise as another figure loomed past the window.

Serena shuddered.

"Whew! One look from that thing is enough to make my blood run cold!" she admitted, a blush rising to her cheeks.

"Mine too!" agreed Lindsey, clutching her knees as her large brown eyes darted around from window to window like little minnows in a pool.

"Mine – EEEEEEEK!" shrieked Kate, facing another eye that was just as big as the porthole she was looking out of.

Mike slapped a hand over her mouth from behind, but it was –

- too late.

The monster bass Fish had heard Kate's scream, and to prove that it had passed the hearing test, it slunk away to get a running start at the Wavequeen.

"T-too?" squeaked a muffled voice from behind Mike's hand. Mike sighed, digging his face into his other hand.

"Great job," he grumbled, removing his hand.

"S-sorry, it just … - I -"

SLAM!

Everybody in the submarine was tossed against one wall. And, despite Serena's warning, everybody screamed.

Another bass, slightly larger than the first - if that was at all possible - towered over the front window. Serena began to stand, her back to that very same window. The massive jaws opened wide to bare pearly white stubs of teeth - sharp as a razor and twice as quick.

"S-Serena..." gulped Jerry, pointing shakily to the window behind the Girl. "Wh-whatever you do, d-don't turn around ..."

Eyes flickered to the window.

EveryCreature froze.

Slowly, Serena revolved on her heel, and came face-to-tonsils with the mutant Fish. Her eyes grew larger and larger as the jaws came closer and closer. Serena herself felt that if her eyes had been any bigger, they would have popped right out of her head. She stifled a gasp as the gargantuan mouth came closer and made to bite down on the glass.

"Oh, no!"

"Grab something!"

"Cover your ears!" whispered the crew.

SCREEEEEEEEEEEEEEEEEEEEEEEEEEEEEEEEEEEEEEEEEEEE!!!!

It was like an old WoMan had taken her long nails and raked a chalkboard with them, only this horrid noise was a hundred times louder. Shudders ran down every spine in the Wavequeen, and every hand slapped to an ear. The screams of the explorers were drowned out by the screeching of the Fish's teeth against the glass.

When the big Fish, admitting defeat against this hard substance and finally withdrew, several white lines Rained down on the window shield. The scaly monstrosity swam off, spitting shards of glass, blood, and broken teeth.

WHAM!

But that didn't mean that the Fish had given up entirely. Everybody went flying into the right wall and the breath was squeezed out of every lung.

A couple of hours later, after the team had screamed themselves hoarse and surrendered to being battered and bruised to unconsciousness, the school of giant, carnivorous bass swam off in search of easier prey.

53

Serena rose sorely from the hard ground beneath her. Her head was pounding like a thousand hammers and searing pain shot throughout her whole body.

"Finally!" snorted Kate. "We thought you would never wake up."

A sigh of relief escaped the throats of Mike, Bob, Lindsey, and Jerry. Serena thought she may have even heard a very small one from Kate.

Jerry stooped to help the Girl stand, which she did very tenderly, leaning heavily upon Jerry's shoulder.

"How long have we been asleep in here?" she rasped, her throat still harsh from screaming.

"We don't know," Mike replied, rubbing his temples in pain.

The rest of the crew was awake and alive, but all very bruised and hoarse. Serena thought she felt a bump on the back of her head and reached back to check. She pressed down on a large lump that she found.

Excruciating pain tore across her head, and she tumbled to the floor with a squeal of pain.

"Are you okay?" Lindsey asked, sitting Serena up and catching a bag of ice that Bob tossed to her from a cooler. She held it up to the spot on Serena's head, and cool relief washed over the sore Girl instantly. She reached up and took the bag from Lindsey, thanking her as the nurse rose to treat a cut on Mike's arm.

"We've found something out, though…" Bob coughed harshly from his position next to the cooler. "We surfaced."

"At last, some good news!" Serena droned, scooting back to lie her head down on her bag of ice. She looked out of the corner of her eye to the front window with its white Fish-tooth marks still freshly intact. It was half sunken in salty, foamy Water. She closed her eyes as, for the first time in awhile, she smiled. She allowed her mind to space out a bit as Mike explained the chemistry behind the Wavequeen surfacing itself.

"Isn't it? It worked like this: Our submarine is like a big bubble…" he began in his hoarse voice.

Oh, don't talk to me about bubbles … Serena thought, thinking back to the big electric bubble Shield they had passed however long ago it was. The buzzing of the busy electric fingers on the surface of the wall seemed to fill her head again, mingling with the pain of her skull-crushing headache and making it all the more miserable for Serena. She seemed to relive the experience once again as she tried to drift off into slumber. As the submarine passed through the Shield again, she opened her eyes in fright. At once, the same feeling of hominess and mystic wonder rippled over her.

Serena was just glad to be out of the grip of the shark-like bass Fish. She sat up and smiled at the angry Rain Clouds that frowned down upon them, spitting large, fat droplets of Rain on the battered and beaten Wavequeen.

"Has it been Raining this entire time?" she wanted to know, looking at Bob.

"Yeah," he replied, "ever since I woke up, anyway."

"What time is it now, do you know?"

"Haven't a clue - my watch died when we passed that Shield. But from looking at the Sky I would guess its early evening," Jerry said, sitting up and glaring daggers at the sneering gray Clouds.

Undisturbed silence hung in the air for a moment or so, giving all six passengers a taste of the odd, freakish tint lingering about the air.

"Oh..." said Mike suddenly, pointing at something in the distance.

"...my..." squeaked Kate as she caught sight of whatever it was.

"...gosh..." breathed Serena.

Before them, rising upon the ship at an alarming rate, was the tip of an unbelievably large coral reef, poking threateningly out of the Water.

"Rock the ship!" Jerry yelled, throwing himself against the wall. "Maybe it'll turn or something!"

"Jump up and down! We might go under again!" shouted Bob, beginning to bounce up and down.

"Don't panic!" screeched Lindsey, pulling her brown curls.

"Here's an idea!" crowed Serena. She waited for the zoo of activity to die down before speaking again. She grinned cleverly and held up an oxygen tank. "Why don't we swim around it?"

"But what about the Wavequeen?" Bob demanded, ceasing his jumping.

Comments of agreement rent upon the stress-tightened air.

"And what if there's more of those … monster Fish things out here?" complained Kate, twirling one finger around her oily black hair. Jerry caught onto the plan fast.

"We'll leave the Wavequeen here, and if we need to we'll come back to her... now hurry UP we're almost-"

"Huh, I *wish* we could just park her here without the fear of her sinking while we're gone..." droned Mike hoarsely, mounting his oxygen tank.

55

"Look out!" shouted Bob suddenly, pointing to the front window.

Too late.

CRASH!

Everyone went flying.

Serena moaned as she rolled over, feeling another lump rising on top of the first one in the back of her head.

"Ohhhhh, wish granted…" she groaned as she got up and noticed a very large gash in the side of the submarine. The front windshield was nearly shattered and had several small holes leaking Water into the Wavequeen. Water gushed into the sub in dangerous quantities as the team recovered.

"This sub isn't going anywhere now," Kate whined, "-except to the bottom of the-"

"Hush up, Kate!" growled Jerry, who looked utterly Thunderstruck by the collision. "Everyone else, don't just stand around waiting to drown!" He glared at them all rather crossly, and Serena though she saw the slightest glimpse of fear etched in his deep Ocean-colored eyes. "Get your oxygen masks on!"

In a flurry of excitement, the order was followed. Serena felt Water lapping at her ankles as she tightened her mask and watched Jerry wrench open the door with a grunt of exertion. More salty Water gushed in as he did so, and the team really had to fight to get themselves out of the sinking submarine before it was completely submerged in Water. They hurried to the surface of the Ocean.

The dramatically torn but still alive exploration team escaped certain death that Day with only three things: their Waterproof survival knapsacks, now looking not-so-Waterproof after all, their scuba gear, and their very lives. All three of which they were very thankful for, although Kate may have had a spot of trouble showing it.

"Great," she scowled, crossing her arms moodily as they watched the last of their faithful Wavequeen disappear in a halo of white bubbles. "We're in the middle of the Ocean with soaking Waterproof backpacks, two hour tanks, and no submarine."

She turned on Jerry with another of her ugly frowns. "Now what do we do, smart guy?"

Jerry sighed, as if releasing his urge to strangle the ungrateful Girl.

The discovery team bobbed up and down in utter silence for a moment, watching the last of their faithful submarine merge to the bottom of its eternal grave. The Rain dribbled morbidly on, as if in mourning for the loss of the

Wavequeen.

"Well, at least we're still alive," chirped Serena.

"And there's no shark-Fish in sight," Lindsey chimed.

"But I know something that is …" said Mike as he squinted through his tiny pinhole glasses, which had amazingly clung to his face without falling off.

"What?" said the team in unison. Mike's hand splashed into the Water to a dead-ahead point.

"The Cloudsail!"

It wasn't long before the group had plunged into the depths of the Ocean and made for the little smudge on the Ocean bottom that was, without a single doubt, Teresa's ship.

There it is! thought Serena happily as she dove lower. She felt very much like a MerMaid with the flippers on her feet. Her hair streamed behind her like a streak of Sunshine in the dark depths of the underWater World. She looked around and saw several other ships and the Wavequeen piled traumatically along the Rock-solid reef.

Not missing a beat, Serena was the first to swim deep down to the old ship and enter through the hole that was ripped in the side to explore. The others followed and they observed the ship in awe for a while, noting the piles of rotted bones and half-eaten clothes that wavered lightly with the current.

Two hundred years ago my own ancestor found her true love, right here on this very deck! Serena thought in exasperated wonder. She had explored her way up to the top deck of the sunken ship, touching and feeling the rotted wood all the way. She now ran her slender fingers along the algae-encrusted railing, wondering how many other people had done the same 200 years ago when the ship still floated upon the sea.

And then a strange thing happened. Serena suddenly closed her eyes, feeling immediately weak, and her thoughts closed all on their own. Her imagination blossomed into a beautiful vision, like a dream. She saw the ship deck, looking much sturdier and younger - and much drier as well. She saw rolling waves of white mist drifting about under the ship as she looked over the railing, bearing it up to the glittering Night Sky. She felt as though the ship were sailing upon a cloud, until she herself heard the gentle lapping of the waves against the underside of the ship.

The stars twinkled brightly, the moon shone luminously, and a light, cool breeze nuzzled her cheeks and her curls as it hurried past. She shuddered. What an odd dream this was – so much so that even the breeze felt real!

And then she saw a Girl – a young Girl about her own age with bright brown eyes and lustrous, bouncy brown curls tied up in ribbons. And she saw a Boy, too. There was a tall, handsome Boy behind the Girl, one hand on her shoulder and the other pointing out to her the Stars in the Sky. He paused and rested his pointing hand on the Girl's other shoulder.

"That's funny," he said, his voice echoing as though it were inside a drum.

"I can't seem to find the North Star…"

The North Star, The North Star… the voice reverberated in Serena's mind, bouncing off the walls of her brain, and in a shroud of creamy blue-tinted mist and swirling glitter as if on the breath of the Wind itself, the vision was gone.

Serena opened her eyes and blinked several times. Had the vision been a dream?

But it seemed so real… she thought, rubbing her aching temples. The lump on the back of her head throbbed unmercifully.

Jerry tapped her on the shoulder, having found her at last, and pointed to a hole in the wall of the cabin of the ship. He led her over to it and ran a finger along the broken edge.

This is where Teresa's friend broke off some wood to float to shore on. his deep blue-gray eyes seemed to say. Serena nodded. A shadow passed over them, and they both looked up to see Kate returning to the surface. In close pursuit were Lindsey, Bob, and Mike. Serena began to follow them, feeling she needed a breath of fresh non-oxygen-tank air herself, when Jerry pulled her back and held up a finger.

Hold on a minute, it said. Serena blinked and crossed her arms.

Okay, what now?

Jerry curled his finger at her and swam-walked in the cabin and down some stairs.

Follow me.

Serena obeyed reluctantly, after a longing glance at the dangling flippers far above them.

Jerry entered a hectic-looking scene on the second deck, where many things were half-dissolved and left lying against one another on the pivoted slope and the side of the ship.

Serena picked through the items in great interest: human bones, broken lamps, sunken clothing, boxes, jars, books, blankets…

Blankets! thought Serena, her eyes widening. *Unless Teresa took her blanket with her, it should still be down here … somewhere …* Suddenly, she began to feel sleepy and weak again. *Why's the … the ship and … and Jerry spinning … so fast … ohhhh …*

And Serena lapsed into another vision in a flurry of purple-tinted Clouds and Stars. This time, she saw a Girl, the same Girl as she had seen before with the Boy, sitting in the same room she was, a crocheted blanket lain neatly across her lap as she scribbled furiously in her diary. She stopped to peek through the porthole in the wall of the ship, and then resumed writing.

Suddenly, an impact of some sort shook the ship. The Girl looked up from her entry in surprise. She got up and talked to the Boy and presumably her parents, scribbled a few last sentences in her diary and then bundled it up tightly and sealed it in a thick jar with a fat cork. She left the deck as Water began to slosh ankle-deep.

Serena remembered the blanket and saw it floating lightly on the Water. It sunk slowly to the bottom of the salty soaked floor as the ship began to tip in the other direction. It slid with the other abandoned belongings across the floor to the other side and sank, half-covering an old traveler's bag.

Orchid-tinted cream and twinkling Stars flashed before Serena's mind and she opened her eyes as if awakened from a particularly pleasant dream.

Jerry didn't seem to have noticed. He was rummaging through an old haversack and scrunched up his nose in disgust as he pulled out an old cloth diaper stained a very lovely shade of brown.

Serena looked around, imagining where the crocheted blanket must have fallen.

It had been covering an old traveler's bag, about mid-way along the wall, she thought, scanning the wall carefully.

And then she saw it – the very corner of a crocheted blanket lightly draped over a greened canvas bag. She Moon-walked over to it and gently pushed aside a broken lantern that prevented the blanket from falling all the way to the floor. The corner drifted lazily to the floor, but not before Serena reached down and grabbed hold of it. Carefully, as not to damage the stitches, Serena pulled the nearly complete blanket up and caught the silver crocheting needle as it tried to slip out of a stitch. She smiled at the blanket she held in her arms, and delicately shifted aside more debris.

Her search was not fruitless – she discovered the string that was threaded through the needle led to a small cloth bag that held several balls of colored yarn. Tucking the blanket tenderly under one arm, she bent and claimed the small bag.

No sooner had she done this than Jerry pulled on her arm and pointed to another spot on the floor where five whole boards had been ripped from the spot by force.

Reverently, Serena folded the blanket and set it down gently atop an old bag. She could hardly believe that she had the opportunity to touch a 200-year-old drowned blanket that the fingers of her ancestor had once knitted. She laid the needle and the bag of yarn on top of it gingerly, then stepped away and followed Jerry to the hole.

She approached the torn gap and ran her hand over the sharp, rotten surface of the ripped wood. She smiled at Jerry, and he nodded at another small section on the wall.

They were down here, too, he seemed to say. *See the broken edges? This ship was very old to be able to break like that.*

Serena nodded and inspected the gaping hole carefully. To prove his point, she bent down and broke off a jutting little piece of wood.

The moment the silent crack of wood was made, Serena's mind shut down completely, and she fell into her third, and, she hoped, her *final* vision.

This time the Clouds that passed her mind were pink, and pastel-colored rose petals were swept along rhythmically as if on the Wind.

The Mist parted, and the Boy, the same one that she had seen in her first vision, was ripping and tearing at the same hole Serena was standing at. He carefully bound the boards together tightly with strips of thick rope, and, to assure the small craft would stay afloat, he tied two air-filled jugs on either side, pounding the corks down into them as though he wished to break them.

Then, after encouraging others to follow his clever example, he bounded from the deck, waist-deep in Water. He met with the Girl, just as she muttered something like a prayer under her breath and flung the jug with all her might into the raging Ocean.

After that, a Lightning bolt shot down from the Sky and touched her necklace. Serena wanted to reach out and help the poor Girl, but knew that she could not. The Girl stood for a long time with the lightning buzzing all over her necklace. Then, the lightning detached itself from the Sky and zapped back into the necklace, which had now not only drastically changed its form, but was now glowing in a most beautiful and strange manner.

The Boy and the Girl, reunited at last, flung themselves onto their craft and consolidated with the others, presumably their families, and tied together the hastily made vessels with spare rope. Then, with the rising Sun before them stretching the first of its rays upon their dirty, tear-stained faces, the few survivors of the now sinking ship embarked upon a perilous Ocean journey in search of Land.

Serena's thoughts swam as the warm, fluffy pink Clouds and fragrant rose petals descended upon her once again, wrapped her up protectively, and then dissolved into a faint Mist and vanished.

The first thing Serena noticed was that she was now lying down on her side and someone was shaking her worriedly. She opened her cerulean eyes to the blurred, then very clear image of a panicked expression plastered on Jerry's face. She sat up and he relaxed, drawing the back of his hand over his forehead in symbolism of relief. He pointed to the surface. She nodded, gathered up her knapsack, and followed him.

~*~*~*~*~

Halfway to the surface, a squirming Mike met them, pointing frantically at the ceiling of waves and beckoning them into a hasty scramble to get there. As soon as they surfaced, Jerry ripped his oxygen mask off and demanded in a frightened tone,

"What happened?"

Serena's eyes grew large as they spotted the answer, which showed itself plainly in the distance.

"Land!" she gasped.

True to her words, there, in the distance, stretched the massive yellow-brown form of a Sandy Beach. It looked to Serena very much like an IsLand. Yes, that was it - a great oblong IsLand that was too skinny to even show on the map! Or was it?

A great lull of silence, like that after a Storm, filled the air. The only sound to be heard was the constant dribble of Rain issued by the Ocean-gray and green Clouds that still hovered above them, appearing ponderous. They didn't seemed to know whether they wanted to Storm now and cause more confusion for the team or to wait for later until they reached the Land in the distance and confuse them even further. The Storm from before had thinned out considerably since it had first arrived.

Suddenly, a shower of questions peppered the still air.

"Where are we?"

"Is that an IsLand?"

"It looks like a Desert."

"No, no, it's a Beach of some kind."

"How far off is it?"

"How are we going to get there with this big reef in the way?"

Jerry held up his hands, the Water rising to his chin, to silence the group. Amidst a last few hurried whispers, they hushed down.

"Alright, we should know only one thing about that little piece of Land over there – and it's this: *That* is strange Territory. It wasn't marked on the map, and we can't possibly tell whether it's an IsLand or an entire Continent until we get there. But let me tell you something - I have a strange feeling that we have succeeded in finding our missing Continent."

Comments of awe and excitement blossomed into the air. The team hugged and high-fived and wiggled in the Water. Jerry had to silence them again before continuing.

"It looks like it's only about two or three miles away from where we are, and I think that if we take off now we could, very possibly, make the place by dusk. We'll have to be very careful going over this reef; we don't know what could be living in there. If there is anything in there, we most certainly don't want to disturb it. I'm just glad it's shallow enough to swim over - but don't try walking on it. It could be very slippery. Alright now, rest yourselves up. We're going to take off here on the count of three."

As a whole, the six team members chanted together, poising themselves to pounce upon the unsuspecting Waters and swim themselves to the very solid-looking Land.

"One ... two ... three!"

SPLASH!

~*~*~*~*~

Serena swam expertly next to Lindsey, who was huffing but still swimming at a quickened pace.

"You know I ... never thought that ... finding a ... whew! ... a missing Continent ... would ever be this ... this physical!" she huffed, spitting the unwelcome taste of salty Ocean Water from her mouth.

Serena stretched her healthy limbs forward to greet the oncoming waves and the Rain that was gradually increasing to thick, fat droplets.

"Yeah, I know ... what you mean ,... Lindsey ... But see ,... that's why Dr. Birkwood ... chose a bunch of younger explorers ... for this trip ... phew! ... because he didn't ... know what kind of ... of troubles ... we would run ... into ... and he knew tha t... someone who had more ... muscle and energy ... would be more likely to ... escape ... than someone who's ... whew! ... older and more … fragile …" she panted.

"… True …" Lindsey wheezed, coughing up the Water. Serena disliked the briny taste of the Ocean Water and did anything within her control to keep it from entering her mouth. She breathed only when she was sure that her head was clear of the Water, and it was then that she attempted to speak as well. Before Lindsey could remedy an actual reply, Jerry floundered up on Serena's other side.

"Excuse me… Lindsey… I need a… a word with… Serena."

"Sure!... whew!" Lindsey gasped, and hung back a little ways.

Serena neither smiled nor frowned but kept herself moving at all costs, determined to reach the Land by the time dusk rolled around.

"So what happened… to you down… down there?" he began in a low whisper. Serena stretched her arms in front of her and swam strongly, mustering up her strength.

"A vision?" he inquired.

"Yeah, I had … three of them …"

Jerry stared at her in wonder, then licked his lips and prepared for the next question.

"What were … they about? I mean, what … caused them? Could you … breathe?..."

"Oh, I … could breathe …" Serena gasped, attempting to lift her head from the Water. "I just sort of … of lapsed into a dream … The first time I saw … Teresa and Jacob star-gazing … And then I saw Teresa … writing in her diary … when the ship … hit the reef …" she paused to catch her breath, "… and then I saw … them … escaping on … on a raft built from … the wood of the ship."

Jerry stroked briskly in thought. "That's weird … Are you sure you … had enough oxygen?"

"Yeah …"

"Maybe you were … just tired or … stressed out … What else did you … you see?"

Serena told him, in detail, her first, second and third visions that she had seen underWater. As the Land grew steadily closer, the team began to wind down somewhat. The Wind picked up as the Sky Clouded over with both Storm Clouds and the growing velvety blackness known as Night. Together, they blinded and blurred the visions of the six swimming discoverers. The storm built up its strength once more and the endless Ocean took up its restless towering of waves.

The team struggled against the oncoming forces with much vim and vigor.

Finally, after what seemed like forever, the young explorers spotted the Land through the white sheets of Rain. Thunder boomed nearby and a great crack of Lightning lit up the Night Sky bright as morning, making the outline of the Land visible to the weary travelers. They had every will inside them to reach the Land before the Storm got any worse, but found themselves fighting the high-rising waves.

Serena was floundering. She wasn't swimming gracefully as she had before, but she was floundering and kicking and fighting to stay above the surface. A large tidal wave towered over her, like a black, foam-crested Spirit on its way to snuffing the life out of its helpless victims. It gained speed and broke over the heads of the poor explorers.

Serena could not breathe. Water filled her senses – her eyes, ears, nose, and mouth. She stretched her arms up over her head and clawed at the life-giving air above her, as though trying to grab hold of it and pull herself up. Finally, she managed to surface between the outrageous waves and did the only thing she saw fit for the situation – she yanked on her oxygen mask and goggles and submerged beneath the raging Storm.

In the dim light from the Moon, Serena could make out five other figures congregating beneath the surface. She hurried toward them. The members of the discovery team were exhausted and sore, but they most certainly were not going to give up now when they were a mere fraction away from solid Land. The only thing between them and the Sandy shore was the angry Storm.

Jerry, depending on his nonverbal language, had quickly formed a plan and tried to convey it to the team in a decently decipherable manner. He had them join hands in a line, and when the next wave hit overhead, he had them jump up into it, letting it carry them forward. Serena felt a little as though she was flying as the waves bore her up, and then plunged her into the deep again. Riding the waves was actually sort of fun, and Serena was sure she would have enjoyed such a sport without the dangerous situation they were in. It was nearly impossible to swim under the furious waves; the current was so strong it would have pulled them back.

The discoverers practiced the plan for only a few short minutes before they were slapped upon the Sand. They scrambled further up the shore, spitting out their oxygen masks and shaking off their goggles.

"Find shelter!" roared Jerry above the howling Wind.

"Where?" Mike shouted. "It's nothing more than Beach!"

"Well, let's have a look around, just in case!" Jerry hollered.

Serena stood and leaned against the Winds as they protested against her. She could hardly see through the white sheets of Rain which were driven sideways by the Wind. She kept one hand on Lindsey's back so that she did not lose her in the wild Storm.

Suddenly Lindsey stopped.

"Hey, guys, come here! I think I found something!" she called, staggering slightly against the Wind. Within moments, the team had congregated to where she stood, staring awe-struck up at a gaping Cave mouth.

Chapter Eight: The Lost Continent

Water dropped from the stalactites in miniature Waterfalls, splashing noisily into wet, little pools that chained together through tiny Rivers. There was a peculiar feeling that rippled through the souls of the discovery team as they gawked up at the yawning, dark Cave. A cool Wind, smelling pleasantly of wet moss and herbs, wafted under their noses and rustled their wet hair, as though the Cave itself was breathing on them and beckoning them to enter.

Serena shuddered as a heavy gust of Wind rushed down to meet them, bringing with it more teardrops from the Sky, rocketing down like angry wasps and pelting the wet earth.

"I-it's a Cave!" Bob said in a voice that sounded hushed and afraid.

Serena looked to Jerry, whose expression simply read that he couldn't believe, after all their bad luck, they were beginning to show signs of surviving on this dangerous mission.

Kate hitched her dripping survival knapsack onto her back.

"Well, it's better than nothing," she retorted. And with that, she began to walk toward the Cave.

"No!" Jerry protested in a loud whisper, jumping out to stop her. He barred her way with his massive figure.

Serena was simply amazed to see Kate thinking positive. She shifted feet, knowing the exact explanation that the black-haired girl was going to receive.

"And why no-" she began with a shout.

"Shhhhhh! Because we don't know what could live in there!" Jerry whispered, shooting a nervous glance over his shoulder. It was quite plain that he did not like having his back to the black mouth.

"Oh, puh-lease," enthused Kate, crossing her arms moodily. Her dark hair hung in wet, greasy strands about her face. "I've had to put up with a Storm at Sea, giant ... Fish, the Wavethingy sinking, stranding us on this *stupid* IsLand, almost drowning to get here, and now you aren't even going to at least let me sit down and dry off by a fire?"

"That's right," growled Jerry firmly. "Because if you would like to risk coming this far just to get eaten by a Bear or a Lion or something, it kinda doesn't seem worth the trouble, does it?"

Kate frowned as Jerry's point hit her. She opened her mouth to snap something else at him, but, not finding a debate suitable enough to fit the cause, she clamped it shut in a tight scowl.

"Now, you guys go lie flat next to that big Rock over there, okay? I'm going to go in and see if there's anything in there, and if there isn't I'll call you."

Serena nodded her head at the wise statement and followed the others to the Rock Jerry had pointed at. She laid flat on her stomach in the muddy Sand.

Jerry approached the Cave.

"He's so stupid!" muttered Kate under her breath. "Thinks he can boss me around just because he's the captain. Well, I'm older than him, and I am perfectly able to take care of mys-"

"Kate!" Mike grumbled in a piteous, exhausted tone. "Shut up!"

Serena noticed as a look of thorough rejection crossed Kate's face. Her cheeks flustered in frustration, growing a deep crimson against her dark skin, adding to the humiliated expression mounting on her face. In a way, Serena was beginning to feel sorry for the snobbish and mean Girl.

Jerry edged cautiously toward a corner of the Cave. He seemed to stop and take a look around its interior before he fully disappeared inside – and even then only for a moment. Serena closed her eyes as she lay beside the Stone, and hoped that he would return in one piece. She didn't think she could bear to lose such a loyal friend after meeting him so soon.

After a couple of minutes, a shout issued from the Cave. Serena was disturbed from her worrisome thoughts as Jerry hailed them.

"Hey, guys! You can come on in! There's nothing in here but dry air and Rocks!"

Cool, calm relief washed over Serena and the other discoverers as they plodded into the Cave, soaked, shivering and famished. At once a fire was made from tinder and flint, and it crackled merrily in the center of the large, dry Cave.

The Cave was very old, as Mike promptly stated upon his examination of the dripping stalactites. Serena herself could have guessed that much, because the very moment she set foot in the place, a musty, moldy odor that carried a hint of age with it greeted her nose. But there was a certain scent to the Cave that unnerved her a little. She could not quite think of a word to describe it, but settled for the closest description as *mysterious*.

She found herself a nice, dry Rock to sit on next to the fire, which was somewhat softened with the presence of a sprightly green Moss. Peeling her scuba suit and nearly-worn tank off, she placed the suit in a pile near the front of the Cave with everyone else's. Returning to the Mossy Rock, she watched as Jerry hung his soaked knapsack up to dry and remembered that she had packed all of her belongings in little plastic Ziploc baggies. And then she remembered, with a taste of dismay lingering in her heart, that not all Ziploc baggies were guaranteed to stay sealed.

While the others explored the Cave and fixed something suitable to eat, Serena wrung her soaked clothes out (the ones that had been in her knapsack and thus escaped the strangling baggies) and laid them out on nearby Stones to dry. She came upon Teresa's diary, which appeared just as thoroughly drenched as her clothes, and found that the protective baggies were nowhere in sight. Serena felt a wave of emotion rush to her eyes in the fear that it had been permanently ruined.

However, she discovered a very odd thing as she opened the front cover, fully expecting blurred and smudged ink.

The text was dry and in perfect condition.

But the outside cover is wet. she thought, sliding her finger over the front of the canvas cover. She thought her mind must have been playing tricks, for the more she felt the front of the diary, the less damp its texture seemed. *What an odd little thing this diary is.*

Serena's thoughts were interrupted by a sudden call.

"Look! Look what I found!" cried Mike from a corner of the Cave. Lindsey, who had been fixing supper, Bob, who had been fervently trying to revive the nearly drowned cell phone (the only dry piece of equipment they had found), Kate, pouting in a corner and muttering dark words under her breath, Jerry, who was feeding the fire, and Serena all rushed to his aid.

"A type of Lizard skin!" Mike exclaimed, obviously excited as he held up a scaly, silver-shining shed skin. He scratched his head as he observed the radiant mixed colors of gold and crimson in the lustrous scales. "But most unlike any skin I have ever seen. It isn't a Snake's – the scales are too large." He squinted through his tiny glasses as he held it up to his face. "I wonder if it belongs to a Godzilla of some sort?"

Kate huffed rudely and returned to her knapsack. Bob inspected the skin for only a moment, and then shuffled off bashfully, his brownish-black hair gleaming on top of his head.

"Very interesting," Jerry remarked, taking the skin from Mike and holding it up to the glowing firelight. Mike beamed proudly.

"What do you think could leave a skin like *that* in a Cave?" Serena couldn't help but wonder aloud, rubbing a corner of the skin to feel its rough texture.

The scales were indeed very large, as big as a half-dollar coin, though more oval in shape and overlapped. The edges of the scales were sharp when touched the wrong way, sharp enough to cause a little paper cut that now showed itself plainly on Jerry's ring finger. However, when stroked the right way, the deep rose- and golden-hued scales gave off a pleasantly smooth, leathery texture. The scales were lightly transparent, as all skins are when they are shed.

Serena shook her head in wonder, and Lindsey traipsed off to finish fixing supper.

"It doesn't look too old, though," Mike noted, "maybe a couple of weeks or so,"

"Hey, look!" Jerry said, pointing to something not far away. He quickly strode over to it and picked it up. It was another patch of skin. Mike scurried over to it, leaving Serena to hold the first small patch.

She carried the skin with her back to the fire and sat on her Rock. She studied it for a moment more, and then set it aside to make herself a temporary sleeping spot.

Throughout the Night, the Storm raged on, the Wind whistling through the Land and the Rain spattering the puddles that continued to grow larger. By early morning the Storm had simmered down considerably, clearing the Sky and whisking away its dark, angry Clouds to go and haunt some other unfortunate part of Land.

Serena awoke before dawn – she did not know why. Perhaps the last bit of Thunder had disturbed her.

But no, the Storm Clouds are long gone, and it is still dark out. she thought. *It's probably just because I have never slept outside on the hard ground before – yes, that's it - all the strange sounds and smells must have been what woke me up.*

Satisfied with her own assumption, she settled herself on her side facing

70

the glowing embers of last Night's fire. The strange skin sat to one side, and she reached out and dragged it to her face to study it.

There was no doubt about it, there was definitely something odd about the skin. Its strange softness, its glittering scales, its autumn colors or its distinctive scent – Serena could not decide which was the most awkward.

She laid her head on her arm, stroking the pretty skin and thinking about the Night before.

They had stayed up late, coaxing Bob to see if he could do anything to make their last cell phone work. (The rest had either been lost or drowned.) It flickered only once, made a strange beeping sound that gradually grew in volume, and then exploded into a thousand little pieces in the Sand. This being their only hope of ever getting back home, the entire crew sulked and trudged off to bed. Kate burst into tears after the cell phone blew up, and, as a consequence, kept everybody up for an additional hour and a half with her sniffing and whining and complaining.

Serena suddenly didn't want to be up so early, and felt that she deserved more rest for all of her adventures. After all that she had done the Day before, she had expected to sleep until past dawn.

Now she stared at the dancing shadows the fire cast upon the Cave wall. She thought she saw a shadow that moved like a real Creature, but pushed the thought away and judged it as silly.

She added more wood to the fire and sat down on the bare floor to think to herself. She leaned back against a Rock and found, to her surprise, something soft beneath the spot where she was sitting. A draft wisped into the Cave mouth and brushed up against her bare feet (for she had needed to dry out her socks and shoes) causing her to shiver. She spotted her now dried socks and shoes next to the fire and snatched them up. She put them on, and feeling the warmth of the fire soothing her toes, she leaned back against the Stone again.

Wearily, she remembered the soft carpet she was sitting on. She felt the texture. It was delicate, cool, and colorful even to her fingertips.

But the ground is made of dirt, she thought, *and it's not a blanket. Maybe it's just some Moss.*

Whatever it was, all Serena knew at that moment was that it was soft and very comfortable, so she laid down and soon fell into a deep sleep.

Something moved.

Serena, unlike the majority of the others, was a light sleeper. As the faint scuffling, scratchy sound met her ears, her bright blue eyes snapped open and she laid still.

A young voice whispered in a crisp British accent,

"What are they, Mum?"

"Humans," rasped an older female voice in reply. "Sun Humans."

Serena gulped as her heart rate shot through the ceiling. Sun Humans? They didn't come from the Sun! She wondered who the British voices were as she laid perfectly still, trying to pretend she was still asleep.

"Should we eat them?" said the young voice again.

Serena's skin pricked in fear.

"No, Sun Humans are almost extinct. Let them sleep and we will scare them off later when they are awake."

More scratching and shuffling. Serena felt a cool, dark shadow creep over her and resisted the urge to get up and flee, terrified. Sweat poured down the back of her neck and she clenched her eyes shut, gulping and trying not to shudder.

"It's got your skin, Mum," the young voice chirped, very near to Serena now. "Should I take it back?"

The voice of the mother heaved a sigh further down in the Cave. "There's no use worrying over a shed piece of skin, Keffle. But, I suppose, if you would like to keep it, you may take it back."

Serena bit her lip, nearly drawing blood. She felt the presence of something larger than her reach down and grasp hold of the shed skin she clutched in her sweating hand.

She could resist no longer.

She opened her eyes.

"Ahhh!" she screamed, releasing the skin and backing off.

"Ahhh!" screamed a little Girl Dragon, dropping the skin at the same time and taking a couple steps back.

Serena's breath came in short, terrified gasps. She looked at the thing that had not moments ago been nose-to-snout with her.

It, that is, Keffle was most definitely a Dragon – with bright orange and yellow scales and leathery orange wings that folded against her back. Her full height reached to Serena's chest as the Dragonling stood on all fours. She wasn't much longer than a common door is tall from tip to tail. She had a short, stubby spinal crest of bright yellow that ran from the top of her head to the tip of her long tail, which was about as long as her whole body, and swayed side to side in a curious, mischievous manner. Keffle sat back on her hind haunches like a cat would, brandishing four small feet filled with needle-sharp claws. On either side of her little head sprouted two rounded stubs, presumably the beginning of horns. But the thing that had Serena taken aback the most was the little Dragon's eyes. They had been very close to her face, and when she opened her own eyes, Keffle's eye color had changed from a curious yellow to a surprised orange very quickly. Now the eyes of the small Dragon burned an even brighter yellow than before.

"I didn't mean to wake you." said the young Dragon in a half-whisper. Serena marveled at the pleasant ring of the little British voice and gulped, sitting up very slowly.

"Th-that's okay." she stuttered, looking about to see if the others were awake.

And realization struck her like 10 pounds of bricks to the head. Her eyes snapped back and caught the gaze of Keffle's blazing yellow eyes.

"D-did you just … talk to me?" she said incredulously. The Dragon, obviously very curious, stood and inched forward. She stretched out her little neck and scuffled closer.

"Yes, why?"

Serena opened her mouth to say something, but with the figure of the Child Dragon growing nearer, she was in the absence of words and closed her mouth quickly.

Suddenly, an overwhelming power of curiosity mounted upon her chest, and she sat up straight.

A Dragon.

A real, live Dragon.

A myth.

A legend.

And she was looking at it.

Keffle sat just feet from her and blinked in awe, her yellow eyes shining.

"Wow," they said in unison, and then caught each other's gaze.

"Now, don't tell me you've never seen a Human before?!" Serena giggled finally, deciding that the little Dragon was harmless. Keffle chuckled and her eyes changed to a merry blue.

"I will if you tell me you've never seen a Dragon." sang the Child-like voice.

Serena's laughter echoed off of the wall of the Cave like many voices.

"Where I come from, Dragons are only a myth," she explained.

"Where do you come from?" twittered the orange and yellow Dragon. She stood and came snout-to-nose with Serena once more. "And why is your hair the color of gold? And why are your eyes the color of the Sky on a Cloudless Spring afternoon? And why do you speak so differently, though I can understand you? I've never seen-"

"Serena!"

Jerry dashed for Keffle, having only just awoken and believing that Serena was under attack.

The Dragonling squealed and made to run, but Serena leaped in front of her before Jerry was even halfway there.

Whoosh!

BOOM!

"AHHHHHHHHHH!"

A 20-foot-long body of claws, teeth, horns and scales landed between Serena and Jerry, uttering a low warning growl.

Serena heard screams echoing from the other side of the Mountain of protective Dragon flesh, and knew the others had awoken. It was not yet dawn.

"Filthy Sun Humans!" bellowed the mother Dragon. "First you steal our front doorstep and then you mean to harm my only Dragonling! I won't tolerate any more of this! Out! Out, I say!"

"Oh, MOTHER!" cried Keffle, her now sad gray eyes glistening with tears. "I only wanted to make a friend!"

The mother Dragon, whose scales were a mix of golden and crimson, reared her head around to face the Human Girl standing between them.

Something worse than fear caused Serena to shiver under the smooth-faced mother's gaze. Executing a nervous smile, she put her hands up to show she meant no harm and slowly began to back away from between mother and Child.

The Dragonling faced her mother. Something about the sight of her Child's wet eyes softened the look in the mother's angry red eyes, and they melted down to a mellow shade of violet.

"Keffle," reasoned the mother, "you have plenty of friends! What about Oudin and Recca?"

Keffle turned her tear-stained face upon that of her mother's.

"But they're just other Dragons!" she sobbed piteously. "I wanted to make friends with a Sun Human."

The mother's brow bristled and scrunched up in a frown. Her wrathful red eyes returned as she raised her head above her Dragonling.

"A *what*? But why in Forever would you want to do something like that? Let me tell you something, young Dragon, one of those … those *savages* tried to attack you! And I am most certainly *not* going to allow any daughter of *mine* to befriend something like *that*! The answer is no, and they are going to leave this Cavehold at once!"

Then, with a snort of utmost satisfaction (which billowed out of her nostrils as two small mushroom Clouds of smoke), the mother Dragon turned to Serena, who was in the process of sneaking around the front of the Monster.

A large, spine-backed tail blocked her way.

"What is your business in my Cave?" the mother Dragon demanded.

"We-we're lost …" stuttered Serena, backing up until she felt the cold Rock of the wall against her back. "We came in last Night t-to get out of the S-Storm."

"I see…" rumbled the Dragon, her eyes swiftly molding into a curious yellow color. Serena relaxed a little at seeing this; anything was better than those shudderingly terrible red eyes. The mother Dragon waited for a moment, eyeing the Girl up and down, then grunted, "Go on…"

Serena could think of nothing more to say. She cleared her throat.

"Where are we?" she squeaked. The mother Dragon lowered her head until she could look Serena in the face. Her Sunny-colored eyes, each as large as a small bowling ball, burned holes into Serena's cool blue eyes.

"Perhaps you do not fully understand me," she muttered. Then, in a loud boom, she proclaimed, "It is *I* who owns this Lair, not you, and it is *I* who is asking the questions here. You have but two choices – to answer them and leave this place with your life or to keep asking silly questions and get yourself, as well as your five little friends here, disemboweled. Which shall it be?"

Serena closed her eyes and tried not to cry. So, she had a two-ton Dragon ready to scorch her to a crisp. She would be brave. So, she was trapped with no way out while this particular two-ton Dragon glared at her with eyes that changed color according to her mood. She could still be brave. So, she…

…*found a big sturdy stick leaning up against the wall, which conveniently just so happens to be hidden behind her back* … she thought, a new hope flushing to her cheeks. Her fingers grasped around the stick, and she opened her eyes to look up at the impatient mother Dragon.

"I choose life!" Serena exclaimed, and in the blink of an eye, she whipped the stick out from behind her back and pole-vaulted over the Dragon's gigantic tail. Dropping the stick, she grabbed her knapsack and high-tailed it out the door with the rest.

Dawn's first bright rays were beginning to bathe the earth in purest Sunshine by the time the six explorers had stopped running. They had taken off in the opposite direction of the Ocean, heading further inLand in search of civilization of any kind. When they finally slowed and paced themselves, they were comforted by the knowledge that they had not been chased. Soon their weary limbs grew tired and they stopped to eat their first meal of the Day.

Jerry threw his knapsack on the ground and set about making a fire. All around the circle, the travelers were catching their breath, taking stock of what they had accidentally left in the Cavern in their hurry and praising good fortune that they were still alive. None of them had ever seen a Dragon before, much less an angry one.

"I don't believe it. A real, *live* Dragon?"

"Oh, it was real enough. Didn't you see how her eyes changed color?"

"Why, *why* did we lose the camera?"

"You know what? I'm just glad to be alive at this point."

"Man, am I glad we got out of there when we did!"

"I'm glad we didn't get scorched! Did you see that smoke coming out of her nose?"

"And those wings! Just like an enormous Bat's wings!"

"Her scales – did you see them? It must have been a piece of her shed skin that we found in there last Night!"

Serena was about the only one who wasn't talking about the mother Dragon. And, quite frankly, she didn't really want to discuss the matter at the time. It had been the most terrifying experience of her life, and for the moment she was trying to gather her wits together and take her mind off of the burning new memory. So she studied the Landscape as she recorded their adventures of the past Day in the notebook Dr. Birkwood had insisted she use.

A rocky outcrop with sandy hills and some scrub grass. The terrain is also very hilly, and so far it has had an awful lot of caves, too. I suppose more dragons lurk in the shadows of these and make them their lairs, but we aren't willing to find out after our bout with Keffle and her angry mother. We try to keep our distance.

Serena closed the notebook and inserted her pen into the spiral loops that held the pages together. She accepted a warm biscuit from Mike and scooted closer to the fire to warm herself against the chilly morning air.

"Well, where do you suppose we are?" Lindsey piped up after several moments of silent chewing.

"Let me put it this way," Serena said, swallowing the last of her biscuit. She took her Sunny curls and brought them on either side of her face in low pigtails. She put on a semi-pathetic expression and said softly,

"I don't think we're in Kansas anymore, Toto."

Chuckles passed around the circle of friends.

"Really," sniveled Kate, "We're lost in the middle of an unknown Continent with Dragons lurking in every nook and cranny, and you're treating it all like it's some sort of big joke?!"

"Well, at least I know how to *make* a joke," Serena mumbled. The navigator fumed fit to burst.

"I think we might be in some sort of utopia," Lindsey suggested.

"I don't know. Those Dragons didn't seem very peace-giving to me," Mike said, reaching out to grab another biscuit from the heated Stone they rested on.

"The little one wasn't so bad," Jerry pointed out. "It was just the big one that we had problems with."

77

"And even then, if we hadn't stumbled into her Lair by accident, I don't think she would have been so aggressive with us," muttered Bob, tossing his head back to get his dark brown hair away from his face. His hairband must have broken or been lost. Serena could now see how long his hair really was – shoulder-length.

"She probably just wanted us out so she could protect her Lair. That's why she didn't chase us," Lindsey put in.

"Or maybe she was afraid for Keffle."

"Like any good mother should be."

Silence fell, as though all six of their minds were in one place but no one had the guts to say what they were all thinking.

And then Serena gathered her courage and spoke the question that was swimming around in all of their minds.

"Do you think we could make friends with one of them and have them tell us where we are?"

"I doubt it," snorted Kate, not missing a beat.

"We probably shouldn't risk it anyway," Jerry replied, ignoring the black-haired Girl sitting next to him, draped in a thin, worn blanket.

"Let's just keep going." Lindsey said, standing to brush the biscuit crumbs from her muddied jeans. "If we find someone civilized, we can talk to them. Personally, I don't care to consort with any more Dragons."

"Okay," grunted Jerry. He got up and shouldered his pack. "We'll just have to keep traveling until we get out of the Dragons' Territory. Then we'll look for some sort of civilization that can hopefully give us some clues as to where we've landed ourselves."

Serena thought this was an excellent idea. And so, it seemed, did everyone else. There were no objections as the team slowly stood and began their perilous quest.

Part Two: The Lands of Forever
Chapter Ten: Dragon Eggs

It was midafternoon and the hot Sun bore down upon the group's laden backs, drilling its rays into their very souls so that they might feel its burning presence.

They most certainly did, or so said the salty beads of perspiration that dappled their weary and dust-showered faces.

"How much further… do we have?" gasped Kate, shielding her eyes against the Sun.

"I don't know," Jerry answered truthfully. He wiped his glistening forehead on the back of his arm.

Serena trudged onward, wondering whether it was this same dry, parched Land that had not too long ago been wet and cool. Oh, just to taste that wet, cool Rain on her face right now, even if only for a moment …

She missed the sharp Rock that jutted stubbornly in the middle of her way, and stumbled over. She almost fell, but Jerry caught her arm.

"You okay, Serena?" he rasped, his throat dry from lack of Water. He dusted off her arm and helped her regain her balance so she could walk again. She blinked and shook her head, trying to ward off the effects of hallucination.

"Yes," she said, rubbing her eyes. "I'm just tired. Thanks."

"I think we all are," Jerry replied, surveying the crew members in front of him. "We've been through an awful lot yesterDay and toDay, and I know that if we had a choice we could sit back and relax. But right now we don't have those types of decisions. We have to survive and find a City or something – it's our only option."

"We will," Serena agreed, nodding her head. She was fully aware of the serious tone in his voice. "We will have to work as a team."

Hours later, the scrub Grass began to thicken and the Caves became larger and more common. The Hills turned to steep miniature Mountains, with small dips of Valleys between them. There were still no Trees, but instead, massive boulders planted themselves in the thin, hard-packed, grainy Sand.

The six crew members trudged doggedly onward, each with their own thoughts and hopes that they would soon stumble across civilization of some kind.

As dusk drew nearer, the temperatures cooled somewhat and the team began to search for someplace to camp.

"No Caves," Jerry had commented, "unless we want to take our chances of getting away from another Dragon."

A solid chorus of "NO" met his waiting pause.

"How about one of these Valleys?" Bob suggested as they rounded the umptieth Hill of the Day.

"Good idea – as long as we steer clear of any Caves," agreed Jerry, putting a special inflection to the word "Caves."

There was little talk as the explorers slipped and slid down the slope, descending upon their temporary camping spot.

Caves dotted the steep, Rocky Hills, like the very pores of the earth. It was hard to find a spot large enough for six people to sleep without the threat of being too close to any certain Dragon's domain, but a cup-shaped, little dip in the Land was finally voted the safest, and the team settled in for the Night.

It was still light out as the group began to make some form of stew for supper. Serena got bored with chopping wild onions (which Mike had found growing in the shade of a Rock) and decided to explore around in case she happened to find Water (which they were becoming low on) or discover some other type of edible Plant or root.

She searched under Rocks and behind Grasses, staying very close to the bowl-shaped dip carved in the Valley. For awhile, she kept her distance from the yawning, black Caves that dotted the Land. But when she spotted a particularly small one that seemed to have twinkling crystals, or even better, Water inside of it, she strayed dangerously close, hoping to find a Water source.

Serena stayed along the side of the Valley wall, and when she came to the small Cave that looked as though no adult Dragon could fit in it, she took a deep breath and peeked inside.

What she saw inside ripped the air from her lungs and left her utterly speechless.

Eggs.

Large eggs.

Hundreds of them.

They were much larger than any egg she had ever seen. She estimated the smallest one to be about knee-high. But there was something special about these eggs that had made her gasp. Something she thought that she would never, ever live to see.

They were completely transparent.

And there was only one Creature within miles that was large enough to be capable of laying such beautiful objects.

"Dragon eggs!" she whispered under her breath. She slid into a crouching sit at the Cave side, her hand still grasping the wall as if begging for support.

The eggs could be described as nothing other than beautiful. The shells were completely clear – for a moment Serena thought they were made of glass – showing everything that gestated inside of them. The colors of the Dragons' scales were one part of the magnificent appearance, and the small flakes of multicolor glitter that floated within, probably chipped scales, formed the other. The most beautiful sight by far, however, was the very interior of the Cave. The Sun glinted off the colorful glitter that swam inside the eggs, casting little spots of light that danced on the ceiling and walls like so many brightly shimmering fireflies.

Serena felt her heart beat fast as she reached out and stroked the nearest egg. The baby Dragon inside flinched, and the sparkles within swirled around furiously in Clouds of spectral colors. Serena withdrew, mortified. Now she was quite sure that the egg would hatch and the baby would set up a series of wails (through which she would flee helter-skelter back to the camp). She braced herself.

But the fetal Dragon did not hatch. No, instead, it uncurled its delicate, little neck, stretched its large-eyed head up to the very spot where Serena had stroked its shell, and opened and closed its weak little mouth. Serena smiled, noticing the tiny, little white stubs inside its gums that would later grow into flesh-ripping fangs. The baby Dragon seemed to smile at her after that, and it nuzzled its soft, little nose up against the shell, begging for more.

A maternal instinct flared up inside Serena as her cheeks flushed, and her heart melted at once.

"Like that, do you?" she whispered and stroked the shell again. She sat on the ground, laying her handful of thoroughly wrung green leaves beside her. As she slowly stroked the shell, the feeling of maternal instinct continued to bubble up inside her. She studied the gleaming blue and purple scales of the baby's coat, and she stroked the egg again, and again the fetus reacted to her gentle touch.

Serena stayed and stroked the baby Dragon's eggshell until it finally fell asleep, at which point in time Serena had been gone for nearly 20 minutes. She was sure the other explorers would be worrying about her by then.

And so, reluctantly, she left the peacefully sleeping baby Dragon and made her way back to camp. After a hearty supper of vegetable stew, she told her friends of how she had come across several nests of Dragon's eggs. Questions arose and fluttered through the air to Serena's ears like hordes of butterflies.

"Why were they unguarded?"

"Were they really glass?"

"How big were they?"

"Hundreds of them?"

"How could a Dragon even *fit* in that little Cavern, much less lay hundreds of eggs in it?"

"Now that one I can't answer," Serena giggled, pointing at the speaker, Lindsey. "But I can tell you that if Jerry will let us, I'll take us all to the Cave so we can see them."

"But what if a Dragon catches us?" Kate piped up, sounding very Child-like.

"They're unguarded, probably abandoned. If some Dragon really was watching them, she probably would have been back by now," Jerry pointed out. He hitched his survival pack up on his back. "We'll just have to take our chances. If we ever make it back, this will be one of the things those scientists will go crazy over."

"Oh my gosh!" Lindsey whispered, stretching her head out over the others

82

that were crouched at a corner of the entrance to the beautiful Cavern. "Ohmy-gosh!"

Words could not possibly explain the sight the glass Dragon eggs made to the eyes of the explorers. Little Rainbow-colored spots of light that bounced off of the sparkles floating in the eggs danced gracefully on the ceiling like a thousand glittering jewels. Serena smiled as she noticed that the eggs were in clusters of two and three.

Nests, she thought. She looked at the five breathless people who were clutching their hearts and staggering into the Cave one by one.

"This is amazing," breathed Mike.

"It's ... it's beautiful!" Kate enthused.

"Watch this!" whispered Serena, and she gently reached out and stroked an egg.

The blue and orange scaled baby Dragon uncurled itself slowly and stretched upward to the spot Serena had touched.

"Wow!" Lindsey marveled, squatting down beside Serena. "It's almost like she knows you ... like you're her mother ..."

Serena smiled. Lindsey stroked another egg, and the baby Dragon un-curled for her and twitched. Serena returned the compliment.

A green light glowed in Kate's brown eyes.

"Can't we take one of them with us? If we ever get back, something like this could mean thousands of-"

"No!" Serena and Jerry said at the same time. They merely glanced at each other and exchanged surprised expressions, and then Serena turned back to Kate. She felt very protective toward the eggs now.

"How are you going to carry it? The other Dragons will surly see it! And what are you going to do if it hatches?"

"I could... keep it in my backpack... and if it hatches, we'll just take the baby with us."

"A backpack is no atmosphere for a Dragon egg! It will crack!" Mike reasoned.

"You probably don't have room, anyway! And what if the baby doesn't want to come with us?" Serena said, glaring at Kate. She looked at the egg in front of her and stroked the top of it lovingly. "What if it needs its real mother?"

"And another thing – what if the Dragon mother comes back and finds that you've taken one of her eggs? Don't you think she'll come after it?" Jerry agreed, stepping forward to look the black-haired Girl in her hollow, dull brown eyes.

"I thought you said this Cave was abandoned!" she wailed, a look of pure deception on her face.

"I said the Cave was *probably* abandoned," Jerry mused in reply. He looked at Serena and hoisted his knapsack up further on his back. "I never said that it was for sure."

This quote seemed to unease the rest of the crew, so Jerry decided to stop at that.

"I wonder how long these guys have been in here," Lindsey crooned in an awed voice. It was quite obvious that she wanted to change the subject of conversation. Serena shrugged, looking deeply into the egg before her.

"They look like they're due anytime, I mean, they look like they're at the end of their gestation," Mike estimated, placing a hand on top of one and squatting down to get a closer look.

"Actually, they're due tomorrow."

"That's wonderful!" Serena exclaimed. She looked up at Jerry. "How did you know that?"

But Jerry's face was white. He gulped.

"I-I didn't say anything," he croaked. Serena turned to Bob, who shook his head, his long hair lapping around his high cheek bones, looking very scared. And finally, she looked at Mike, whose tiny, little eyes were larger and scarier than Serena had ever seen them.

Reality dawned on her like a fallen Tree - someone else was in the Cave with them.

She gulped and closed her eyes, then said aloud,

"Who are you?"

The question echoed off the deep walls of the Cavern.

Then, from the shadows in the very back, a figure with large, swimming red eyes moved forward into the light.

"Just the question I was wondering," growled a green and blue male Dragon, digging his large claws into the soft dirt. He was even larger than the female that the discoverers had seen at the beginning of their quest, and he wore a large green collar with a sparkling blue gem in the middle on his thick neck. His angry breaths came out as little puffs of smoke from his nostrils.

Serena gulped again and looked at Jerry. He turned to the 30-foot-long Dragon.

"We're Sun Humans," he said boldly.

"I can see that just as well as you can!" the Dragon sneered. "What are your names? What is your business here?"

Serena bristled at the Dragon's barking demands and stepped forward bravely.

"Our names are our own and our business is nobody's," she said coolly. Her voice echoed and bounced off of the shining walls.

The Dragon's red eyes shot daggers at her, and in a flourish of green and blue scales, he was nose-to-nose with the young Girl.

"Don't get cheeky with me, miss!" he snapped. "State your name and destination now before I let Daylight into your pathetic, little skull! What are you doing here?"

Jerry glanced at her out of the corner of his eye. She caught his sneaky wink and hitched her knapsack tighter on her back.

"Actually, Mr. Dragon, I do believe we are..." She took a step back. "Running!"

Energy sprang to her legs and she blazed out of the Cavern following the rest of the group.

Never had Serena run so fast in her life. She stretched her legs out, taking long strides and nearly flying over the hard, Sandy ground. She watched Mike pounding heavily away at the ground in front of her, Bob bobbing forward on his long, skinny legs, and Lindsey shooting away from them like a living bullet. Kate, because of her short stature, fell a little behind and ran next to Serena and Jerry.

But the Dragon did not pursue them. He merely poked his monstrosity of a head from the entrance of his Cavern and shouted,

"Come hither, you foul, egg-robbing rotters! I'll show you a whole new place to ransack! The inside of my stomach! Begone, you cowardice, brain-sucking-"

"Oh, shut up you sad, under-grown Snake with legs and wings! If you're so big, why don't you leave your cozy, little Cave!"

"Kate, NO!"

"Leave him be!"

"Do you want to get us all killed?"

Kate had stopped at the top of a rise several yards from the small Cave. Her greasy black hair hung in oily threads about her long face as she stood and scowled distastefully at the tough-looking male Dragon. She propped her arms on her hips as a five-year-old Child would when told to go to bed.

"Why don't you bubble-brained spawn of the devil just crawl back into the dank little holes you came from and-" the Dragon snarled in a booming voice.

"Oh, yeah? Well, why don't *you* just take your precious, little eggs and-"

"You leave the eggs out of this!"

"-before I take that sorry little string you call a tail and tie it in a knot, then shove it up your nose sideways in place of what you call a brain!"

"Well why don't you grow some common sense and learn that you can't trespass on private property-"

"Private property, my foot! I don't see any signs!"

"I believe the Cave speaks for itself."

"And I also believe that you need to go boil your ugly, fat head-"

"STOP!" Jerry thundered. Some startled Birds fluttered away quickly from behind a bush. "Kate, back to camp, now! Dragon, we're sorry we intruded, and it won't happen again."

And without further amiss the matter was settled.

Serena felt very guilty as she set up her sleeping spot for the Night. She had apologized to the entire troop for leading them up to danger, and they had all forgiven her – except for Kate, who merely stuck her nose in the air and made to act as her mother.

"You could have gotten us all killed!" she declared, admiring her dirt-encrusted nails.

"Well, I'm sorry, Kate, but there's nothing more I can tell you."

Kate turned and looked the blue-eyed Girl in the face.

"That's the second time you've led us into trouble! Remember the incident with the other Dragon?"

Serena was near to fuming, but she remained calm, determined not to let Kate know her true feelings. She sat down on her makeshift dirt bed.

"That wasn't my fault, Kate. It was nobody's fault that we just so happened to accidentally stumble into the wrong Cave." She turned over onto her back and stared up at the Stars with her hands comfortably behind her head. "And if you're looking for something more than a simple, honest apology from me, you aren't going to get it. Because, Kate, there's nothing more for me to say other than sorry."

Kate scowled and prepared to blurt forth another blame, but Jerry came up beside her and hushed her.

"It was my fault we got into trouble with the Dragon." he said softly to the two Girls. "And I'm sorry. No more guilt trips for toNight, and tomorrow, Kate, I would like to have a word with you."

Kate flushed and smiled wickedly, then went to bed. She looked very happy with herself.

Chapter Eleven: The Dragons' Lairs and the Hippogryph

Morning came sooner than any of them had expected, so they promptly packed up and were on their way before Kate could start another squabbling fest with the Dragon. He had perched his scaly body at the entrance of his little Cave, snarling dark words under his breath.

It's a dull morning. It must be these horrible Clouds that are hampering our Spirits, Serena thought as she trudged along beside Lindsey. Then she noticed something she hadn't before. *And quiet ... it's also very quiet this morning. Everybody seems to be thinking their own thoughts toDay, never minding about sharing them. Oh, well. Silence is a good thing after that spat we had with the Dragon yesterDay.*

She shuddered at the thought. Had that Dragon been able to squeeze through the entrance to his Cavern without damaging any of his precious eggs, Serena believed that he actually would have fried them up and served them to the baby Dragons once they were born.

That's right! The baby Dragons were due toDay, he said. I wonder when they will hatch. Oh, what a pretty sight that will be when they do!

Serena enjoyed the solemn silence as she plodded ever onward, mounting great Hills of near-barren Land only to plummet down the other side and begin their descent again on the next Hill.

And, true to Serena's words (or thoughts, that is), nobody spoke at all until they were well away from the Dragon's Lair and its eggs. They all seemed to be holding their breath about something, waiting for something to happen, expecting excitement to bubble up out of any Cave. Perhaps the bout with the Dragon had made them more aware of just how dangerous this Land really was, and they were trying to escape the notice of any particularly observant Dragons, be they adult or Child.

As the morning wore on, Serena watched the sunken gray Clouds that shrouded the bright Sunshine drift off Westward, heading back to the Ocean. After the warm rays of the golden Sun washed off their backs and warmed their souls, the team seemed to lighten up and smile. They enjoyed the inspiring, delicious rays of warmth.

But they were not the only ones who enjoyed the Sunlight. Often, as they passed Rocky, Mountainous Hills and ledges or smooth Sand, they would see a Dragon or two lying flat on their stomachs, basking, like the enormous mythological Lizards they were well-known for in Fairy tales. Their bright-colored scales were glinting, their hideous, gargantuan Bat-like wings out-stretched, and their gleaming red, orange, yellow, and all other mood-colored eyes peered out at them in warning.

Serena did not mind the looks in the Dragons' eyes; she simply stayed her distance and admired them there. For some odd reason, the simple scene of a Dragon basking in the Sun seemed beautiful to her - deceiving the myths that said Dragons were heartless, ugly, greedy Beasts that killed any living, moving being that came within their sight. Already she had found that supposed moral to be false, upon her small chat with little Keffle. She had found later that the Dragonling was actually interested in her and her customs, her World. So Serena came to an understanding that Dragons had the same souls as men - some were good and some were wicked and some were just in between.

~*~*~*~*~

Only around mid morning did anybody dare to speak in the silence of the dry Lands.

Jerry grabbed Kate's arm and pulled her close to him, so she could hear him as they walked.

"I would like to have a little talk with you."

Kate seemed flattered, and blushed up to her ear tips. She looked at Jerry with admiring eyes.

"Well then let's have this little talk, shall we?" she said softly and as in-nocently as she could. She batted her eyelashes madly.

Jerry drew up a nostril and removed his hand from her arm as though she were on fire.

"Kate, I did not expect you to lash out at the Dragon like that," Jerry said finally, looking away from her in disgust. The eerie silence was broken as the guilt hung on Kate heavily. Her face fell and something resembling tears glimmered in her eyes.

"I had to do something! I wasn't going to just let some smelly Lizard push us around like so much-" she started.

"No! You did not have to start us on bad terms with him like you did, even after you were told not to," Jerry coaxed, trying to be quiet so the other journeyers could not hear them. But Serena heard them fine, as did everyone

89

else. Nobody seemed to want to talk. And, as humiliating as it sounded, every-body appeared to want to hear this "talk" that Jerry was having with the Girl that had gotten on every one of their last nerves since the first Day at landing on this strange Land.

Kate's head hung like a sad puppy.

"What would you have done if the Dragon had come after us?" Jerry continued. He looked in her direction. "You could have gotten us all killed!"

"The Dragon was too fat to get out of the Cave!" Kate protested, kicking at a small Rock. She stubbed her toe on the very next and made to curse aloud, but, seeing Jerry's blazing eyes, decided against it.

The team jumped into the pit of another Valley and mounted another rise. Kate was silent for only a moment, and then started up a series of ranting.

"And besides, I wasn't the one who started us on bad terms with the Dragon - Serena was! Remember when she said our names were our own-"

Kate met Serena's gaze as they walked. Serena stared at her, showing no emotion – not sympathy, not anger, not jealousy. No emotion at all. She smiled and raised her eyebrows politely, listening to Kate's tattling blame as though she were quite interested and wished very much for her to continue.

"Yes, but Serena was simply stating a fact. Honestly, do you think it would have gotten us any further if we had told that Monster where we are go-ing?" Jerry broke in. "And besides, she wasn't directly insulting him the way you were when you called him … ah, well, names."

Silence hung on the air, and again Kate hung her head like an injured, dis-heartened Animal. She sighed, sniffed and looked up at Jerry with a mixture of rebellious rage and pathetic beseech set in her dark, hollow eyes. But Jerry was not finished. Quietly, he leaned forward and looked her straight in the face.

"I don't ever want to hear or see you disobey another of my orders again, do you understand me?" he hissed.

Kate scowled her ugliest and glared hatred at Jerry for a long time before nodding. She said no more.

By mid-afternoon the team found themselves on a high Cliff that over-looked a vast Prairie that stretched as far as the eye could see. A gnarled, twist-ed old Tree stood naked upon the crest, surrounded by a thick briar of berry bushes that stretched down the ridge and tapered off into the dusty wilderness of the Dragons' Lairs. There was something about this bountiful Land that drew the mouths of the tired, hungry travelers to feast off its sweet crop. The decision was promptly made that this was to be their new camping spot. So the six weary explorers stomped out their own little nests in the tall thickets.

Serena was glad she had packed a plastic poncho with her survival knapsack. The first thing she did after stomping down the twigs and leaves was to pull the thing out and model it, with the help of some strong sticks she found by the dead, old Tree, into a protective roof over her little bowl-shaped nest. She found two sticks with a small Y on the end of them and dug them into the ground at a good interval apart. Then she took a long stick and laid it in between the Ys of both sticks. Over this, she draped the poncho and tied it down with a strong, flexible rope at its corners.

Looking around, Serena saw that the other team members were creating similar shelters. Mike seemed to have forgotten or lost his poncho, so he used his scuba suit (which he must have crammed in his knapsack upon leaving) and cut it up to make a tent-like structure. He waved over at Serena when she complimented him on his witty craft, then hurried over to a clearing that Jerry had made to start a fire.

Dusk drew nearer, and Serena finally emerged from her small hutch, happier now that she had recorded their bouts with the Dragon and his eggs. It was like she had left the matter behind with the notebook. She laughed when she looked back on some of the insults Kate had thrown at the Dragon and put them in the back of her mind for later use herself, should the occasion arise.

Confidently, she arose from her spot and wandered out in the waist-high thicket. She climbed her way over to the gnarled, old Oak Tree, and with the agility of a Squirrel, she shinned up the trunk and sat down on a thick limb close to the top.

It began to sprinkle again, for it had stopped of its own accord for only a while, and Serena had wanted to savor the clear atmosphere for as long as she could. However, now that she had journeyed across the thicket and earned herself many scratches and rips just to get to the gnarled, old Tree, she didn't want to do it all over again to go back. For some odd reason she felt that if she were to go back, as soon as she set foot inside her makeshift hutch the Sky would change its mind and stop Raining.

Serena sat alone in the Tree, staring up at the face of the colorful Sunset. Like a red berry dipped in honey, the Sun sank into its fiery halo of light, promising that it would rise again tomorrow. The Rain continued to quench the thirsty earth.

The Sun is shining, and it's Raining out, she thought. She smiled as she spotted a small Rainbow. *Kind of like Mother Nature smiling through her tears.*

Serena, both surprised and pleased with herself at having unintentionally invented her own poetry of nature, look to the Sky to see if she could do the same for it.

Parted gray Clouds…hmmm… Like two friends of the Sky that are furious at each other, and to show so wreak havoc upon the misfortunate Lands below and … what is that?

The young Girl squinted, quite sure now that something was flying at her from between the two departed friends of the Sky. Something bright and colorful, with large wings of an Eagle and a long red-brown tail.

Serena stood, one hand on the trunk of the Tree and the other shielding the Rain from her eyes. Drops of Rain clung to her long lashes as she peered out through the dribbling sheets of precipitation. Leaning past the trunk of the Tree, she looked back at the camp in the brush; everyone seemed to have shrunk into their own little tents for the time being. An ashy patch in the social circle that Jerry had stamped out smoldered thin, gasping, little strings of smoke, marking its departure as the Rain quenched it. Serena wanted to call on Mike or maybe Jerry, but she knew they would be busy getting things ready for dinner and decided not to bother them. They had all had a rather rough Day.

So, she turned back to whatever it was that may have been flying at her. The colorful thing drew closer. Serena noted that it had a beak and feathery wings. Yet the thing had the back end of a Horse, which looked terribly odd galloping on the air in back of the long, thick, clawed talons that made the front legs of the Animal.

I know the name of that Creature! the Girl thought. She racked her brain as the winged Beast grew so near that she could see the Raindrops clinging to its long lashes.

It starts with an H, she thought, hugging the Tree trunk closer. *And it is said to be the cousin of a Gryphon .*

As the Creature alighted on the end of the branch, tucking its colorful, feathery wings behind it, the name of the strange Animal suddenly popped into Serena's head.

"Hippogryph." she whispered, bringing her other hand up with her first on the soft, rotted bark of the twisted, old Tree.

The Animal looked up as if just noticing the Girl for the first time.

"Yes," it said in a deep, rough female voice. "Sun Human."

Serena blinked, hardly believing her eyes.

Here, before her, was another mythical Creature.

The Hippogryph blinked as well, her brown eyes shining under the last rays of the Sun. Her head was that of a rusty golden Eagle. Her red and orange feathers gleamed, and the deep rustic red of her hind quarters shimmered, adding to the splendor of her appearance. Her back legs were hoofed with black lobes; her front limbs thin and tainted a striped orange. On her knobby, Bird-like front feet jutted terrible, razor-sharp talons, each one as long as a Mountain Lion's claw and each as black as Night. Her chest was comprised of softy downy feathers; her curved beak of the brightest orange tipped with black. The tail of the Hippogryph swished behind her in long black strands and her dark brown, nearly black, eyes studied Serena closely. Her wet, befeathered head, wings, and front body glimmered lustrous under the waning Sunlight.

Serena was very curious about the Creature.

If I were a Dragon, right now my eyes would be yellow ... she thought with a smile. She longed to reach out and touch the Hippogryph, to reassure herself of its mortal existence. She waited several silent moments before advancing, not quite sure that it was a harmless Creature or not.

Yet curiosity won her over, and Serena reached out to touch the Hippogryph.

"Are you... real?" she wondered aloud in a half-whisper.

The Hippogryph chuckled in her low tone.

"As real as you are, pretty Flower."

Astounded, Serena left the protective trunk of the gnarled Tree and ventured out on tip toe. Ever so tenderly she reached out and stroked the top of the Hippogryph's hard beak. The texture of the beak felt smooth and natural, and Serena loved the Animal at once.

"You are a beautiful Flower yourself," she said softly. The Bird-Horse Creature seemed to smile, then she stood on all fours.

"No, you, my Child, are beautiful. You will go well with my collection."

Serena's smile faded rapidly to a look of complete confusion. What did the Hippogryph just say?

Oh no. Serena thought, fear gathering in her heart.

"Yo-your collection?" Serena stuttered, withdrawing her hand and making to move back to the trunk. She flushed as the truth dawned upon her. This lovely mythical Creature was thinking of stashing Serena away with her many other treasures that she confiscated from passing travelers and hidden somewhere in her lair!

"Er, I'm sorry, Hippogryph, but I'm not a part of anybody's collection…"

"Oh yes, you are…" snarled the Hippogryph in her low voice and stretching her wings delicately. "You are a part of my collection now."

"No!" Serena shouted, surprised at the volume of her own voice. Her breathing increased as she furrowed her brow and glared at the Creature perched not four feet away from her. Enraged by the expression of finality on the Hippogryph's beak-pointed face, Serena turned and began to tip toe back to the trunk.

But the Hippogryph reached out with a long, sharp claw and caught the back of the young Girl's shirt.

Serena screamed.

"Yes," rasped the Hippogryph, and she lifted herself into the air, one talon on each of Serena's fair-skinned arms. Serena screamed again as she felt herself being hoisted into the air, kicking and wrestling helplessly. Then she shrieked as the thick, long talons sunk into her arms, like knives pressing threateningly on her skin. She kicked madly, and in the fuss, her left shoe fell off and dropped to the Golden Prairies below. A single tear slid down Serena's cheek as she realized the tremendous distance between her and the hard ground. Closing her eyes instead of looking down, she curled her legs up underneath her, hoping to make herself seem heavier, if it was any at all possible.

Where is Mike? And Jerry? Oh, I should have called them! she thought, wiggling in the Hippogryph's grasp.

Then, a dangerous flame burning in her glassy blue eyes, Serena's face snapped up to the hovering Hippogryph and glared daggers at her.

There has to be some way I can convince her to let me go, she thought. *Maybe if I try to kick her in the face or something, so she can't see.*

Quick as lightning, Serena sent herself into a swing, trying to avoid the bucking back legs of the Creature. Then, she swung her feet up in front of her and gave the enraged, panicking Beast a good hard boot right in the eye from her right foot – the only foot left with a shoe. This sent the Animal squawking, and in her pain she released the screaming Girl, just as Serena was swinging another kick.

Screaming, Serena felt herself do a backwards somersault in the air. She was free!

Almost.

94

Realizing that the Girl had nearly escaped, the Hippogryph struck out with her beak and caught a mouthful of shoe. She tried to blink Water and blood away from her throbbing, bruised eye. The female Hippogryph growled and made to take off into the Skies once more, but Serena still had a full spleen to vent upon the possessive Creature.

From her upside-down position, Serena felt the blood rushing to her head. Shaking off sudden dizziness, she continued to swing back and forth.

Haven't had enough yet? Maybe this will change your mind...

She buffeted the Hippogryph several times in the stomach before stopping, a wicked plan occurring in her clever brain. A pretty smile of triumph crept up upon her features, and she closed her eyes, biting her lip hard.

If I can just use my free foot to pry my shoe off ... she thought, but then thought of a better idea. *Maybe if I kick her in the throat* ...

Serena crossed her fingers and kicked hard with her dangling left foot.

And the Hippogryph gave up after feeling a painful crack form on the bottom of her beak. Serena plunged earthward, free, but now completely shoeless.

Well, that was terribly clever of me ... she thought, twirling onto her back in the air and covering her eyes with both hands so that she could not see the height from which she was falling. *I am now free from the grasp of the Hippogryph, but now I will certainly die from the fall*

Die. The word flickered across her mind and rippled through her soul. She shivered. *I am going to die. Will the team carry on the journey without me? What will they say when they find me ... gone? Who will inherit Teresa's diary from me?*

I cannot die! Serena cried in her mind. *I cannot! I am too young to die! There are so many things I have not yet accomplished in my life! Oh, to think that one Day I would grow up to fall in love, to marry and to have children! To have a little Girl – I would name her Angelique, and perhaps a boy and to name him after his father! To become a pediatrician, or at least to get a job and support my new family! To grow older and have grandchildren and tell them the stories of when I was young! I am young! I cannot die!*

It was these very horrible thoughts that swirled wildly in the Girl's head, just as the air around her swirled, a menacing threat to remind her of her coming departure.

The Wind rushed past Serena's face, howling in her ears ceaselessly, tousling her golden curls as they streaked after her, and causing Water to gather in the Girl's Sky-colored eyes. But Serena's eyes were wet for more than that reason.

She felt the nearness of the ground approaching her. Shadows overcame her mind and her world. A strangled sob escaped her throat as she prepared to draw her last breath …

Whoosh!

"Oof!"

And Serena stopped falling. Something had caught her and was now ascending slowly back up to the Cliff.

Surprised, Serena whipped her hands away from her face.

And gasped.

Chapter Twelve: The Halfbreed and the FrogStorm

A Boy.

Her age.

Pale skin, pointed ears and shiny, curly blonde hair.

And the largest, greenest eyes she had ever seen.

He looked down at Serena and a smile drew up one corner of his mouth. The young Boy set her gently back on the Cliff at a safe distance from the edge.

Serena was lost for words. Without thinking, she checked that her head and appendages were all in place, then looked up at the Boy with a very surprised expression.

But not quite as surprised as the expression on the Boy's face when Serena flung her arms around him in a thankful hug.

"You saved me!" she enthused in a loud whisper. The Boy, who was dressed in a forest green tunic and dark brown leggings, smiled winningly and held her at arm's length.

"Yes," he mumbled in a shy tenor, "I suppose I did."

He spoke with a crisp British accent.

Serena's heart was near to bursting with pride for the courageous young Man.

"Thank you!"

The Boy smiled and his cheeks flushed lightly from the unexpected praise.

"Er, you're welcome," he replied, looking at her as though saving a Girl from falling to an imminent death was nothing out of the ordinary.

From the snowy blonde hair that poured in handsome curls over his head to the scuffed, rough fabric of the moccasins covering his toes, the Boy looked like a true, old-fashioned Warrior. His Sand-colored moccasins rose to just beneath his knee, tied up tight for hard traveling. Thin brown leggings outlined his sturdy-looking knees and thighs, reminding Serena of the trunk of a Tree, and met up with the green, leafy skirt of the very bottom of his long green tunic. Around his small hips stretched a thick, tough belt that held a scabbard, an Emerald-strewn hilt that protruded from that scabbard, and four small drawstring bags, each a different shade of green. His dusty tunic had a wide, ragged collar that stretched down his chest as though someone had cut it open.

It revealed a muscular physique in both his chest and his bare arms because his tunic had no sleeves. On his back was strapped a quiver of green-feathered arrows, while slung over his shoulder was a large bow. Around his neck was strung a Golden chain, to the end of which hung a precariously sharp tooth of some kind. His twinkling green eyes reminded Serena of the kind of green that young leaves portray in the early Spring.

Serena protested a gasp as her eyes fell on the pointed tips of his ears, and the shrunken earlobes. Instead, she put a hand politely over her mouth, thinking to herself that she had just found her third mythical Creature as she whispered,

"Are you an Elf?"

The handsome young Boy, who had been eyeing Serena's strange outfit just as she had been studying his, suddenly snapped to attention.

"No," he said, fumbling about tightening one of the four small pouches that clung securely to his belt. He looked back up at her. "Are you a tom Boy?"

The question was out of simple curiosity, and Serena laughed nervously as she shook her head.

"Boy? Don't you mean Girl?"

"No, I mean a Boy. In this case a tom Boy, a Girl who dresses and acts as a Boy."

Thinking this terminology strange, Serena blushed and shook her head. She had never been a tom Boy, or whatever it was he had said, and she most certainly had never acted like one either.

"No … so what are you then, if you aren't an Elf? Are you a … a male Nymph?"

The Boy guffawed loudly and slapped his thigh.

"Heavens, no. I'm a Halfbreed! Hah hah hah! A Nymph?! Really!!"

Feeling a little embarrassed at her previous remark, Serena stepped closer to the Boy out of curiosity.

"Wh-what's a Halfbreed?" she whispered softly. The Boy wiped a tear of mirth from his cheek and lifted her chin.

"Do you not get out at all?" he asked, and before Serena could protest, he replied, "A Halfbreed is half-Human, half-Elf."

She caught his field-green gaze.

"So, tell me, what might a pretty Damsel such as yourself be doing all the way out here in the wilderness, in Man's trousers, and *alone*, I might add?"

Serena's mind was beginning to spin. First, a talking Dragon, then an aggressive Hippogryph, and now a half-Elf? She couldn't think of anyplace she had studied that called Girls Boys!

Dusk was ending as the Sky turned different shades of purple, red, orange and indigo.

"I'm … I mean, *we're* lost …" she said, glancing back over her shoulder and nodding at her team's encampment not far away and further down the slope. "We're looking for civilization so we can go home."

The Boy seemed to study Serena for a moment or so before responding.

"I see … and just what City might you come from in garments such as these?"

He pointed to her ripped and dirtied jeans and T-shirt.

She laughed, but stopped when she saw that he wasn't.

"Y-you're serious?" she said, astonished.

"You're not?"

"You don't know where I come from?" she added with a chuckle.

The Halfbreed stood straight and crossed his arms, glaring at her from under bushy light brown eyebrows.

"I don't know what you are trying to play with me, young miss, but you had better stop it. Now please, state the City you've come from and I shall escort you and your crew back to the whereabouts of the place."

Serena pursed her lips.

"Alright then."

She crossed her arms and stood with her feet shoulder-length apart to make her look bold as she copied his posture.

"I'm from Springfield, Illinois."

It was the Boy's turn to look puzzled.

"Sprinkle-what? Where's that?"

Serena raised one eyebrow.

"Sangamon County, United States of America?"

She studied his confused gaze, and her other eyebrow flew up.

The way her mind was spinning was beginning to affect her heart as the organ began to thump at a drastic pace inside her.

"Uhm, North America? … Earth?" she squeaked.

"Oh, Earth!" he said suddenly, looking up and pointing into the Night Sky.

Serena was utterly flabbergasted!

This strange place had two Moons!

The Boy directed her gaze to the larger, bluer Moon that dwarfed the little white Moon.

"That's Earth," he said.

It felt like someone was squeezing her heart, trying to milk it of misconceptions. Her chest was so tight that it hurt. Serena could not tear her eyes from the Sky even if she had wanted to.

That little blue Moon was her home! Her *life*!

"Then ..." she whimpered, an air of tears hovering in her voice. "Then ... just where are we?"

The Halfbreed stood in front of her and stared her straight in the eyes.

"You are really from Earth?"

Serena nodded, suddenly becoming very frightened. Tears of frustration and confusion brimmed in her Sky blue eyes as she looked at the Boy. He stayed silent, and she wanted to scream at him for being so quiet when all she wanted was to know where in the World they were! But her courage left her completely; she felt vulnerable and unprotected.

"Where am I?" she repeated in a soft, scared voice. She searched for some sign of explanation in the Boy's beautiful green eyes.

"Forever," he whispered back, wiping away a trickling tear from her cheek. "You are in the Lands of Forever."

Suddenly, a rustle in the bushes startled them both. Jerry bounded out just as the Boy leaped over the Cliff and floated back down to the shimmering, Moonlit Prairie of Gold.

"Who was that?" he demanded.

"*That!*" Serena cried, ignoring his question and pointing at the big blue Moon that shone like a beacon in the Night Sky. She grasped his shirt and thrust her whole arm up at the blue Moon. "That's Earth!"

A long silence passed as Jerry studied the Moon.

"Are you kidding me?" he chortled after the pause that seemed an eternity. "Why are you crying? Where are your shoes and socks?"

Serena felt like snapping back at the mother-like comment, feeling very able to take care of herself. But she held herself back as he gasped, staring stunned at her toes.

For there, sprouting slowly amidst her bare, dirty feet, was a peculiarly bright green Moss, with several Rainbow-colored Moss Flowers poking their way up to smile at the Moon-bathed Cliff.

Serena gave a disgruntled gasp that sounded much more like a small yelp

100

of surprise. Wasn't this new World full of surprises! She didn't know what else would happen next. The unmistakable Moon called Earth seemed to smile down on her in rays of blue as she felt her heart give a sickening twitch after the discovery of the Moss Flowers. Warm tears flooded to her eyes. Why had this happened? What had she ever done to deserve being abandoned to a completely alien Planet? What had any of them done to deserve this? Jerry saw the tears that ran down her dusty face as she looked up at him with huge blue eyes.

This place is so strange, I don't know if I can take this any longer... Serena thought, her chest heaving around her pounding, bleeding heart.

Then, with another petrified little scream, she fled the scene and dived into the bushes to seek the warm comfort of her self-made nest.

~*~*~*~*~

Plunk!

Bonk!

Spack!

Ssshlupp!

Serena's eyebrows lowered in her sleep and she turned over, trying to pull her blanket over her head.

Plicket!

Clap!

Smack!

Squilsh!

"Croak!"

"Rrrrrrrrr ..." she groaned, flipping onto her back.

I really wish that sound would go away! she thought drowsily. Finally, after what seemed to Serena an eternity, she sighed and decided to get up.

"Ribbit!"

"Croikle!"

"Kreeeeeloik!"

"Richit!"

Serena's ears pricked, and she lay completely still. Daring herself, she opened one eye.

And opened both very wide.

And came face-to-eyeballs with a fat, little Frog that hung only inches from her nose!

"Croooooikit!" it grunted heavily, for there were several more Toads atop this little one.

Serena sighed again. Apparently, the stick that had held up the plastic poncho had broken and now the ceiling drooped in upon her. Only the strong ties on either side of the poncho kept it, along with thousands of tiny speckled Frogs, from caving inward and drowning the Girl in a pile of croaking amphibians.

Gently, she scooted herself out from under the loosening trap and, snatching her things on the way, backed out of her nest with discomfort. Jerry and Bob were already up, laughing at the look that now crossed Serena's bedridden features.

Frogs.

And Toads.

Everywhere.

Little ones, big ones, croaking, slimy, wart-skinned Frogs.

And the strange thing was …

They were falling from the Sky!

"What …" Serena squeaked, dropping both knapsack and blanket onto the Sea of croaking Frogs. All around the thicket hopped, ribbitted, and landed a multitude of nothing but green and brown Frogs.

"F-frogs!" shrieked Kate, who was just now awakening from her spot. She sat bolt upright as a fat brown Toad croaked loudly and landed with a wet splatter! on her head.

"Eeeeeeeeek!" she screamed, slapping the Frog away. "Falling from the Sky?"

"It's a – a FrogStorm!" Mike crowed, pausing to construct a word for this new type of precipitation.

Lindsey laughed, rising from her own nest and brushing a couple of little Frogs from her shoulders.

"Amazing! Frogs falling from the Sky!" she chuckled, catching one tiny amphibian and lowering it to the ground. It hopped off without missing a beat.

Curious, Serena caught a Frog and let it jump out of her fingers. The Frog seemed ponderous and hesitant to leave, but it finally bounced off to join the other amphibians that carpeted the thicket in green and brown warts.

"How do they … not die landing like this?" she inquired. Mike studied a fat Toad as it soared earthward and splattered into a puddle beside him. Serena noticed now that it was not only Frogs that were falling from the green Clouds that mottled the Sky in dark patches, but also fat dribbles of Rain that came along with them.

"Hmmm ... they seem to be able to control their landings," Mike observed. He squatted and shielded his eyes from the Frogs and Rain. "Fat ones fall faster but have more cushioning, and little ones are lighter, allowing them more time to twist around to the spot where they want to land."

"Look!" Bob exclaimed, pointing to a specific Frog far above them. Serena looked up, and laughed in disbelief.

The Frog spread its webbed feet wide, and scooted itself through the air as though it were on wings.

"Amazing!" she said in a hushed, whispering voice of awe. She shook her head. "They're using their webbed feet kind of like wings-"

"to scoot themselves along in the air so that they can land where they want to," Jerry finished, leaning on Lindsey to help himself out of the thicket. "Simply remarkable."

The team, still a bit awed at the sprinkling of Frogs, soon helped Serena to clear off her poncho of the warty amphibians and find another thicker, sturdier stick to rebuild the shelter once more. All of the other tents in the briar had had their fill of Frogs and laid flattened on the bare ground where Kate, Lindsey, Jerry, Mike and Bob had rescued their knapsacks from the avalanche of amphibians.

Serena's was the only nest that had not caved in completely, and small as it was, they all six managed to squeeze inside long enough to devour a breakfast of aged, stale Pop Tarts. When Kate complained, Jerry offered to fry up a batch of Frog's legs just for her. Kate's bottom lip quivered. She slapped a hand over her mouth and dashed out of the shelter. Friendly chuckling rippled across the circle of travelers.

After breakfast, the crew hurried about packing up their few belongings and preparing themselves for a long Day's march through the Golden-Grassed Prairie. The tall-backed Cliff hovered over them in the distance, and the Golden-hued Prairie Grass rose up before them in eight and nine foot stalks.

As they walked, they talked freely of the strange mystery of where they were. Serena explained to those who weren't present about the talk she had had with the Halfbreed Boy.

"He told me, 'Forever. You are in the Lands of Forever.' He was startled by something in the Bushes and flew off just as Jerry came out of the thicket. Oh, yes, he actually flew!" she finished, seeing their astonished faces.

"Forever, huh?" Lindsey said, parting a shimmering stalk of eight-foot-tall Prairie Grass to allow the team to pass into a small clearing. A scraggled, old Tree was growing on one side of the clearing, the only Tree they could see from their position.

"That's what he said," Serena shrugged. "So, I guess the Lands of Forever is where we are."

"We'll stop here for lunch," Jerry decided, squinting up at the smiling Golden sphere of light that hovered directly over their heads. Relieved that Jerry had let them rest at last, Serena plunked down at the base of the Tree. Lindsey, her brown curls bobbing, sat next to her.

As she searched her knapsack for something edible, Serena's thoughts turned to the weather.

This Forever place sure gets some awfully strange weather. Almost every Day we were in that Dragon Desert place, it Rained. How does it stay so dry and lifeless with all that precipitation? And how do Frogs manage to get up in the Clouds to Rain down on unfortunate travelers?

Serena sighed, pulling out a crusty-looking sandwich.

"Weather's been sort of crazy lately, hasn't it?" Lindsey said, pulling out her own soggy peanut butter and jelly sandwich.

Serena's face lifted into a smile.

"You must have read my mind," she giggled. She voiced her thoughts aloud to her friend, and then said, "I just don't see how it could be Raining Frogs – literally – this morning, and be Sunny and warm this afternoon."

Lindsey shrugged, her hair swishing as she shook her head.

"I don't know, but we've changed our position, too. That could be part of it."

Serena nodded, about to reply, but stopped with her hardly-eaten sandwich halfway to her mouth.

A muffled whine had sounded behind them in the Prairie.

She sat up straight, her brow furrowed, then looked at Lindsey with a quizzical expression.

"Did you hear something?" she asked in a hesitant voice. Lindsey looked up, catching a piece of crust as it fell from her sandwich.

"Hmm-mm," she replied, shaking her head.

Serena leaned over and looked behind the trunk of the scraggled, old Tree, her Golden curls wisping into her face.

"I thought I heard a sort of cry or something," she said, turning back. Then, shrugging and deciding that her mind must be in the mood for tricks, she rose her sandwich again.

"Buhoo hoo hooo!"

And again she stopped, the sandwich halfway to her mouth. Sighing, she dropped the food on top of its plastic cover on her knapsack and got up.

"There it goes again… and I'm sure I heard it that time!" she mumbled, making to start into the Prairie.

"Wait, I heard it, too!" Lindsey said in a loud whisper.

Serena looked over at Jerry, Mike, and Bob, who were standing with their backs to them and observing the Prairie, and Kate, who was sitting by herself in another corner watching them.

Lindsey leaped up, dropped her sandwich next to Serena's and came behind Serena to shepherd her into the Prairie. "Let's go check it out."

Silent moments passed as the two Girls searched through the tall Prairie Grass. Serena tried to follow the direction that the sound had come from, always keeping the top of the Tree in sight lest they get lost.

"Sounded like it came from over here," Serena said finally, breaking the silence. She parted some Grass and slipped between it. Lindsey followed her, but stopped when they had walked a good distance from the clearing. She grabbed the back of Serena's shirt and pulled her back.

"Wait … Serena …" she whispered, glancing nervously over her shoulder. "What if we get lost?"

"We'll follow the Tree back to the clearing," Serena said, pointing to the leafless skeleton of the top of the Tree.

"I know … but… I think we've gone far enough, don't you? I think we should turn around."

Serena grasped Lindsey's forearm and looked her in the eye with a very serious expression on her face.

"Lindsey, if you're that frightened, you can go back."

Lindsey's roaming eyes snapped back to meet Serena's cool spring Water-blue eyes. She flushed lightly.

"N-no, I just don't like being out here in case we get in trouble. And besides, we haven't even heard that sound once since we took off to look for whatever was making it-"

"Wahaaaa! Sniff sniff… Boohooo hoooo!" the sound came from very near, even louder than it had been before.

"I spoke too soon."

Lindsey straightened like a board and Serena turned toward the direction of the sound in a flash of blonde curls. On tiptoes, she crouched low and slunk towards a specific cluster of Prairie Grass. Lindsey hesitantly followed her.

Tenderly, Serena pulled back the clump of Prairie Grass, and revealed a little Boy, no older than six or seven, sitting with his back to a Rock. He was frightened of them, and made to get up and run with the broken toy bow he held in his lap.

"Wait!" Serena said softly, emerging fully from the Grass. She found something familiar about this little Boy when she squatted to look the whimpering Child in the eye.

"Who are you?" he demanded in a bold, little voice, deeply accented in the British language. Serena stopped and stared into his fear-stricken green eyes. Now she knew who he resembled.

"The Halfbreed Boy!" she gasped suddenly, looking up at Lindsey.

The Boy gulped and took a warning step forward, lowering his scruffy little brown eyebrows. He brandished his broken bowstring.

"S-so what if I'm a Halfbreed? 'Tis of no concern to you!" he piped in his chirpy, Childlike voice. Serena looked back at the little Boy with a smile.

"Do you have an older brother?" she inquired.

The Boy lowered his eyes to his bow and twanged its broken string distractedly. "Yes," he murmured. He looked up at her with the large green eyes of a Child. "Why?"

"Oh, I was just wondering," Serena answered, glancing at Lindsey out of the corner of her eye. She turned back to the little Boy.

"What's that you have there?"

The Boy's bottom lip trembled and his eyes brimmed with tears.

"A … a bow …" he wheedled, twanging the broken string. Serena's smile faded. She blinked. What kind of government allowed 7-year-old Boys to run around with bows and arrows? Or did this place even *have* a government?

"What's your name, little guy?" she questioned fondly, coming to sit next to the Boy.

He wiped away a trickling tear, but did not object.

"Theo. What's your name?"

"My name is Serena."

The Boy sniffed.

"I've never heard of a Girl named Serena," he smiled, looking up at her with those huge green eyes again.

Serena giggled, shrugged, and beckoned Lindsey to sit down with them.

"Well, I've never heard of a Boy named Theo, either," she chirped. Something about Serena's comforting laugh made the Boy smile.

"Theo, my name is Lindsey," informed the brown-haired Girl.

"I've never heard of that name, either," he chuckled. Serena and Lindsey laughed in unison, quite enjoying the Boy's comic company. Soon, Theo's tears were long forgotten.

"So, where is your brother, Theo?" Lindsey wondered.

"Nelson? Oh, he's off to get me another string for my bow."

"How old are you?"

"7."

Serena nodded, getting up.

"Well, I'll just bet you're hungry sitting out here all by yourself, aren't you?"

Theo responded by licking his lips and standing with Lindsey.

"You bet I am."

Lindsey and Serena both smiled.

They led the little Boy back to the clearing to meet the crew. Serena hoped that somehow the little Boy's brother would find him here. She wished dearly to see him again.

Before long the team had warmly accepted little Theo into the group. He was fed what little food they could spare, and, seeing as they did not have the most plentiful supply of food, the little Boy scurried over to behind the old, gnarled Tree and introduced them to an edible Flowering Plant. Mike's notebook shot out on the spot and he immediately took note of the new Plant.

Meanwhile, Serena sat scribbling thoughtfully in her own notebook, her back resting against her meager knapsack.

We've now moved into a sort of golden prairie. Trees are few and so are plants of any kind, aside from the conditioned stalks of prairie grass that grow as tall as a cornfield. And, of course, the delicate moss flowers that are constantly sprouting at my feet. It seems not to matter to them which soil I am standing upon, they will blossom just about anywhere, even now as I am sitting with my back against my knapsack.

But this strange prairie is not only a prairie – it is also filled with large fields of plains and flatlands. This small clearing we are stopped in is just an example.

The little boy that Lindsey and I found, Theo, has taken his fill of lunch and is presently showing Bob and Mike how to operate a bow, although the string is broken. He says that his brother, Nelson supposedly, is off on a quest to find him a new one. This is the strange Halfbreed boy who saved me from certain death on the cliff we were previously encamped upon.

Serena was disturbed from her work as she looked up with a start.

"Pack it up, guys, we're moving on!" Jerry shouted. Serena closed the notebook and turned to open her knapsack so she could put her writings away.

Standing behind her travel pack was the 7-year-old Halfbreed Boy, staring down at her with very large green eyes. In his hands he held his broken bow.

"Might I join you?" he asked shyly, turning over the dry dust with his bare feet. "I don't know when my brother is going to return, and I do so wish to go with you."

Serena sighed and smirked at the same time. She unzipped her knapsack and slipped the notebook inside.

"Will he know where to find you if we take you with us?"

Theo's face broke into a wide, Boyish grin.

"Nelson knows where to find me anywhere!" he bragged, "He's got such a good sense of direction, you know, he could tell you which way was East blindfolded and gagged underWater!" The boastful, young lad drew his chest out for special effect.

Serena felt warm mirth bubble up inside her. She poked Theo's protru-dimg stomach, making him deflate in a very theatrical manner.

"Oh alright. We might just need a brave Warrior to protect us against Dragons or Hippogryphs, or whatever else may be out here."

Theo beamed with pride and hitched his bow over his shoulder.

Serena shook her head. He did look so much like his older brother!

As she walked, Serena observed the information that she had received from Theo. And, in this case, was still receiving.

"I still don't believe you lot are from Earth," he twittered. He looked up at her, and shook his head. "Though I suppose it makes sense."

Jerry appeared on the other side of the small Boy.

"How's that?" he wondered aloud. Theo turned and looked at him. "You crashed on the coral reef, right? The one off the Coast of the Dragons' Lairs?"

Jerry and Serena nodded in unison, eager to learn more.

"Did you pass the Shield?"

Jerry's face flushed a bright pink as he let out a long sigh and caught Serena's gaze. Both of them remembered the electric bubble that they had passed Days ago.

"We really are in another World," he admitted, giving up at last. "The evidence is too … too rea l… too fool-proof."

"But how-?" Serena paused and closed her eyes. Gathering both her thoughts and her courage, she began again. "But how could we possibly go from being in the middle of an ocean on Earth to being in the middle of one in Forever?"

Theo shook his head.

"If you were a real Foreveran, you would already know that. I give up! You are from Earth."

"We already know that!" sniffed Kate from in back of them. Apparently, she had been eavesdropping. Theo kicked a Rock bashfully and seemed to cower as he trudged along, looking very rejected. Lindsey nudged Kate hard in the ribs.

"Leave him alone, will you!" she hissed, out of Theo's earshot.

"Never mind her, Theo," Serena said softly, patting his back soothingly.

He brightened a little.

"Anyway, how *did* we get here?" Jerry questioned.

Theo looked up again as they passed into another small clearing.

"Every hundred years, the Continent of Forever drifts down from its place in the Sky as the North Star and lands on that spot in the Earth's ocean, called Atlantica or something. It stays there for three full months, and then it rises from the Waters and goes back up into the Sky."

"How come we can't see it – I mean, when it's rising and falling from the Earth and while it's resting on the surface of the ocean?" Mike inquired. His face screwed up as he thought about what he had just asked. "Surly, it's not - "

"Not invisible!" Theo agreed, laughing. "We'll, it isn't. The reason you cannot see it is because," he stopped to make a long sigh that clearly stated that he was preparing for a long response. "Because a long time ago, before any of the Foreverans lived here, a Charm was cast over the whole place, so that Mists surrounded the edges of the Ceaseless Ocean. The Mists are called the Endless Mists. Like a chamcleon changes his skin depending on his surroundings, the Mist will change to look like absolutely nothing is there. It is no more than a silly illusion."

"What about when a ship sails into the Mist? Will it go into Forever?" Serena wondered, observing the shimmering Golden stalks that surrounded them. They suddenly reminded her of her own hair.

"No," said Theo ponderously, leaping over a Rock. "A part of the Charm that was cast was that the Endless Mists could also be … oh, confound it, what was that word Nelson called it? Oh, yes! Sel-ect-ive-ly perm-e-able." The young Boy had to stop to sound the word out, and, when he was certain he had pronounced it correctly, continued, "It means that it chooses which ships can pass into the Lands of Forever and which cannot. Those that can will sail into a Storm, pass through the Shield, and come out into the Ceaseless Ocean on the other side of the wall of Mist. Those that cannot are taken in by an invisible Portal and come out on the other side of the whole place without even knowing it happened."

Jerry looked up at Serena, his brow furrowed in confusion.

"So… what you're saying is that… this Continent has a mind of its own… and it chose us to pass beyond the Mist?"

Theo nodded absentmindedly, his eyes focused straight ahead. He seemed to be very alert just now for some reason. He ran the rest of the way across the flat Plain they had entered and dived back into the Prairie.

"Hm … must be past his bedtime or something." snorted Jerry, looking at the Sky.

It was early evening, and already the Sky before them was beginning to grow a rich, dark navy blue with the coming of dusk. Serena's feet were blistered, cut, and dirty. They hurt terribly, as did the small bump on her head that had occasionally spread into head-cracking headaches. Every muscle in her whole body felt bruised, every bone weak and tired. Yet despite her weary position and the dreadful state of her hair and clothes, Serena pushed on, determined to unearth some way or another to find her way home.

The worn crew of explorers finally stopped at another small clearing to set up camp for the Night. Ten feet from the clearing there stood a tremendous heap of Rocks, the very tops of their gray heads poking up over the auburn Prairie Grass, now a glimmering shade of fire under the last rays of Sunlight.

Serena couldn't have been more relieved when Jerry called it quits for the Day. All Day she had longed to soak her screaming toes, which were now every other color except for peach from being stubbed countless times on her way.

The very last rays of warm Sunshine kissed the explorers' weary faces goodNight as they huddled around a crackling fire in the middle of the clearing. Mike retrieved a bag of the berries they had picked back up on the Cliff. These they roasted over the fire on sticks, enjoying the sweetness of the berries after a long Day's march.

Suddenly, a distant rumbling shook the ground. Serena's berry, as well as some of the others', fell off her stick. Kate stood, dropping her stick in the fire in alarm.

"What on Earth…" gasped Bob.

"In *Forever!*..." Serena corrected, standing as well.

"Could it be another Storm, perhaps?" Lindsey wondered.

"No, the Sky is too clear for that," mumbled Mike, eating his berry right off the tip of his stick and then casting the thing into the crackling fire.

At that moment, as though on cue, Theo rushed into the clearing and hastily began kicking and throwing dirt on the fire to extinguish it. Jerry shielded his face from the flying Sand particles and stood with the rest.

"What are you doing? What's going on?!" Jerry demanded, grabbing the Boy's arm. Theo wrenched away, moved to another spot, and continued to hurriedly scratch at the dark soil, digging like a Dog in a Flower Garden.

"Sauropod migration! Put the fire out unless you want to be smashed underfoot!" he rasped, the dust rising about his face.

Trying to make sense of what Theo had said, Serena leaped to the task of extinguishing the wayward fire.

All the while, the distant rumbling grew ever nearer, until the team could pick out the single footsteps that shook the ground like Thunder.

BOOM! BOOM! BOOM! BOOM! CRASH! BOOM! BOOM!

Dark, Moonlit shapes loomed out in the not-so-distant Plains, crashing over Trees and causing quite a ruckus. The ground was shaking so much that the team could hardly keep their balance. Serena fell on her knees, petrified, then managed to scramble up in a panic. *Dinosaurs! Real Dinosaurs! Extinct Creatures! Dangerous Creatures!* She stopped to look up and gather her knapsack – but then froze,

Her feet were planted firmly in the Sandy Grass. With the Moon shining on her large, petrified blue eyes, she spotted the gargantuan shapes that loomed ever nearer.

Chapter Fourteen: Thunder Giants

"Dinosaurs?" she breathed - if her voice hadn't been so soft it would have passed for a squeak. There, towering in front of her stood a long-necked Sauropod, a Brachiosaurus if she wasn't mistaken. Its little head was perched atop its long neck and swayed from side to side in rhythm with the din of the enormous footsteps. Its skin was leathery and grayish-slate blue, and its tremendous tail lashed out like a whip behind the wide monstrosity that Serena knew was its colossal stomach. Its four legs, each as thick as the trunk of a very fat old Tree, and as tall as a Tree itself, pounded the ground mercilessly underneath its gigantic bulk, leaving in its wake deep footprints large enough to be small Ponds. Longer than three City buses and taller than any Tree Serena had ever seen, the Sauropod thrust back its head and released a throaty, low, ear-piercing roar to symbolize its arrival.

"Out of the way!" yelled Mike, rushing straight at a screaming Lindsey.

Serena, seeing the Brachiosaurus heading for the clearing with several others behind it, sprung into action. With her heart pounding, she grabbed her knapsack and threw it onto her back, then made to scramble willy-nilly out of the clearing like the others. But she felt as though she was forgetting something. Looking back, her heart dropped like a stone into her stomach.

Theo was standing next to the freshly extinguished fire, every muscle in his little body tensed, but yet not a single limb moving. Just from the look into his wide, fear-stricken eyes, Serena could tell that he was petrified stiff. And there, with its long, cold shadow hovering over him like a lingering Nightmare, was the Brachiosaurus. Its leg was lifted and ready to smash down right on top of him.

Terrified, the golden-haired Girl opened her mouth to scream, but nothing came out. Driven by her will to protect the little Boy, she dashed straight out into the clearing and pushed him out of the way just as a Monstrous foot stomped down in the place he had been standing seconds before. The ground shook like an earthquake and the sound was so tremendous that Serena's ears rung.

Sprawled on the ground next to the heavily breathing Theo, Serena suddenly found her voice.

"Look out!" she coughed, spitting gritty Sand from her mouth.

113

Then, a giant, leathery elephant's foot, though more than several times larger, landed itself squarely in front of Theo, nearly missing his own tiny feet. He shrieked loudly and moved back closer to Serena, who thought that if his eyes had been any larger they would have popped out of his little head. She slowly stood up, catching out of the corner of her eye two other Tree-sized legs planted firmly beside her. Rising to her full height, she turned around slowly, mouth agape , staring up at the large stomach that felt much more like a ceiling to her at the moment. The stomach clenched itself as the Brachiosaur straightened its neck and let out the loudest roar Serena had ever heard – she was afraid at first that she was going to go deaf. The sound reverberated in the beast's bronchial tubes and echoed across the horizon. Then, one of the back legs lifted to take another step.

Serena's mind clicked and she scooped up the shivering Boy in her arms. She darted out from under the sweeping foot swifter than a Deer in full flight.

A voice rung out to her side above the rumbling din of the Sauropods.

"The Rocks! Everybody to the Rocks!"

It was Jerry, climbing atop the jagged gray Boulders that sat to the side of the clearing.

Serena adjusted the trembling Boy comfortably to her hip and started for the Rocks.

"I've n-never been tha-that c-close to a S-Saurop-pod before." stuttered Theo, burying his wet face in Serena's soft hair. Serena patted his shivering back as he laid his chin on her shoulder, hiding the view of the Sauropods with her abundant curls.

"Well, now you have and you've survived. You're a hero, now!" she crooned softly, warmly hugging the poor Boy. His legs, still tight with fear, curled around her and locked on the other side of her thighs.

"No, y-you're the hero. You – you saved me, Serena!" spluttered the little Halfbreed, grasping her shining ringlets and peeking out to see if the Dino-saurs were gone yet. Serena felt a shudder ripple down his small spine, and he buried his face yet again in her hair. He was becoming quite shaken with emotion. Serena wondered if he wouldn't become scarred for life because of this single event.

It is better for him to be scarred for life with the memory than not to have a life at all. Serena thought, continuing to soothe him as she approached the Rocks. Being one of the first ones there, she lifted Theo up to Jerry and hoisted herself onto the smooth-faced Boulder. The ragged Rocks that lined the base of the Boulder were soon occupied by the rest of the team. Theo was seated securely between Serena and Jerry, watching the massive forms cross the clearing by the light of the Moons and the Stars. A shiver shook through his little body and he leaned against Serena, burying his face in her hair again. Soon he was on her lap.

Serena watched the forms too, promising herself a very exciting, descriptive entry to the notebook she kept for the scientist. Hesitantly, the great Creatures moved, shaking the earth as they did. Their footsteps reverberated into the very bones of the team. The Sauropods swung their huge heads back and forth, gurgling bass-voiced rumbles in their throats. One passed so close to the Rocks that Serena could hear its Wind-like breathing. She sat staring in awe, the figures of the Sauropods twinkling in her eyes as they boomed away, like living earthquake and Thunder.

Thankful that everyone had survived uninjured, Jerry hushed the excited jabbering set up by the team as they congregated around the Rocks.

"Were those… meat-eating Dinosaurs?" shuddered Kate.

"No, Brachiosaurs are only Herbivores. Gentle giants, I guess you could say," Mike replied, thrilled to say the least.

"Huh! They certainly weren't very gentle with me! I almost got trampled!" Lindsey exclaimed.

"It's a good thing we put that fire out! I think they were attracted to the light," Bob rasped, hoarse from barking warnings.

"You would be too if it was dark out," wheezed Serena with something of a nervous laugh. She was hoarse for the same reason.

"Alright! Quiet, please!" Jerry shouted over the distant rumbling. The discoverers fell silent and looked up to the Boy perched on the Boulder. "Thank you, Theo, for warning us. Okay, we'll need to find another secluded clearing to spend the Night. It appears this one has seen its better Days."

Standing on the Rock, Jerry propped a hand on his hip and used the other to shield his eyes from the shimmering Earthlight (which Serena learned was like Moonlight, only blue) that washed over the Plains. He squinted with his eyes to the surrounding horizon. After a short pause, he pointed Northeast and proclaimed,

"There – over there's a little clearing." He made to jump off of the Rock, but his eyes snapped back to the clearing as he spotted something unusual. "Whoa, wait a minute – what was that? Something just landed in it!"

Unexpectedly, Theo climbed up onto Jerry's back and perched on his shoulder. He looked hard at the spot, then jumped down quickly as realization seemed to dawn on him.

"Nelson! My brother! He is hurt!" he yelled, and then jumped off the Rock he had landed on and vanished into the Moonlit Prairie Grass. "Come on!"

A lump of emotion having fallen upon her chest at hearing his words, Serena slipped off the Rock silently and was the first to dash after the Halfbreed. She felt very sure-footed running barefoot though the Prairie Grass, feeling her heart throbbing within her. Ignoring blistered feet and sore muscles, she panted to keep up with the fast, little Boy. She heard the fumbling and bumbling of the others behind her as she sped ahead, worried about what fate had befallen her new friend.

Nelson sat in the clearing, casting aside his moccasin and cleansing the gash on his calf with herbs from one of his four pouches. Theo arrived first, kneeling by his brother's side to help bandage the wound. Then Serena emerged in a flurry of rosy cheeks and bouncing Sun-blonde ringlets. She immediately flung the knapsack from her back and produced from it the first aid kit.

"What is that?" Nelson wanted to know, wincing as Theo ripped at the tear in his leggings to get a better look. Jerry, Mike, and Bob arrived, panting heavily, followed by Lindsey and Kate, puffing as well.

"Medicine from Earth. It will help you heal faster." Serena answered. She opened the kit to reveal bandages, cleansing cloths, ointment and other medical emergency items. Using her knapsack, she elevated his left leg to pave the way for Lindsey, the nurse of the team.

"Let me have a look," Lindsey gasped, squatting beside Serena. Serena moved over to allow the nurse to do her job. Immediately after pulling on plastic gloves, she set to work cleansing, treating, and bandaging the wound.

"Nothing serious," she observed, "though it does look pretty deep."

"What did this to you?" Serena rasped, moving around the brown-haired Girl to snatch up Nelson's hand. Nelson watched Lindsey spread a clear salve over the bleeding gash, then blanched and looked up at Serena piteously.

"I ran into trouble with a Chimera, though, I don't suppose you know what that is."

The other five curious explorers dropped their knapsacks and moved into

116

a circle around Nelson.

"Is this the rest of your crew?" he flinched, sitting himself up on his elbows.

"Yes," Serena chuckled. She waved a hand to point to the members as she introduced them. "That's Kate with the black hair standing next to Jerry, who didn't mean to scare you off by the way. Then there's Mike with the glasses and Bob. Lindsey's here next to me, and I don't suppose you would know your own brother, would you, Nelson?"

The Boy chuckled half-heartedly as he tried to sit up some more. Failing, he rested back on his elbows.

"How did you know my name?" he inquired. Theo sat down next to his brother, rising dust to his face. Nelson coughed. "Oh, you," he grumbled. "I got your string."

Theo smirked and clapped his hands.

"Oh, yippee! Where is it?"

Nelson blew a flyaway piece of hair from his eyes.

"Sitting over there with my bow and quiver."

The little Halfbreed Boy needed no second bidding.

"I never did learn *your* name, though," Nelson said, staring innocently up at the Girl who was studying the sharp tooth that hung around his neck. She set it back down gently upon his chest.

"Serena," she said with a smile. She looked over to admire Lindsey's work. "And the next Chimera that wants to pick a fight with you is going to have to go through me first."

"Alas, the poor Beast," Nelson mumbled, attempting a fake cough. Serena smiled wickedly at him and tweaked his nose.

"What *is* a Chimera, anyway?" Mike wondered aloud, watching Lindsey close and insert the first aid kit back into Serena's knapsack.

Nelson laid back down on the hard-packed soil, staring up at the luminous yellow Stars with his arms tucked comfortably behind his head.

"They are horrible beasts with the head, front legs and chest of a Lion, the abdomen and back legs of a Goat and the tail of a Snake. The one I encountered must have been guarding young ones or something, otherwise she wouldn't have attacked me the way she did. Sneaky, awful Creature!" he cursed.

"That is a terrible wound; does it hurt much?" Lindsey inquired, standing and brushing her hair from her face.

"Not so bad now – it smarts a little. I would like to hear more about your

117

trip here, though."

So the team briefly told him about their trip from the Ceaseless Ocean to the present and asked him about his destination. He said he had none, but he was willing to travel with them because of his new wound and to show them to the closest civilization.

Bob yawned sleepily and sat down.

"I agree," laughed Mike, sitting down beside Kate. "It is very late."

"Let's get some sleep. We'll talk more in the morning," Jerry suggested.

And with that, the crew of explorers, plus their two newfound friends, laid down to sleep for the Night.

Serena spent another fitful Night of sleep out on the Prairie, though for some reason she felt safer with the presence of a two true Foreverans.

She was up before anyone else that morning, climbing a Tree that stood on the edge of the clearing to watch the Sun rise in the East. The weather warmed considerably as the Moon and Earth disappeared over the Western horizon, and the bright yellow rays of the Sun poured over the shadows of darkness and warmed the soil of Forever for another hot Summer Day.

Serena heard a rustle behind her and looked down to see Nelson half-walking, half-floating over to her, holding his injured leg off of the ground.

"Good morning, Sunshine!" she greeted him in a sing-song voice that dripped sarcasm.

"Why, good morning, morning glory," rumbled the British-accented tenor in an equally theatrical voice. Serena wondered as she watched him drift up to the branch how he could be so sarcastic while he was still in so much pain. She helped him steady himself on the branch.

"Did the medicine help?" she asked, tottering precariously forward to glimpse his injured leg. As though beckoned, he turned on his bottom and placed his legs in her lap, then laid down on the branch with his hands behind his head. He smiled happily.

"Yes, it does feel ever so much better toDay. However, I do believe 'twon't be completely healed for awhile."

Serena loosened his moccasin and pulled it down a little, then lifted back the flap of blood-stained brown leggings to look at the bandaged wound. Noting that it had stopped bleeding long enough to be stuffed chock-full with an-

118

tibiotic ointment and wrapped tightly in gauze, she nodded satisfied approval and replaced the legging fabric and the moccasin.

"Good. And just where did you find that mother Chimera?"

Nelson perked up a little, riling himself up for a good story.

"Well, I was walking along through the Prairie Grasses not far to the North, here, and I heard a little roar off to one side. So, I got out my bow and arrows and flew up into the air to see where it was coming from. That was a bad idea because that rotter jumped right up out of a Tree, grabbed my calf and dragged me to the ground to start mauling me. I had to drop my bow and arrows in order to get her off of me, but when I did, I had to grab them and take to the air before she lunged at me again. I flew all the way here, because she chased me for a long while, but when I moved out of her territory or too far away from the nest for her liking, she stopped and turned around. Blasted beast! I hate Chimeras!"

Serena giggled as he explained in detail his very moves, then shook his head and looked at the ground, pushing the memory aside.

Silence took over, which was broken when Serena asked,

"Where do you and little Theo live, then?"

Nelson removed his legs from her lap and allowed them to dangle over the branch. He seemed hesitant to reply.

"Well ... nowhere, really. We were Princes once, but we ran away from the Kingdom and forced ourselves to live on our own. We really don't have any place to stay, so we just sort of drift around from Town to Town helping travelers and living our own lives."

Serena touched the Boy's arm.

"You say you ran away? From where? And what for?"

Nelson went strangely silent for a moment, staring at the ground sadly, reliving unwanted memories. Then he looked up at Serena with the same large green eyes as his brother. Something deep inside Serena suddenly went soft.

"I – I really don't want to talk about that," he half-whispered, looking down at his dangling moccasins, "Maybe later."

"Hey, loveBirds!" Lindsey jested beneath them. "Time for breakfast! Come on down!"

With a smile and a nod of understanding, Serena helped her friend down from the Tree to hobble over to breakfast.

After a hearty breakfast of fried Bird's eggs and roasted grains (both supplied by Nelson and Theo) the group of eight set off through the Golden-hued Hillocks and Plains.

Jerry, Mike and Bob traveled silently behind Lindsey and Theo, who were speaking lightly of the Sauropod incident. Kate was following Serena and Nelson with her arms crossed, looking a little disheveled from the recent events. Ever on the lookout for more Sauropods or some other strange Creature, Serena plodded along beside Nelson, learning more from him about Forever.

"So, you said that my eyes are the color of a SeaLore's rear end." she said, recalling a name he had called her at breakfast. "I can't imagine any Animal I know having a blue-"

"No, no, no!" chanted Nelson, laughing. He watched her peek warily up over the tops of the Grass. "A SeaLore isn't an Animal - it's a Spirit. A Spirit of Water. 'Sea' refers to the fact that it is made of Water and 'Lore' means it is legendary."

"Ohh…" Serena sighed, looking back at him. "So, then what does it look like?"

"Well…" he sighed, pausing to condense the words so she would understand them. "It's similar to a face in the Water - usually a Human or an Elven face." He stopped to scratch his head. "I'm not very sure about that, actually. You see, I've never truly seen a SeaLore for myself, but I hear they like to reside in shady Pools and Lagoons. Of course, there aren't many Water sources here in the Golden Plains. I suppose I shall see one some Day," Nelson explained.

"And you said something once about a SkyLore, too," Mike eased in, having left Bob and Jerry to research this new Animal. He took his tiny glasses off, cleaned them on his T-shirt, and put them back on. Then he pulled a handheld notebook and a pen out of his pocket as Nelson obligingly spoke.

"There are five kinds of known Lores to the Foreverans: SeaLores, SkyLores, TreeLores, CaveLores, and MountLores. Skylores are Wind Spirits that often inhabit Clouds or great Winds. The rest I'm sure you can figure out – I daresay the the prefixes are dead give-aways."

"Oh, I know one! Like a TreeLore would be a Spirited Tree!" Lindsey said, her gray eyes shining.

"And a CaveLore would be a Spirited Cave," Bob figured. He rubbed the stubble on his chin, as all of the older boys had begun to grow something of a beard. "And a MountLore-"

"What would that be, Nelson?" Jerry wondered. "A Spirited Mountain?"

"Not quite a Mountain," the Halfbreed laughed, "but they're usually found in the Mountains. I've been told they are smaller models of Mountains, with eyes and other facial features. Downright scary when you think about it."

He took out a smooth piece of some sort of candy and popped it in his mouth.

"Can they-" Serena started.

"What are those little pouches for?" wondered Kate, suddenly barging between Serena and Nelson.

"Stuff," was all he said. Then, looking past Kate, "Hey, Serena!"

"Wait!" Kate urged. "What was that you put in your mouth?"

"Food," Nelson replied irritably, pushing the treat around in his mouth.

"What kind of-"

But before the black-haired Girl could finish her sentence, Nelson mumbled a quick,

"Excuse me, miss," and flew right over her head to land on the other side of Serena. "Sorry about that," he apologized.

"That's alright." Serena giggled.

But Kate's cheeks flushed a bright red as she stomped off, thoroughly humiliated in front of the Halfbreed Boy.

"So, just what are those little pouches for?"

"Now let me see… this one-" he pointed to the lightest shade of green of the four bags, a pale color and obviously the first one, "is where I keep my healing Herbs; this one," he gestured to the pouch next to the first, a slightly darker pouch the shade of healthy Spring Grass, "is where I keep some of my keepsakes; this one," he pointed to the third, still darker pouch, which was a vibrant shade of Emerald green and was the same pouch from which he had produced the candy, "has in it some candy and bits of dried fruit and meat in case I get hungry; and this one," the very last, darkest green bag, the shade of a shadowed Jungle canopy, "I keep what little money I have in case I need something from in Town. Most of the time, though, Theo and I just do stuff on our own."

Serena couldn't help but wonder - was the currency in this Forever place different from the money on Earth? She voiced her thoughts to the limp-flying Halfbreed Boy.

"Well, I don't know," he said. "Do Dinkels sound familiar to you?"

"Dinkels?" Serena giggled, "What kind of a name for money is that?"

She heard Jerry and Lindsey chuckle behind them.

Nelson smiled, opened his Jungle-canopy green pouch, and took out three coins. He held them flat in his hand, and sensing a lesson for the blue-eyed Girl next to him, explained the name and value of each. The others, specifically Jerry, who seemed especially interested in the money, crowded around.

"This is a Dinkel. It isn't worth much." He pointed to a rustic Bronze coin about the size of a dime. Holding up another one, a shimmering Silver coin as large as a quarter, he said, "This is a Farlo. It's worth much more than a Dinkel, but not near as much as," he stopped to hold up the last of the three, a shining Gold coin about the size of a half-dollar, "a Welnon."

"Amazing," Serena remarked, admiring the glittering object as he flipped it up in the air and caught it neatly in the pouch.

All morning the weary band traveled along, each learning something new about this strange new Land known as Forever. Nelson and Theo hardly stopped talking about the place, teaching their six eager young pupils all they knew of the Land.

"So how is it exactly that you two can... *fly?*" Bob asked, seeing Nelson fly over a Rock that he mustn't have felt like stumbling over.

"Pardon? Oh, flying – well, Theo can't really fly just yet," he nudged his brother playfully as the younger scowled up at his big brother, "but he's learning. We've got five different levels of Magical Creatures in Forever - FiveStars, FourStars, ThreeStars, etc. - and those that don't have any kind of Magic are called Starless. You would probably be Starless, I'm guessing, unless you used an object to perform Magic, like a bottled Charm. Then you would be considered a OneStar. We're ThreeStars, Theo and I, because we're Halfbreeds. Our Elven parent was a FourStar and our Human parent was Starless. TwoStars are Creatures who hardly have any hereditary Magic at all, like MerMaids and Unicorns. And FiveStars are Creatures who have the most Magical Ability in Forever, like Sorcerers-"

"How exactly do you measure how much Magic a person – oh, excuse me, a Creature – has?" Lindsey had to know.

Nelson shrugged.

"It's kind of based on what race you are and how much hereditary Magic is running in your family. For instance, most Brownies and Elves are FourStars, and most Halfbreeds and Nymphs are ThreeStars. We usually decide how much Magic a Creature has on what kinds of things they can do with it. FourStars can disappear and transform but ThreeStars can't. The Mother of Forever can do anything she wants – I think the Magical Ability comes with the title of Mother. Lots of Creatures are using their Magic to travel right now, because we're in kind of a... a Continental crisis," Nelson went on, his face red from the Sun.

"Whoa! What? Are we in danger?" Jerry exclaimed from in back of them. Nelson stopped momentarily and looked at the dusty team leader.

"Not at the moment, we're not. I'll explain later – let's keep walking and see if we can find that old path."

Serena watched a pair of spectral-colored Birds wing overhead, happily chirping.

"I don't see any crises here, Nelson." she said seriously, looking back at the fair-faced Boy. The medicine had indeed taken effect on his calf, for he now walked instead of half-flying as he was doing before.

"Looks can deceive," he said and then paused, scratching his temple and tossing his head back in an attempt to tame his wavy bangs that hung unevenly over his brow. He looked behind him at Lindsey, who was staring at him uneasily. "At the moment we're safe. Lindsey – is that right? – you can stop looking at me like I've got a boil on my forehead," he laughed, "If something happens to Forever, it will happen in due time."

Lindsey giggled and stepped up next to Serena.

"Sorry. You scared me."

"I apologize."

Lindsey looked at the Sun, which was shining hotly on all of them.

"So why is this place called Forever? Can you live forever or something?"

Behind them, the rustle of paper alerted them to Mike's rapidly filling notebook.

"The reason this Land is named Forever is because of one thing. One Fountain. A specific Spring."

"The Fountain of Youth!" twittered Theo, jumping up and down next to his brother as they progressed along the Plains.

Kate stopped in her tracks, chuckling.

"The what?" she cried disbelievingly. Her mirth subsided immediately as she found Nelson glaring at her. Gulping in humiliation, she began to walk alongside Bob once more.

Jerry apologized for her.

"Sorry, Nelson, it's just that where we come from, The Fountain of Youth is nothing more than a myth. Oh, what was his name… some Spanish fellow mistook it for a Spring in the Bahama Islands."

Serena knew his name but could not think of it at the moment.

"Ponce de Léon," Bob put in from the back, his lanky figure swaying as he walked.

"That's him!" Serena exclaimed with a snap of her fingers. She looked back at Bob, who was trudging along determinedly. "Thanks, Bob!"

"Ponce de Léon," Nelson murmured, racking his brain for any information on the name. "Only now do I wish I'd paid attention to that Witch of a school Mistress,"

"He was the first to voyage across Forever to Sparkline Mountain and the Castle of Diamondia," recited Theo hesitantly. "He spoke a in-de-ciph-er-a-ble language from Earth and his entire memory was erased of his travels in Forever when he passed out through the Shield, except for the one name that he himself had found. That was the name of the great Spring that ran within both the Mountain and the Castle – The Fountain of Youth."

"Are you sure he's only seven?" Serena half-whispered to Nelson, who was astounded at this sudden outburst of knowledge from his younger brother.

"I think so." he coughed in return, stifling a chuckle. Theo smiled faithfully up at his older brother.

"I heard that," Theo seethed through the smile.

Serena decided to change the subject before they witnessed any sibling rivalry.

"Ah, if it's not too much to ask, Nelson, but what did you mean when you said that Forever was under a crisis?"

Nelson straightened and looked at the Sun. He seemed hesitant to discuss the subject, but nonetheless prevailed.

"The Lands of Forever has only one true ruler, and she is known as the Mother of Forever. A couple of months ago, as Forever was descending down to Earth as it does every hundred years, the Mother became deathly ill. Such a situation can only be a sign that we are in great need of another ruler. That

124

illness that has fallen upon her is the only known sickness that the Waters of the Fountain of Youth (called Spring Water) cannot heal. The Daughter of the Mother of Forever has been trying ever since the sickness fell to claim the crown from her, but so far has not succeeded."

Serena lowered her head just in time to step over a Rock that would have tripped her bare, calloused feet. She moved gracefully over the Sand and the sharp, poking Weed Grasses that blanketed the ground. The Moss that sprouted from the soil she stepped on made her marching minimally easier going, cushioning her footsteps.

"We're sorry to hear this," she said at last, looking at Jerry's puzzled face. "But are you sure that the Daughter of the Mother is the correct Heir to the Throne?"

Nelson scratched his chin.

"She has got to be!" he exclaimed. "There is no other WoMan in Forever that is fit for the Throne." Seeing Serena's puzzled expression, he explained, "By that I mean there is no other WoMan in the Lands of Forever with the blood of the Mother running through her veins. The Daughter of Diamondia has no other female siblings, and the Mother herself has no siblings or cousins or even parents. I cannot think of any other Creature that is applicable to claim the Throne."

Serena watched the tannish curls of Theo as he skipped ahead of them, his little quiver of feather-tipped arrows bouncing on his back.

"Are you sure that it must be a Mother of Forever? Why can't it be a Father?" Lindsey said from behind them. Nelson turned to look at her. It must have been the Sun shining in his eyes that made him flush when he answered,

"You know, that's a good question. I'll have to ask the Mother that when we get there."

Serena felt her skin freeze.

Jerry must have felt the same.

"We? When we get where? Where are you taking us?"

"To-" Nelson began, nodding in a SouthEastern direction.

"The path! Nelson, we found the path!" Theo hollered, bounding back to the group of Travelers.

Nelson smiled, quickening his pace and encouraging the others to do so as well.

"Good! I knew the bend in that old path was up this way somewhere. We can stop there for lunch."

Jerry suddenly sprinted up to the front line of the group.

"Hey, wait a minute!" he yelled, halting the team. He turned to Nelson. "Where are you leading us? This is not your group of explorers; I'm the captain here!"

Nelson shrugged coolly.

"Alright, so you are. But tell me, almighty captain, do you happen to know the layout of the Land?"

Jerry paused a moment, staring almost enviously at the sharp points on the ends of the Boy's ears that poked out from his mop of curly tan-blonde hair. His clear green eyes seemed to bore holes into Jerry's head as he crossed his arms, patiently awaiting a response.

"Well … not really," Jerry admitted in a hushed voice, "But that is beside the point! That is why Mike is our wildlife specialist, and he-"

"Ah, but is he trained to know the ways of your so-called 'mythological' Creatures? Surely he wasn't trained in the ways of the Animals on Earth?"

A smile crept up on Nelson's half-Human half-Elven features. Mike shifted from foot to foot and then looked innocently up at Jerry through his tiny glasses.

Jerry coughed nervously.

"Er, well… I suppose he was," he agreed reluctantly.

Nelson's smile widened, and he uncrossed his arms as he strode up to Jerry and placed a friendly hand upon his shoulder.

"I can tell that all of you are very eager to get back to your homes. The only way to send you back at this point is to gather some Spring Water for yourselves and wait out the hundred years that Forever is in the Sky. Then you may sail out again on the Ceaseless Ocean and through the Endless Mists to land back on your home planet. I am here to help you do this."

The team gasped almost in unison.

Terror dawned on Serena's heart. Kate spoke what they were all thinking.

"But," squeaked Kate, grasping Jerry's arm, "but by that time, the scientists will all be dead! And so will we! We can't-"

"Not with the Spring Water." Nelson interrupted, removing his hand to place it on his hip. "As long as you keep taking it every 10 or 20 years to reduce your age, you could very possibly live for eternity. That's why these Lands are named Forever."

Kate's arms fell to her side and she looked at the ground heartbrokenly.

"Is there any other way?" Serena inquired, feeling sorry for Kate despite

126

their rival ways.

Nelson slid an arm around her shoulders and began to walk with her again, following Jerry and Kate, who seemed to be deep in thought.

"I know only one other way to transport you and your group back to Earth."

"And what is that?" Serena asked eagerly.

Nelson cleared his throat, looking at her full in the face.

"To consult the Mother of Forever herself, and see if she could arouse her Powers to send you back to the Earthen World."

Serena's hope vanished.

"But she is sick," she sighed softly, studying the Sandy, hard-packed ground of the sharp bend in a path that they now approached. Already Theo, Jerry, Kate, and Bob had settled under the shade of a partially sizeable Tree, mumbling in voices of disdain.

"Yes," Nelson replied. "She is very ill and unless we should find a cure for her or another ruler for the Throne soon, she shall perish and the reigns of Forever will fall into criminal hands."

Serena sighed deeply as she, Lindsey, Mike and Nelson joined the circle on the side of the large path.

.*.*.*.*.

Serena's troubles were temporarily pushed aside as she engaged in a delicious bowl of biscuits and soup, cheffed by Nelson and Mike, who had become rather attached through their travelings.

"Add a bit of buttercup milk for seasoning..." Nelson explained, deciding to teach the wildlife explorer about his special Plains Soup. He continued to add more seasoning and flavor to the soup while Mike took notes on his second batch.

Serena thought the soup was very tasty, with lots of seasonings and tang, but also filling. She felt bloated even after her first bowl and stopped there to watch and see who could possibly dare themselves to down a second helping. As she sat and eyed Lindsey and Mike, giggling, she wondered where the bowls and the cauldron had come from. Certainly they weren't there when the group arrived.

"When we were talking about going to this Fountain place earlier in our team huddle," Jerry explained, "and he thought we all had our backs turned to him, that Nelson Elf wiggled his fingers and created them out of thin air!"

"Wow! What kind of Magic did he say he was?" asked Lindsey.

"ThreeStar, I think – because he's a Halfbreed. If he was a full Elf he would have FourStars," Serena replied, looking over her shoulder and watching Mike scribble furiously in his notebook.

Just then a scuffling noise and a sound of many voices reached their ears. Turning to the right side of the path, the eight Travelers were just in time to see a large mob of strange half-Human Beasts wander around the bend to meet them. Nelson stood and left the bubbling contents of the pot to Mike.

Serena and Jerry stood at once, both knowing just what these odd Creatures were -

Fauns.

In ancient Greek myth, Fauns were half Man, half Deer - with the upper torso of a Human and the waist down of a Deer or a Goat, she thought in awe, studying the elder Faun, the only one with any signs of age upon him. Nelson was addressing him with respect.

In a sign of honored greeting, Nelson placed a hand over his heart, closed his eyes and nodded his head slightly. Sensing this must be some sort of respectful greeting (in the same way Americans would shake hands), Serena watched Nelson and the Faun smile at each other.

Chuckling in a nasal, low-pitched, and somehow Childlike voice, the elder Faun placed his hands on his hips where his loin cloth straps tied and said,

"Now inna Faunish."

Nelson's Boyish grin widened and he put his pointer finger on his nose while raising his right hand to head-height. Watching the Faun do the same, Serena observed Nelson as he crossed his eyes, bloated out his cheeks like an overstuffed Chipmunk, and stuck out his tongue.

Then, in unison, Nelson and the Faun wiggled the fingers of their right hands and made disturbing noises - *like that of a disgruntled Duck being stepped on,* Serena thought - with their tongues.

This was too much for little Theo, who promptly fell to the ground clutching his sides as he laughed out loud in his husky, little voice. Tears of merriment streamed from his face, and when he finally got up to dust himself off, he only fell to the ground again, laughing uncontrollably, because a little Faun Boy his own age was greeting him with the gesture.

Trying fervently to hold back the laughter that threatened to explode out of her, Serena studied the group of Fauns. They stood only shoulder-height with Nelson and had different shades of black, brown, red, and white hair to match the fur on their upright Deer flanks, which were covered in short, soft fur. None of them looked any older than about 20 years old, and nearly a quarter of the population was made up of thigh-high Faun Children - Girls capering in swishing Grass skirts and homespun braziers while the Boys ran in circles chasing one another in little loin cloths and nothing more. The adults were dressed the same and seemed always to be giggling, jumping, and dancing about something or another.

From a safe distance, Serena examined their backwards knees and their complete lack of shoes because of their two-toed hooves. On their backs were strapped haversacks, and, for some new mothers, squalling babies. There had to be no more than 15 of them in all.

"'Tis good to see you, Wildder." Nelson commented after a short conversation with introductions and revealed destinations. He invited the group over to have some soup for lunch and left to talk to Serena as soon as the explorers had taken to the group. Giggling, Serena watched as Mike's notebook Magically reappeared, Bob and Lindsey attempted to say hello in Faun, and Kate shrieked and hid behind Jerry, who spoke openly with the Creatures. Serena stood with one hand on the trunk of the Tree, somehow either too awed or too shy to introduce herself. After all, her first two encounters with Magical Creatures had both been disastrous.

"What-" she began, peeking over Nelson's shoulder at the feasting Fauns.

"It's alright, Serena. They're quite friendly," he blurted quickly, leaning against the trunk. "I've met them traveling along this pathway before; they are destined for the Castle Forcromb further up this road. It is said that it has a Portal there that will transport us to any other Portal in Forever. The problem is that the only Foreverans that are allowed to use it are Kings and Queens, and those of high Power. Very seldom do they allow mere travelers to use them."

Serena felt her Spirits plunge, and then lift again just as quickly as they had come down.

At least, she thought with a wry smile, *we have a destination.*

She looked back at Nelson, who was watching the troop of Fauns eagerly devour every last drop of his famous Plains Soup.

"What did the leader, the elder one, say?"

Nelson rubbed the back of his neck and stared at the beautiful Moss Flowers sprouting at Serena's bruised feet.

"He said that the Princess of Castle Diamondia has tried again toDay to claim the crown from her Mother," he said slowly. Then, looking up at Serena with sad green eyes, he added, "She failed."

Serena sighed mournfully.

"I am sorry," she confessed. Nelson offered a smile and then looked at the Sky.

"Nevermind it, Serena. It'll all turn out, you'll see. Now, time to move on," he said, straightening and looking stern. "You should gather your things – we will press off as soon as we have packed away the remains of our lunch."

Serena nodded and watched him walk away to call attention.

Chapter Sixteen: Mosslyn

As Nelson gathered up the group of Travelers, Serena sauntered over to her knapsack and hitched it up on her back for another long trek. A Faun Girl, about her age with dark brown pigtails and Childishly large brown eyes stooped by her feet and picked up Teresa's diary, which Serena had dropped. She held it out to her with a smile.

"Thank you!" Serena enthused, relieved that the Girl had noticed. She didn't know what she would do with herself or what she would tell the team if she lost that diary. The Faun Girl grinned.

"Aw, it awright!" she bleated in a high-pitched, slightly British-accented voice. Her rosy cheeks lifted to her Human-like pointed ears. "Yoor welcomed!"

Serena then attempted to make the greeting gesture in Faun, placing her right pointer finger on her nose and waving her left hand comically, crossing her eyes and bloating her cheeks to make the duck sound.

The Faun Girl giggled until her freckled cheeks were pink.

"No, no, no!" she chortled, waving her hands in front of Serena's face. Serena stopped and smiled.

"Did I come close?" she asked.

"Uh-uh," giggled the Faun Girl, shaking her head. "That was bad."

"Alright then, how do you do it?"

Without a second bidding, the tan-skinned Faun Girl taught Serena how to say hello in Faun. Serena had to stop many times under the pressure of her own laughter, sounding much more deep- throated than that of her new Faun friend.

After mastering the gesture, Serena grabbed the Faun Girl's wrist and, chuckling in great fun, led her to the front of the group of Travelers.

"My name is Serena, by the way," Serena said as she found a comfortable traveling spot next to Nelson.

"Well my name's Mosslyn! Pppppp! Please ta meetchya! Heeheeheehee!" the Girl giggled, stopping in the middle of her introduction to pull off yet another funny, little Faun gesture.

"What part of Forever do you come from, Mosslyn?" Serena wondered.

"No-whereses really. Heeheehee! We just sortsa roams arownd wherevers we pleases, and, heehee! I guesses now we's goin' ta Forcromby's Cascle. Where are you's a-goin', Seblena?"

Serena shrugged, liking the young accent of her Childlike new friend.

"I think we're bound for the Diamondia Castle, wherever that is. Isn't that where the Mother of Forever resides?"

"Ooooh, yesyes, that's where she liveses. Poor Mommee of Forever, she so dreadfully sick an' ill right nows. Ya know where the Diamondsia's Cascle is, now, doncha Seblena? Heeheehee!"

Serena shook her head at her comical friend.

"No, but Theo told me that if I followed the current of any of the Rivers it would eventually lead me there."

Mosslyn's large Childish brown eyes studied Serena as the Faun jumped up and down with excitement.

"Theo Boy's a smartee one he is! Heehee! Yesyes, he right, alla Rivers in Forever runses backawords, and dey all leadses to da great purty Mountin 'a Jewelses calleded da Sparkline Mountin. It sitses inna ververy middo of Forever – itsa biggestest, bootifullest Mountin ya ever sawed! Heeheehee! Alla Riverses in Forever leadsta there, then-a they awl run uppa sideses uvva Mountin like whoosh! Heehee! Aw sparkly purty the Watta runnin' uppa Jewelded Mountin – da Watta takeses wif it litto bitty Jewelses yuppy yup it do! Heeheehee! Thennit pours over da sideses inna big circa Watafawl cuz da Mountin be hollowses, see, anna alla Jewelses sparkly purty fawl withum Watta inta da Misty Lake. Oooh, such a bootiful sightsta see! Heeheehee!"

So that's how it works, Serena thought. Eager to learn more, she consulted her small, bouncy friend again to decipher her young-sounding language.

"But Mosslyn, if the Sparkline Mountain is hollow and has Water running up all sides of it, then where does the Diamondia Castle sit? And how does someone get to it?"

Mosslyn took a deep breath and ceased her energetic bouncing to lunge into a slow skip to keep pace with her friend.

"A Diamondsia's Cascle sitses up onna litto platform that hassa necksy dat rises up throughs the Mistses uvva Misty Lake, frumma veryvery middo. Da necky hassa litto hollow inna middo too, anna Wattas anna Jewelses frumma Misty Lake atda bottumses goes up throughs the necky thingy an' comses out inna da Fountin 'a Yoofs inna Cascle. Heehee! So purty sparkles twinkly! Heeheehee! Da whole neck anna platform anna Cascle itselfs is made uppa real Diamondses, anna Cascle is see-through likea glass. Heehee, itsa biggestest Cascle in Forever, even biggerer thin da Cascle Dawn onna Giantses' IsLand cawled Mornin' IsLand to da Norf. Heehee! Anna only way ta gets dere is ta climba uvver Mountins arownd da Sparkline Mountin cawled da Perpetchool Mountins, andta ridea backs uvva Pegasus Horsey-Birds an' takeses ya's backs too. Heeheehee! So shiny purty bootifuls it alls is! Whya you's not know about a Sparkline Mountin anna Perpetchool Mountins anna Diamondsia's Cascle, Seblena?"

Serena sighed and laid a hand on her friend's shoulder.

"It's a long story," she began.

The rest of the Day the large group of Travelers trekked up the path of warm Sand. Now Serena truly realized why the Fauns had dressed so native – fur was very hot when it came to the sizzling Summer Sun. And with all of the unbelievable energy the Fauns put out during the Day, Serena was not at all surprised to find them hot and tired at dusk.

Mosslyn turned out to be an absolute Fountain of knowledge on the history and geography of the wonderful place called Forever. Whenever Serena began to ask a question, Mosslyn had already spurted forth a River of answers before she could even finish.

Serena learned that Forever was not only an inLand Continent, but also several IsLands that bordered the dips in the Coastline. She learned that there were many wonders in Forever, just the same as there were on Earth. There were Trees called Magical Banyans, which grew on their fair branches every type of fruit, berry, and occasionally even nut, known to Man, plus mixed breeds of fruits and invented fruits of its own. There were hot Pools called Aquaria Springs in the South where Creatures from all over came to relax and bathe in its warm, soothing Waters. There were Trees and Mountains that could talk and move, and an IsLand known as the Mysterious IsLand that constantly changed its Landforms and shapes, and spun itself, circling the inLand Forever completely once every year. There were two types of Animals in Forever: the Four-Leggers, which were ordinary-sized, mute Animals much the same as those on Earth, and the Two-Leggers, who were Human-sized, upright, literate Animals that dressed and talked the same as Humans.

Flying ships, singing Trees, spinning Castles – the place sounded like a typical fantasy paradise, at least it did to Serena. Serena was absolutely astounded at all of this. She was very impressed at the excitement and adventure of this new Continent. And for the first time, the thrill of being out on some grand, heroic adventure alit in her chest, and she warmed to its adrenaline-pumping presence. In fact, she felt as though she would have ventured out sooner to find Forever, had she known the place even existed. Mosslyn chuckled when Serena voiced her thoughts.

"Heeheehee! Evun if you's dided adventure outta da Earthy world, you's still notta finded it! Heehee! Cuz a bootuful landsa Forever wood bee's wayway up inna Sky… Ya knows it'sa Northy Starpurty, donchya?" the little Faun Girl giggled, playing with the two long braids that graced her Childish appearance.

Serena smiled at her energetic new friend, silently deciphering the poorly articulated language of her species. She stopped to take off her travel pack as Jerry and Nelson, coincidentally, called halt for camp at the same time.

"Well, now I do," she mused, smiling at the Faun.

Mosslyn grabbed her wrist.

"Comeon over to a fires, Seblena! Heeheehee! We's can cooksy up some yummy appleses! Heehee!"

'Seblena' allowed Mosslyn to lead her over to one out of the three would-be small campfire sites. The Faun pulled four delicious, ruby-red apples out of her canvas haversack. Sticks and poles where whittled and passed out, and before long, Nelson, Jerry, and Wildder each had their own crackling fire alongside the path. The team from Earth was split between the three fires - Mike and Kate sat at Jerry's fire and Bob and Lindsey at Wildder's with their new Faun friends. Serena was the only team member at Nelson's fire, but with Mosslyn and some other Fauns – young male Fauns, who sat and stared at them, twittering in great fun.

Mosslyn and Serena roasted two apples apiece over the fire and ate them delicately, discussing the styles of Foreveran Girls.

"Mosta Girlies in Forever wears aw dese corsetteses anna frocksies anna bloomy-pants anna petticoatses, but some wear silky see-through gownses wiffa sparklies anna longlong angel sleeveses anna trainses. Me, doe, I donna likes dose hot dresses, heehee! Cuzza on de hot hot Summer's Dayses me legses get awl hot an' warm unner de big foofy purty skirtses – dat's why I on'y wears a thinthin Grassy skirtsy – see so I don't get aw hot an' warm an' roastses likea dat apple fruits you gots dere. Heeheehee!"

Mosslyn bit into her roasted apple, and Serena watched the juice run down her chin. The Boy Fauns gave an uproarious laugh from across the fire.

134

Giggling at the silly, dancing Creatures, Serena opened her mouth to explain what style of clothes Girls on Earth wore, but someone behind her stopped her.

"Hey Serena!"

In a flash of fire-lit curls she turned to look behind her. Jerry strode over to her in a business-like manner.

"Yes?" she said politely, awaiting his request.

"Did Nelson say anything to you about a Portal that can take us to Sparkline Mountain?"

Serena hadn't a doubt that he had received knowledge of the Sparkline Mountain and the Diamondia Castle. She fussed with her stick and replied,

"Yes, he said that there was one at the Forcromb Castle."

Jerry stopped in front of her, his gray-blue gaze studying her dancing blue eyes.

"Do you think we have any chance of getting into one – I mean, of them letting us use one?"

Serena shrugged, pulling her stick out of the fire to observe her steaming, shriveled apple. Two boy Fauns across the fire were mime-acting Serena and Jerry kissing, the three around the actors screaming and laughing and instigating the two. Shaking her head and looking away from them, Serena turned back to her apple. Finding a side that was not quite done, she revolved it and poked it back into the sizzling flames.

"I highly doubt it. Nelson told me that only Kings and those of a royal sort are allowed to use them."

Jerry's shoulders sagged, and he frowned over at the Halfbreed Boy, who was busying himself with entertaining a group of admiring female Fauns.

"Well," Jerry said after a pause, "we're just going to have to find some way of getting in there."

A thought popped into Serena's mind, and she prepared to tell Jerry her idea when from the background sounded,

"Seblena Girl!"

Mosslyn had suddenly begun tapping Serena's shoulder, and the Boys across the fire were prancing and pointing at her.

"One moment, Mosslyn." She turned to Jerry. "Do you think we could dress up as Kings and Queens and sneak in there?"

Jerry rubbed his chin thoughtfully.

"Perhaps, but where will we find the costumes? Wildder told us that it's only a Castle up there – no Cities or Towns or even Villages. I don't-"

135

"Seblena!"

The Boy Fauns soon joined in.

"Heeheehee! Izzatter name?"

"Hay, Seblena!"

Serena was growing irritated with those Boys across the fire, but she ignored them.

"Please, Mosslyn. But even if we did dress up they might see through our costumes," Serena doubted.

A mischievous smirk played on Jerry's thin lips.

"Not if we-"

"Seblena!" shouted Mosslyn right in her ear.

Both turned to look at the interruption.

"What!?" they replied in unison.

The Boys across the fire were wrestling one another, now, straying perilously close to the fire in their scuffle. Apparently, there had been a disagreement. Serena was just glad they had stopped hooting at her.

"The rulerses at Forcromby's Cascle gots a Cyclops eye – anna Fortune Tella toos. Dey's see right throughs you planses even now as wc talks! Heehee! Anda by da ways, you's apple fruit's burnin' flameses!"

Directly after dinner Serena went to bed. The Fauns prepared to stay up late, but Jerry and Nelson would not have it. Those who wished to party were pushed further out along the path, at least out of earshot. Mosslyn went with them. The team settled down for a long Night's sleep in groups for safety purposes. Lindsey, Jerry, and Nelson were in Serena's group, later joined by Mosslyn some time early in the morning. Lindsey had made friends with the healer Faun of the group and a few others, Jerry had spoken to the Boys that had jeered across the fire at them and scared them off, and Nelson was friends with all of the Fauns. The sounds of the settling campsite were of fires being fed, Child Fauns protesting bedtime, and three or four mothers telling stories or singing lullabies to the protesting Children.

Serena had soaked her blistered feet in a warm bowl of Water Nelson had kindly made up for her, and that relieved some of the pain in her soles. She was very tired after her long Day's journey, and looked forward to a restful slumber. Serena smiled as she settled down beside Lindsey, bidding her a good

Night in a low whisper. Sleep wasn't long in coming.

Serena's dreams were pleasant.

She thought this as she rolled over, noting how nice it was to sleep peacefully after several Night's fitful slumber.

In her dream, Serena was flying. She was wearing a long, beautiful silken white gown that sparkled and fluttered about at her ankles. Her Angel sleeves made her feel like the most graceful Bird soaring through the air in flawless loops and twists.

Through Misten Clouds of many different pale and lovely colors she flew, over and under, through and around, side to side, upside down and all over. Serena's Spirits lifted as she did when she fluttered upward, feeling the breath of the cool morning air on her cheeks. Her curls played around her face like tendrils of Mist, and she felt the trains of her twinkling skirts billowing out beneath her like a fragile tent of cloth.

And then the feeling of being one with the colorful Mists of the Sky left her, and was replaced by a strong, cold emotion she knew only too well as morbid foreboding. Something was wrong.

And indeed, something was wrong, for Serena began to fall. Her skirts, hair and appendages flailed as the last of her flying Powers left her. She opened her mouth to scream, but nothing came out. She turned to look beneath her, and there, in the distance below, stood two forms, both with their arms outstretched to catch her. One figure was blurrier and smaller than the other, and a long shadow far beneath her may have possibly been a third figure. In another few seconds the Mist would part and show their faces.

But …

Serena was abruptly awoken with a large hand smelling deeply of herbs and fire smoke restraining her mouth. Her eyes snapped open and she prepared to scream.

She found herself looking deeply into a pair of large, beautiful and yet vaguely familiar, green eyes.

Nelson.

"Shhhh …" he hushed, returning her silent gaze. His lips barely moved as he whispered. "CatEagles are on the prowl. We must move off the path immediately. Forget your knapsack; don't go after it. If you leave it as a distraction, they might not notice us leaving."

He removed his hand slowly as she nodded in agreement.

"Go – wake as many of the others as you can without making any noise.

Have them congregate quietly out in the Prairie on the right side of the path," he breathed, slinking off to wake more Travelers.

Now, Serena had no idea what CatEagles even were, but from the way Nelson had said their name, they didn't exactly sound like the most polite Creatures in Forever.

It was a very foggy morning. The ground was coated all around with the swirling white Mists that would later rise to provide sight to the group. Luckily, Nelson had nodded his head in the direction of the right side of the path, so Serena had a good idea of which direction not to go. Curious, she edged a bit closer in that direction, and through the Mist she could hardly spot a feathered form of a huge Cat, rummaging through her very own knapsack. Heeding Nelson's warning words about the CatEagles, she turned over and quietly awoke Mosslyn and Lindsey.

Before long, Serena had aroused seven or eight other sleepers, mostly Fauns, and had them crawl carefully over to the shelter of the tall Prairie Grass. She herself slid around in the Sand on her hands and knees, trying to move as slowy as she was possibly able. She crept up on Kate, and, praying for a quiet awakening, placed her hand over her mouth and shook her.

"Mmmph! Thrrrnnnaaa!" the Girl choked beneath her hand. Her dark brown eyes narrowed at Serena above her scrunched nose. She ripped her hand off and prepared to set up some remark of defense, but Serena slapped a hand over her face again and explained to her the situation with the CatEagles. For the first time, Kate grasped Serena's arm as though begging for comfort.

"No!" she mouthed, fear in her eyes. "What are CatEag-"

"Shhh!" Serena hushed her, and directed her off to the others. "We'll explain later. Right now you need to get out of here as quietly and as quickly as you can!"

Kate nodded and crawled off on all fours. Serena scratched her head – Kate had not protested at all. That was uncharacteristic of Kate, but Serena was not to complain.

Finally, when she was quite certain that all 23 of the questors were awake and in the Prairie, Serena began to head that way herself.

But something stopped her dead in her tracks.

Teresa's diary, she thought, and felt a wave of fear ripple across her skin. Something about that diary was very attached to her, and she to it. She lowered her eyebrows.

I have to get it back.

138

Stifling cold shivers of discouragement, Serena turned on her knees and lowered herself to the ground. She felt very much like a Snake wriggling in the Sand on her belly, and didn't too much like the feeling of being one of the scaly things. She merely pushed these thoughts aside in hopes of rescuing the frail diary of her ancestry. Scratching, ripping, rustling and an utterance that sounded strangely between a purr and a squawk hung in the otherwise still air as Serena drew closer to her raided knapsack. The feathery figures that obstructed her view loomed even larger before her eyes as she came closer.

At last, she stopped in back of a twitching feathered tail, colored red and auburn with a little fan of supposed tail feathers sprouted from the very end. What a strange sight it was, so much so that Serena almost laughed out loud at the strange little thing.

Suddenly, from another side very close by, another tail slithered out of the white Mist. Menacing threat though it was, Serena kept herself moving, determined to find the precious diary.

Something… over there… whispered a voice in her head, and an object caught the corner of her eye. A slingshot.

Pity, a Faun must have lost it. she thought.

Then, an idea formed.

A risky idea, almost crazy, but one that made her shake with suppressed laughter. She crept over and snatched up the slingshot, and quickly found a couple of small, sharp Rocks lying nearby.

Sticking the slingshot in the back pocket of her jeans with the Rocks, she slinked over to the two tails that twitched mischievously and Catlike in the air. With a grin of self-satisfaction, she set to work.

Barden the CatEagle lifted his gargantuan head from a destroyed knapsack. Clacking his orange beak and twitching his befeathered Owl-like ears, he dove into another and was rewarded with a small canvas diary.

"Well, well, well!" he snorted in a deep British accent, "Wot do we 'ave 'ere?"

"Wot is it, Barden?" piped Limple, the other CatEagle. "Wot'd ya find?"

"'Tis none of your blisterin' business, Limple. 'Tis mine." growled Barden in return, twitching the small stubby whiskers of a Mountain Cat.

Suddenly, something sharp stung his claw, making him drop the diary. He whirled upon his brother.

"Wot did you do 'at for, whiskerbeak? You made me drop the blasted thing!"

Little did Barden know that as he confronted his fellow CatEagle, the diary was moving away from him. He failed to notice the small white human hand that pulled it along.

"Do wot for, featherbrain? I ain't done nothin' wrong."

Barden stood. Anger bubbled in his veins as he studied the ground critically for his lost prize.

"Great, now ya made me lose it! You're never going to be a very good plunderer if ya keep that act up!"

Limple cowered for only a moment, until something pointy hit him in the eye.

"Reoooooaaawwwwk! Naow you've done it, you filthy feather pillow!" squawked Limple, wheeling around to buffet his older brother.

But Barden was too quick.

Or, at least, he thought he was.

He took off to lunge into the air, spreading his large Eagle's wings out to their fullest – but something stopped him. Mysteriously, his own tail had become tied in a nasty, little knot with his brother's, and because of this he was yanked back to the ground to land in a heap of crumpled feathers. Limple pounced on his older brother, seizing his chance.

"Truce! Truce! I didn't do it, I tell you!" Barden pleaded trying to kick his brother off of him.

"Thaaaaat's right! You just go ahead and lie some more, you slack-gutted, bloated Pignut! Why I'll …"

Serena didn't need to hear the rest of the conversation to know that the two CatEagles were well-distracted. And she had Teresa's diary.

No sooner had she unnoticeably slipped away into the Prairie than she and several others who had watched her erupted into a fit of rib-cracking laughter.

And so it was, when the hilarity of their narrow escape had subsided, that the large group of journeyers continued their quest in the Prairies. They traveled Eastward, away from the path and the threat of any more invading CatEagles.

However there were two things that bothered Serena the most that Day. One was they now had a dangerously low supply of food and Water after nearly half of the haversacks in the group had been confiscated and torn apart. The second was their decision to keep heading East until they ran into the Castle Barrift with the City Dooditan resting at its feet. The setback of this new destination? It was a full five Day's march across the Golden Plains and a wide stretch of FlatLand Meadows to get there. And with the state the whole group was in now, Serena highly doubted they would reach their goal without either being starved to death or being eaten first.

"Heehee! We'll also be passings the border atwixt Winkel and Marlo Realmses!" Mosslyn informed Serena later that Day. She rebraided her long hair as she skipped along.

"I didn't know Forever had separate Realms." Serena responded, noticing how much lighter her shoulders now felt without the added weight of her knapsack upon them.

"Oh yesyes, she does! Heehee! She has gots the inLand divided ups inta 12 Realmses, sorta like-a de Stateses you tolds me abowt onna de Earthly planet. She gots, oh, lemesees now… Winkel, which us's all in anows, anna Marlo, anna Liberica, anna Ticheria, anna Zorna, anna Bartle, Thunderia, anna Belkor, anna Youngland, anna Thunderia – oops, I awready seds dat ones, heehee! Anna Aquaria, anna Mistendale, anna Foxwood Realmses. De IsLandses don't gots no Realmses, dey just one awl together! Heehee! Winkel's a Land uvva Winkin' Eyes, acuz dere's eyes awinkin an' a-blinkin' inna Forests a Many Eyeses. Anna Marlo's a Land uvva… aw, geez, I fergotted! Oh, yah! Itsa Land uvva Spirits, cuz it gots lotsalotsa MountLores anna CaveLores anna TreeLores anna SeaLores anna SkyLores! Teehee! I's gladly I paided attentions ta my scholarses! Heehee!"

I wish my studies on Earth had been half as interesting as what Mosslyn seems to have experienced. Serena thought as she nodded politely. Mosslyn went off into a prattle of sorts about which Realms were her favorites and which ones she didn't like. In fact, Mosslyn was speaking so quickly in her excitement that Serena could hardly understand a word she said. After all, the language of the Faun race was something her poor ears was still getting used to. Serena could only smile at the quaint, Childish speech of her little friend

141

and nod politely. She tossed her Sunny locks out of her face and looked at the ground, observing the Moss and its brightly colored, little Flowers that sprouted in her wake. She wished dearly that she had a pair of shoes to protect her ailing feet.

A distant rumbling silenced the excited jabbering of the traveling bunch.

"Sauropods!" shrieked Theo, and he immediately dove himself into Serena's outstretched arms. Serena picked up the whimpering Boy and patted his back, watching Nelson rise into the air to peek into the Prairie.

"Nope." he said, just as the whole group prepared to high-tail it. "Guess again!"

The Sun glinted off his blonde curls, making them gleam like a ray of the Golden sphere itself.

The rumbling ceased gradually, until the earth was still once more.

The only sound after that was the noise of Mike flipping pages in his rapidly filling notebook. Bob's eyes were like a Deer's in the headlights of a car. Lindsey had Serena's waist and Mosslyn crowded close to a shivering Theo, unsure of what was to come. The other Fauns played along with the game, guessing what the sound may have been.

"ThunderCloudses!"

"It'sa MountLore!"

"Inda Prairie! Nuh-uh!"

"Izzita Giant?"

"Wuzzit a bigabig growl frumma Monster?"

"We give up." said Wildder the Faun leader, pushing his way to the front.

"What is it?" squeaked Kate, who had a hold of Jerry's arm and was in the process of cutting off his circulation. Jerry shook her off.

"Unicorns," replied Nelson to the awe - and relief - of his waiting audience. He squinted and shielded his twinkling green eyes against the late afternoon Sun.

"Looks like there's Bicorns and Tricorns over there too. Come on, let's all go have a peek!"

He landed next to Serena to claim his younger brother as the group began to move slowly, whispering excitedly all the way.

"Real Unicornses! I thoughts most of dem liveded inna de Forestses! Heehee!"

"De Horn Hunterses must be outs thickly this Summer Seasons, yesyes!"

"Prettypretty Unicornses anna Bicornses anna Tricornses! Heeheehee!"

142

chattered the excited group of Fauns. The discovery team was astounded beyond speech and so remained silent as they followed the Fauns.

"Hush up now, friends, or they'll hear you!" Nelson called out in a loud
whisper. The sound dampered as they drew closer.

Serena looked at Nelson, who had his brother perched firmly on his back
as he crouched in the Grasses.

"What are Bicorns and Tricorns?" she whispered, almost mouthing the
words. In a low whisper, Nelson replied as Theo jumped off his back to join
the front runners.

"Bicorns are Unicorns with two alicorns, and Tricorns have three."

He paused to walk around a group of admiring Fauns and poke his head
slowly out between the Grass. Serena herself followed his example and peered
out at the Herd.

The full Herd.

That was also very colorful.

There were the Unicorns, of course, their alicorns shimmering strikingly
under the Sunlight. The alicorns themselves looked like a smooth piece of
twisted ivory that had silver sparkles glittering out between the spiral creases.
Then there were the Bicorns, who, instead of having only one alicorn, had two
gleaming horns about four inches apart on their soft brows. Tricorns were the
same as Bicorns aside from the fact that they had one more alicorn jutting up
from between their nostrils in the very middle of the bridge of their nose.

Serena thought the colors of the grazing Creatures were beautiful, also.
She noticed that the Colts and Foals were a bright Golden color, the half-
grown were Silver in hue, and the full-grown adults were such a pure, flawless
white that Serena knew they must be Magical in order to keep the dust of the
Plains from staining their silky coats.

But the colors that struck Serena as the most fantastic were the colors of
the Animals' manes and tails. Any bright and pale color of the Rainbow was
naturally dyed into their hair. Some manes were solid colors while some were
more than one color mixed. They were long and flowing like Serena had been
taught in Fairy tales, overgrown, almost draping on the ground. She noticed
with interest that their eyes were changing colors as they swung their heads to
look at each other.

The same as the Dragons... she thought with a jitter of excitement. *They
must be mood dependant...*

Serena was right. She watched as the great Herd nibbled and grazed away earnestly at the plentiful green Grass. She marveled at them with great wonder and admiration.

"They're beautiful…" she whispered softly, clutching her curtain of Prairie Grass. A nearby Bicorn lifted its head from its grazing, shaking its bright, glimmering Ocean and Sky blue mane. Then, with a loud whinny and a swish of the long, highlighted tail, the Bicorn swung its big head and looked Serena straight in the face.

Fear mounted in her heart as the color drained from her face.

She was discovered.

Slowly, very slowly, she lifted the corners of her mouth into an innocent smile, which soon faded as the Bicorn turned its sideways body and faced her head-on. He chortled a neigh and pawed at the ground, as if standing to attention and awaiting orders.

Her heart pounded with apprehension. What was she going to do? The Bicorn made no move to attack. Reluctantly, Serena decided to make the first move.

Curious, she began to step out into the clearing, but a hand grasped her wrist - Nelson. She looked back at him and took his hand, then squeezed it in reassurance. She said nothing with her voice, but with her eyes, she told his green gaze,

Just let me do this. I'll be fine.

He smiled at her and squeezed her hand back. Serena felt a sudden burst of exciting Power within her when she did this. Pondering at this odd new sensation, she turned back to the clearing.

Then Serena emerged completely from the tall Grass and stood to admire the beautiful Creature before her.

She blinked.

The yellow-eyed Bicorn blinked back, and stomped its front hoof.

Serena, now even more curious than before, stepped forward and reached out her hand, very slowly.

Come! Come to me! she thought for no reason in particular.

And, to her utter astonishment, the Bicorn did come, but slowly. It nodded its large head, tousling its vibrant mane of bright pale blue. It stepped forward hesitantly and carefully, finally nuzzling its pink-nostrilled nose under her outstretched hand.

Serena heard silent gasps sound from behind her. Resisting the urge to pull away shyly, Serena stroked the nose of the magnificent Creature.

Serena's blonde curls glittered under the Sun as she turned her head and looked back at Nelson, smiling anxiously.

"Look, Nelson!" she breathed through her smile.

"I see," Nelson nodded, smiling to himself as he studied the scene. He leaned forward to her and whispered, "They prefer a Maiden's touch."

Before long, Lindsey and Mosslyn had joined Serena in stroking the Bicorn's mane and nose, and soon, several other Girls and Women came out to admire the white-furred adult Bicorn.

After that, Serena somehow drew both a Unicorn and a Tricorn over to her, and even some of the Boys who came out were not rejected. Nelson watched from the Grass how easily another Unicorn was lured over; Serena simply looked at the pretty Creature with an outstretched hand and it came to her. Nelson sighed and cocked his head to one side, an odd smile of passion drawing up one corner of his mouth.

"Nelson! Nelson! HEY!" prodded Theo, jabbing his brother hard in the thigh to get his attention. Nelson looked down, his cheeks flushed in anger. Or embarrassment. Theo couldn't tell which.

"What?" Nelson growled irritably.

"May I go pet the Unicorn?"

Nelson sighed.

"That's really more of a Maiden thing, Theo. But, I suppose, if it will allow you to,"

Happily, the young Halfbreed Boy skipped out into the clearing and stood beside Serena, watching her as she delicately combed through the Unicorn's pink and purple mane with her slender fingers. Theo tugged on her jeans, and the Unicorn braced itself, ready to run.

Relax, I know him well. He will not harm you, Serena told the Creature in thought. It sighed and obeyed immediately. She had found that the only way to communicate with these Creatures was to speak to them through thought, and somehow, though they preferred to remain silent to her, they heard her and obeyed her every will.

Serena lifted Theo up onto her hip, so he could stroke the Unicorn's brow. She smiled and looked back at Nelson, who was watching her protectively. And, she thought, he was smiling at her in a way she had never seen before - compassionately.

Chapter Eighteen: Follow the Rainbow

As dusk approached, the large group of Travelers chose a tiny clearing to make camp. After marveling at the Unicorns, Bicorns, and Tricorns, they had struck off Eastward once again, not wanting to pause in their travels for too long, lest they lose essential distance. The group was split up again - each with their Faun friends. Mosslyn was off giggling with a group of Faun Girls her age, dancing around Bob and his Faun friends and marveling at his height. He merely chuckled and offered to kneel so that they were the same height. Mosslyn thought this was hilarious and slapped his cheeks merrily. Mike was complaining to Lindsey about getting a writer's cramp in his hand as she helped him to solicit the Fauns about their lifestyle.

"Wes stays ups anna parties *awl Night long*!" giggled one young male Faun.

"Mmm hmm, I see, and how long do you usually sleep each Night?" Lindsey asked, giggling at the Boy's crazy antics.

"Four or five hourses!" crowed a young mother Faun, her skirt swishing as she spun around and around until her husband caught her and saved her from spinning into a fire.

Kate had overheard that, and her mouth dropped.

Serena smiled as Jerry approached her with a couple sizeable pieces of dried meat. He sat down beside her next to the fire with his own dried jerky.

"It's been quite a Day, huh?" he mumbled after a pause, beginning to devour his supper. Serena gulped down the first chewy part of her evening meal.

"Quite a week, you mean." she replied, tearing off another piece ravenously. She felt famished. And as she thought about it, it *had* been about six Days since they had started off on the quest.

Six Days! she thought in awe, *Almost one full week. And in that short amount of time we've encountered Dragons and seen their eggs, met a Hippogryph, awaken to a full-blown FrogStorm, befriended two half-Elves, narrowly escaped being trampled by a bunch of Sauropods, made traveling buddies with a wandering tribe of Fauns, outfoxed a pair of CatEagles, touched a real, wild Unicorn, Bicorn, and Tricorn, and also survived through it all! And it's not even the end of the week yet! Who knows what we will find tomorrow?*

"What did you think of the Unicorns?" Jerry asked, scattering the Girl's thoughts.

"And the Bicorns and Tricorns?" she replied, looking at his fire-lit face. His blue-grey eyes reminded her of the dark Night Sky. "I thought they were beautiful! Wasn't it a wonderful sight to see all the colors of their manes and tails – it was so bright I could have sworn they had to have taken the Rainbow right out of the Sky and rubbed it into their hair!"

Jerry laughed, tossing a stick into the fire. He bit into his dinner once more before responding.

"Yeah, and their eyes had a pretty freakish tint to them too. It makes you wonder … how do they change their eye color from blue to yellow just like that?" he snapped his fingers and swallowed. "Makes you think they must be Magic or something."

"They are," said Nelson, sitting down on the other side of Serena.

Jerry made to interrupt him, but Serena silenced him with a pleading look.

"How so?" she asked, studying his countenance under the light of the fire.

"Well, I suppose you could say that it's their horns that give them their Magic. I think so, anyway, because whenever their horn is dislocated from their body, they always die within 24 hours of its removal. Oh, but an alicorn is a wondrous thing to have! They say that if you place it on a table with poisoned food or drink, it will begin to sweat – many Kings these Days own one to display at royal feasts."

"Hmph! Well *I* always heard that they could purify Water. I was never told that-" Jerry began.

"But we come from a different Land than Nelson does." Serena said, tucking her hair behind her ear. She looked at him with excitement. "Jerry, in our world Unicorns are only a Fairy tale – a myth - but in this World they are real!" She paused to take another bite. "How do we know if someone didn't just make that up?"

"Because it's true." Nelson said simply, agreeing with Jerry. "Alicorns do purify Water, and they can heal certain sicknesses, too." Nelson stopped and looked at Serena seriously. "But I bet you don't know what they use Cyclops' eyes for, do you?"

Serena thought for a moment, and remembered something Mosslyn had said about them.

"They don't use them for Fortune Telling, do they?" she wondered aloud.

"Exactly! You're right!" Nelson laughed, sitting back and smirking in

147

wonder at her. "How ever did you come to know something like that?"

Serena smiled and told him of how she and Jerry had planned on sneaking into the Forcromb Castle's Portal to get to Sparkline Mountain.

"Oh, ha ha ha!" he laughed when she had finished with her short tale. "Really! I cannot believe you were daring enough to try and pull that one off!"

Serena felt slightly offended at his remark.

"Well, I don't suppose you think you could do any better calling the President of the United States and asking him if you could use his Air Force One to fly to Europe!" she snapped.

Jerry laughed loudly as if this were the funniest thing he had ever heard.

Serena felt guilty at once as she saw complete puzzlement fall on Nelson's Boyish appearance. She noticed Jerry still chuckling as he got up and strode over to talk to Mike and Bob, now surrounded by dancing Faun Children that were beseeching the Boys to hang off of their arms and backs and be swung around. Mike even had a toddler Faun sitting on his head amongst his nest of unruly black hair. Serena turned back to Nelson with embarrassment written on her face.

"I'm sorry," she breathed honestly. She reached out and took his hand, inspecting his rough fingernails. "Please forgive me, I didn't mean to lash out at you like that. It's just … I think we've all had a very long week, and we're all very tired,"

"I understand," replied Nelson, lying his other hand on top of hers. He sized them up, now noticing how very small of a hand she had. "I probably shouldn't have said that either - somehow I knew it would upset you. But I said it anyway. I'm the one who should be begging forgiveness."

Nelson frowned uncharacteristically at the dying fire.

"I'll forgive you if you forgive me," said Serena softly with a smile.

"You're forgiven," Nelson grinned, his green eyes filling up her vision. Serena forgave him immediately with a bigger smile. Surly this was the best friend she had ever had in her life!

"I suppose now it's time to turn in," Nelson commented with a look at the Sky. "You can lie down and settle in for the Night. I'm going to throw a couple more logs on and then I'll be back. Get some rest, now."

With that, he patted her hand comfortingly and rose to fetch more firewood. Serena felt resistant to let him go; his presence was so comforting and brotherly, perhaps even warmer than the fire itself.

Soon, a warm Summer Rain began to fall at an even pace. Nelson had seen this coming earlier as they had made their camp and constructed something of a tent out of someCreature's cape. All around, similar structures arose, and five or six Creatures squeezed into only one of them. Kate, Lindsey, Mike and Bob would be sharing Nelson's tent with Serena. She found a warm little spot close to the side of the tent to lie down.

What a true friend Nelson is, she thought as she laid on her side, Teresa's diary tucked safely in her pocket and her hands beneath her head. *I wonder if he thinks of me as a true friend too.*

~*~*~*~*~

Again Serena was having her dream of flying. Up through the spectral Mists she soared, her skirt, sleeves, and hair fluttering behind her like trailing ribbons. She enjoyed her flight, and when she began to fall, she remembered the three shapes that had been beneath her with their arms outstretched. She still could not see their faces, although she was close enough to be able to see the first figure's form. It was a male, she could tell by the broad shoulders and small waistline. The second she could not yet see, for it was down somewhere further than the first figure. The third was extremely blurry and even further down in the Mists than the second. In this way, it appeared to Serena that the three figures were standing on different levels of the Mist.

She was very close to the first figure now. Any moment she would come close enough to touch his face and swat away the Mists that surrounded him to see who it was.

But then…

It must have been the ominous chuckling that awoke Serena from her sleep. Or perhaps it was the bouncing of something small and hard off of her nose. Whatever it was, it was getting extremely annoying, and it caused a deep-throated groan to sound from the Girl's throat.

"Teeheehee! Dee pretty Lassie up yet is shee? Heehee, heehee! Time to get oop naow, and smell thee Sunshine!"

It can't be Mosslyn, she thought, her eyes still clenched tightly shut. *The sound isn't Childish, and it's a lot lower, too.*

Another small pebble contacted with her forehead, followed by more merry laughter.

"Teeheehee! *Gingel is ah fiendish fellow*
Dresses in green, never yellow!

149

So clever and so sly is he,

    Catch heem naow and git his muneee!" caterwauled whatever
the voice was, in a chuckling tone.

Can't sing... and it has an Irish tone to it, too,

Bonk! went another Rock, mildly grazing her ear on its way past.

Another low groan escaped Serena's throat.

She turned over, hoping to avoid any further bombardments from the
taunting Creature.

"Nah nah nah nah naaahhh naaaaaaahhh! Teeheeheeheehee! Betchya
can't gyit yoor tender leetle fingars around mah neck, can yee, ya wee Lassie?
Teeheeheehee!"

"You just keep saying that, you little nuisance!" Serena grumbled.

She heard another Rock come flying at her, but this time it hit her in the
spot she least expected - right on the lump on the back of her head, which had
been healing quite nicely until then.

Pain spread throughout her head like a bucket of honey pours over fruit,
and through closed eyelids, the Girl saw multicolored Stars. Serena could handle no more.

"That's it!" she snarled, turning over onto her stomach and making to get
up. She glared out of the dripping tent, dry, yet angry. But, she stopped. Something strange had caught her eye.

Before her stood a fat, little Man, probably no bigger than waist-height on
Serena, wearing a pair of green short overalls and a green shirt beneath it. He
wore a green hat as well, from under which poked curly, thin locks of cherry-
red hair. The Man had side burns and the beginning of a bristling, tangled red
beard, and a limp-looking four-leafed clover hung out of the black belt around
his hat. He was completely barefoot save for the few red hair that grew atop his
enormous feet, which looked far too large for his fat little body.

His dark brown eyes studied Serena from her position on the ground and
he twitched his bulbous little nose.

"Ah, thee pretty wee Lassie has awaken aftar awl! Heehee! For a moment
thare, ah took haer to bee dead! Teeheehee!"

Serena stood and exited the tent. Indeed, the little Man stood only to
about her waist. She placed her hands on that waist and leaned forward, looking the red-haired little Man right in the eyes.

"And just who do you think you're calling 'wee', you misbegotten lump
of manure? What are you anyway?"

150

The insulted little Man drew himself up to his full height.

"Ah im genuinely sooprised yah don't know, yah blasted Damsel! Ah wood thank yah wood know a good Leprechaun when yee see one."

A Leprechaun?!

"A WHAT?" Serena cried incredulously. As though on cue, Mike woke up behind her, gasped, and, still rubbing sleep from his eyes, located his notebook. When Serena looked at it with a smile, she saw that each page was almost black with the ink he had used. Hurriedly, he kneeled and began to sketch the tiny fellow and write notes on him. Serena turned back to him.

The Leprechaun crossed his arms and giggled infuriatingly.

"Ooh, fairst you was playin' dead and *naow* yer hearin's gone awl bad. Such a dreadful shame, 'tis, for one so yung ta lose 'er ears."

"Rrrrr, you ingrown little nuisance! My hearing is just fi-"

"Oooooh, de wee Lassie's gettin' inta insoolts, naow, is shee? Haha, weel, then, yoo'll be a lousy, misshapen, ale-guzzlin' Horsefly!"

"Misshapen?" said Serena in surprise, advancing on the chuckling, bouncing Leprechaun. "If anyone in misshapen here, I do believe it's you!"

She emphasized her point with an unpleasant jab on the nose.

"Because you are nothing more than a mud-sloshing, brainless... green-toed... fungus-flopping... Sand-chewing... Frog spawn!"

The Leprechaun drew in a breath as if being stabbed by a sword.

"Tsk tsk tsk... ye're a fine good insultress, ah'll give ye that, bot ye'll have tac do much beeter than that to brang daown the King of Insultin'! Handa that is ai, Gingel! Yae are a flabbergasted, flame-suckin' pot-bellied, past-forgottin' limp-legged sour cucumber!"

Serena had to stop herself many times through his recitation from reaching forth to strangle the cackling little Man. She stepped back, noticing now that many more travelers were awaking to watch the contest. Some Fauns, though tired-looking, started up a chant, "*Seblena's gonna gyit Gingel*! *Seblena's gonna gyit Gingel*!" Their heads swung back to the fuming Serena as though watching a tennis match.

"I'm so flattered, Gingel – something like that is giving me credit compared to what you are! You... bottle-nose ... bag-bottomed ... flop-eared ... inconsiderate ... half-baked excuse for a stump! You oafish ... low-down ... bug-eyed, flame-whiskered, giant-footed, hairy-toed, droopy-nosed, squatty-figured," Serena stopped to draw in another breath and to come closer to the wide-eyed Leprechaun, listening happily to the Fauns (and hearing Lindsey,

151

Kate, Jerry, and Bob join in with them as they awoke). Soon their chants grew to a roar that rose in competition with Serena's voice. "Rotten-egg-eating, soggy-brained dung weasel that cares for no one more than his own self-loving narcissist, egocentric self except for maybe his-"

"Enoof!" squealed Gingel, tears pouring down to soak into his bright red beard. The Creatures behind Serena cheered loudly. Gingel waved his hands in surrender and fell to his knees. "Ah beseech ye, Lassie, noo moore!"

Serena crossed her arms and stepped back, a pretty smile of victory hovering on her lips. Nelson strode proudly up to her, laying a hand on her shoulder. The group hadn't stopped cheering just yet, and Serena was wondering if they were going to.

"Nelson, why are they clapping so much?" Serena lamented, not quite understanding the immediate attention she was receiving.

"You have defeated a Leprechaun, Serena," he extended an arm to show her the sobbing Gingel, who was shaking his head in his hands. The Prairie Grass behind him swayed in the Wind. "You have captured him, in other words. Most Leprechauns taunt travelers by making them chase them, but apparently *this* one thought he was better at insults."

Realization struck Serena and she gazed wide-eyed at Nelson for a moment.

"You mean he – Gingel, that is - he has a pot of Gold hidden somewhere, and now he must lead us to it?" She grasped his arm tightly.

"No, 'tis you he must lead the prize to – and only you - for you are the brave soul that defeated him. See that Rainbow over yonder?"

Serena looked into the East, the Sun rising behind a magnificent, colorful Rainbow that seemed to be turned sideways somehow.

"Yes?" she replied. Nelson smiled and patted her arm.

"That little Rainbow is going to lead you to Gingel's pot of Gold. So, if you lose him while he is leading you to it, all you must do is follow that Rainbow, and eventually it will lead you to his Gold."

Serena beamed with pride, but that brilliant grin soon dissolved into a puzzled frown, and she consulted her companion once more.

"But what if that prize is in a far away Land? How will I be able to find my way back to the group?"

Nelson glanced over his shoulder at the crestfallen Leprechaun in caution, and then leaned very close to Serena and whispered in her ear, "I'll follow you in the air so he doesn't see me, then I'll lead you back here to the camp.

Don't let him know or he will refuse to show you."

At last, the Travelers behind Serena began to tame down and pack up camp. She accepted a few crackers from Lindsey and ate them with a small cup of Water before she stretched herself out and prepared to follow the Leprechaun.

"Good luck!" Bob told her, patting her back before turning to help Kate take down the tent. The black-haired girl scowled at her and remarked,

"Yes, and I hope you come back with more than a hand full of Magical beans."

Serena had to laugh at that, and she saw Kate crack a smile too.

"Ohhhhh, me purdy liddle lost trezures! Boohoohoohooo!" sobbed Gingel, pounding the dust. "An' I werked so hard ta gyit it too!"

Mike found her and grinned, thrilled to say the least.

"If you could, try and see how fast he actually runs, and where he hides his Gold,"

"Of course, Mike."

"And if anything about him changes, or his Gold, tell me as soon as you get back!"

"I will do that, Mike."

"Thanks a lot, Serena!"

Grinning, the wildlife expert hugged Serena and sauntered over to breakfast.

"Don't strain yourself, Serena," Jerry told her, coming over to rub her shoulders before she accepted to follow Gingel, who was still squirming on the ground and moaning about his 'lost treasure'. "If it's too hard for you, just come on back. Would you like me to follow you so you know how to get back?"

"No, but thanks. Gingel wouldn't show me his treasure if I had you follow me," she stopped, watching the Leprechaun's tantrum out of the corner of her eye as she whispered in his ears, "Nelson is secretly going to follow me in the air so I don't get lost."

Jerry pulled a face, but patted her back and smiled to try and cover it up. He wished her good luck.

"Ach, 'tis no use blubberin' over lost Gold," sniffed Gingel, standing at last. He turned his tear-stained, red face up to Serena, and frowned miserably. "Weel, common thin, me wee Lassie, 'tis better tae give it to ye naow than tae wait for ye tae start yer merciless rantin' agin."

Serena smiled wickedly and scanned the ground behind him.

"So, Gingel, just where is this hidden treasure of yours?" she asked, noting the dispersing crowd. They backed up to give her room to take off, just in case the Leprechaun tried anything silly. Some Faun Children, including Mosslyn, waved at Serena. She waved back at them and turned back to Gingel quickly. She intended to keep her eye on the little Man; Nelson had told her that Leprechauns were extremely agile and tricky.

"It's hidden, acourse, me pritty Damsel. So if ye wishes tae find it, ye may's weel larn tae keep oop!" He turned and stomped off into the tall Prairie.

Oh, please, Serena thought mockingly as she began to follow the little Man into the shimmering hair of the Prairie Land. *With a pudgy, little stomach like he has, how fast could a little Man possibly run?*

Gingel, glancing behind him every so often at his sprightly pursuer, tried to quicken his pace some as he noticed her gaining the distance between them.

Puzzled, Serena increased her rate of walking as well.

Dodging the gnarled turn of a Tree, Gingel grunted in dissatisfaction as he doubled his pace.

Serena copied him and avoided the Tree too.

Still not happy with his own rate, Gingel stepped up to a quickened skip.

Serena did too.

Glancing over his shoulder at her, he heaved himself into a jog.

Serena did too.

And a faster jog.

Serena did too.

Dodging Trees, jumping over Rocks and darting to and fro, the little Man tried vigorously to shake off his quick pursuer.

But Serena dodged, jumped, and zig-zagged just the same as he did, and strove hard to prove it.

Finally, Gingel broke into a full-fledged run, and Serena sprinted behind him, very determined not to let the sneaky Leprechaun out of her sight.

Grasses, Trees, and Rocks flashed by her like a distant memory as Serena stretched her limbs and streaked gracefully after the stumpy, little Man like a Deer in full flight. She stared up at the beautiful, radiant Rainbow that sailed over their heads, leading them to the hidden Gold.

On and on they went, pushing the tall Grasses out of their way as they hurried past. Jumping swerving, darting and dodging they ran, fully aware of the other's harsh breathing and loud, slapping footsteps.

Serena, seeing the little Man merely four feet in front of her, stuck her tongue distractedly out of the corner of her mouth in concentration and put on a burst of speed to catch him. Closer and closer she came – she could taste victory already as she raised her hands to capture the little fellow right by his generous middle.

But then he veered swiftly to the left while Serena wasn't paying attention, and she sailed past, feeling the triumphant smirk slide off of her face just as Gingel slid out of sight.

Cursing under her breath, she screeched to a halt and plunged into the direction the Leprechaun had taken.

After awhile chasing this path, Serena began to grow tired. Panting heavily, she came to a stop and leaned against a nearby Tree. She heard her heart pounding like a colossal drum in her ears and grasped at her heaving chest. The air was sharp in her lungs.

Something moved behind her, and she turned in a flash of tangled blonde curls.

Nelson dropped into a crouch from the Tree above her, and stood.

"Oh, Nelson! It's hopeless – I'll never find that rotten little-" she cried.

"Shhh!" he urged, placing a finger over her lips. "Remember the Rainbow?" Serena smiled, nodded, and looked up. The Rainbow was so close now that Serena could almost reach up above her head and touch it. She made to, but Nelson took her hand and discouraged her.

Serena felt the blood rising to her face as she prepared to protest, but before she could, another sound was issued from another mouth.

"Teeheehee! Methinks we did good, Goldypot, losing de wee Lassie, teeheehee!" cackled an all-too-familiar voice. Serena stared shamelessly into Nelson's smiling green eyes. Then she turned and placed a hand on the bark of the twisted Tree.

Slowly, she peered her two narrowed eyes around the trunk, and spotted Gingel, perched upon a Rock as big as he was in the middle of a little clearing. The dazzling, fluorescent Rainbow ended straight on top of the glowing pot of Gold the Leprechaun held. A hand landed softly on her back as she crouched, ready to pounce.

"Not yet," Nelson whispered, watching the happy Leprechaun jostle the

155

small cauldron of money on his lap like a Child. The money clinked loudly, bathed in the iridescent rays of the Rainbow and the sound mingled with the wicked laughter that stained the air.

Serena could feel her back legs straining to release her into a spring, and she lowered her head more, reducing her eyes to slits.

I'll catch you yet, you filthy under-grown worm, she thought, utterly seething with unreleased rage for the little Man. She clawed the hard-packed dirt, waiting. And watching.

All at once, Nelson patted her back gently and came very close, then whispered,

"Now!"

An unknown force welled up within her at the same time and she shot off like a Stone from a sling shot.

"Aeeeeek!" squealed a disgruntled Gingel, and he leaped off of his Rock. He shot off from the spot, his precious prize held out far in front of him. The Rainbow stretched and followed the little Man as he dashed away, streaking after him and splashing Serena in the face with its Magical colors. She enjoyed the Rainbow rushing past her skin as she hurried after the little Man; it felt very much like her skin was tasting a very lovely, very pleasurable taste. She felt her skin growing somewhat damp from the oncoming Rainbow, but ignored it in her hurry.

And so they engaged in another quick-paced chase.

At this rate, he won't get very far without tiring – with that big cauldron of money and his own fat little stomach – he's bound to wear himself down eventually ... Serena thought, progressing over a Boulder. She savored the Rainbow tousling her hair. Her pace hardly slowed as the Prairies thinned to reveal a flat little opening in the Land – and a great yawning hole that could be nothing other than another magnificent Cave.

"So this ... is his little ... secret hideout ..." panted Serena as she stopped before the place. The Rainbow left her, and she flipped her curls out of her face.

She stopped.

She flipped her curls again.

They were stained the colors of the Rainbow!

Her eyebrows, eyelashes, and hair had all been temporarily dyed in varying shades of red, orange, yellow, green, blue, and purple, all mingled together but yet none of them mixing. She brought about one of her curls in front her, examining its variation of colors. It looked very much like a slew of brightly colored dye had been poured into her hair and twirled about to form the rippling lines of color. Deciding to ignore this aspect of the chase, she threw the curl behind her.

Serena licked her dry lips and was about to enter the Cave after the Leprechaun, but a sudden hand pinched her shoulder and held her back.

"Serena! No!" gasped Nelson from behind her. "Don't you dare go in there!"

Serena studied the Cave a little before attempting to reply. She found that the place had absolutely no stalagmites or stalactites. She took a step closer, ignoring Nelson's urgent warning, and sniffed the air.

Much to her surprise, a rather objectionable fragrance hovered on the air. She sniffed it again – it smelled quite disturbing.

Dried blood ... she thought, eyes wide with fear. *That's what that smell is* ... *it's* ....

"Death," Nelson breathed, catching her as she backed into him accidentally. "Stinks, doesn't it? I smell it too."

"But, why…" Serena started, but stopped as the ground began to tremble. Petrified, she turned to Nelson in a flurry of Rainbow curls for an explanation-

-But the Boy was laughing - uproariously!

"Nelson! What is going on?" Serena cried, fear mounting on her chest. Her heart thundered inside her as she began to back away from the mouth of the Cave, watching it warily and expecting a devil of a Dragon to emerge from the opening any moment, boiling with rage and ready to roast the two alive. But one thing rather unnerved Serena – why was Nelson laughing?

Before long, her questions were answered. Nelson slid an arm around her waist and lifted her easily up into the air - all the while the great tremors continued to rattle the ground viciously.

Higher and higher Serena felt herself hoisted. The Breeze tousled her multi-colored curls and brushed softly against her cheeks, as though trying to comfort her.

She watched with eyes as large as a barn Owl as the "lips" of the Cave trembled horribly and began to clamp shut. A scream issued from the Cave just as the ground sealed itself shut. The Rainbow that reached down into the throat of the Cave began to dissolve slowly as the dew began to evaporate. Serena opened her mouth to scream at Nelson to let her go (hoping to save Gingel although she disliked the Leprechaun), but she failed to hear even herself over the loud rumbling.

A disturbing shift of Rock in the throat of the earth, which sounded to Serena suspiciously close to a gulp, followed, and then the Cave opened its dark mouth once more, a breath of rotting death streaming up from the opening. It stunk up the air all around Serena, and she shuddered and tried to close her nose to the unpleasant smell. Nelson carefully lowered them both to the ground once again.

As soon as Serena's bare feet touched the ground, she tore herself away from Nelson's arms. She took a breath and prepared to speak, but, casting a terrified glance over her shoulder at the reeking mouth, simply closed her lips and strode back over to him. His calm gaze unraveled the knot of fear tied up in her chest.

"W-what is that thing?" she stuttered, turning to nod at the Cave. "Another sort of Spirit?"

"Yes," Nelson said, still fighting off chuckles of mirth. "Funny how one smart, little Leprechaun could manage to be stupid enough to run into the only CaveLore in the area." And he laughed all the louder, holding his sides.

Serena didn't need to ask an explanation of him. Looking back at the CaveLore, she could already tell that it was an invincible Spirit, a Cave.

"A-a CaveLore," she repeated, venturing nearer.

"No!" Nelson's merry expression quickly changed to that of worry. He grabbed her arm to keep her from moving any closer. "No, Serena! CaveLores are dangerous. You can't tell when they will decide to swallow you up, or whether they will at all. Look what it did to Gingel!"

Serena turned to look at Nelson to reply. She opened her mouth.

"I KNOW," grumbled a deep, Rocky voice.

Serena slapped a hand over her mouth. Was that her own voice, or had some other person spoken?

Her thoughts were soon answered.

"HE WAS A LITTLE DRY … COULD HAVE USED SOME SALT. BUT VERY FAT AND QUITE FILLING ALL THE SAME," thundered the slow, loud voice again.

Serena's blood ran cold and she froze. With her hand still covering her mouth, she slowly revolved to look up at the CaveLore

- the *speaking* CaveLore.

Serena stifled a gasp that sounded something similar to a sob.

The corners of the Cave mouth lifted up in a fiendish grin.

"AH, BUT THAT LEPRECHAUN WAS A TASTY LITTLE MORSEL! SEEMS SOME PART OF HIM OR ANOTHER HAS BEEN LEFT BEHIND – IF YOU KNOW WHAT I MEAN!" The CaveLore executed a dry, gravelly laugh, to Serena's horror. "I JUST CAN'T SEEM TO GET WHATEVER IT IS OUT OF MY THROAT,"

With that, the very ground trembled and the Cave released a dry, rough cough. Serena fell under the vibrating ground and scrambled in a backwards crawl towards Nelson, who sat mortified as he gaped up at the CaveLore. Serena brushed her Rainbow-colored hair out of her face and stared up at the Spirited Cavern.

Finally, she found her voice.

"I-I'm sorry you have s-something caught in your th-throat, CaveLore…"

She paused to gulp and grab Nelson's sweating hand for support. "B-but we can't help you."

"In fact," Nelson blurted, turning to catch Serena's gaze. "w-we must be going now. We have some very … ah, important work to do."

Serena looked Nelson straight in the face. He winked slyly and she caught on fast. She drew another breath to speak.

But the CaveLore cut her off.

"OH, BUT YOU CAN HELP ME, YOUNG MAIDEN IN MAN'S TROUSERS! SEE, IF YOU COULD KINDLY CLIMB DOWN INSIDE MY MOUTH TO RETRIEVE THE OFFENDING ITEM, I WILL SOLEMLY PROMISE NOT TO SWALLOW YOU."

Nelson's eyes stated very truly his opinion on the proposition. He glared up at the CaveLore in distaste.

"I am very sorry, CaveLore," he snarled, picking himself and Serena up, "but we are not the foolish types of Travelers to believe such rubbish and put ourselves in a death trap." His face was filled with offensive scorn as his fingers curled around Serena's hand. She knew that soon they would bolt into the Prairie and back to the camp.

But an idea sparked inside her head.

"Wait!" she cried, just as Nelson prepared to take off. He looked at her, puzzled. She returned a calm wink, and turned back to the frowning CaveLore. "We *can* help you, CaveLore, if you aren't lying. We can find the spot above the ground that would be your throat, and jump on it. It would be sort of like-"

"Burping the baby!" Nelson laughed. "Serena, I must admit – you are a clever one!" He tweaked her iridescent curls fondly.

"YES, YES, VERY CLEVER," boomed the great voice of the CaveLore. It sounded a bit disappointed, but soon brightened. "WELL, I SUPPOSE … IF YOU HONESTLY BELIEVE THAT IT WILL WORK,"

The two young explorers eagerly bounded around the mouth of the Cave, giving it a wide berth, and began walking around in back of it until it stopped them.

"THERE, RIGHT THERE. THAT'S IT," it droned in a deep tone beneath them. Serena had to catch herself so that she did not fall from the tremor that shook the ground when the Spirit spoke.

Exchanging smiles, Nelson and Serena began to bounce up and down on the spot. Serena's multi-colored hair was beginning to fade very slightly, because the Rainbow was vanishing. They continued jumping for awhile, until the CaveLore drew a deep, shuddering breath.

"Wait," Nelson warned, feeling the rumbling grow as the CaveLore inhaled in gasps, as though it were preparing for a particularly violent sneeze. He put his hand up and they both stood still.

Nelson studied the ground he was standing on for a moment, then took one pace forward and threw all his weight into a final, well-aimed stomp.

"BRAAAAAAAAAAAAAAAAAAAAAAAAAAAAAAAAAAAACK!!!"

Serena and Nelson were thrown forcefully to the ground again as the CaveLore belted out an outrageously loud belch.

And, from out of its wide-stretched mouth came -

CLUNK!

Gingel's pot of Gold!

Nelson and Serena stood at once, their eyes growing as Bronze, Silver, and Gold coins flew everywhere. The Rainbow that had previously been attached to the mouth of the CaveLore suddenly burst into a great flash of beautiful, bright colors. It followed every last coin as it fell to the ground. Serena and Nelson looked at each other and smirked.

"So, we get our prize after all." Nelson chuckled. Serena slid down a narrow slope and he followed her. She nodded.

"Take it easy, CaveLore." she chirped, patting the moaning Cave's side before rushing over to the spilled cauldron which was bathed in the rays of the Rainbow. The CaveLore coughed once or twice more, producing a small shower of coins each time until one last Gold piece leapt from its mouth and the Cave continued its miserable groaning.

"Yes, we hope you feel better soon!" Nelson twittered as he joined Serena in collecting their scattered reward.

A single harsh, exhausted moan escaped the Spirited Cave before it opened into its deceiving Cave position once more.

After following the fading Rainbow and fetching every last coin of the spilled money, Nelson and Serena took to the Skies, seeking a fast way back to camp rather than running.

With Nelson holding her securely from behind, Serena scanned the countryside. She held the handle of the cauldron in both hands, and was surprised to find that it weighed a bit more than she thought it would.

How that idiotic Leprechaun was able to carry this thing in front of him and keep his speed up is a wonder, Serena thought, savoring the view. It was going to be another very hot Summer Day. She smiled and closed her eyes as a Breeze rippled through her iridescent hair and rushed by her pinkened face. How very much this felt like her dream ! A thought struck her. *How Nelson can manage to carry me, the money, and himself up in the air is more than a wonder! It's astounding, it's,*

"Remarkable," Nelson breathed above her.

Serena flushed suddenly, opening her eyes.

"The Countryside, that is," he explained. "Those Prairies somehow always look so much-"

"-more beautiful up in the air," Serena finished for him. *And*, she thought, *they do.*

"Well, yes," Nelson said after a pause. He laughed. "'Tis almost as though you've read my mind, Serena!"

Serena had to smile at that. She knew very well that she couldn't read Nelson's mind, nor anyone else's for that matter. But, over the past few Days that she had known him, she had become so very attached to him as a newfound friend, she was beginning to see the way that his mind worked. Quite often, she had noticed, she and he were thinking the same things, and because of this they had a specific understanding of one another that friendships often lead to.

"Lovely hair you have toDay, Miss Maiden," Nelson suddenly chuckled. Serena smiled.

"Oh, you like it, do you? Say, Nelson, what caused that Rainbow to stain my hair the color it is?"

Nelson shrugged, adjusting Serena comfortably.

"Oh, I don't know. It will fade probably by the time we reach the camp. See, now, the Rainbow is already vanishing,"

And vanish the Rainbow did, along with the colorful streaks of brightness it had left in Serena's hair. She felt that she preferred her natural Golden color anyway.

Before long, Serena found herself conversing with Nelson about flying. She found that he had gained his Powers in flight from one of his parents (who was a full-blooded Elf) and that all Elves (and almost all Halfbreeds) could fly. Yet seldom did they, as they preferred to travel by Portals and Unicorns, and other more fashionable means of effortless transportation.

"What about Theo?" she asked, watching the amber Plains moving beneath them.

"Theo has not yet mastered his Powers of flight. But he will – he has already begun to hover above the ground when he truly tries. If he were a full-blooded Elf, he would be flying perhaps by the age of three."

Serena giggled, looking up at him.

"That is very young," she noted, and sighed. "You know, I've always wished I could fly."

Nelson grinned as the camp came into sight.

"You've wished, am I right? Never tried? Oh, wait, I forgot – when you jumped off that Cliff …"

Serena nudged him playfully as he descended to the clearing.

"I didn't jump, Nelson, a crazed Hippogryph dropped me!" she giggled. Mosslyn met up with Serena and gasped at the pot of money. She ran her little fingers through it eagerly.

Nelson stepped back and puffed out his chest proudly.

"And I saved you," he crowed, beaming with pride.

Serena came very close to him and slitted her eyes. Behind a smile, she whispered,

"But only because you can fly."

As the Day wore on and the weather grew warmer, Serena searched fervently for something to tie her hair up with - her hot, thick blonde hair.

I don't know why I never thought of this before, she thought, twisting a few shards of Prairie Grass together. Carefully, she used the long strand as a hair ribbon and drew her heavy carpet of hair up in a high ponytail. She double-knotted the temporary hair ribbon, and tied it in a pointy little bow that stuck out stubbornly from atop her lengthy curls.

Bob appeared to take note of what she was doing, as did Lindsey and Kate. Soon she found all three of them copying her idea and thanking her for her cunning initiative.

Her bangs still dangled from either side of her face now, and after awhile she grew tired of them as well. So, as Nelson stopped the group for lunch, she suddenly remembered the few hair pins she had stuck in her pocket while she was still on the submarine. She pulled the two pins out of her pocket and pinched her annoying bangs up with them.

"There," she said officiously, dusting her hands off in a business-like manner. "And you had better stay!"

"What?" piped Jerry. He dropped the cauldron of money that he had offered to carry for her. "What did you say?"

"Oh, nothing. I'm just talking to myself again," she replied. She patted Mosslyn's back as she skipped past her over to Bob to try and hang off of his back again. Serena bent to pick up the cauldron.

"Again?" Jerry retorted with a laugh. Ignoring him, Serena lifted the cauldron heavily. She looked over as Lindsey and Kate tried to help a mother Faun control a toddler with a fit of temper. She pulled the cauldron up enough for her to get her arms around it.

"Thanks for carrying this for me. I would never have been able to do it on my own." she admitted.

Flattered, Jerry replied,

"Oh, it was nothing. Say, when do you think we'll reach that Barrift place?"

Serena shrugged as she carried the cauldron over to Wildder, the leader of the group of Fauns, and Nelson, who sat close by with two young female Fauns re-bandaging his healing wound. They giggled, blushed, and flirted outrageously, bashfully batting their eyelashes and softly stroking his cheeks.

"You musta beens *terribly* brave!" exclaimed the first one.

"Oh, yesyes, suches a *heroic* Warrior you is, Nelson!" gushed the other.

"And *dreadfully handsomes*, too!" giggled the first again. She stroked his overhanging curls admirably, batting her long brown eyelashes.

"Please, Ladies!" chuckled Nelson as he batted them away and flushed pink.

Rolling her eyes, Lindsey, who had successfully managed to help the mother Faun calm her hyperventilating Child, perched beside the flattered Halfbreed, offering tips to the two Maids.

"Right, Barrift. You know, that would be a good question for Nelson." Serena stated to Jerry, growing flush in the face at having seen the Faun Maidens and Nelson. But she could not help but laugh at the adamant Girls as they rebandaged his leg and showered him with compliments. Returning to her previous predicament, she snapped back to face Wildder, dropping the cauldron at the feet of the Faun leader. "Perhaps you should go ask him."

Jerry shifted uneasily and glared at the Boy while Serena addressed Wildder with the traditional Faun greeting, which she had grown accustomed to.

164

"How should we divide this up?" she said afterwards.

"Heehee! Whatchya mean, avided it up, Seblena? 'Tis awl yers, anna none of its fer usses!'"

Serena smiled at the Childlike speech of the Faun.

"Well, Wildder, I can't just carry it all by myself. I've just decided to split it up between all of us. Then we can use this cauldron to make some soup."

"Oh – heeeheeheee! What a splendidious idea, missy Seblena Maid! Hows much money coinses is we all gonna getsy?" The old Faun leader rubbed his generous middle section.

Serena glanced down at the cauldron, doing a quick bit of math in her head.

"Hmmm," she said, scratching her head. "I would estimate at least a handful of coins to every Creature present – less Welnon than Farlos and … what are they called?"

"Dinkels," Theo piped helpfully, skipping by with a Girl Faun in hand.

"Yes, Dinkels. Thanks, Theo!"

"Ooooh, dat's a lottalotta moneyses!" bubbled Wildder, dancing from side to side and clapping his hands in great fun. "When ya gonna give aw de moneyses away, Seblena Dame?"

"Now that you mention it, it would probably make the load a lot lighter if I just did it now."

Smiling, Serena reached down and plucked out four big Gold coins, six middle-sized Silver coins, and eight little Bronze coins. These she awarded to the outstretched palms of the Faun leader, and then picked out the same amount for herself and Jerry.

"I don't want to ask that leaf-Boy how long it takes to get to Barrift – he probably doesn't really know anyway," Jerry commented under his breath, just loud enough for Serena to hear. He shoved his share of the money into his jeans. Serena looked up in surprise, feeling very offended at his remark. Nelson was their friend. He was helping the entire team in their endeavor to get back to Earth. Why would Jerry make such a quick assumption about Nelson? Was it because Nelson was a different race? Was it because Jerry wanted to have more control over the situation? Or was it because he was jealous of Nelson's knowledge and kindness? Jerry's words had sliced at her, and out of the anger of pain, Serena defended her friend.

"He's *not* a leaf-Boy, for one," she snapped matter-of-factly. She retrieved Teresa's diary from the back pocket of her jeans and emptied her handful of money into the small, flat keepsake pouch on the inside of the front cover. Carefully, she put it back. She looked back at Jerry, her bright blue eyes blazing. Kate appeared suddenly behind her.

"And for two, he happens to have an extraordinary sense of direction that not many people have. He is giving of his time and talents to help us get back home," She stopped and narrowed her eyes at him. "I see no reason for you not to be appreciative of him. That is, unless you're *jealous*."

Jerry's brow furrowed and he looked over at Nelson, who was now telling some story or another to a collection of very young Fauns. The team captain snorted.

"Who, me? Jealous of *him*? Haha! Sorry, no! I just don't like him, that's all. I mean, just look at him! He's dressed in rags, doesn't have a home, and thinks he knows about all there is to know! He's nothing more than a ... a *scamp*!"

He turned to look at Serena, who by now was absolutely fuming. In fact, so furious was this young Girl, that all that she could do was to poke the offender hard in the chest with her pointy little finger and seethe,

"Yeah? Well let me tell you something, buster! That *scamp* also happens to be my best friend! And he *should* be yours, too, after what he is doing for us right now!"

Moodily, Serena snatched up the handle to the cauldron and prepared to dole out the money. She turned back to face the red-faced Boy and call out to him,

"When you grow up a little and decide you have the nerve to apologize, I'll be willing to listen!"

And with that, Serena stomped off to pass out her cauldron of well-earned money.

After lunch, Serena doled out all of the money that was in her cauldron, and cooled down a bit upon the discovery that there was enough Gold Welnon to go around one more time. Every soul in the camp received five pieces of Welnon instead of four. The small cauldron was packed away to be used later for soup or stew.

Serena tended to keep her distance from Jerry for the rest of that Day, and spoke to him not once. Kate asked her what was the matter, and Serena told her. Kate sided with her and offered to stick up for her the next time Jerry was putting Nelson down. Lindsey and Mosslyn comforted her too, and she thanked them greatly for their kind and inspirational words.

The Golden-hued Prairie rose up on either side of Serena as she followed a bounding Mosslyn through the Plains. She was deep in thought. But Serena was not thinking about her complications with Jerry (for they proved to be too irritating and distracting for her, and she came upon the decision that she had better things to think about.) No, this Girl was having thoughts of the Mother of Forever, and how much longer she had to live.

She has an illness that even the Water of the Fountain of Youth cannot heal… she thought, *so the cure for her sickness must be for a new ruler to take the Throne. Does the next Mother of Forever have to be in the bloodline of the first? Can it be a Father of Forever? Does sh e- or he - have to reach a certain age or perform a specific task? I wonder if Nelson could tell me.*

Serena leapt over a small Stone, and as soon as her feet hit the ground, a new thought struck her:

Could the Mother of Forever have a distant, unknown relative somewhere?

And another uneasy thought:

But what if that distant relative, the one and only Heir to the Throne of Forever, has died somewhere? What then? Will the Throne of Forever fall into the claws of tyrants?

And the worst, most uncomfortable thought yet made Serena stop dead in her tracks, eyes wide:

And if the Heir to the Throne could be a Boy … could it in any way be … NELSON?

~*~*~*~*~

Serena shook her head and began a quick-paced walk to catch up to the group.

No, no, it couldn't be.

But it must be! He said he ran away from a Castle somewhere. If he's the brother of the Princess, then he could be the real Heir to the Throne! Could he be the one who put the sickness on the Mother? But wait a minute - If he ran away from the Diamondia Castle ... why would he be going back, unless he was returning to get ...

Serena gulped.

Revenge.

Serena's thoughts shattered like a scattering flock of Birds as an upside-down face greeted her cheerfully.

"What's keeping you, Serena?" chuckled Nelson, his Sandy locks dangling away from his face in a ridiculous style, reaching for the ground.

Serena smiled and tweaked his nose, dismissing any thought of Nelson wanting to hurt somebody. After he had saved her, she had no doubt that he was not out to kill another soul. She settled for the thought of his going back to Sparkline Mountain to apologize for running away, and to claim the Throne. She walked around him to keep up with the group.

"Oh, nothing in particular," she sighed. With a whoosh and a flash of green cloth, Nelson was walking beside her. He was now limping only very lightly, and Serena noted this as she looked down at his freshly bandaged wound.

"So how is your calf healing?" she asked quickly, before the Boy could formulate a reply. He caught his breath.

"Oh, 'tis doing quite a bit better. Thanks. 'Tis healing fast, as least that's what Lindsey told me. She also said that in a couple of weeks it will be completely healed, but that I'll always have a scar."

Serena tightened the bond around her Sun-filtered hair and stooped to pick up a Stone that she didn't feel like tripping over. She hurled it to one side of the Prairie before responding.

"Well that's good. Not that you'll always have the scar, but that it'll be healed before too long. How long did she say it would be before you would stop limping?"

Nelson drew a breath and watched a lone bumblebee buzz into its hive in a Tree.

"She didn't really say anything about that, but I'm guessing from my own knowledge of healing injuries, that it won't be long before I stop completely."

Serena nodded in satisfaction.

Moments of silence passed as the two listened to the chatter of the group behind them grow steadily closer. They were catching up now.

"So what will we do when we reach the City Dooditan?"

Nelson looked at her with his almond-shaped green eyes.

"Well, first, we're going to find ourselves some shelter where we can clean up, get some hot meals, and rest. But," he paused to look her seriously in the eyes and say, "The next Day we have absolutely got to go find you and the other two Girls something more suitable to wear in public. They may believe you are a spy if you dare to show your face in Men's trousers."

Serena didn't know how that could be possible, to take her for a spy just because she was wearing blue jeans. Yet she needed to consider the source – Mosslyn had said that the inhabitants of this place wore clothing from the Earthen Middle Ages to the 1800's. And so, nonetheless and for safety's sake, she agreed to find herself a frock and a bonnet.

Later Lindsey looked ready to cry as Serena told her about the deal that Nelson proposed to her.

"Complete with heels and those … those petticoat things, and - oh, no! - we aren't going to have to wear," the brown-haired Girl leaned close and whispered, "girdles, are we?"

Serena slung her body onto the hard ground and dug out a small dip in the ground to serve as a sleeping place for the Night. Kate made herself a spot next to the two Girls, joining them for the first time since they left Earth.

"I hope not! But I was always told that they were called corsets," Kate told them, smoothing the ground.

"Girdles, corsets … same thing! I really don't think we should have to wear them. I think they are embarrassing," Lindsey groaned.

Serena laughed, sitting up as Jerry strode over to make a fire for supper. He glared at her as he passed.

"Yeah, what's Nelson going to do, make us wear them?" she retorted, ignoring the Boy who had bent to start a campfire. Mirth bubbled up inside Serena.

"Wear what?" Jerry wanted to know. He squatted to blow on the tiny red sparks that he had made on the pile of kindling and wood on the ground. He

169

coaxed the embers to a little flickering flame, and, receiving no answer from the two chatting Girls, broke into their conversation purposefully to interrogate Serena.

"Are you still hung up with that leaf-Boy?" he snorted, hands on his hips. Serena frowned at having been cut off, and apologized to Lindsey before Kate stood to look Jerry square in the eye. Her brown eyes blazed with unreleased rage as she glared right into his face, boring bolts of terror down into his very soul. His eyes widened, and he made to back off, but she grabbed his arm, testing his circulation. Serena watched from the ground, glaring at him.

"I have three things to tell you, Jerry Johnson. One, never call Nelson a leaf-Boy ever again. Two, yes she is still, as you say, "hung up" with him because he is much better company than your critical mouth, and three, never butt into somebody's conversation - it is very rude."

Then, turning at winking at Serena, she made to seat herself on the ground once more. Serena smiled back at her, glad for the protection. Kate looked pleased that she had had the chance to be mean to someone with a reason.

But was Jerry's turn to catch her arm. Serena knew Jerry had made a wrong move. He pulled Kate up with a grip that was white-knuckled, and glared straight at her with burning blue-grey eyes. Serena stood, her hands over her mouth. She did not want the matter to go this far. Lindsey stood too, and backed into Mike and Bob, who had been setting up camp with a group of Fauns off to their left.

"And I have a few things of my own to tell you, Miss Katelynn Pentol. For one, I am still the captain of the discovery team, and Serena's body guard. Therefore you have no right telling me what I will and will not do, and I have every right to know what kinds of idiots she may be consorting with. That Boy – Nelson – you don't know him very well at all! For all you know, he could be a cold-blooded killer,"

"That is where YOU ARE WRONG, JERRY!" Kate shouted, poking her pointed little finger into his chest as though wishing to spear his heart with it. Her voice rose to such a deafening climax that everyCreature in the camp dropped anything they might have been holding and gawped at her with wide eyes. A handful of young Faun Boys started chanting "fight, fight, fight!" and Serena knew the matter had gone awry.

Serena buried her face in her hands. What had she done? She had told Kate everything, and now Kate was using it to her advantage to make Jerry leave. Kate was greedy for power, and felt threatened at having someone else telling her what to do. Oh, why hadn't Serena seen this coming? Why had she trusted Kate?

"IF NELSON WERE A KILLER, WHY DO YOU THINK HE WOULD HAVE SAVED SERENA?"

Silence stole over the three-fire camp ground. Serena, Lindsey, Mike and Bob all stood with white faces. Jerry's mouth dropped and he took a step back. And although she very much agreed with Kate's last outburst, Serena stepped forward and placed a hand on Kate's back.

"Kate, really, this is unnecessary." she sniffed. "Please, just leave him alone. This doesn't have to be a-"

But Kate slapped her away. Serena stayed where she was, determined to prevent a fight. She looked back at Jerry, who was glaring at her with fire in his eyes.

Kate, absolutely bursting with rage, advanced on Jerry. "YOU ARE NO LONGER THE CAPTAIN OF THIS TEAM!"

Serena jerked forward, but found that Mike and Lindsey had a hold on her arms.

"NO! LET ME GO! KATE, STOP!" she screamed.

"Kate, what are you doing?" Lindsey cried.

"You don't have that sort of power!" Bob shouted.

"Kate, give it a rest!" Mike retaliated. Serena looked at Jerry, hot tears falling down her face. He was staring at her.

Is this truly how you feel? his gaze seemed to say.

"NO! JERRY! NO!" Serena shouted.

But Kate went on, the fire lighting in her eyes. Jerry's face snapped back to meet hers.

"WE HAVE NO WAY OF GETTING BACK TO EARTH! HAVEN'T YOU REALIZED THAT THIS MISSION IS HOPELESS?"

Serena, tears pouring down her face, struggled to get away, screaming at the top of her lungs,

"NO! NO! WE CAN GET BACK! KATE, WHAT ARE YOU SAYING? STOP, PLEASE! YOU'RE HURTING ALL OF US!"

The others behind her yelled similar remarks at Kate, though still holding onto Serena and keeping her from entering the fight.

Kate did not even look at them but continued screaming, ignoring the team's loud pleas to stop.

"JERRY, HOW STUPID ARE YOU? NELSON IS TRYING TO HELP

US AND YOU ARE ACCUSING HIM OF BEING A MURDERER!"

"KATE, STOP, NOW! PLEASE, LEAVE HIM ALONE!" yelled Serena.

"YOU ARE A SHAME TO THE TEAM, JERRY, A HUMILIATION TO THE HUMAN SPECIES!"

"Don't take that from her, Jerry!" Mike said. Serena could not stop herself from screaming. She felt that she was screaming even more than Kate was.

"SHE DOESN'T MEAN THAT JERRY! OH JERRY, DON'T LISTEN TO HER! PLEASE, KATE, DON'T TEAR OUR TEAM APART!"

But Kate was not listening to her. Jerry stared at her, looking back at Serena after each accusation. Serena was crying now, and Mike and Bob pulled her back into their protective arms to keep her from bursting between them.

"WE DO NOT NEED YOUR SARCASM, CRISTICISM, NOR YOUR ORDERS ANY LONGER!"

"SHE'S WRONG, JERRY! WE NEED YOU SO MUCH! DON'T LISTEN TO HER! DON'T LEAVE US!" Serena almost choked on her own tears and sunk to the ground, panting.

Fuming, Kate turned to return to the ground and found the entire party watching her. Pursing her lips in frustration, she turned on her hip and told Jerry shakily, "Serena is 16 years old. With Nelson, the team and me, she is perfectly capable of taking care of herself. And by the way, Jerry, your leg is on fire."

No sooner had she spoken these words than Jerry felt a stinging pain on the back of his right leg. Kate had scared him so much that she had driven him backward into the fire - the bottoms of his jeans were aflame!

Serena watched with callous guilt as he dropped to the ground and rolled the flame off his leg. But it seemed to roll over with him, and refused to extinguish.

Guilt bathing her in its poisonous green steams, Serena was about to get up and help him, but out of nowhere came a flying torpedo of Water which attacked the offending flames with full force and smoldered them to nothing with a satisfying sizzle.

And there, standing over Jerry with a dripping pail in his hand, was Nelson.

The green-cladden Boy offered a hand to help Jerry up, and he reluctantly, after glaring at Serena, accepted it. The former captain of the discovery team saw something shining in Serena's eyes, something other than the glassy tears that slid down her face. Something between fear, guilt, and unbelievable sorrow glistened in her eyes. Why had she even told Kate what was happening?

Her hands clamped over her mouth, Serena felt a change blossom within her and quite suddenly, found herself weeping uncontrollably. Bob held her close and Lindsey brushed her hair away from her face.

With the action being done and over with, the camping ground soon picked up on their own conversations once more.

But Serena knew very well that the action was not over. When Bob and Mike let go of her, she sheepishly wandered over to where Jerry stood, his leg still steaming, and looked up into his eyes.

"Serena did not mean anything Kate said, Je-" Nelson began for her, placing a friendly hand on his shoulder.

"No." Jerry said, pushing the hand off. He looked back at the tear-stricken Girl, and narrowed his blue-gray eyes. "I want to hear it from her."

"I'm so sorry, Jerry," Serena sobbed and rasped at the same time. She found herself somewhat hoarse from her yelling. She looked back at Kate, who had seated herself on the ground and was chewing ravenously on a sheet of jerky and glaring triumphantly at Jerry and Serena. Serena narrowed her eyes at the Girl. Was there another reason she had said all those things? Perhaps, she wanted not only Jerry to leave, but Serena, too. She already knew that half of Kate's plan had failed. Serena had no intentions of deserting the team. She looked tearfully back at Jerry, "I am so, so sorry. I had no idea. When I was telling Kate, I thought she was being friendly and understanding … I had no idea she was going to attack you like that … and it was all my fault that this happened. I'm so sorry, Jerry, will you ever forgive me?"

A moment that seemed like forever passed. Jerry's face contorted into several expressions, as though there were a million things he would have wanted to say, and then finally, he spoke one word.

"No," he declared finally. With a scowl, he plunged off back into the Prairie.

~*~*~*~*~

Serena had no other emotion left in her but sorrow. Certainly she had opened her mouth too far and said one too many things to Kate. But she had felt so offended for Nelson, and she had truly believed that Kate was only going to stick up for her. She never meant for anyone to get in a fight. Now, the damage was done - Kate was very happy with herself and everyCreature around her seemed to go out of their way just to avoid coming in contact with her. Even Lindsey moved away from her, and she moved Serena's things for her too.

Oddly, Serena felt as though an inexplicable change had taken place within her. It was as though all of the anger and humiliation she had ever owned or felt had seeped out of her through Kate's outburst. It was as though it had all floated up to the dark Night Sky and its twinkling Stars, never to return again. Kate had detected her anger and frustration and magnified it a thousand times toward Jerry, almost acting for Serena. But Serena could never act like that – never had she and never would she ever act so irrational, unreasonable and foolish. And, as embarrassing as it may sound, even when Serena tried to make herself angry at Jerry again, not a single drop of resentment extracted itself from her shattered heart.

It was all gone.

It had all swept out of her as swiftly and softly as the warm Summer Breeze that rustled her tear-stained fire-lit curls.

Serena, for the first time in her life, felt truly serene.

Out of humiliation, she bowed her head and stared at her feet. What horrible things she had done! She was ashamed of Kate's behavior and her own actions toward Jerry, the state of their leaderless team, and especially of herself. She knew it was her own fault Kate had eliminated Jerry from the team. Kate only needed one reason to yell at him, and being incredibly imprudent, Serena had supplied her with that one reason. Serena should have felt furious toward Kate at that moment, but somehow she felt nothing at all. She wished more than anything just to talk to the Girl and to try and help her and her tremendously insensitive rage.

Nelson dropped the pail and approached her. Tenderly, he hugged her and allowed her tears of sorrow to flow out of her system and onto his tunic. For a long time they stood and hugged, understanding each other's feelings, like the best that friends could ever be. The lights from the fires went out as the camp settled down for the Night, and it grew almost dangerously silent. Finally, Serena lifted her head and looked up at Nelson.

"Shouldn't someone go after him?" she whispered, feeling her swollen throat.

"Nay," Nelson whispered back. He stroked her Golden, fire-illuminated curls. "He will be back."

"But what if he …"

"Shhh," he pressed a finger against his lips. "Wait and see." he breathed.

The Prince of Forever, she thought at once, *and he can see into the future!*

"I trust you," she whispered, and she felt his hand in hers.

And that was the last either of them heard of each other because a pair of green-skinned hands seized them both and forced them to slam violently to the ground.

Chapter Twenty-One: Chains

The next thing Serena knew, she was gasping for air on the ground with some-one manhandling her from behind. She was on her stomach with her hands behind her back. She tasted the unpleasant flavor of dirt on her lips.

"How many we got, Pelnor?" grunted a wheezy voice from behind her. The cold hand heaved her up to kneel, and then pulled her up to stand. Her voice was very sore, and her throat was raw from yelling and crying, so she figured it was for the best that she kept silent and didn't even try to whisper.

It was extremely dark out; their fires had been extinguished in the tussle. Serena was scared. She had no idea where Nelson, Mosslyn, Lindsey, and (feeling a stab of guilt in her chest) Jerry were.

"Uhhh … Wensol! Didjya count the blaggards up?" called a different voice off to her right, heavy with a British accent.

"Aye, dere's twenny-two 'ere, enuf ta earn us a purty Welnon er two in the City. Fifteen Faunfolk, five Sun 'Umans … an' two 'Aflbreeds," answered a third voice, far off in front of Serena. She guessed this was the filthy goon who had sacked Nelson.

"Good," ranted the voice behind Serena. "Get the manacles and put 'em in the line with the others."

Serena felt herself yanked carelessly along through the black Night. She turned her face pleadingly up to the Sky, begging for Earthlight. A thick, vast Cloud had swathed out the Moon's brilliant beams.

And then she heard the sound.

The odd, displeasurely clinking sound of chains against chains. The un-comfortable crying, whimpering, and groaning of beings within these chains. And the harsh, crackling laughter of the three Goblins that had turned the en-tire camp over to slavery.

As the Goblin that had ahold of Serena bound her hands with manacles and her ankles with shackles, the Clouds over the Moon Earth moved aside. Serena saw, slumped in front of her, the almost-black braids of a Faun Girl's hair. She knew without a second glance that it was Mosslyn.

Serena heard clicking behind her, and knew that Nelson had been added to the line as well.

"We ain't got enough chains fer this'n Neder. Shood we finish 'im off?"

growled the second voice that Serena had heard. She looked over and saw a stringy, stick-figured Goblin. She figured his name to be Pelnor, from the way the first Goblin, Neder (who appeared to have more hair than either of his accomplices), had addressed him. A third Goblin, with Owlish, large black eyes, was dubbed Wensol.

Serena should have been absolutely bristling. She should have felt like lunging out and maiming lanky Pelnor for even suggesting that they kill the shivering little Faun Boy he held roughly in his hands. Yet that calm, reasoning feeling took over her thoughts again, and she slumped in her chains. She did not want to do anything stupid that would result in a brutally punishing outcome.

Neder, obviously the leader, pondered for a moment as he stroked his oily, long black hair.

"Yeah, Neder! We ain't 'ad fresh meat in a long time!" complained Wensol, emerging under a ray of Earthlight. His eyes shone greedily and he sniffed his warty nose. "An' we deserve a liddle treat fer are 'ard work!"

"Eh, I dunno, Wensol," Pelnor put in. He jabbed a long, skinny finger at the small Boy's thin waistline, "'e don't look like much mor'n skin an' bones ta me. I reckon 'e woodn't be good eatin' either. You ever 'ad Faun meat?"

The Boy whimpered piteously and sniffed aloud.

"Pweese don't eat me! I tastes weel bad, yesyes I dooses!" he squealed.

His beseeching pleas pierced the still Night air and hung on the ears of all listeners.

Finally, Neder spoke.

"Nay, we'll make do fer toNight on sometin' else. Every slave 'as a price to 'im, I always say, an' asides, dat liddle pipsqueak cood grow up ta be a real keeper if'n we play are cards right. Wensol, get some 'o dat rope an' tie 'im up. Set 'im in the backa de wagon. I'll watch 'im fer now."

Without another word, Wensol fetched some rope from further up the line somewhere and returned promptly. As he tied the protesting little Boy up, Serena leaned out around Mosslyn's back and strained her eyes to see. Faintly, past all of the poor Creatures in front of her, she could see the outline of a two-wheeled wagon with many small lumps that she guessed were the haversacks and belongings of the bedraggled Creatures. The supposed provision sacks were lying uncovered in the back. Beyond that, she thought she saw the backs of some Humans, strangely bare, sitting in the front of the wagon. There were two of them, a male and a female; the female had very long brown hair that

177

tumbled in waves down her back.

Serena's cheeks should have burned.

Deceived! By my own kind! she knew she could have thought. Her blood should have been boiling, but again, the indescribable feeling of calmness soothed her beating heart. She bowed her head, and sighed. *Oh, well, it's all over with now. There's no use in wasting tears over it. I wonder where they're taking us.*

Serena soon found out.

~*~*~*~*~

All Night the traveling band of slaves moved, ever Eastward through the Prairies. Near midNight, Serena guessed, was when they witnessed a change in terrain. By the Moonlight she could see the shimmering Golden Plains behind her as she left them and marched into a type of Meadowland.

Serena also found that manacles and shackles were not the most comfortable restraints in Forever. They scratched and rubbed at her wrists and ankles, blistering and bruising at first, but then opening the wounds and rubbing her skin raw. It was a very unpleasant experience for her, and more so because of the sweat that ran down her arms and legs, penetrating her stinging, burning new wounds.

It soon appeared that Neder, Wensol, and Pelnor did not only have Serena's troop captured, but also several other misfortunate Creatures; when the Girl counted all the slaves including herself, she found that there were 35 in all. She quickly did some math in her head, and found that there must be 13 of those poor slaves that she did not know.

But Serena did know what they were, those slaves that were chained the closest to the back of the wagon that dragged them along. She was the second to the very last slave on the line, and wondered what kinds of mischief she could get by with in the back. She looked with pity upon the 13 slaves in front, heavily watched by Wensol and Pelnor, who had perched their skinny selves in the back of the wagon facing the line of prisoners, their eyes as sharp as Eagles. The other 13 slaves were some kind of life-sized Fairy, with wings and all. She thought she heard Pelnor call them Pixies once, and settled on that to be the proper title of their species. The Men were dressed in worn tunics with leggings (although some wore breeches and hoes) and doublets, and some had capes. The Women were dressed in tattered, long, flowing dresses that out-

178

lined their slight figures, very unlike the poofy dresses Mosslyn had described to Serena. The dresses the Pixie Women wore were thin, and the skirts and sleeves were silken with some sparkles still twinkling. The beautiful gowns had seemingly been ripped at the sleeves and bottoms, indicating that they had at one time possessed long trains and wide angel sleeves that drooped to the ground.

But the things that caught Serena's attention the most were the Pixie's wings. She admired the beautiful, iridescent, transparent wings that drooped from their backs, much like butterfies' wings, but much thinner and more pointed at the tip. The wings resembled a Dragonfly's wings in this manner and were grown on the Pixies' backs straight between their shoulder blades. The wings were also more colorful than any other wings Serena had ever seen, like stained glass in many shades. Tiny sparks fell from the elegant structures like dust. However, since the wings were not in use, they were folded back and temporarily forgotten.

The Pixies were pale-skinned but Human-like, and their ears were slender and pointed at the tips, like Elves. Every color of Human hair matted their weary brows, and Serena thought of how tired they must be.

Poor things, she thought, and to get her mind off of such sorrow, she turned her attention to the two Goblins perched on the back of the wagon. Her sorrow should have turned to contemptuous loathing, but ended yet again in another sweeping gust of coolness and understanding.

What an ugly species. she thought despite her inimitable calm, for the two horrible slave drivers could be nothing other than Goblins. Their skin was a dark bluish-green, leathery and dry. Short, dark hair matted their heads, limp and oily. Their eyes had no color and were but two shiny black beads drilled into their wrinkled foreheads. They had no facial hair at all, but long, pokey noses and jutting chins, giving them a grim appearance.

But they aren't grim, Serena reminded herself. She stumbled suddenly and Nelson caught her from behind.

And Nelson! If he is the Prince of Forever, then why isn't he helping us? Certainly he has the Power, she thought a bit farther on this as she regained her footing. *Oh, I know. He is concealing his identity ... that must be why.*

"Thanks!" she breathed to him. In her mind's eyes, she saw him nod.

No, these Goblin-Creatures are nothing more than cowards after what they have done to us! Picking us off one at a time when Kate was having that fight with Jerry, and Nelson was being an understanding friend. Why, oh, why must we be confined to such evil?

"Seblena girl, please try ta keeps up – I can'ts pullses ya da whole way deres," Mosslyn whispered from in front of her.

Immediately, Serena tried to walk a little faster to save her friend from any more pressure to her manacles and shackles. The side of Mosslyn's head showed as she looked back for a reply.

Serena opened her mouth to say she was sorry, but all that came out was a strangled wheeze - she had lost her voice.

Mosslyn's eyes showed pity.

"It's okay missy Seblena, I knowses you cants talk."

Serena sighed and felt relief wash over her that her friend knew what she had been trying to say. She wondered how the others in her team were faring at that point. Mike and Bob, who had done all they could to prevent Serena from harm during that dreadful fight, Lindsey, who comforted her and spoke nothing to her but friendly words, Nelson, who must be feeling the most awful of them all after hearing that he was the subject of the verbal fight, and Kate, who had betrayed Serena and the entire team. Somehow, Serena felt no anger at what Kate had done, but rather forgiveness. Perhaps Kate just needed a second chance. Oh, if only she had a second chance! She would not have told Kate a single thing. Mulling over the evening's foul outcome, Serena resolved to forget the conflict and move on to more important things.

The chains rubbed against her wrists and ankles painfully.

Then she tried to think of some way to escape.

Was there something on her, anywhere, that could somehow fit into the locks of the manacles and shackles? Her earrings? No, she had left them in her knapsack for better comfort while she slept, and the same with her bracelet and necklace. Then the knapsack had been stolen by the CatEagles.

Maybe there's something in my hair.

Serena almost stopped dead in her tracks.

Of course! The hair pins! But how will I conceal them from the Goblins? Surely when dawn gets here they will check us for any weapons or means of escape.

Her eyes widened for a second time as another thought struck her: her mouth! She couldn't keep the hairpins in her pocket because the Goblins would find them, so she would stow them in her mouth! But how would she be able to talk?

I can't talk! she remembered hopefully. Immediately she glanced up at

180

the two sharp-eyed Goblins farther up the line.

Good, they're not watching us back here.

She reached up slowly, careful not to clank her chains, bent her head and pried the hairpins from her hair. Her curly bangs sprung to her face at once.

Checking again for the Goblins, she turned her head sideways to Nelson. He looked up, his face dirty and worn. She wondered if he had been thinking about his position and what he was capable of doing if he decided to break his false, helpless identity.

"What is it?" he whispered, coming closer to her. She held up the pins.

A smile drew up at the corners of his mouth. He reached for them, but she pulled them away. She nodded her head up at wide-eyed Wensol and stringy Pelnor, scanning the line of slaves in front and mumbling in droll undertones. He withdrew quickly, nodding vigorously.

"Yes, it is better to wait until they aren't watching." he breathed, trying not to attract their attention. "But how will you hide them? They will find them if you put them back-"

Serena waved her hands frantically, interrupting him. She pointed to her mouth, then moved her hand to her tender throat. Nelson nodded.

"You cannot talk, so you will put them in your mouth! Clever!" he hissed excitedly.

"Quiet back there, or I'll give you something to cry about!" bellowed Wensol from the cart, his shiny black eyes seeming to bulge with his pulse. Serena rather thought he resembled a giant BullFrog in that manner.

Quickly, she popped the pins into her mouth and settled them under her tongue. She blanched. They tasted of oily, unwashed hair and cold metal. But the taste soon washed off and Serena was left to suck on two thin, uncomfortable hairpins. After awhile, the coolness wore away also, and Serena nearly forgot the pins were even there.

~*~*~*~*~

As the Sun began to rise over the Hills of the Meadow and yawn in the faces of the dizzy, tired slaves, a soft sound met Serena's ears. She looked up, her twinkling blue eyes opening wide in surprise. The first rays of the Sun were stretching over the luscious Meadow they had passed into during the Night. An exceptionally soft musical sound fluttered about on the air, as tender as the wings of the Butterflies that came in hundreds on the Wind. The Flowers

181

were all the most beautiful shades and spectral hues, same as the Butterflies, each with its own colorful design. The Grass was the lightest, healthiest green Serena had ever seen, and was thick and soft on their feet. Dew shimmered in the wonderland of indescribable natural beauty, and glistened off of the nodding heads of the Flowers. All kinds of Flowers - tall Flowers, little Flowers, large, single Flowers, tiny, clustered Flowers, all sizes and shapes and colors of Flowers, dotting the young-looking Grass in graceful clumps of pink, blue, purple, yellow, orange, white, red, and all other colors in between. Serena marched along, dazed and blinking at the birth of these things of great beauty before her.

But she had to keep moving and keep walking to the time of the rhythmic clinking of the chains that bound her hand and foot. Her mouth was parched and dry, and she was very hungry, having missed the evening meal the Night before for now obvious reasons. She moved the pins around in her mouth, switching them to more comfortable positions and sucking on them to relieve her tremendous thirst. Her throat was still very swollen and sore, but, then, so were her wrists and ankles. She was filthy, and smelled absolutely awful. But, most of all, she was tired, and craved sleep badly. Hearing sighs and coughs and grunts of discomfort told Serena that the rest of the team and all those Fauns and Pixies in front of them must have been feeling the same way.

Serena looked down at her dirty, blistered feet. Little footsteps of Moss Flowers trailed after her, brighter colored and livelier now than she had ever seen them, and they melted into the Meadow once she was gone.

Soon we will be stopping for those wretched Beasts to search us, she told herself, and looked up as the line slowed and they stopped. *Oh, dear. I spoke too soon.*

Something caught her eye as the Goblins leaped off of the wagon and unhooked the line of slaves from the open back of the vehicle. Something she had not noticed (or seen, for that matter) before.

Centaurs.

Two of them.

Male and female.

And both of the poor Creatures were harnessed to the front of the cart.

Serena suddenly felt very guilty, for now she realized that the two Human torsos she had seen were not full-fledged Humans sitting in the front seat of the wagon. No, these torsos were attached to the chests of Horses' bodies, whose hooves pawed the ground impatiently.

Neder, his long hair swinging in his long face, led the slaves over to a nearby fruit Tree, which was strangely gnarled but held drooping green branches loaded with something Serena had not seen in a long time.

Fruit.

But not just any kind of fruit.

Colorful, striped, dotted and designed fruit of all shapes and sizes.

Serena gawked in awe at the laden branches as the Goblins tied the front of the captives' line to the trunk of the Tree. She saw some original fruits – oranges, apples, pears, and cherries. But she saw some others she had never seen before – an orange, soft-skinned fruit shaped like a pear with purple stripes running around it; a blue fruit, bluer than the Sky, that looked like a blue tomato; a purple fruit in the shape of a banana with pastel pink spots on it; a white fruit in the shape of a perfect spiral like a Snake coiling up, with pricks of green berries studding its outer layer.

"Eat!" ordered Neder, and with a grunt he started to stalk away toward the wagon.

"How?" Nelson boldly called after him. He held his hands above his head. "We cannot reach the branches!"

Neder stopped and glared at the brave Spirit, then a wicked smile crept up upon his ugly blue-green features.

"That's yer problem, 'Alfbreed, not mine!" sniveled the stocky Goblin, and then he strode off, cackling and looking very pleased with himself.

Some of the slaves collapsed with exhaustion upon stopping. Theo was crying and Lindsey was holding him, stroking the poor Child's hair. Mike, although bedraggled and hot, was talking casually with one of the Pixies as though he was not surprised to see them at all, and Bob was rubbing Kate's back, for she was green in the face and looking very sick indeed. The Fauns, though chained, were still somewhat bouncy and jitterish, having a wealth of energy and not knowing where to put it with their new restraints. Most of them were crying most Childishly, especially Mosslyn, and Serena had to hug the Girl several times before she would calm down so they would not get in trouble for being too loud. The Pixies mostly were laying down and sleeping, some glaring longingly at the fruits with tears standing in their hopeful eyes. But they seemed rather used to being slaves and having to travel all Night long.

Nelson growled and looked up at the lively green branches, full and glittering with jewels of fruit. Serena knew that if he used his Power to retrieve the fruits, he would be revealing his identity not only to the Goblins, but to the

Pixies and Fauns, as well as the discovery team. They would simply have to find another way to get to the fruits.

Serena tugged on his sleeve. She had an idea.

"Put your foot in my hands," she choked, finding herself capable of whispering. "And lift yourself up to that branch and shake it so the fruit falls."

He nodded and tried the mechanism – it worked. He flew to a standing position in Serena's outstretched hands. She held him strongly (for he was half-flying to make himself seem lighter) as he reached up with his hands-

- and stopped, for his wrists were chained in the line to Serena's hands. The line of slaves, or those who were awake and well, had been watching them with anticipation. As a unit, they let out a sigh, looking at the sad predicament. Nelson's manacle chains hung taut, barely reaching the length of his body as he pursed his lips in determination and stared bitterly at his restraint. An idea seemed to pop into his head and he stood again, half-flying, and reached up with his mouth. He grasped the branch firmly with his teeth (to the astonished gasps and happy giggles of the slaves) and shook it vigorously – and in return, the strange, lovely-smelling fruits Rained down on the hungry, ravenous slaves. They bit into them gratefully, calling their thanks to the brave Boy and Girl who had solved the tempting puzzle.

Serena had to remove the pins from her mouth in order to down two blue fruits, a handful of awkward (but tasty) mint-flavored green cherries, and a bright pink apple with orange spots that tasted of cider. But, as soon as she had finished and cleared the particles from her mouth, in when the pins again. She resumed her position on the ground to lean against Nelson and sleep.

Serena was having her dream again. Up through the whimsical, pale Mists she swirled, feeling her heart beating as one with the Mist, until …

She was falling once more, skirts and hair flailing. She turned to meet the first figure, now confident that she could unmask his identity before her dream ended. Closer and closer she fell, the Mist rushing by her cheeks at an alarming speed.

The figure leaned out to catch her. The fog parted - it was Jerry.

But Jerry is lost and gone! she thought with a jerk, and twisted to try and land in his outstretched arms. She looked into his face as she grew ever nearer. It was pale and ghostly white; his mouth was fixed in a straight line, neither smiling nor frowning, but simply stern. His blue-grey eyes were glazed over strangely, and his gaze was directed not at her but at the Mists straight in front of him. His expression was absolutely meaningless. There was no look of happiness, sadness, fury or any other emotion in his face.

Serena reached out to shake and awake him as she made to fall into his arms.

But Serena did not fall into his arms. At the last moment, Jerry withdrew his hands and stepped back on the Cloud of Mist he was standing on. And Serena fell past him, dazed and blinking in disbelief. Here her dream ended.

The weary Girl had only been asleep for a mere 10 minutes before a shadow trickled over her and bent to get a good look at her.

"Hey, Pelnor! C'mere!" grumbled the Owlish Wensol, startling the young Girl into wakefulness. Her crystalline, blue eyes studied the ugly face of her captor as he bent over her, staring her straight in the face with his huge eyes that shone with the luster of a shined shoe in the morning light.

The other Goblin hobbled over to his fellow slave driver.

"Wat? This better be importint!" he snapped, scratching his skinny side. He looked at Serena and his eyes widened as if only just noticing her for the first time.

"D'ya thank we cud use this'n ta make food fer us, an' put that scrawny, whinin' Faun kid in 'er chains? She looks like she might sell purty good fer a Servant Maid," noted Wensor. Pelnor nodded and gripped her about the cheeks with his long-clawed, bony green hand. He was so stringy that she once even wondered if there was any fat on him at all. She should have wanted badly to bite his hand away, but with her new sense of serenity, she merely stared back and refused to open her mouth for fear they would find the hidden hairpins. She pursed her lips tight.

"Aye, we got us a purty one here, Wensor," Pelnor agreed with a thin smirk. Serena slipped her head out from under his cold grasp carefully and backed up into the sleeping Nelson. Nelson awoke and looked at her, then the Goblins.

"Wat's yer name, liddle Girly?"

Serena refused to talk or even open her mouth lest they discover her secret. Glancing over at the team members (most of whom were sleeping, save for Mike, who was glaring at Pelnor like a Wolf looking at its next meal), she gulped her sore throat. Looking back at the scrawny Goblin, she blinked.

"Well? Tell us, Damsel! Speak, er we'll-" Wensol begant to withdraw his

185

whip from his belt in warning, glaring at her with his broad eyes.

"Dawn!" yelped Nelson, leaping up protectively in front of her. "Her name is Dawn."

Pelnor tapped the whip, signaling for Wensol to put the tortuous item away. The goggle-eyed Goblin refused and continued to brandish it, hoping to milk every last drop of information out of this defensive Boy.

"Why don't she tawk? An' why in Forever is she warin' a Man's trowsers?" he demanded.

"She … she is from a strange country. She is mute," Nelson replied hesitantly, looking back at Serena with a quick, swift wink. He turned back to the two blue-green Goblins. "I would think that any Creature with half a brain would be able to tell so if she does not answer you."

Offended at this remark, Wensol shook his whip in Nelson's face.

"It's you ya filthy slave, that ain't got nuthin' but 'alf a brain! Who's in chains 'ere? Who outsmarted ya?" he snarled, raising the whip threateningly. Nelson's face fell, and Serena could not believe what she heard next.

"Ah, 'tis no use arguing over. You caught us fair and square. You're right," mumbled Nelson, and he promptly seated himself, swatting away a bare core."Go ahead and use Dawn for a cooking Maid - she was the best cook in our tribe, you know!" His face brightened as he seemed to be recalling good memories, although Serena had to stifle her laughter because she knew he was lying through his teeth. "Makes a mean mint tea – real good for after you've been toiling hard labor like the stuff you fellows do. Helps you sleep like a baby, too."

He made a large, obvious wink to the two Goblins and nodded, mouthing, 'take her' to them before settling back again.

"You won't be sorry," he yawned.

And then it was Serena's turn to play her part in the act. Surprised at first, she had learned from his sneaky wink that he was trying to get the Goblins to release her so that she could go back to him and hand him the hair pins some time when their captors were not watching.

Looking deceived, she shot a look of menacing contempt over at Nelson, returning his wink. Pursing her lips, she glared up at the two Goblins, shrugged and let out a silent sigh. She then lifted her wrists, looking reluctant to be giving them over to them. They looked at each other and sighed, then the emaciated Pelnor stepped forward, drawing a key ring with two keys on it from his belt.

186

"Go gyit dat pipsqueak kid frum da wagon – an' bring da rope, too," he grunted, taking hold of Serena's chains. Serena watched carefully as the Goblin used the larger key to unlock her shackles and the smaller one to liberate her from her manacles.

The poor Girl was very relieved when the bonds were removed, rubbing her sore, blistered wrists and ankles tenderly. She looked back at Nelson again, who was now sucking on the stem of a Flower he had picked, with his arms tucked behind his head. Looking at Mike, she found the wildlife specialist looking ready to cry out. She winked at him and that seemed to ease him. He quickly leaned over to whisper something in Bob's ear, and the tall Man nodded, looking at her proudly. She smiled at them optimistically.

No sooner was she freed from her imprisonment than the small Boy was brought forward, unwound from the ropes that had confined him. Pelnor immediately fitted the Boy in Serena's place and threw the rope to Wensol. Serena watched in wonder as the manacles magically shrunk to his size - perhaps a tad bit tighter for added discomfort. The Goblin hastily tied Serena's hands together at the wrists, right over the red, raw wounds left by the chains. She blanched and made an uncomfortable face as they tightened them, but refused to open her mouth. She looked over her shoulder and caught the gaze of the little Faun Boy, who was having his rope wounds treated with Nelson's herbs.

His large, twinkling brown eyes were smiling at her, as if to say 'thank you' for relieving him of the ropes. She managed to smile reassuringly, but felt positively awful that the Boy would now have to endure those skin-peeling manacles.

Chains are no better, she thought, shaking her head sadly as Pelnor led her away. *Chains are no better.*

"Wensol is checkin' dem new 'uns fer weapons an' such." greeted Pelnor the Goblin as he found his leader, Neder, chopping some sort of dried meat up for a stew. Neder looked up at the young Human Girl the Goblin held captive on a leash of thick, strong rope.

"Good. Whozat? An' wherezat Faun kid we 'ad tied up in da wagon?"

Pelnor explained his simple exchange as he tied the rope of the poor Girl, Dawn supposedly, to a nearby Tree. Neder nodded, his long, oily black strands of hair dangling in his face as he abandoned his work and stopped to study the Girl.

"So ye kin cook, den, kin ya slave? Hmph! Wotchyer name?" he snorted. Dawn lowered her head and looked at the ground. She was mute and could not speak.

Pelnor, looking absolutely ravenous (in expression and body structure) tried to sneak a piece of meat and succeeded, and chose another.

Neder advanced, his shoulder-length hair dangling like twisted pieces of rope from his scalp. His hair style contrasted sharply with the other two, who hardly kept a few wispy threads of oily locks as long as their ears.

"Cummon, now, Gurl, tell me yer name. Wherea ya frum?"

Still Serena held her tongue. She looked up at the Goblin innocently through her curly bangs with swimming clear blue eyes.

Neder was getting impatient and made to draw his whip. Serena backed up like a frightened Dog, but Pelnor answered him, seeing the pleading look in the Girl's blue eyes.

"Er, ah … 'er name's Dawn, Neder. Don't 'it 'er naow, she cain't tawk."

Neder's eyebrows flew up like two gray Worms leaping in the air.

"Mute, eh?" he sniffed. He took a long, critical look at Serena, eyeing her like a Farmer eyes a Rabbit in his Garden, then told Pelnor, "D'you know 'ow many slaves'll try an' make ya tink der' mute jus' 'cuz 'ey don't wanna tell ya where der' goin'? Yew blisterin' block'ead! If she wuz rilly mute, 'er troat'd-" he stopped, his hand around Dawn's throat. Tears brimmed in her eyes as he paused and felt her sore throat. Pelnor watched in fascination. Neder did not finish his sentence, but merely looked at the other Goblin, who took the liberty of scratching his skinny side again.

Serena couldn't stand the pain any longer. Regardless of her restraining ropes, she reached up and pried the Goblin's hand from her neck.

Then, playing as though it were a serious crime, she shrunk away and slouched back by the Tree trunk.

"Well," muttered Neder, "I guess she really is a mute, udderwise she woodnt'a got away like dat."

"Aw, look, she's embarrassed!" howled Pelnor in a mock-sympathetic voice. Serena coaxed tears to her eyes and covered her face, pretending to sob miserably. Inside, she wanted to laugh.

"Well, no use worryin' o'er a slave who cain't tawk – she's a right purty one, dough. She'll sell good," Neder noted. He turned in a flash of greasy black hair and looked at the rising Sun over the beautiful Meadows. "Git Wensol ta round up da rest 'o dem wretches an' hook 'em onta da wagon. We'll be takin' off shortly 'ere."

Pelnor nodded his ugly head and blinked his beady black eyes, then scampered off to spread the orders to his fellow Goblin.

Neder picked up the board he had been cutting up the dried meat on. Half of it was gone. He frowned as he scooted the remnants of it into a little bag, and stuck his knife back into its scabbard. He gathered the things up and prepared to pack them away in the wagon, but he saw the Girl watching him curiously.

She flushed bashfully and looked away. He pondered a moment, then leaned down next to her.

"It was Pelnor who took dem pieces 'o meat, wudn't it, Dawn?" he rasped. She could have choked on his sour breath.

Slowly Serena nodded her head, and then made gestures with her hand to him not to tell Pelnor she had told him. Neder smiled and winked at her.

"Aw, I won't tell 'im, I promiss. I'll show 'im, dough! Show 'im wot 'ap-pins ta Goblins dat try ta sneak be'ind my back!" he hissed venomously.

Serena liked that very much, and nodded her head vigorously with a wide grin to show so. She felt that one of the best ways to escape unnoticed was while the Goblins were fighting with one another, therefore she would try everything within her abilities to set them up, similar to what she had done earlier with the invading CatEagles.

"Hawhaw, thar's an ideer fer ya! You watch ma back, Gurl, spy on 'im fer me, an' I'll make sure yer sold ta good masters an' mistrisses. Hawhawhaw! Ma liddle spy! I likes dat!" Neder guffawed loudly.

189

Serena made voiceless giggles to accompany him, as though she liked his idea well. She, in fact, despised his plan. She knew very well that she was not going to be sold. For she had two little hairpins lying in wait for her, hidden from the Goblin's sight. Those two little hairpins would make all the difference in the World.

The rest of that beautiful morning the fraudulent, mute "Dawn" staggered alongside the cart, her ropes tied securely to the side of the wagon. Even though the Grasses of the Meadow were soft and thick, and she had her ever-blooming Moss Flowers to cushion her tender feet, the march was still very harsh.

She glanced back at the other slaves frequently, hoping to raise the hopes of a single one of them while she marched alongside the wagon. A few Pixies looked up at her once, but the Fauns and her own team were too far away for her to pick out. She did hope that Kate was feeling better, and she could not stop worrying about Nelson, who must have still been feeling especially down because of the fight that had broken Jerry away from their team which then cleared the path for the Goblins to catch them while their shield was not up. She imagined all of the Fauns still sniffling and whining, and poor little Theo and Lindsey dragging themselves along with the horrible iron chains. At one time, Serena found a young Pixie lad looking at her curiously. She smiled gently, exposing one of the hairpins. His cheeks blushed even redder under the Sun as he realized what she was up to, and leaned forward quietly to pass the news to the Pixie in front of him, winking at her meanwhile.

During that cool, quick-passing morning, Serena learned several things.

For one, she discovered that she had a fatal flaw in her plan: hairpins could not undo rope knots. She was horribly disgusted at herself for letting this mistake pass right under her nose unnoticed. But, since there was really nothing else she could do other than let it go, she had to let the matter slip.

She also found out the Goblins' strategy for catching all 22 of her group without setting up an alarm. She overheard them talking about "the prosperous catch", neverminding her, of course, because she was "mute" and she was already captured. It appeared that the Goblins had shot tranquil darts and dragged them off one at a time in the dark, putting out all the fires and making it look like everyone else was asleep. The only reason they had not drugged Serena, Nelson, and the little Faun Boy was because they were the last few,

190

and they were running low on darts. By the time all the captured victims had awoken, they'd had the last two chained and the Boy tied up and had set off on their long, hard march through the Night.

Another thing that Serena found out was the origin of the dainty, pretty song that floated on the air. The Flowers were making it! She discovered that the Flowers had a tendency to "sing", as Pelnor had once said, whenever the warm light of the Sun touched their stretching, colorful petals.

"Yeh, be glad it ain't Rainin'." Neder had told his complaining accomplices, "They sing evin louder whennit Rains."

And the last and final thing she learned that Day was that a frock, bloomers and wealths of petticoats were very uncomfortable on hot Summer Days.

Neder called halt around noon or so, dragging a large wooden spoon and a scummy-looking, big cauldron from the back of the wagon. Both items looked like a health inspector's nightmare. The greasy Goblin untied Serena from the wagon and brought her over to the two items to direct her to cook.

"Hay, Neder! Come an' lookit wot I faound!" shouted Wensol from the shade of what looked like a naturally-grown Orchard. Neder gave a disgruntled sneer, then yanked Serena behind him as he approached the yelling Goblin.

"Wot naow?" he growled, noticing a tall thicket behind Wensol.

"It's a liddle Pondy thang. Water looks real clear an' we need ta refill da jugs anway. It's kinda deep… looks like it mighta bin a well at some poinna time."

Serena followed the waddling Neder over to the thorn bush where Wensol was beckoning. She peeked over its thorny ridge and found a small, clear Pool with a slippery, Moss-covered Rock crumbling on one side. The waist-high thicket surrounded all sides.

She thought it was an extremely welcome sight, and longed to rip off her bonds and plunge into the crystal-clear Waters, drinking it all in. But she knew better, and waited patiently for Neder's response, gazing into the blue depths.

She did not have to wait very long for his answer. Neder seemed ponderous as he studied the new, tempting Water source and he scratched his rich head of hair. A shadow of doubt passed over his rough-skinned features, but was soon replaced with a wicked grin.

He turned.

And looked at Serena.

~*~*~*~*~

Serena felt her face grow red hot under his cold, heartless glare.

"Der's four clay jugs in da backa that wagon right der." He smiled, waving at the two-wheeled wagon. "I wantchya ta fill 'em all up. Now."

The Girl did not hesitate, but obediently carried out his orders. She lowered the jugs into the crystal-clear Waters by tying a rope around their necks one at a time and hauling them up after they had sunken enough to be filled. Four of these large jugs she filled and placed, dripping, into the back of the wagon to screw fat corks into their wide tops. Then she stood, awaiting Neder's next command by the side of the cart as he rummaged through its contents. Finally, he seemed to find what he wanted, and pulled out a fluffy-looking brown pillowcase drawn tightly shut with a thin cord.

"'Ere." he growled, throwing the soft bundle into her arms. "Naow I wantchya ta go inta dat liddle Pondy thang an' wipe some scum offa ya. Yer filthy. An' I don't wunt filthy 'ands fixin' my supper. Change inta dat when yer done, too. It'll be cleaner den dem blue trousers yer wearin' naow."

Serena nodded absentmindedly, her mind spinning. What was in the sack? What about the diary? Could she hide the pins somewhere else? (They were becoming quite a nuisance.)

As her face burned from both embarrassment and the hot Sun bearing down upon them all, she carefully made her way over the sheltered Pond with the bundle of supposed clothing. And as she did, she peeked warily over the thick, tangled thorn bushes before venturing forth.

Carefully, she leaned over the thinnest portion of the wall she could find and tossed the bag onto the flattened top of the large rock. Wensol watched her with his large, unsettlingly observant eyes.

"Well, go on, den, mute slave! Neder ain't waitin' all Day fer you ta gyit done an' fix us sometin' ta eat!"

And he gave the poor Girl a hard boot in the behind as she leaned to gaze into the depths of the Pond.

SPLASH!

Quite suddenly, Serena found the Water rushing up to meet her. It filled her every sense.

Not my mouth… she thought, screwing her eyes and her lips shut tight as

192

she floundered to the surface. *I cannot afford to lose those hairpins…*

Serena shook Water from her eyes and hair and steered herself over to the tall Rock. Behind it she quickly bathed herself and her dripping hair. She found a small, flat Rock that she could stand knee-deep on as she reached out to discover what was in the drawstring bag.

Much to her relief she did not find a potato sack or something equally humiliating. Instead, she found a faded light blue dress with many underclothes to go along. She frowned, knowing that it would be harder to move in and much hotter than her old jeans and T-shirt, but at least it was dry, and smelled better than what she had. And, donning a smile, she would no longer be persecuted or interpreted as a spy for wearing her torn, ripped jeans. Now she had to worry about the rest of her team – Kate and Lindsey were still wearing their jeans, and, she was sure, getting disgruntled looks about them. Hesitantly, Serena obliged to wear the dress.

It took her a bit to figure out just exactly how all the layers were supposed to go. After awhile she got it right, and almost smiled when she saw how puffy the skirt looked.

Almost like a little tent, she marveled in thought. She looked at her old jeans with a silent sigh, and suddenly remembered Teresa's diary and the money she had hidden inside it. Careful not to disturb the now-snoozing Goblin outside the thorns, Serena pried her treasure from her old clothes and allowed them to sink to the bottom of the Pond.

The diary was not wet, much to her astonishment, but very clean and dry. She opened it; the text was still as perfect as the Day Teresa had written it. Shaking her head in disbelief, she closed it reverently and stared hard at the object.

It must be the outer canvas lining that keeps the pages dry, she thought, tying the faded pink and blue ribbons into a little bow.

With a mischievous smirk, she flipped up the front of her poofy skirt and examined the inner lining. She noticed a very small hole in one of the many layers, and ripped it open just large enough to make a little pocket for the diary. She opened it up silently and, with a cautious glance over her shoulder, took the hair pins from her mouth, washed them off in the Water, and clipped them onto the inner lip of the small pouch on the inside of the front cover of Teresa's diary. Then she slipped the small, dry diary into the pouch in her skirt and prepared to get out.

But how? she thought with a jerk. *Wensol is asleep, and I am supposed to be mute.*

She let out another silent sigh and climbed up onto the Rock to sit on the bag. Chin in hand, she began to think to herself.

Well, I might as well think of some other way to escape aside from the hairpins. I'll have to distract them somehow long enough to get those ropes off of myself and give the hairpins to Nelson.

Her blue eyes roved over the thicket as though in search of a key to give her an idea.

And then she spotted it.

A Plant, with round green leaves that drooped to the ground, and a very tiny white Flower sprouting from the top of its head. Serena almost gasped when she realized what it was – it was a wild Plant called Snoorbil, one that Nelson had pointed out to her on the side of the path with several other odd new Plants.

"Snoorbil likes to grow just about anywhere." he had told her, squatting to show her the drooping, circular leaves. "Herbalists and Healers use them on their patients to calm them from pain. When you crush the leaves of the Snoorbil Plant and feed them to someCreature, it sends them straight to sleep and makes them snore very loudly. It isn't harmful, though."

Serena smiled.

Hadn't Nelson said something earlier that Day about having her fix them some mint tea later that evening?

Eventually, Wensol awoke and pulled a cheery-looking Dawn from the Pond, dragging her to the site and ordering her to make a soupy sludge for the slaves to eat.

Immediately she obeyed, slipping tasteful seasonings in while they had their backs turned. She tried to make the lumpy mess less foul-tasting than the Goblins insisted she make it.

Then she passed it out, shoveling heaping spoonfuls into the outstretched bowls of the poor slaves. They ate with their fingers and most of them followed her sneaky wink and acted as though it tasted horrible. Nelson was close to laughing when he saw her sly wink, but he and a few others acted as though they were going to be sick because of the glop. This only brought more entertainment for Neder, Pelnor, and Wensol.

194

Immediately after lunch they moved on, and Serena was tied to the side of the cart once again. The dress was much heavier and hotter than her old jeans and T-shirt had been. But she felt very proud of herself for many reasons: the ropes around her wrists had loosened while she had prepared the food for the slaves just enough for her to slip out (though she waited for that); she had gained the trust of all of the slaves and the Goblins; and she knew just exactly how she was going to free herself and the others.

In the early evening, the train of slaves stopped in a little Banyan Orchard to settle in for the Night. The Goblins complained loudly about their aching feet and legs, but Serena soothed them with a promise to make them some warm mint tea after supper. Bug-eyed Wensol and paunchy Neder gladly accepted, but sinewy Pelnor wasn't so fast to admit he wanted some.

"How da we know ye ain't gonna put poison innit ta kill us?" he spat, wiping away the steaming teapot Serena had drawn in a small patch of Sand.

Her hands flew to her cheeks as she felt them burning, and she shook her head, eyes wide in reassurance that she would never do something like that. Then, she patted Pelnor's back and wrote in the dirt,

Where would I get poison? I would not do something that despicable even if I could!

"Dipicsa-what?" Pelnor gurgled, scratching his dry, wispy-haired head. "Wot's 'at s'posed ta mean?"

Serena forced herself to smile understandingly instead of bursting out laughing at the Goblin's poor vocabulary.

It means terrible, she wrote in the Sand. She looked innocently up at Pelnor and held up her hands to show that they were tied, symbolizing that she was his captive. Finally, the bug-eyed Goblin broke into a grin.

"Yer a 'onest Maid, Dawn. Fine thin, I'll 'ave a cup too."

Serena's face lit up and she bowed her head in gratitude as the Goblin passed her.

So as dusk drew to a close, Serena set to baking a delicious meal for the three ravenous Goblins. In fact, it was more like a small feast to show her innocence and generosity to them. On a flat Rock over the fire she cooked roasted meats, warm fruits dipped in a small supply of honey they had confiscated from the knapsacks, and even a small nutcake she baked from the nuts and fruits that grew plentifully on the bordering Banyans. She tried to keep the food well out of sight from the poor chained slaves.

The slaves were tied to a Banyan Tree, once again in torment of the beautiful, strange fruits that peppered its branches. Nelson used what few Elven powers he possessed (or so he claimed, but Serena knew the real truth) to get some fruit down for them, but that was still not enough.

Serena wished dearly that she could help them, but was presently occupying herself with something she had waited to do since noon –

- make some tea.

As soon as she had cleared the empty platters away from the ground where the three Goblins sat, she set herself to work on the soothing, warm tea.

And although she had never made tea without a tea kettle, she could honestly say that it wasn't all that complicated. After cleaning the cauldron, she brewed a fine mix of herbs with some mint she had found in the supply. She stirred in some honey to sweeten it. Turning her back to the three jabbering Goblins, she crushed the leaves of the Snoorbil Plant that she had hidden in her skirts after picking it earlier that Day. She stirred the creamy paste evenly into the three ceramic mugs and discarded the evidence by digging a shallow hole in the ground with her foot to bury the remains and the Stones she had used to crush it. She quickly covered the hole and patted it down before the Goblins could see what she was doing.

"That tea redy yit, Dawn Maid?" called Pelnor lazily. Serena could tell that already he was very tired. With a smile, she turned with the wooden tray and approached the fire.

She watched in solemn silence as her three captors guzzled the mint tea by the firelight, some of it dripping down their chins.

"Weeeell, at least dat 'Alfbreed wuz troo to 'is word!"

"Yah, dis teas's explemperly!"

"Wat's dat mean?"

"I dunno. Good!"

They belched and smashed their cups on the ground.

Serena stood patiently by the wagon she was tied to with her hands folded neatly.

They groveled and bragged, and slumped sleepily to the ground.

Sweat not from the heat of the fire, but from her anticipation beaded on Serena's brow. Would the Snoorbil Plant work?

The three Goblins talked and talked and finally, when Serena felt as though her plan had failed, Wensol's head drooped on his chest and he began to snore.

Loudly.

And then, as if on cue, Pelnor and Neder did exactly the same.

Very loudly.

Serena smiled.

Her plan had worked.

Ropes fell to the tiny Moss Flowers in the spot the Girl had previously occupied.

Chapter Twenty-Three: Escape

Serena edged closer to Neder as he slept, making very sure that she did not disturb his slumber. She had no idea just how deep the Snoorbil Plant was supposed to make its victims sleep, or how long for that matter, so she was especially cautious in approaching the Goblin.

Senses alert for anything, Serena carefully loosened his belt and removed the key ring. Then, without a backwards glance, she was gone to the line of slaves.

In less than half an hour, every slave along the line had been freed, and the chains were unhooked from the back of the wagon. Each of the team members hugged Serena, even Kate. The Fauns continued crying (though now with happiness) and the Pixies stretched themselves and thanked Serena profusely. The poorly-fed slaves immediately made for the wagon to collect their things that the Goblins had taken, but Nelson prevented them.

"Wait!" he ordered them in a loud whisper, jumping out in front of the wagon. "We mustn't begin taking our things from the wagon; it may cause enough noise to wake them!"

"Nelson! Let the poor Creatures retrieve their belongings!" Serena said, taking his arm pleadingly. "Come with me. I have an idea that will aid our safe escape and take revenge!"

Curious, Nelson followed the grinning Girl.

And soon found her clever plan to be more than just clever.

Hours had passed since the slaves had been freed, and still the group lingered at the campsite, feeding, resting, and loading up on the tasty fruits of the Banyan Trees. The camp was Moon-bathed and, despite the chronological time of Night, it was quite bright out, due to the looming blue Earth and its tiny white friend, the Moon.

New voices penetrated the air – voices that previously had been cut off and forced to be suppressed inside their owner's mouths by way of leather whip. Other sounds littered the air, too. The serene silence of the Meadow rang in everyCreature's ear (for the Flowers did not sing at Night). The Summer crickets and katydids trilled their melodies to the luminous Stars, wrapped in their black blanket of Sky, mingling with the ear-splitting, obnoxious snoring of the three drugged Goblins. The Fauns and Pixies were bandaging their chain wounds, stocking up and resting themselves before the group decided to disperse. Kate looked to be feeling much better as she sat and received a bun from Mosslyn, while Lindsey buzzed around treating wounds. Mike and Bob were filling knapsacks at the wagon and passed them out to Fauns and Pixies. Children jumped and ran, excited to be away from their iron burdens at last. Theo was among them.

Serena and Nelson oversaw the progress, chatting on the subject of where to go. Nelson seemed to think that it was better to keep heading East to the City of Dooditan, but Serena suddenly felt very uncomfortable about it.

"That could be the very place they were leading us!" she argued, "How do we know that we all won't be trussed up again as soon as we get there?"

"That is a good point," said a strong-looking young Pixie. It was the same young Pixie who had winked at her earlier. "We never can tell who to trust in the Cities these Days. I thank you for freeing our expedition."

Serena smiled as the Boy stopped in front of her. Obviously, he was the leader of the 13 Pixies. Remembering the Foreveran Greeting, she laid her hand over her heart and nodded her head respectfully.

"I'm Serena," she said. The Pixie returned the gesture.

"My name is Elkhorn, loyal servant to King Alanon of Bendar."

"Bendar!" Nelson exclaimed with a snap of his fingers. After a pause to wait for a floating snore to get out of his way, he introduced himself quickly to the red-haired Pixie and explained, "We need some place to stay other than Dooditan, and our supplies are waning. We are in need of clothing, weaponry and rest. Would you mind-"

"Absolutely!" grinned the grey-eyed Lad, flexing his pointed, iridescent wings. He took Serena's hand and kissed it. "After the risk this pretty Damsel has ..." he stopped abruptly, waiting out the thunderous belch of a snore that erupted behind them to disperse "... endured in order to free us, my Creatures and I are eternally in your debt."

Nelson's fire-lit green eyes were wide, yet not wider than Serena's blue ones. Here, bowing in front of her as though she were of royalty was a full-grown male Pixie, dedicating his life and many others' lives to Serena's will.

The Girl bent and tapped the bowing Pixie. Slowly he looked up at her. She smiled, and offered him a hand up.

199

"Your debt will be repaid to Nelson and I as you lead us to your King at Bendar," she stopped, waiting for a crackling snore to pierce the air and allow her to speak. "The only other thing I will ask of you is friendship, and then you shall be free."

Elkhorn's freckled face lit up and the pointed tips of his ears turned red.

"What a gracious Maiden ..." the Boy paused to let another loud snore pass in the distance, "... you are, Serena!" He turned to leave. "You could be a possible suitress for the young Prince!"

Serena did not know exactly what this meant, but she certainly did have a good idea. She shrugged the thought off and fell to the task of finding herself another knapsack. She was glad, at least, to be far away from the bellowing, hacking, snoring Goblins, at least enough to hear herself think. She did not pause to wonder if she had possibly used too much of the Snoorbil Plant on her former captors.

There were several empty haversacks in the back of the wagon, presumably the remaining possessions of deceased slaves. Serena chose a small one, and stuffed it to the brim with fruits from the Banyan Tree, rope, dried meat, a strange Goatskin pouch of Water, and many other necessary items. Nelson accompanied her, finding his bow and quiver, his sword, his dagger, and his belt pouches. And, of course, his little brother.

"We're free, Nelson! Free! We can go anywhere and do anything we want to now! Oh, where are we to go? What shall we do? We are free!" Theo crowed, bouncing up and down excitedly like a Faun, his Sandy blonde hair flopping about on his Moonlit features. It was still quite dark out.

Nelson sat his excited younger sibling upon the back of the two-wheeled wagon, and bade him to sit quietly as he bathed his chain wounds. He soon gave in to the young Boy's interrogations and began to explain where they planned on going.

While Nelson and Theo discussed their future plans with Wildder(who happened to seek aid from the Halfbreed Prince as well), Serena suddenly remembered the Centaurs that were harnessed to the front of the wagon.

Pulling the keys away from Nelson, she hurried around in front of them and greeted them with the Foreveran Greeting.

"Many apologies, my friends! I-"

"Yeak! She speaketh!" hailed the male in a frightened tone, recoiling in horror.

"Calm thyself, Skywood!" chided the smooth-voiced female, her long

200

red-brown hair swishing at her cheeks as she addressed the male. "Had ye half a brain ye would already know the Child is with voice!"

Serena noticed the pretty blush in the young WoMan's face, probably from embarrassment at her fellow Centaur. The Centauress turned back to her.

"Ye needn't apologize to us, young Dawn, for the key you holdeth in thy hands are of no use to us. You see, thy foul-mouthed Goblins hath cast away the keys to our harnesses, and so it is for all eternity that we – my brother and I - shall be as one with this accursed wagon."

Serena smiled, looking for someplace to put the keys. With an evil smirk, she found one, and set them on the jutting arm of a Tree. Then she turned back to her new Centaur friends.

"That can be remedied. By the way, my name is Serena, not Dawn. It was only a spur of the moment bluff to get us out of here."

"Clever!" exclaimed the male. "Yet how dost thou intend to 'remedy' our captive situation? We beeth confined-"

"That is nonsense; I have a way to free you!" Serena exclaimed. She quickly detected the forgotten hairpins.

"My name beeth Fernwood," smiled the green-eyed Centauress, pawing the ground with her strong front hooves. "And my brother yonder goeth by the name Skywood." Grinning fiendishly, she leaned forward. "Albeit sometimes I wonder if his head really is one to dwell with the Clouds."

A disgruntled roar escaped the throat of blue-eyed Skywood.

"I hath heard thou'st scoff, sister!" he rambled.

Serena giggled, replacing her ancestor's diary back in her safe-keeping pouch. In her hand she held two small hairpins.

"What beeth the small tools that thou holdst in thy hand, Serena?" Skywood wondered. The Girl smiled and called Nelson over to assist her.

"This is Nelson," she said, patting her good friend affectionately. "And these," she held up the hairpins, and presented the straightest one to Nelson, "are called hairpins." She looked at Nelson and smirked. "I hope you're good at picking locks."

Nelson laughed and tossed his hairpin up in the air, catching it swiftly before jamming it expertly into the keyhole in the buckle of Fernwood's harness.

"Only the best!" he boasted proudly, working the hairpin around. Serena did the same with hers in Skywood's belt-harness. She had never picked a lock before, and found it very complicated and confusing.

Oh come on ... she thought wearily to the lock, *I've had enough trouble*

201

toDay ... and if you would just stop being stubborn ... and ... OPEN!

Beside her, Nelson coughed, nicely disguising a laugh.

CLICK!

Shhhhhhh!

Serena looked at Nelson's bright green eyes. He raised his eyebrows proudly as the harnesses of the leather and pure metal suddenly unlocked and crumpled to dust. Both harnesses, in unison, fell around the Centaurs' hooves like showering Rain, and landed in small heaps of dull gray ash.

"Wow," Serena gulped, hardly believing what she had just witnessed. She blushed furiously, still looking at the prideful young Lad. Certainly he was the one and only Heir to the Throne of Forever!

"You really are the best at picking locks!" she teased, handing him the other pin to keep for later.

His inherited Father of Forever Powers. He had to use them to make the harnesses fall off! Serena knew, looking into his Starlit green eyes. He hid the two hairpins in one of his small belt pouches and bounded off to bandage the other chain wounds. Serena turned to talk to her two new acquaintances.

Skywood and Fernwood were both taken into slavery as young adolescents, and their tribe was much farther to the South than they were now. They told Serena that they planned on heading in that direction at once, and thus would accompany them to Bendar.

By the time all of the escaped prisoners were ready to begin their travel, it was little more than an hour past midNight. But Serena and Nelson had only procrastinated for so long on certain terms: they first needed to fill themselves and bandage their wounds and then pack supplies for the journey to the Fortress of Bendar. And, of course, once they did set off into the Moonlit Meadows of Night, they would have the comfort of knowing that they would not be chased.

By the time the three snoring Goblins awoke, they would be finding themselves chained up in their own manacles and tied to the trunk of a Banyan Tree. Their wagon would be stripped bare, the captives long gone, and their very own keys – their keys to freedom – hanging 10 feet away, straight in front of their noses, dangling tauntingly from a small branch.

~*~*~*~*~

One hour after midNight, the large group began their long trek South.

202

Serena plodded along happily between Skywood and Elkhorn, listening intently to their life stories as she observed the dark, Moonlit Meadow.

It was quite interesting and wonderful, the sights of the sleeping Flowers and Trees under the blue-hued Earthlight. Everything was lit up with a pale light blue, brightening the ways of the Travelers as they marched their way South. All the rest of that Night and all of the next Day this restless trekking persisted, come the beauteous dawn and set the fiery dusk.

Serena heard all sorts of stories as she journeyed through the soft Grass coated in droplets of dew from the previous Night. It appeared that the Pixies – all of them – had originally come from the Fortress of Bendar. They had been outside of the Fort conducting a search party for a small Boy who had become lost while he was out picking berries. Just as the small party found the Boy huddled sleepily in the hollow of a Tree, three Goblins had surrounded them and captured them all just as quickly and slyly as they had caught the group Serena was in. They had been confined to the chains and pushed Northward, then veered sharply to the East after catching up with the Faunfolk and the explorers.

The Centaurs had been in the slaving trade for years. Ever since that fateful Day when they had been captured as half-grown Colts together, they had pulled the wagon of the three horrible Goblins. It had been so long, they told Serena, since they had seen their Tribe far down to the South, that they were not very sure of the Tribe's exact location.

"Yet, we shall find them," Fernwood had promised, "come Rain and fire!"

Wildder and his Fauns had at once changed their destination to Bendar in short pursuit of Nelson and the discovery team. Serena was still getting used to looking forward to her third known destination, and who better to do so with than with Mosslyn and company?

"Oh, I hearses it is veryvery bootifuls at da Forty-dress a Bendar!" Mosslyn squeaked in excitement as she skipped alongside Lindsey and Serena. Mike had finally found his notebook and was following Elkhorn around, making small notes here and there. Theo was practicing his flying as Nelson instructed him, Kate was talking animatedly with a Pixie Maiden quite younger than she, and Bob was evidently attempting to dodge the jumping Faun Children around him by talking to Wildder. Once Serena heard the old Faun leader giggle as the youngsters clawed at Bob's jeans.

"Heeheehee! Aw, common, Bobbies – dey woan't hurta yoo's if'n ya just giveses dem dere back-rides!" Bob sighed and squatted so the closest Faun could board his back while two more hung from his strong arms. A group of Pixie Maidens giggled and waved their handkerchiefs at him after seeing this, making the young Man blush.

Serena yawned as she looked at the setting Sun off to her right. They had not hesitated to put great distance between themselves and the Goblins that Day. She did not know when their former captors would awake, and if they could devise a clever plan to free themselves.

If they could, they could be after us right now! she thought with a shiver. *Although, they weren't that smart in the first place, since they didn't notice that I was drugging them with the tea,* Her pace slackened a tiny bit, but then quickened as soon as it had slowed due to her final thought on the matter: *Better to be safe than sorry.*

The Centaurs Skywood and Fernwood were a tremendous help with carrying travel sacks and small Children. Each had three little knapsacks and three or four Children – four Faun Children and two Child Pixies, plus Theo when he decided he wanted a ride. Serena was amazed at their strength and grace as they moved along with those long, slow strides to keep pace with the group.

They didn't even stop to eat that whole Day – they merely slowed their pace and nibbled fruit and dried meat as they moved. Serena knew that the fear of being captured again was on all of their minds, and that was why no one dared to stop.

By midevening the group approached what appeared to be a fast-flowing River. The current ran off to their left, heading SouthEast. Serena figured that to be the direction in which Sparkline Mountain and Diamondia Castle lay. Nelson studied the dark shapes that loomed beneath the surface in menacing swarms, and hopped back from the bank in alarm.

"Bassteeth!" he hissed, looking over at Serena. "We've found the Basstooth River, impossible to cross for so many Foreverans!"

"There are bridges further down the banks on either side." Fernwood put in helpfully.

"Nay," said Elkwood, pulling up the sleeves of his tunic. "We should not be needing them."

"How so?" Serena asked curiously. Elkwood turned to her and suddenly threw his arms around her waist. He picked her up. His great wings spread out delicately behind him.

"Ahh! What are you doing?" the Girl shrieked. Elkwood began to lift into the air with her.

"It is easy! We will fly one another over the River to the opposite bank."

Serena considered his idea, stopping her squirming for only a short moment. She groaned and tried to slip out of his grasp.

"That is a very good idea, Elkwood, but I should not wish to be the first to go. I would like to stay on this side to be sure everyone crosses," she pleaded. Elkwood smirked and dropped her to the ground. She felt herself bounce on her rear end and come to a sit next to a Boulder that protruded from the muddy River bank.

"Suit yourself!" he cackled, and flew off to his task.

Elkwood didn't know the real reason Serena had protested his transportation – she was absolutely mortified of being up high over a large body of Water.

Chapter Twenty-Four: Over the River and Through the Woods

Now, Serena had no idea how the Pixies planned on assisting the two Centaurs across the Basstooth River, but she soon found out as the pair just so happened to be the last to go before her. A group of muscly Pixies took two ropes and inserted one behind the forelegs of a Centaur, and the other before the back legs. This mechanism proved successful, and Serena stared distastefully at the swirling blackish Waters of the River after she was sure the two had made it safely to the other bank. As they landed, they supervised the making of another camp – for now they were sure that once they crossed the deadly River, they were safe from any unwanted Goblin pursuers.

Serena knew she was still in danger, but she didn't care. All that filled her mind at the moment was the swishing, lapping, shimmering surface of the foam-crested waves, surging like miniature typhoons upon the banks. Their dreadful dwellers with their gnashing, razor-sharp teeth and beady black eyes rode these waves as a Man rides a Horse, mouth agape and ready to bite into any flesh that dared to come close enough.

But Serena knew she could not escape her problem forever, and finally agreed to go only when Nelson offered. For some odd reason, she felt much safer with him than with one of her newly-acquainted Pixie friends. She gulped even as the Boy landed on the bank next to her. She had been sitting on that hard Boulder she had landed by, watching the others across the bank waving at her and setting up camp. She waved back, then sat alone, staring fearfully into the dark, swirling Waters of the broad River, and the long, black shapes that swam beneath its surface, waiting, always waiting, for a chance to rip something carnivorously limb from limb. Her eyes were nearly as wide as the churning River itself, yet they were a much lighter blue than its Night-dark Waters.

"What's the matter?" Nelson asked, squatting some distance from her to observe a small Weed. She looked around and realized that they were the only two left on that side of the Basstooth River. Already she could see Mike squinting up at the Sky and observing the Clouds, and Bob aiding Lindsey in rebandaging some of the wounds inflicted by the chains on some of the Children. The Fauns whooped and hoorayed as they started a fire and the Pixies, who were more mellow Creatures to be sure, set their camp up a little ways away from the Fauns, who planned to stay up late and party because of their recent escape. Serena guessed that she and the rest of the discovery team would be making camp with the Pixies. Mosslyn waved at her cheerfully from across the bank, and she waved back.

"Nothing!" she blurted with a toothy, innocent smile. Nelson seemed to know better.

"Something is bothering you," he stated, glowering at her with eyes as green as the Plant he held in his palm. He dropped it, watching it fall. Serena felt her face burn and turned away quickly.

"Maybe I'll ... I'll tell you later," she promised. "Er, let's get over this ... this River first,"

Nelson smiled and approached her, sweeping her feet off of the muddy ground. As he ascended, Serena knew this was to be a fearful crossing, and covered her eyes with her hands.

She did not see the Boy's smile grow.

"Oh, I know what it is," he mumbled, rising higher than he normally would. "You're scared of being over the Water, aren't you?"

Two blue eyes appeared between Serena's slender fingers.

"How'd you know?" she asked, feeling rather embarrassed.

Nelson laughed, looking up at the darkening Sky. Dusk would not be long in coming.

"Oh, I just know. Oops!"

Serena felt herself lurch toward the Water, but Nelson had seemingly only been adjusting her to a more comfortable position. She let out a small yelp and grabbed at his neck.

"Oh, you don't like that?" he chortled, his voice dripping with sarcasm.

Serena's face showed obvious scorn as her head slowly slid back to look at his grinning face.

"No! I mean, yes! I mean, Nelson ... AGH!"

Nelson dropped her purposefully, but caught her wrists just as she began to plunge.

She screamed helplessly.

"What did you do that for?" she squalled, watching her feet dangle beneath her Wind-fluttering skirt. Her gaze moved to the choppy, deep Waters, and then her screaming eyes screwed themselves shut tight.

Don't look down ... don't look down, she told herself.

"Nelson ... please ... please put me down,"

207

"If you say."

"Ahhhh!"

This time the Boy caught her ankle, and Serena felt her skirt flip up around her. Her hair dangled uncomfortably in her face as she screwed her eyes shut again, willing herself neither to look at the gruesome River nor give her lunch to its swirling waves. She felt her face grow very red. Her new underclothes were exposed, no thanks to the guffawing Boy who now grasped her ankle.

"Ah, so that's what it looks like under a Maiden's skirt!"

And now he was mocking her.

Her face grew redder yet.

"Nelson! Oh, for heaven's sake! This is ridiculous! You are ... you are just atrocious! I insist that you release me now or I will – eeeeeeeek!"

Nelson let go again, but first swung Serena up in the air. He flipped himself onto his back and caught her on the stomach with his feet. He put his hands behind his head comfortably as though he was no more than a Shepherd Lad on a Hillside, spending a leisurely afternoon watching the Clouds roll by. Serena felt pinched in the stomach, having slightly lost her breath. She glared daggers at the mischievous Boy, who was staring at her fondly.

"I didn't mean to drop me, you moron!" she coughed.

"Oh, surely we can overcome this tiny little fear, can't we?"

"No, we can't!" Serena rasped, and leaned forward to grab the front of his tunic menacingly. Nelson smirked all the wilder.

"Why are you doing this to me, Nelson?" she whimpered, trying to stay on his good side.

"You always said you wanted to fly!"

"But not over a boiling River of carnivorous Fish!"

She had had it. Serena came very close to his face, literally dragging herself on top of him to get his attention. "I demand that you bring me down from this place to-"

"If you so desire, oh Damsel!"

"No, Nelson! AAAGH!"

Serena's nails raked the Boy's tunic as he flipped his body to stand in the air. To her relief, they grasped his belt, but, to her dismay, they traveled to his ankles with her gripping hands.

SWISH!

"Agh!"

It was Nelson's turn to yelp.

Serena smiled, despite the churning Waters beneath her. She looked up at the beet-red Halfbreed Boy. She had unmasked a pair of swaddling white underpants. Her mirth further expanded as she formulated a devious reply.

"Oh, so that's what it looks like under a Boy's leggings!" she cackled.

"Alright, alright! Truce!" wailed Nelson, and he lowered them both to the bank, a fair distance from the gawking camp. Once Serena was safely standing on firm ground, the mortified Boy hauled up his leggings and tightened his belt, all the while glaring menacingly at Serena. She grinned. She could tell by his beet-red cheeks that he was mildly angry with her for exposing his interior clothing to the entire camp. But, she could also see a twitch in the corner of his mouth that told her he wanted very much to smile.

"You didn't have to do that," he grumbled, straightening his tunic.

Serena shrugged.

"I had no choice. It was either become dinner for those slobbering Fish or humiliate you – and I chose the latter."

Nelson's green eyes pierced holes into her.

"Well … you have more skirty things than I do, so that's not f-"

"I should hope you don't have any!" laughed Serena before he could finish. She tried to picture Nelson in her mind wearing a delicate pink dress. She laughed as she never had in her life. "It would be awfully scary if you did!"

Nelson scowled, but then his face finally gave in to that hidden smile Serena had seen cowering behind his frowning mask.

"So, I've embarrassed you and you've well humiliated me. Sounds fair to me. Do you want to call it even?"

Serena accepted with a smirk, and turned to join the camp.

"Oh, and by the way," she giggled, stopping to poke the Boy in his stomach with a sharp finger. He gasped dramatically as though she had wrenched a hole into him and he was rapidly deflating. She continued on her way. "Nice underwear."

That Night the Moons hardly shined and the Stars were absent from the Sky. Dark Clouds blotted them both out, causing darkness all around the camp. Three small campfires crackled merrily along the bank, warming the faces and the souls of the weary Travelers.

"Tomorrows we go ta finds da raily-road dat leadses trew de Forest uv

Many Eyeses, to da Forty-dress a Bendar,"

Serena recalled what Wildder had stated earlier that evening. Of course, she was very excited about getting to rest at the place for a Day or so before continuing on into the Forest of Many Eyes. But something about the way Elkhorn threw sidelong glances at her made her uneasy about going to the Fortress.

Since he had talked to her, she had found that he meant for her to be a possible future bride for the Prince of Bendar, whose name was Errenon. Serena did not agree with the suggestion, nor did she oppose it. The poor Girl had never even thought about marrying and starting a family at such a young age. The more she thought of it, the more uncomfortable she felt about the whole deal. She would simply have to refuse and go on her way to Sparkline Mountain.

And what about the Mother of Forever? How much longer could she live to save the Throne of Forever from being overcome by tyrants?

We must get Nelson to the Diamondia Castle with as much haste as we can muster. If he is the future Father of Forever, he must claim the crown before it is too late. she thought anxiously, glancing over at Nelson.

Nelson still had no suspicions whatsoever that Serena even thought he was the real Heir to the Throne. But Serena was sure, very sure now, that he was. And the more she thought about it, the more it all made sense. It was like a huge puzzle falling into place before her eyes. He had seemed very uncomfortable speaking on the subject of a possible solution for finding the Heir. He had been reluctant to answer the question of whether the Heir could be a male. He had said that the Princess of the Diamondia Castle had no sisters, but he said nothing of her having any brothers. It appeared to Serena that he may not have been banished from the Castle (which, for a time, seemed to have been possible) – but had indeed run away with his younger brother (who must have been much too young and inexperienced to be the Heir) when he felt he was no longer needed. He had thought that his sister, the Princess, was surly the true Heir to the Throne, since she was female, but by the time he had found she was not, he was already as far away from the Castle as he had dared to go.

And now he is going back to apologize and claim the Throne. Serena thought with a smile. She huddled closer to the fire between Nelson, Lindsey and Mosslyn, and closed her eyes. *To become the Father of Forever.*

And then she fell into a deep sleep.

~*~*~*~*~

210

The next morning was a dreary one indeed. The hovering Clouds that had blocked the view of the Earth, the Moon, and the Stars turned out to be a pack of precipitation-infested Storm Clouds. They showed this plainly by sending forth sheets of cold Rain accompanied by bolts of white Lightening and claps of Thunder that reverberated into every soul.

Serena awoke later in the morning than she had expected. When she first awoke, she thought that it was still Night because the Clouds that shrouded the horizon and the very Sky above their heads was so dark and unbelievably thick. As the first fat droplets began to pelt the River bank Sand into mud, Elkhorn, Nelson, and Wildder began to package their things and gather their troops.

"We will have to keep going no matter what weather betides us!" shouted Elkhorn above the gale.

"The Winds are picking up as well, so let's try to stick together and not wander off on our own!" Nelson added, agreeing with Elkhorn.

"Any small Children that cannot walk on thy own may seek refuge from the fierce Winds on our backs!" called Fernwood.

Serena herself felt that she was to be blown away by the whistling Winds. Her skirt and hair added resistance to her, as though they wished to join the Winds themselves. But nonetheless she downed a bitter yellow and green mottled fruit, hitched up her knapsack, and followed the slow-moving group. She looked around at Kate and Bob, who were using their forearms to shield their eyes from the Wind and Rain. Those who had capes were using them as shields, and those who didn't were toughing it out with their arms, like Kate and Bob. Mike had been smart and taken off his T-shirt to use as a shield, though it hardly offered much more protection than his arm because it was so wet.

NoCreature spoke until that afternoon when they finally reached the railroad tracks that would carry them to Bendar. Serena learned from Lindsey what one of the Fauns had told her about the Evertrain.

"It stops wherever it is needed," she half-yelled over the endless, raging Winds and Rain. She blinked RainWater from her eyes and lifted her arm higher. "And it is happy to accept whomever needs it!"

"But what about Robbers and Thieves?" Serena asked loudly, wiping Rain from her face and wringing it from her hair and skirt. She was very wet, not to mention uncomfortably cool.

"Sometimes the Evertrains are supervised by Guards and Soldiers, but sometimes they are not! That's the risk with taking an Evertrain to Bendar - we do not know whether we will get a good Evertrain or a bad one!"

"I certainly hope for safety's sake we get a good one!" Serena shouted back. Lindsey nodded vigorously and sat to wait for their transportation. They had finally reached the glistening iron tracks.

It was not a long wait. Only about 15 minutes after Serena had learned of the Evertrains, she and the rest of the group were accepted to one that stopped sharply with a long whistle, but no smoke.

She knew they were all very glad to be going under the cover of the Evertrain; all of them were soaked from tip to toe, hungry, and worn. She wrung her clothes out in the aisle of one of the cars as she looked around at the great thing.

The Evertrain, inside and out, was much different than the locomotives Serena had been taught about on Earth. She had noticed outside that their wheels had spokes, but no arms to move them, and there was no smokestack or smoke to be seen about it. Curious, she consulted a drenched but relieved Nelson on the matter.

"These Evertrains were once fed Spring Water from the Fountain of Youth," the Boy explained, shaking his head to spray Serena with a shower of Rainy droplets. She shielded her face with her hands.

"Do they have to keep being fed the Spring Water, or will they just run forever?" she inquired.

Nelson shrugged absentmindedly and seated himself into one of the cushioned, wooden, bus-like seats. Serena sat down beside him, staring out the glass window of the car. Lindsey and Mosslyn sat in the seat in front of them, wringing Water from their hair and skirts. Across from them, a Faun couple stretched and prepared to feed a squalling baby. Pixies everywhere sighed and smiled, patting each other on the back. One female Pixie was crying she was so happy.

"We finally made it! We're going home!" she sighed, shaking water from her sparkling wings. Serena could only smile at the joyful Girl. She could hardly wait to see what "home" was for this fabulous Magical Creature.

Serena turned and watched the Meadows begin to move outside, slowly at first, but soon the Evertrain began to lurch forward smoothly, and gradually they began to hurtle along on the tracks. Serena felt the ride was mildly bumpy, but for the most part she was very comfortable in her seat. She watched the darkening World outside being flooded by the never-ending Rains and shaken by the cracking Thunder.

Thunder ... like the Sky ripping itself in two, she thought, *Somewhere out there in that horrible storm are three Goblins tied to a Tree in their own chains, a Boy named Jerry who is unwilling to forgive, a CaveLore with a stomach full of Leprechaun, a beautiful clan of Unicorns, Bicorns, and Tricorns, a wandering herd of Sauropods, a Hippogryph with a cracked beak, a Dragon with a Cave full of newly hatched baby Dragons, and a school of ferocious shark-bass Fish, all waiting for the Rain to stop and the Moon to shine.*

Serena let out a long, tired sigh, and then the lights on the car went out. Nelson grabbed her arm in a panic, and she flung into his arms.

"What's going on?" she cried. All around were screams and cries.

Then she was knocked unconscious with something hard.

Part Three: The Heart of Forever
Chapter Twenty-Five: The Grandiloquent Prince

Am I in heaven?

This was Serena's first thought when she finally awoke. She was dry, warm and clean. Her bump that she was sure she had felt rise after she had been hit over the head was gone.

Serena sat up. She was swathed in a flowing silken white gown, with long angel sleeves and a beautiful train that ran over the bed of white, fluffy fabrics and draped to the floor. The bed itself was nothing more than a soft, deep bowl of warm, silken material that was purest white. It sat like an egg-shaped cradle on top of a smooth white trunk that held it up sturdily.

A lock of Golden hair fell in her face, and she smelled it. It smelled like the most fragrant Flowers. She reached up and touched one of the white Flowers that had been woven into her hair.

She heard the sound of Birds chirping. Was she outside? Cautiously, she poked her head up over the half-egg-shaped bed, and the sight that met her eyes made her gasp.

It was the outside … inside!

Around her grew tall, straight, perfect Trees with soft, cushioning Grass that did not have so much as a leaf, twig or acorn in sight. Flowers bloomed everywhere, mostly against the walls which were painted as though the Forest went on, and the ceiling was designed as a Cloudless Spring afternoon. There was no Sun in this striking room, but in the middle of the ceiling was clustered a big ball of what looked like bubbles of light.

More of these bubbles lit up the large Forest-grown room, illuminating small Animals such as Rabbits and Squirrels scurrying from perfect Bush to perfect Bush. Colorful Birds sang in the Trees, just as spectral Butterflies alighted on the delicate Flowers. Multi-color Toadstools sprouted from the health-conditioned Grass, all different shapes and sizes of them. The whole place smelled of pleasant herbs, Pine, Cedar and Flowers. Serena sat herself a little higher from her bowl-shaped bed, and saw more white beds dotted here and there. It was then that she noticed there were other people in the Nature-grown room –

- Pixie folk.

They were mostly females, all swathed in the same colorful, nearly transparent silk gowns as Serena, all with Flowers woven into their Human-colored hair. They were barefoot and had pointed ears that poked out from between the soft curtains of their long hair, and almond-shaped eyes. But Serena loved their wings most of all – some folded back and some displayed open, transparent and delicate, their little sections colored as stained-glass windows. Serena sighed. If only she could fly.

"Ah, so you have awaken!" said a soft voice behind her. Serena turned around in her bath of soft, dry white fabric that smelled deeply of apple Blossoms.

"Y-yes," she replied just as soft, studying a young Pixie Maid in a light Orchid gown. She stood before Serena with her long, slender hands folded neatly in front of her, as though awaiting orders. A little white bubble of light floated beside her head, illuminating her flawless Pixie features.

"This is good," the Girl continued, "that you have awoken. You have slept for nearly two whole Days now, and we where beginning to worry that you would never awake. This is the morning of your third Day in Bendar."

"Bendar," Serena whispered the name, more to herself than to the informative young Pixie Maid.

I have slept for two whole Days, she thought in pure astonishment. *I have never slept that long in my whole life! Where is Nelson? And the Fauns and the Centaurs and my team from Earth? And the Mother of Forever*! she thought with a jerk. She looked at the Pixie Girl, eyes wide.

"Is … is the Mother of Forever still alive?" she had to know.

The Girl smiled sadly.

"Ah, yes, the poor dear is still with us. The Princess has tried thrice since you have arrived here to claim the Throne, but not once has she succeeded."

215

Relief washed over Serena like the cool wafts of Cedar and Pine that caressed her senses.

"I am very sorry to hear this," she said, and sat up some more in the deep, fluffy white silk sheet fabric. "Do you know what has become of my friends the Fauns, Centaurs, Pixies, Halfbreeds and Sun Humans?"

"Yes. They are all here in the Fortress of Bendar, but in different chambers. You are the last to awake, Serena, so you are the only one here in the sick chamber that is not seeking rest. Your good friend Nelson the Halfbreed has anxiously been waiting for you to awake, checking on you every other hour. He says he has your diary, but nothing more. Some of your Sun Human friends and a female Faun have also been to see you whilst you slept. Sometimes the line in here became so long with visitors all wanting to see you that the King had to assign them each a time in which they could see you. Some of them were still afraid you might pass, I think. All of your belongings except the clothes on your back were lost in the Evertrain raid on your way here. And to think that those horrible Creatures could leave all of you lying out on our front doorstep for the beggars in Fifftor to maul! Such amateur, inconsiderate, ignoramuses they were!"

Serena did not know how the Girl's voice remained soft and sweet while she spoke these words. Evidently, though, she had a line of visitors, and the Pixie Maiden acknowledged her for being very well-known. She admired the Blossoms of light purple Freesia that was woven into the Girl's straight dark brown hair that tumbled down to the back of her knees.

"Is Fifftor the City that lies just beyond the Fortress?" Serena asked as she settled her back against the pure-white bed.

"Yes," replied the Girl simply, and looked over Serena's head at the other Pixie Maidens who were tending to the other crib-like beds, similar to how the Butterflies tended to the Flowers. Serena followed her gaze.

"Ah, here is your friend the Halfbreed Boy," smiled the Girl just as Serena spotted Nelson hurrying toward her in a fresh green tunic and leggings. He had also acquired a sharp-looking green cloak that swished behind him as he strode along. His green eyes met hers and he quickened his pace.

"I shall leave you now to report that you are awake. Prince Errenon will be pleased." chirped the Maiden Pixie, and she flapped off on her iridescent, multi-color wings.

"You're awake!" Nelson exclaimed. He threw his arms around her at once, and she pulled him, giggling into the white bed. "I was so afraid that we

216

would lose you!"

"I thought I was in heaven!" Serena said, peering over the side of the bed at the scene that had made the thought believable.

"You very nearly were the first Day you were here!" chuckled Nelson. He brushed a clean lock of Sandy blonde hair from his brow. Serena looked at him as wide-eyed as an Owl.

"I – I almost died?" she said incredulously. Nelson nodded sadly.

"That bump on the back of your head was bleeding so badly that you almost perished from loss of blood. But the Pixies bathed the wound in fresh Spring Water just in time, and you lived to see another Day. Our only problem was that we didn't know when you would awaken to see it."

Spring Water, she thought. *And I'll just bet every time he visited me he put some more power back into my limbs from his own bank. What a Magical Creature indeed I have befriended – he has saved my life!*

Serena shook her head as if in apology, and picked up a corner of Nelson's new cloak. She marveled at its softness, warmth and strength as she sheepishly wondered,

"What have you been doing for two whole Days while I slept?"

Nelson shifted in the soft, bouncy white fabric and sat up with his legs folded.

"Oh, nothing really. We've been biding our time, helping the Pixies with Watering the chambers, cooking meals, and entertaining that dolt of a Prince, Errenon. Pretty little Fortress, isn't it?"

He inhaled deeply. "Smells just like a Forest in the morning after a Spring Rain."

Serena laughed her approval and tweaked her friend's nose.

"So, where is my ancestor's diary, you Thief?"

Nelson cringed, although smiling, and pulled the ribbon-tied diary from within his tunic.

"Oh, please don't use that word," he pleaded. "At least not until I gain my pride back. The filthy blaggards stole my favorite dagger and would have taken my sword, too, if I hadn't drawn it first and beheaded one of them."

Serena gasped and covered her mouth too late to hide it.

"You – you killed it?"

Nelson raised his eyebrows, as if this were nothing out of the ordinary.

"Well, of course I killed the dirty rotter! One less Raider to steal from us!"

Serena still could not believe he had killed one of the Robbers, but she eventually let the matter slip upon reaching the understanding that she had never killed something in her life. Here in Forever, contrary to what she had been taught on Earth, killing was a matter of self-defense.

The conversation moved on to the subject of where to go after their rest at Bendar and how long to stay there.

"We will move on into the Forest of Many Eyes. Well, technically we are in the Forest of Many Eyes now, but only on the very inside of the Northern ridge. Then, I suppose, we will make a beeline for the Diamondia Castle by cutting through the Blue Marsh and the Windy Meadow. Then we'll climb the Perpetual Mountains and hitch a Pegasus or two to Sparkline Mountain, and we'll go from there," Nelson explained, having done some definite research on the subject. "And the Fauns and Pixies have decided to stay here at Bendar for awhile. The Centaurs will be moving South tomorrow morning, and it is soon that we shall follow their example – only we will strike out SouthEast, toward Sparkline Mountain."

Serena sighed as she heard a bit of commotion outside her white bed. Curious, she peered up over the tall side and gasped at what she saw.

"Oh, please," Nelson enthused in a low voice.

"You're telling me!" giggled Serena, looking back at her friend.

Approaching Serena's white bed in a Jewel-studded tunic with an embroidered doublet and breeches with hoes, and a long, flowing cape was the Pixie Prince of Bendar, Errenon. Majestically placed atop his dark brown locks was a glittering coronet, while held proudly upright in his hand was a betwined, scraggled staff with a gleaming green Jewel perched atop its end. His wings were splayed wide open, and his eyes twinkled a marvelous dark brown – almost black, in fact. His lips were pursed in utmost superiority. Errenon strode grandiloquently forward, chin held high, a look of stern importance on his face.

"Ohhh brother!" Serena sighed just out of his hearing range. Nelson's gaze caught hers and he winked sarcastically. She smiled uncertainly back at him.

"Ah, the beautiful Maiden Serena, a Sun Human, I see," hailed the Prince in a deep voice. He halted just before the egg-shaped white bed, planting the end of his staff into the soft Grass.

Serena looked up at him innocently.

Of course he is mildly handsome, she thought to herself, *but does he have the brains?*

"So, you have finally awaken from your long sleep. How do you feel, my precious Dame?"

Serena looked at Nelson, who was smiling fraudishly at the Prince. Ignoring him, Serena replied,

"I feel fine, actually."

Errenon fluttered his wings and folded them back carefully.

"You are not hungry or tired at all?" he questioned, appearing amazed.

Serena shook her head.

"Excuse me for not introducing myself, Serena," continued the Pixie. He snatched up Serena's hand and kissed the back of it. "I am Prince Errenon, son of the mighty King Alanon of Fort Bendar. I am very pleased to meet you."

Serena smiled at the pompous Prince.

At least he is polite, she thought.

"Well, it's nice to meet you too, Errenon. How did you come by my name?" Serena asked softly.

"Oh, I have my sources. His name is Elkhorn - my personal Servant – and I believe you freed him from slavery from some Goblins?"

Serena played with the corner of Nelson's cloak, which she still held in her hand.

"Yes, but it wasn't only me. My good friend Nelson here also helped me free them."

The young Prince looked at Nelson as if seeing him for the first time. He studied the Boy for a moment, and then said,

"Very well. Thank you, young Sir, for helping this lovely Maiden free the slaves. You are dismissed." He said this very quickly.

Nelson sat up straight as one of the perfect Tree trunks outside the bed. Serena, puzzled, looked at Errenon.

"Dismissed?" the two said at the same time.

The Prince dug his staff deeper into the long, soft Grass.

"Yes, Sir Nelson, dismissed. I would like to have a moment with young Serena alone."

Serena should have felt have felt like grabbing Nelson to herself and repelling the rude command. But that feeling was there again, and kept her from doing anything of the sort. And, since she knew that if it were not for the Pixie folk she would not even be revived at all, she felt the only way to thank them was to at least obey the orders of their Prince. With a long glance of apology, Nelson sighed and flew up out of the white bed. He landed, and with a last look over his shoulder, strode off into the sweet-smelling Forest.

Errenon turned back to a not-so-impressed suitress.

"He is your brother?" he inquired.

Now I see where Nelson gets the 'dolt' idea here, she thought, flustered at the thought of Nelson being her brother.

"Oh, no!" she corrected him. "My friend. He is my best friend."

Errenon nodded.

"Well, my delicate Dame, shall we walk?"

Serena accepted and made to stand, but fell into the softness of the fluffy bedding. She looked around, confused for a moment, then looked at the Pixie Prince before her.

"Just how do you get out of these things?" she wanted to know, searching for an exit. Errenon gave a muffled laugh, then spread his wings wide.

"Oh, of course! I forgot, my Maid, that to get out of a Pixie Basket you must fly! Silly me – forgetting that Sun Humans cannot fly."

Serena knew he meant no harm in the remark as he fluttered into the air to pick her up gently around the waist. But to Serena this came as quite offending because of her wish that she could fly. She remained silent as the Boy set her down gently on the Grass. Only then did she notice that her feet were clean and healthy, no longer blistered and painful as they had once been.

The Pixie folk must have soaked them in Spring Water, she thought, watching the green Moss return to her and admiring the colorful, small Blossoms within the Moss.

"Ah, how enchanting!" smiled Errenon as he spotted them. "A Damsel whose touch to Nature is so soft that Moss Flowers Blossom at her feet!"

Serena smirked fraudishly at the flattering comment and began to explore the Forested room.

"Are all of your rooms like this?" she asked. The Prince stooped to pick up a small Rabbit that had obstructed his way.

"Oh yes, the whole of Bendar is a living Nature. We have got some absolutely gorgeous Gardens and Orchards on the bottom floor, which is where we grow our own vegetables and fruits. My father has recently installed a Brook and a small Pond down there, too. Would you care to see?"

Serena accepted both the Rabbit from his arms and the proposal to go down and see the beautiful Garden room. She was about to leave when she remembered something very important, and set the Rabbit back down to retrieve it.

Teresa's diary.

"What have you forgotten?" Errenon wondered as she leafed through the soft white bed fabrics. She still had not found it.

Perhaps Nelson took it for me to keep it safe, she thought.

"A diary," she answered truthfully. "And it appears that I have not only forgotten it, but also lost it."

Something as equally hard as a Rock fell on her heart. What would happen if she lost that diary?

"Is this what you are looking for?"

Serena turned.

Errenon was holding up the diary with a prideful smirk plastered on his face. His dark eyes studied her reply.

"Oh, Errenon, where did you find it?" Serena exclaimed, feeling relieved. She reached out to accept the diary, but Errenon held it away from her.

"Now, now, my Jewel, let's not be grabby," ordered the Prince in a taunting tone. "You may address me as Prince Errenon, if you will, and besides, Pixie Law states that all weapons must be taken away from visitors lest they be spies of any type."

Serena's respect for the Boy was waning.

"Weapons? That's not a weapon! That is my ancestor's diary, Sir Prince Errenon! I demand to have it back this moment!" Serena commanded in a cool voice. She held her composure calm, although she did not know how she managed to do this.

"Ah, but the Pixie Laws here at Bendar state-"

"The Pixie Laws can kiss my foot, Prince Errenon. You and I both know that a simple diary is no weapon. Please give it back to me now."

Errenon drew back from her, his lips pursed in determination. He held the diary high away from Serena.

"You have insulted my ancestry, Damsel! I should like to keep it."

Serena should have felt her cheeks growing red, yet she still remained calm.

"I have insulted your ancestry, have I?" Serena laughed. "You have more deeply insulted mine by refusing to give my ancestry to me!"

Inside, Serena's pride burned so badly she wanted to cry.

Of course! she thought. *I will play the part of an emotional young Maiden like he expects me to be!*

"There is very good reason for my not allowing you to keep the diary,

221

Serena. For instance, you could be writing down information in there that is meant to stay in Bendar! Now, what's this?" Errenon began.

Serena's cheeks had suddenly grown pink and hot tears were willfully drawn to her eyes.

"That diary is the only thing I have left of my family," she sniffed in a shy voice, wiping away a tear. The tear flew to the ground, and Serena failed to notice the beautiful Rose that sprouted where it landed. "If you take it away from me now, I will have nothing left to remind me of my heritage."

Pity softened Errenon's hard brown eyes. He prepared to say something, but Serena cut him off with a soft yelp.

For, quite suddenly, she had seen a hand shoot down from the Tree directly above the Prince's head and snatch up the 200-year-old diary.

Serena looked at Errenon.

"Now see what you have done?" she wailed. In reality, she knew very well who the person in the Tree was. She was only waiting for him to climb down.

Dramatically, Serena threw herself at the trunk of the Tree and covered her face, trying not to laugh.

"Now I have nothing left to symbolize my family heritage," she sobbed, her back trembling heartbrokenly.

Errenon strode over to her and patted her back.

"There, there, now, beautiful Flower. Do not weep! Whosoever has taken your diary into the Tree will soon be captured, for I will spear them myself with my bow and-"

WHOMP!

The diary hit its message home in the hand of Nelson as he sprung limberly to the ground beside Serena. Errenon took a couple of steps back, rubbing his temple where the diary had struck. Nelson had aimed it front-side down (Serena could see) where he knew the money was hidden in the pocket, and so the impact on the Prince's head was indeed very hard.

"Whoops!" smiled Nelson, his arm slithering around Serena, who had immediately regained her composure. "Sorry about that, Prince Airy-Nun."

Serena had to bite her lip to keep from laughing

"Why you..." growled the Prince, shaking a fist at them.

"Sorry Nelson, but that still didn't knock any sense into him." Serena whispered with a giggle as they made for the door. "I do believe he's hopeless."

Serena curled up in one of the light blue Pixie Baskets comfortably in the visitors' dormitories. Its soft, transparent, silky blue fabrics smelled deeply like a cool Summer Rain and reminded her of the Sky. Tomorrow she, Nelson, Theo, Mike, Lindsey, Kate and Bob would move off SouthEast through the Forest of Many Eyes.

But for now, all Serena wanted to think about was the fun she'd had that Day at Bendar with Nelson and the team. Lindsey cried when she found that Serena had awoken, Kate merely smiled, and Mike and Bob both expressed their deepest relief. Theo would not let go of her hand for the first couple of hours, he was so happy to see her. All of them had been redressed – Lindsey in a pink frock and Kate in a purple one, Mike in a red tunic and Bob in an orange one. Theo was dressed the same as his brother, only in lighter shades of green. It was very strange for Serena to see those she knew from Earth dressed in ancient attire, but they even told her that they sort of liked it and that it wasn't all that bad.

After she, Nelson, and the united team members had left the sickroom (where Errenon had crawled into one of the Pixie Baskets to await service for the small red spot on his head), the Halfbreed Boy had personally escorted her down the Grass-carpeted and Tree-grown halls to the Garden room. Serena had noticed as she walked down the halls that they were all as nature-strewn and beautiful as the sickroom she had been in. Different kinds of straight-trunked Trees, (Birch, Oak, Ash, Pine, Cedar, and Rowan) fringed the sides, with Bushes of berries, clusters of fluorescent Flowers, and multi-colored Toadstools blending right in. Irises, Daffodils, Roses, Violets, Carnations, PrimRoses, Tulips, Impatiens, Lilies and all other manner of sweet-smelling Blossoms garbed the place thickly with their cheery Rainbow colors. The Grass, Serena thought, could not have been any softer or greener, since not so much as a twig, leaf, nut, or Animal dropping appeared anywhere. Butterflies tended to the Flowers, Squirrels chattered in the Trees with the chirping Birds, and small Chipmunks, Rabbits, and even some Deer littered the whole place. Tiny Ponds with colorful, little GoldFish were occasionally spotted here and there, their crystal clear Waters glistening under the little white balls of light (called Glow Globes) that showed up everywhere there wasn't a window. Some followed Pixies and other Creatures around, providing light to them. It was quite plain to her that the whole place was absolutely crawling with ancient Magic.

The Garden chamber, Serena thought, was exceptionally beautiful with all of the fruitful Banyan Trees and rows upon rows of green vegetables and Flowers. Nuts and berries were harvested daily, and grew back so quickly that they had to be picked again the very next Day. And, true to "Prince Airy Nun's" prediction, a winding, plentiful little Rivulet ran from one corner of the room to the other, ending in a miniature Waterfall and another small Pond in one corner. Stepping Stones that changed color when you stepped on them formed pathways through the thick, dense Gardens and Orchards, and there was even a little bridge to accompany the babbling Brook.

After that, Nelson and the team showed Serena to the kitchens, where heavenly-smelling aromas drifted up to greet their noses. Serena finally allowed Nelson to serve her some scones and Banyan cakes (made from the Banyan fruits), and enjoyed them aplenty as she admired the kitchens. The ovens were carved out of fat Oak Trees, the cabinets all were vine-entwined boxes, the stove was set over large, square, flat Rocks, and the counters with smooth, polished wooden surfaces were one of the few things that were not overgrown with Moss. Tall, twisted Banyans were grown into the walls straight from the Mossy, petal-strewn floor, heavily laden with the delicious gems of fruit, which were frequently picked fresh and washed before being used for puddings and other sweets.

The music chamber was a profoundly small room, compared to the chambers Serena had seen before, and held a variety of interesting new instruments. In this chamber, the music Serena had heard from the Flowers in the Meadows returned to her ears, now more light and beautiful than ever. Here in the music chamber, elders came to listen to young Maidens sing, bands play, and both to sound together. At the same time the group had brought Serena, a small group of Pixie Children were lined up to practice their singing. A piano-like instrument made out of reeds, Tree bark and a huge Rock (that was the seat), along with a Vine-stringed instrument that resembled a harp accompanied the five Children. Their little voices were clear and melodic, and sounded very much like small bells ringing in the air.

Next, the unpredictable seven entered the nursery and the playroom which were conjoined by a little hallway. Tiny Pixie Children bounced and some of the older ones flew just about everywhere, plucking berries and fruits and gobbling them up eagerly, dropping from Trees, chasing the Rabbits and

Squirrels, and wallowing in the wide Meadows of Flowers. All around the two rooms, full-grown Pixies could be seen chasing after their young, or teaching them in quiet little corners, or tucking them into the miniature Pixie Baskets that were built lower to the ground, and in brighter colors than the adult Pixie Baskets.

After that, they visited the training dojo and the forgery, both of which were also conjoined by a small, Mossy hallway. Overall, Serena was impressed with the Pixie Warriors who indulged in amazing feats of clever fighting through hand-to-hand combat or stick fighting, or just plain wrestling. The Warriors in training, whose age range stretched all the way from six to sixteen years old, came to practice archery, slinging Stones, and other advanced combat techniques taught by the older Warriors. It appalled Serena that they allowed small six-year-old Children to handle blunt swords that were almost as tall as they were, and it came to no wonder to her that there were no Animals in this chamber. The forge was hot and was about the only chamber she had seen so far that did not have Grass or Trees or so much as a Butterfly. Instead, the chamber was fashioned out of a crystal Cave, one that glittered and sparkled its beauty to the blacksmiths. On the Cave's walls were hung all types of weapons – clubs, swords, daggers, slings, bows and arrows, javelins, lances, spears, pikes, and much, much more. Something about the grim dreariness of this room made Serena uncomfortable.

And so the team showed her three much larger, more beautiful chambers, all with lots of space filled with endless Woods and Meadows, Butterflies, Squirrels, Rabbits, and even some Deer romping about in plenty. One chamber was called The Valley, and was styled to look like a luscious Valley between two ice-capped Mountains. Here was an enormous room where Pixies and visitors of all shapes and sizes visited and greeted around. A few chairs and tables could be seen, and Serena saw that this room was also the cafeteria of the Fortress. Banyan Trees were plentiful, and another thin Stream wove around the room, with small colorful Fish playing under its surface.

Another room was the Grand Hall, which really wasn't a room, but rather a broad hallway with tapestries and pictures of the history, ancestry and creation of Pixies on one wall, and long, stained glass windows on the other. The last was the Council Room, where Chieftains discussed plans for battletime, but was really just a meeting room for the elders and specific groups when not in use. One long table and several Toadstool chairs sat in the very middle surrounded by tall, straight Trees on all sides. Only the mute Animals inhabited this room.

Nelson and the discoverers went on to show Serena the library, where bookshelves were made from Trees, and all was quiet except for the rustling of Pixies in surrounding Trees and the turning of pages. A small chamber connected to the library was reserved for schooling and lessons.

The cellars were even decorated with Trees, soft Grass and Flowers. Stacked in groups here and there were large barrels of wines, ciders, ales and other delectable drinks. The team was offered a bubbly-looking purple drink and accepted it gleefully. Serena thought it tasted like grape soda pop from Earth, and Theo had a second cup he liked it so much.

Then Lindsey went to show Serena the Girls' bathing room. Clear little Pools with multi-color bubbles sat everywhere on the fresh green Grass, and there were no Trees but a few scattered shady Oaks. Flower Bushes lined the walls, and from them the Pixie Maidens produced towels and lotions, oils and wash rags, and all other manner of clothing and such. The air smelled heavily of dainty, Flowery perfumes, shampoos and other lovely aromas.

And last, the chamber Serena was now curled comfortably in was the visitors' dormitories. Other dormitories and small rooms dotted the Fortress through and through, but Serena felt the safest in the whole place in this one room.

But why?

Because she knew that Nelson was safely tucked away in a light green Pixie Basket just a few feet away, and that he was still alert for her safety even though he was supposed to be asleep.

"Serena?" came a soft tenor voice. She knew it was him. "Are you still awake?"

"Yes," she replied, turning over in her sweet-smelling fabrics. "Why?"

"Do you like Bendar?"

"Of course," she replied. "Bendar is a wonderful place. Why, do you not like it?"

"No … it's just … I was just wondering," she heard him stutter. "Would … I mean, how would you feel about staying a little longer?"

Serena felt a blush rise to her cheeks. Nelson was the Heir to the Throne – and she had to get him to Sparkline Mountain before the Mother of Forever closed her eyes for the last time.

"Well … as much as I would like to stay here, I really think we should move on," Serena tried to keep her voice to a low whisper, as not to wake the others. "I believe Mike, Bob, Lindsey and Kate are all very homesick…"

She listened to the rustling of Nelson turning over in his Pixie Basket.

"Serena, do you … miss your home on Earth?"

Serena had to think about that one. Finally, after a silent sigh, she replied, "Not really."

"Why?" the Boy inquired. "Didn't you have any family or friends?"

"Well … I am an orphan," Serena explained, and told him of Bertha and how she had been home-schooled.

"Oh," crooned Nelson sympathetically. "But … how did your parents die?"

"I was told that they died when I was a baby. They were in a car accident."

Briefly, as not to leave him in the Clouds, she explained to him what a car was.

And then Nelson asked her the most bizarre question she had ever heard.

"Do you think … maybe … that your parents could not have died, but have secretly been transported to Forever?"

Serena let out a soft giggle.

"No," she whispered. "How would they? I know where both of their graves are; I've visited them many times. I have even seen the car that took their lives in a junk yard."

Silence reigned for a few moments, and then Nelson finally said,

"I am sorry that both of your parents died."

Serena smiled.

"That is kind of you, Nelson. Thank you. Now let's get some sleep, so we are refreshed and ready to travel in the morning. Good Night, Nelson."

"Good Night, Serena."

Moments later, a series of soft snores announced Nelson's departure from the conscious world. Serena turned over again and nuzzled her face into the Rainy blue material, inhaling deeply. She itched to asked Nelson about his own parents, but didn't want to give anything away. She knew he was what all of Forever was looking for.

Of course, Nelson knows how I feel about losing a parent – his own Mother, the Mother of Forever, is dying now as we speak. Oh, I am so tired now.

What a wonderful place Bendar is. she thought as she felt herself drifting off into sleep. *I wonder what the Diamondia Castle will look like.*

Chapter Twenty-Seven: Departure

In Serena's dream, she was flying again. She soared up and up, higher and higher, through the iridescent Clouds of Mist. She felt one with the Winds that carried her all about, until, once more, the feeling of forlorn deception took over and she began to fall.

She fell and fell, trying to scream for help all the while, but noCreature came to help her. In the distance loomed the three figures, each one a little more distant and lighter than the one before it. She knew the first one was Jerry, and she was right as he stepped back and let her fall as he had before.

The second figure, however, she did not know. Could it be Nelson? The outline was broad and tall with a long cloak and something poky sticking up from the top of its head. It also held in one hand a twisted staff with a gleaming green Emerald on the top.

Prince Errenon.

Although Serena did not exactly like the Boy, his wrongs could be forgiven as easily as a Pixie could stretch his wings and fly. She fell ever closer and found that his pale face was ever paler than before – nearly as white as the Mists now - and his eyes were glazed over just as Jerry's were. His staff was leaned against a Cloud, standing upright, waiting for him. His arms were outstretched, and his wings were displayed widely with all of their spectral stained-glass colors, beautiful to say the least. Serena fell closer and closer to him, the Wind whistling in her ears, burning her cheeks pink, and drying her lips. She closed her eyes, very sure now that he was going to catch her, for there was no way now that he could miss her.

Unless, of course, he put down his arms and stepped back, just as Jerry had done.

Which he did.

Serena fell on, scared that she could possibly hit the ground and kill herself without anyCreature taking a care that she did so.

But wait!

There was one figure left, further down from her, that could catch her before she fell to fatal results. She fell and fell, but seemed not to be getting any closer to the figure. Then she urged herself onward, pursuing the last figure to catch her so that she might not perish.

It was then that Serena, in real life, felt something brush against her eyelash. She flinched, her dream floating away like a Cloud in a Mountain Breeze.

It happened again, and she rubbed at her eye. Was it an insect or a bug?

No, Bendar had no insects other than Butterflies inside, she told herself in thought. Then something brushed against her eyelash once more.

Stifling a sigh, she rolled over and buried her face into the soft, sweet-smelling fabric. It smelled so pleasantly sweet that she would have immediately fallen asleep once more had that persistent, obnoxious little something not alighted on one of her curls distractedly.

This time Serena did not stifle her sigh. *Maybe one brave little Butterfly thinks that I am a Flower ... and Boy, is he wrong.* she thought, and lifted her hand to slap it away. Instead, the back of her hand smacked something like Human skin, and she sighed again.

"Go away, Nelson..." she grumbled, hiding a smile. Nelson, who was floating on his stomach just above her, blew comically on her hair. It wisped over her face like the Wind itself in a more curled, Golden version.

"Malevolent MerMaids and no, I shan't! 'Tis well time for you to get up! You've slept in past the break of dawn already and scared the rest of us into thinking you were unconscious again," babbled the hovering Halfbreed. He flipped onto his back and allowed his cloak to fall heavily on top of the Girl. "But of course I knew you were only sleeping,"

He tucked his hands behind his head comfortably and stared at the ceiling that resembled a Cloudless blue Sky. His expected response came muffled.

"Oh, yes? How is that?"

"Because you were snoring!" Serena heard him crow to the dormitory.

She reached up and grabbed his cloak, pulling her offender down. He made a strangled yelp as he landed softly on the fabrics.

"I was snoring? You should have heard yourself over there! I thought a Storm was rolling in before I realized that Thunderous sound was only you!"

Serena had the Boy trapped on his own leash – his cloak. He smiled, one hand on his tingling throat, and he sat back against the Pixie Basket.

"You must have extra healthy lungs to be able to wake me up like that then!" he rasped fraudishly, grasping his cloak. Serena let go of it and came nose-to-nose with the Boy.

"It wasn't me who woke you, Nelson."

His lips trembled and he looked surprised.

"It wasn't?"

229

"No."

"Then who was it?"

Serena smiled, admiring her friend's clear green eyes.

"It was yourself!" she cackled, and leaped away as Nelson grabbed at her.

Nelson suddenly grew alert as the sound of hooves reached their ears. Serena peered up over her Pixie Basket and spotted Fernwood, her brown hair twisted in several braids and woven in pink Flowers, approaching them.

"Thou hast awoken!" she chirped, a wide smile spreading on her face.

"At last!" sighed Nelson, and promptly dodged a well-aimed smack.

He chuckled and then took the Girl about her waist, lifting her out of the warm, comfortable Pixie Basket.

"A pleasant meal to break thy fast is waiting in yonder kitchens for thee," Fernwood put in, playing with one of her braids. "Oh, and Prince Nelson, my brother and I hath decideth to venture South after thou hast partaken thy morning meal."

Nelson nodded and set Serena down on the soft Grass. Immediately, bright, beautiful Moss Flowers bloomed at her feet, and a curious Chipmunk scampered over to her. Smiling, she picked it up and followed Nelson and Fernwood to the Valley.

Serena had a most scrumptious breakfast – fruits and berries dipped in honey, sugar-glazed scones and tarts, steaming, freshly-baked sausages and breads, and, her personal favorite, the Banyan cakes that tasted like the colors of the Rainbow in her mouth. She did not realize just how hungry she really was until that fragrant, alluring aroma saluted her nose as she first walked in. Mike and Bob piled her plate high, insisting she try a bit of everything that was laid out on the long Stone table. This she did without a second bidding, bouncing jovially on the large, spotted Toadstools which served to the feasters as seats.

After breakfast, the Maid in the purple Orchid gown somehow learned that the team would be leaving soon. At once the Maiden sent out two other Pixie Maids to pack Serena a haversack with food, clothes, rope, and other necessities required for venturing.

"We shall wash you and find you a more suitable traveling dress, also," the Girl (who, Serena found out, was named Lilac) had told her as she led her away to the bathing rooms. Serena, upon hearing this conclusion, prepared to protest – they had a limited amount of time left to travel, and she wished not to be wasting a single precious moment. And yet Lilac persisted, and chose shampoos, lotions, soaps and perfumes from a surrounding Bush.

"It will not take us long," she reasoned, and gathered the things up in her arms like priceless Children.

Serena finally surrendered to the Girl and allowed herself to be tended to by the sweet-smelling Pixie Maidens. In a record amount of time (or so it seemed to the bewildered Serena), they managed to wash, dry, oil, and garment Serena, all in a calm manner. Yet Serena had to confess that the bath was certainly the most soothing she had ever had, and the towels were the softest she had ever felt, and the soaps, oils, shampoos and perfumes were the sweetest she had ever smelled. She wished dearly that she could, as Nelson had suggested, linger in the Heavenly place, but drove herself ever onward on the situation of limited time.

Serena marveled at the hair drying Spell that one of the Girls worked through her hair. She simply ran her hand flat over it, and it collected little droplets of water which she flung to the conditioned Lawns. Serena was clad in one of the uncomfortable contraptions the Pixies called a corset, and she was not very pleased with it. But, not wanting to hurt the kind Pixies' feelings, she obliged and was soon dressed in a light blue frock, the bell-like skirts reaching just below her knees for easy travel, and the shoulders poofed out in short sleeves. The bodice portion was very tight and mildly uncomfortable, the waist being fitted with a built-in sash that tied in a hugely decorative and poofy silken bow in the back. Another blue bow was fitted to her hair, drawing it away from her face in a long, towering ponytail. By the time Serena emerged from the bathing rooms, she felt as though she absolutely reeked of sweet perfume that was named after a light blue flower (that also doubled as a bug repellent) – called Skybell. Her knapsack was ready for her as soon as she entered the Valley, and so was Nelson and Theo.

Nelson had to look twice before he was positive of what he was seeing. Was this beautiful Maiden the same that not four Days ago had been confined to filthy men's trousers? He blinked as she drew nearer. She was looking questionably at the big bow in back of her skirts. She felt like a doll.

"The rest have gone into town to buy weapons." he whispered. Serena nodded, and laid a hand on Lilac's shoulder just before she left.

"Wait." she pleaded softly, and the Pixie turned. Serena smiled into the friendly, Sandy brown eyes. She held out her hand and dropped two Gold

231

Welnon into her hand. The Girl's eyes grew considerably, and she looked up at Serena, mouth trembling, but speechless.

"I only wish I could give you more." Serena said, and patted the Girl on the back. "If it had not been for you and Bendar, I would not be standing alive right now. Thank you very much, and take care, my friend."

Lilac hugged Serena and suddenly found her voice.

"Nay, thank you, Mistress Serena, and may your blessings come as plentiful as the Blossoms at your feet," she half-whispered. Serena smiled as she watched the Girl walk off, staring, astonished, at her new prize. Her wings, sleeves and train trailed behind her on the soft Grass.

Nelson put a hand on the poofy shoulder of Serena's silken dress.

"We must leave now, if we are to travel a good distance toDay."

Serena nodded. She could tell from the Boy's anxious grasp that he was just as eager to leave the place as she was, although they both sorely wished they could linger.

Serena hoisted her new haversack up onto her back and followed Nelson to the front gates. A very small, but nonetheless well-Gardened Lawn stood beside the tiny path that led from the thick, wooden double doors to the iron-barred gates of Bendar. Serena looked over her shoulder at the place as Nelson accepted his weapons from a gate Guard. Fully expecting the place to be covered in Vines and Moss, it came to her great surprise that the place was but an ordinary Stone Fortress, with armed Warriors patrolling the battlements in a business-like manner.

What a strange, yet wonderful place Bendar is, she thought wondrously as she followed Nelson into the City of Fifftor.

There was no doubt about it, Fifftor was most certainly a very large organization. And yet Serena failed, miserably, to find the very organization in the place with beggars scattered in handfuls here and there, filthy little Children running to and fro in the streets, and Horse's leavings caked to the brick roads.

Fifftor's inhabitants came in every shape and size: there were Pixies, Nymphs, a few Elves, Brownies, Gnomes, Dwarves, and upright, speaking Animals, plus many more. Serena had never seen such diversity in Magical, mystical Creatures before all at once in her entire life, and could not help but to gawp at them in astonishment. Instead of Horses, Travelers rode on the

232

backs of Unicorns, with a couple of Bicorns and Tricorns thrown in for good measure. Serena knew, as she watched a rich-looking Elf pass by them in a shimmering, beautiful cloak and a suit of great price, that Unicorns were not a cheap sort. She admired the line of Elves as they paraded past; they were all men, and all extremely handsome. With long, pointed ears, all with sparkling clear green eyes and palest skin and hair, each and every one looked the picture of something brought to life from the Heavens. Now Serena saw where Nelson had acquired his inimitable good looks; either his father or his mother – whoever had been an Elf.

On the front stoop just in front of the gate, Nelson and Serena stood, waiting for the long train of Elven warriors to disperse.

"Where are we supposed to meet the rest?" Serena found herself wondering.

"Actually, they were supposed to meet us here with the supplies," replied Nelson, and promptly moved to the Stone wall that encased the Fortress of Bendar in a thick shield of brick. He sat down with his back against the wall, fingering the Emerald-hilted sword at his side. Serena sat down next to him.

It wasn't long before the two friends encountered a party, although it wasn't from Fifftor. Mosslyn, Elkhorn, and Prince Errenon greeted them from behind the iron-barred gates. Wildder soon showed up beside Mosslyn. They learned that the discovery team and Theo had said their goodbyes while Serena was being redressed.

"We comed to biddy you's a farewellings," piped Mosslyn, gripping the iron bars at the gate. Her small face poked between the two bars at Serena, her honey-colored eyes shining with tears. Elkhorn and Errenon stood beside her. Nelson took to his feet and greeted them, saying,

"We thank you, Wildder and Mosslyn, for being our faithful companions on our way here. And though our paths may part, our hearts will always remain as one in friendship."

"Just the point I was about to bring up," Errenon interrupted suddenly, holding up his finger for patience. He stared shamelessly at Serena, who courteously stood and saluted him with a bow.

Nelson coughed in attempt to hide a laugh.

"You're supposed to curtsey!" Errenon added in a low whisper.

Serena sighed, wondering how many times she would have to salute the spoiled Prince before he would be happy. She dipped into a graceful curtsey.

Prince Errenon smiled and grabbed her hand.

"I am profusely sorry for our, hm, misunderstanding at the first impressions, my beautiful Jewel. I would hope that you could, perhaps, forgive me?"

Serena stared into the Boy's dark, dark eyes, and knew that he, being a Child of royalty, expected forgiveness as a necessary response to his plea.

"Of course," she finally said, looking aside at Nelson, who was distractedly watching a Toad hop about, chasing a Grasshopper on the ground.

"Ah, what a generous, courteous soul you are, Mistress Serena. Now, I know that you and your, ahm, friend here are eager to push off, but I beseech you to reconsider. Stay a few more Days here, lovely Damsel, and grace us with your warming presence."

Serena could not believe what she was hearing. Obviously, Errenon was trying to flatter her into staying! She held her composure well. But she was not able to resist a broad grin that, if not monitored could have burst into a series of rude laughter. Errenon's sweating grip squeezed her hands anxiously. Being brought up in royalty, and also considering his high position over her, he was fully expecting her to accept his offer. Serena looked around at the other four countenances watching her with large, hopeful eyes. Nelson's spring-green gaze met hers. That gaze seemed to fix the deal. She was certain, later, that he had used his Prince of Forever Powers again to make the decision she fully intended on making herself.

"I – I am terribly sorry, Sir Prince Airy – er, Prince Errenon, but my friends and I have important business elsewhere that must be tended to," she heard herself blurt after a short pause, and she began to draw her hands from his perspiring grasp.

He struggled to hold her hands and took a deep breath.

"Alas, so our ways must part. I do hope ever so much that our paths will cross again Mistress Serena."

The blonde-haired Girl smiled almost knowingly.

"Perhaps they will, Prince Errenon, perhaps they will."

And with that she yanked her hands from him and turned to embrace Elkwood, Wildder, and especially Mosslyn, each in turn.

"Why canta you's stay wif usses eneemore, Seblena?" sobbed Mosslyn. "I wantsa you's ta stays!"

Serena hugged her tightly, then took something from her knapsack that she had made earlier for Mosslyn – a small braided bracelet made from her own hair. She tied it around the Faun's wrist, and in return, Mosslyn clipped a string from her own hair (which for once was left unbraided in tumbling waves weaved with yellow flowers) and tied it around Serena's wrist in a small braid. Knowing this might be a hindrance or even get lost in travel, Serena placed a note in her mind to remove the bracelet later and put it in Teresa's diary with her money and hair pins.

"I may not physically see you ever again," Serena whispered softly, wiping tears from Mosslyn's Child-like face, "but in your heart is the memory of us being together, and there you can always find me."

Nelson tapped her shoulder just as Mosslyn burst into tears and ran off back into Bendar, her sunshine-yellow gown with its long sleeves and train streaming behind her with her long brown hair.

Serena felt horrible at having to leave her weeping friend behind in Bendar. It was then that she realized that crying and running away at the departure of a good friend was merely another aspect of Mosslyn's Childish culture, that she would accept the concept sooner or later.

She turned at Nelson's beckoning and found Lindsey, Kate, Mike, Bob, Theo, Fernwood and Skywood approaching them from the town. Wildder, Elkhorn, and Prince Errenon melted back into the Fortress of Bendar.

Serena noticed that all of them had been cleaned and clothed appropriately for traveling. Kate now wore a purple frock and Lindsey wore a pink one, both of their bell-shaped skirts billowing out in ruffles and lace, like long umbrellas. Bonnets similar to the one Serena had were now fastened around their heads as a shade from the Sun, and bound their clean, perfumed hair. Black slipper-shoes were tightened fast to their little feet. The Boys, too, had been washed and cladden in tunics and leggings, each with a heavy cloak to use as a blanket at Night. Their hair was neatly combed, and they each now carried a gleaming new sword tucked in a fancy belt around their hips. Even the Centaurs had been nicely dressed for the occasion: Fernwood wore an ordinary bodice with a skirt that reached over her Horsey bottom half, with a small hole for her long, beautiful tail. Skywood had a similar piece of clothing that resembled a tunic, and he also had a long cloak.

"We collected some nice weapons." Theo reported officiously as he slipped down off of Fernwood's back. He brandished a white grin as he saw that his brother had acquired his bow and arrows once more.

"Ah, yes ... seems that the Blacksmith happens to be our own kind," smirked Skywood. He held up a polished spear that he now carried with him as a walking stick. "He beggeth us to remain here, but our clan is not here in the City, and so it shall be that we part."

Nelson nodded and agreed casually, watching the Sun warily in the Sky like a business Man eyes a watch face.

"We would buy Unicorns for easier travel, but they're too expensive," Mike said. Bob tightened his orange cloak. "It seems that only upper class Foreverans and those of royalty have the financial liberties of purchasing them."

Skywood twisted the end of his spear into the dust, reminding Serena of Errenon and his scepter.

"Well, so our paths must split." Nelson said at last. He made a swift nod of his head with one hand over his heart, the other gripping his bow. "May good fortune follow you on your way."

Skywood and Fernwood returned the gesture.

"And may thy lives fare as well as thy Blossoms bloom on the Banyan Trees in Bendar."

With that last remark, the two Centaurs turned and started South through the City of Fifftor, while Serena followed the group of six towards the East, the Sun shining brilliantly on their faces.

Before them stood a massive Forest.

The Forest of Many Eyes.

Chapter Twenty-Eight: The Forest of Many Eyes

It soon occurred to Serena that the Forest of Many Eyes was much more beautiful than it sounded. The Sun shone in bright beams from in between the canopy of Trees – bathing the Ferns, Toadstools, sticks and loam of the Forest floor in spots of cheerful Sunshine. The place smelled of Trees and fruit, for tall Redwood Trees and several wild Banyans grew alongside the other Trees. Some of them were so terribly tall that Serena had to strain just to see their lowest branches. Theo picked extra fruit from the bountiful Banyans as they traveled along.

There was no marked path in the Forest, although there were plenty of Deer trails and Animal tracks, most of which Nelson spotted before anyone else and pointed out to them. Mike enjoyed seeing an Earthen Creature's tracks for once. Sometimes Serena felt, as she lifted her skirt to jump over a fallen log, like they were going to get lost since there was no path, and the Forest seemed so endless, the very thought seemed reasonably possible. But Nelson reassured her that he knew his way, and so she trusted him.

"I wonder why they call this place the Forest of Many Eyes," Lindsey wondered aloud, looking up into the bright, leafy green branches with her shining grey eyes.

"It's because we are being watched." answered Bob, reaching back to touch his trimmed hair, which had been drawn back into a tight, low ponytail with a black ribbon. Apparently, he had come into contact with information concerning the place while at Bendar. "Every move we make is being watched, and every word we say is being heard."

Frantically, Kate began looking about, her purple bow slapping her cheeks.

"Who's watching us?" she demanded to know. "I don't see any eyes."

"That's because you cannot see them in the Day time." Mike put in, digging a temporary walking stick into the ground. "They are invisible while the Sun is out, but when the Moon rises, you can see all of their eyes watching you. Blinking, all sizes, colors and shapes of eyes, just waiting for you to fall asleep so they can come out and steal from you. It is said that some only steal your provisions, while others prefer to steal your lives."

A sudden chill crept down Serena's spine and she quickened her pace.

"Who are 'they'?" she whispered.

"Don't whisper, Serena. They can hear you anyway," shrugged Mike casually.

"The Prowlers of the Forest," Bob explained. Mike's walking staff crunched in the soil. "Some are Animals, and some are Monsters. A long time ago, a Spell was cast in this Forest. Some of the Animals in this Forest were turned into hideous Beasts, while some other Animals simply mutated. Those that had been Cursed were forced to conceal their ugliness from one another in the light – for some were so fiercely ugly that a Creature could die just from getting a single glimpse of them. But during the Night, that part of the Spell is hampered, and they become mortal. This is when they prowl the Forest and steal from helpless Travelers. They are called Prowlers."

Lindsey did not hold back her shuddering.

"Burrr! So how do we protect ourselves from them?"

"We post lookouts and sleep in turns with our weapons close at hand," Nelson called from the front of the group. "And we keep the fire going all Night. If it were to be exinguished, we would be robbed of our possessions and our dignity."

Serena did not like the sounds of this place during the Night, but she quickly learned that during the Daytime the Forest looked absolutely dazzling and harmless. Or, at least, for the time being.

Around midDay Nelson called halt for lunch, and they stopped right in front of a fallen Redwood Tree that they had come upon. The thing was monstrous – as tall as a wall and as long as a River. Luckily it was one of the thinner ones – if it had been any larger, they would have been forced to go around it.

After a quick lunch of dried fruit and Banyan cakes, Nelson set to the feat of finding a way to climb the side of the half-buried Tree. The blood-red bark was thick and grooved, and Nelson finally figured that it was suitable for climbing.

Serena was one of the last ones to start climbing, not quite sure that this was something she wanted to do. But, after much reassurance from Nelson that he would be close to her to catch her should she fall, she set to the task confidently.

The bark was deeply grooved, forming somewhat of a small, vertical staircase for her, but the texture was also wet and loose from rotting away in the Rain.

Further and further she climbed, trying to keep something of a distance between her and the other climbers ahead of her. Higher and higher she went, until finally she was the only one left climbing; the rest were standing on the top, surveying the Land before them.

And then, without any notice at all, the worst possible outcome of her climbing efforts came to life -

a fault in the wood just ahead of her cracked, and she felt the entire bark of the Tree underneath her shift.

She froze, eyes wide and body stiff with fear.

The bark was falling off of the Tree!

If she moved up, it would crack and she would die. If she moved down, it would crack and she would die. If she moved at all, the bark would crack and she would die falling with it. She gulped.

"N-Nelson?" she squeaked and looked up at him. But all of her companions' backs were turned to her, and their mouths were hanging open, awestruck. Obviously, something other than the danger of Serena's life had caught their attention. Mike and Bob drew their weapons and passed two daggers to Kate and Lindsey. Nelson and Theo drew their bows.

Serena had to move now or the bark would not be able to support her weight. It had already begun to slide earthward. Taking a deep breath, she scrambled up the last of the wood just as it cracked and picked up speed on its fall. She reached the top of the peeling bark and jumped –

- and barely caught a ridge from the remaining bark on the top of the Tree. The bark she had formerly occupied hit the ground, scattering in all directions with a Thunderous crash. The slime on the ridge made it slippery, and Serena knew that with the sweating of her own hands and her weight on her fingertips the way it was that she could not hold on for much longer.

"Nelson! Help!" she shrieked, just as the bark began to crack again.

But Nelson was occupied with something else – he was shooting off arrows at a speed hardly imaginable.

Serena could not pull herself up – she was not strong enough. The wood cracked audibly again.

"Nelson! Can't you hear me?! Help! Someone, HELP!"

Serena screamed her last just as the bark broke off.

Then a hand caught her.

"Oh, Nelson!" Serena panted as the Boy hauled her up. "Thank you!"

"Take this, hurry!" he ordered, jabbing the hilt of his sword into her hand. He paused momentarily as their hands touched, then flushed as red as the Tree bark and drew another arrow.

Only when Serena turned did she see what had kept the six so distracted. Monkeys.

Huge Monkeys.

Huge purple Monkeys.

Huge purple Monkeys with blazing orange eyes.

Huge purple Monkeys with blazing orange eyes and a will to kill the seven people who stood on top of their Tree.

"Oh my-" she began, but got no further, for the enormous mammals were already scrambling up the crimson bark at record-breaking speed. They were Giants of Monkeys, at least seven feet tall, with ears that stuck out boldly on either side of their heads, long, whip-like tails, and razor-sharp claws and teeth. They growled and grunted, heaving themselves further upward to their goal.

Nelson and Theo were shooting off arrows at top-speed, Bob and Mike were cutting off claws and heads as soon as they came in range, Lindsey was stabbing frantically at the hands that appeared too close to her, and Kate was shrieking and dancing, stepping on their claws. Serena stood frozen, unwilling to wield the sword and kill something. Instead, she leaned over behind Nelson, and found that the redwood Tree was half-buried, but only on one side. And, to her astonishment, the Tree was perched on a Treeless Hill.

"The log," she whispered to herself. Serena grasped Nelson's shoulders as he let fly another angry arrow.

"Nelson! The log is on a slope! We can roll it if you use your Powers to do it!"

She caught her breath at what she had said.

"What Powers?" Nelson wanted to know, his face reddening again.

"Your … Elven Powers!" Serena stammered hesitantly, not wanting him to find out that she knew his deep secret.

"Serena, I don't think I can-"

Serena glanced out of the corner of her eye at the advancing violent, violet Monkeys as she shook his shoulder confidently.

"But you have to try!" she hissed, and she stared deeply into the Boy's large green eyes to get her point across.

You can do it, Prince of Forever, you know you can! she thought as she watched him move behind the others and place both hands on the bark surface. She closed her eyes, knotting her fists white around the hilt of Nelson's sword. The green Jewel glowed brightly in the Sunlight.

He can move this thing ... oh, I know he can! Nelson, move the log, quick-ly! she thought nervously. Nelson, red in the face, tossed his blonde locks out of his face, looked up at her and winked with a sneaky smile, then gripped the log hard. And, to her bewilderment, the log trembled and shifted.

The Monkeys stood stock-still. Everyone froze.

"Turn around and get ready to run, friends!" Nelson shouted.

The Monkeys screamed and began to flock off the log like ants scampering away from a hungry Frog.

Mike laughed, Kate whimpered and Lindsey cheered as the Redwood Tree was pushed from behind by some unknown force. The log began to roll – very slowly at first, and then so fast that Serena did not know if she could run so fast on top of the log to keep up. Her companions panted beside her – all but Nelson and Theo, who followed the log in the air.

Down and down the Tree rolled, smashing all in its path to a pulp. Serena gasped in horror as she saw the devastation of the log as it rolled further downHill. Monkeys were flattened and pressed into the Forest floor like raisins pressed into a honeyed cake. Black blood trickled down the Hill in pursuit of the Redwood log, rushing in little Rivulets and Streams that gathered at the Valley bottom.

Serena's skirt was a great deal of trouble to her, and she had to pick the front of it up slightly to allow her to move more easily. Her hair bobbed behind her, her heart thudded in her chest, and sweet triumph could already be tasted in her mouth. Her feet pounded the rough, twisted surface, jumping over knots in the wood and dodging small holes. The log slowed as the land leveled, and finally came to halt in a very small ditch. Four other Redwood Trees barred it from going any further. The five were thrown off with the impact to land on their backs in the soft loam of the Forest.

All fell unconscious.

Serena heard voices.

Human voices.

Her head hurt like nothing ever before, causing her to utter a soft moan of pain.

Another thing she noticed as consciousness flooded into her – she was being carried – no – she was flying!

She opened her eyes.

She was flying, but in Nelson's arms. The Boy was carrying her, traveling over the ground in the air, next to a native-dressed Human who had blue-tinted skin. Beads made of bone and large seeds rattled from his loincloth and satchel, and he walked barefoot through the Forest with a hard staff slightly taller than he.

"Sah ruoy dneirf nekowa?" he said in a tongue Serena did not recognize.

"Yllanif, sey," Nelson replied, smiling down at Serena in relief.

"Who-" Serena croaked, looking at the blue Human.

"This is Rockwicha," Nelson said. "He is one of the local Sky Humans from the Boulder Tribe, and he is going to help us get to the Blue Marsh."

Serena smiled and nodded her head with her right hand loosely over her heart in greeting. She was still feeling very weak. Rockwicha returned the gesture.

"Eht srehto llahs nekawa noos," he assured Nelson, and sprinted off to join the rest of the Sky Humans in front of them. Serena could tell from the lighting in the Forest that it was near dusk, and it eased her throbbing temples to know that they would soon have to stop for the Night to light a fire and ward away any Prowlers that may feel hungry.

Serena studied the Tribe of Sky Humans as Nelson filled her in on all that had happened since she had been asleep. And Sky Humans they were indeed, for their skin and even their hair had a bluish tint to it. Different shades of blue skin, eye, and hair color flashed in the crowd of nine or so Sky Human Warriors.

They were a strong-looking people, men wearing loincloths and for some, moccasins. The women wore skirts and braziers; some wore full Deerskin dresses. Their hair was left down in a natural position with beads and Flowers woven into most. They carried woven wicker baskets on their backs, and each had his or her own satchel that they wore across their chest. They looked very much like the Native Americans from Earth, Serena thought, and what a humble people they seemed, though most men carried spears as walking sticks. Serena could not understand their tongue.

"The Sky Humans found us just in time," Nelson continued, seeing her fascination with the people. "Theo and I were just getting ready to settle down

242

for the Day with you when they showed up. They said that those Monkeys had them surrounded when they saw us on their log, and rushed to protect their domain. The Sky Humans got away safely before the Tree began to roll downhill, and do you know it did wipe out all of those miserable purple vermin! There was black blood trickling down that Hillside in Streams, because of all the carnage-"

Serena placed a hand over her friend's mouth to stop him from downloading the horrid visual Serena was gaining from his description.

"Ew llahs pots ereh rof eht Thgin!" shouted Rockwicha as they came to a small clearing. The only word Serena had understood was "pots," and she then wondered if Rockwicha wasn't calling a halt and telling his people to get the pots out for cooking.

Nelson, who had carried her all this time without once offering her to walk on her own, sat Serena up against a Rock while he began to set up a fire. The Girl watched, regaining her senses slowly. The Sky Humans made their camp in the middle of the clearing, and it was around this camp that they constructed a circle of torches, like a huge gate. These they lit with the small fire Nelson made in the center of the camp. It was very much like a ring of fire, or at least Serena thought so, as she accepted Nelson's cloak and a hot mug of tea from Rockwicha.

The big Man sat down next to Serena as she sipped the hot tea.

"Ahciwkcor," he said, calmly pointing to himself in an attempt to teach her the language. She narrowed her eyes and cocked her head to one side. What did he just say?

Rockwicha pointed to Nelson, who was busy passing out more wooden mugs of hot tea to Lindsey and Mike, who had just awoken and were sitting up to take in the refreshment.

"Noslen," said Rockwicha.

And suddenly, Serena understood: he was speaking backwards!

It must be his language, she thought, and smiled and nodded to show that she understood. Then she pointed to herself, trying to formulate her name backward in her head meanwhile.

"Aneres." she said hesitantly, articulating very well to make sure she was right. Rockwicha spoke slowly for her.

"Aneres. Ti si doog ot teem uoy."

Serena decoded this and came up with a hesitant reply.

"Ti si doog ot teem uoy oot. … Knaht uoy rof… gnikat su ot eht …. Eulb

243

… Hsram."

Rockwicha smiled and waved his hand as though it were nothing.

"Ew era no ruo yaw ot ruo pmac rehtruf Tsew fo ereh." He stopped to poke a yellow and blue striped fruit on the end of a stick. "Dna ti si su ohw dluohs eb gniyas knaht ouy. Fi ti t'nerew rof uoy, ew dluow eb Yeknom wets thgir won!"

Serena was very glad the Man spoke slowly and deliberately – that way she could sound out what he was saying and write it down in the Sand to read. She laughed at what she saw, erased the markings and wrote a response to aid her in the speech.

"Fi uoy erew, I dluow epoh yeht dluow ekohc!" she laughed, and scooted over so Nelson could sit next to her.

"They speak backwards," Serena stated, sharing the cloak with him. Nelson smiled.

"Ah, so you've noticed. You are a clever one, I must admit. I thought that I would have to explain it to you, like I had to the others."

Serena smirked and took another sip of her mug.

"Rockwicha says that the Sky Humans' camp is further West of here."

Nelson nodded, stealing a sip from the same cup.

"Yes, they were out on a fruit gathering expedition when the Monkeys found them."

"So, why could we see the Monkeys when they attacked us? I thought Bob said they were only mortal … during … the Night?"

Serena's skin suddenly pricked and hair on the back of her neck stood straight up. She gulped as she looked past the light of the torches, into the pitch-black shadows of the Trees.

Eyes.

Many eyes.

Large eyes, small eyes, round, narrowed, and slitted eyes. Eyes in clusters of two, three, five and eight. Eyes every color of the spectrum, all with dilated pupils, and all watching Serena suspiciously. Warily. Expectantly.

Nelson noticed the Girl's unease and put an arm around her in comfort.

"Not all of the monstrous beasts out there were forced under the Spell that made them invisible. Quite a few were left alone."

Serena shivered and snuggled closer to her warm friend.

"I don't like this Forest, Nelson. When we are out of this place, I never want to come back."

"Don't worry, Serena," whispered Nelson directly into her ear. He stared at the blooming Flowers at the Girl's slippered feet. "After this you will never have to come back to this Forest, ever again."

Something about the tone of his voice, or the smoothness of his words ,made Serena trust him completely. And there she fell asleep, leaning on his shoulder.

The rest of the next Day the group traveled through the hideous Forest of Many Eyes. The team was aghast at the challenging new language. Kate and Theo did not even try to pronounce the words, but Lindsey, Mike and Bob were all determined to learn. In a group of three they practiced saying things to one another to see if they could decode them.

"Eht Yks si uelb," said Lindsey.

"We already know that! Try this one: Ym hcamots si gnilworg," Mike proclaimed, swatting a bug away from his sharp red tunic and cape. He straightened a matching red hat with a fancy feather on his head. The feather swayed blithely as he moved.

"Your stomach is ... what? Oh, growling! Well, M'i yrgnuh oot!" Bob figured.

"Woh gnol litnu ew hcaer eht pmac?" Lindsey wanted to know.

"I don't know… I mean, I t'nod wonk. Uoy dlouhs ksa … oh Man, I don't think I can say Rockwicha's name backwards. Help me out here, guys!" Bob laughed.

"Siht … Tserof si… ypeerc," Kate finally said. The others fairly agreed with her, glad to see her join the group.

Serena, although she was walking some ways away so she could think to herself, agreed as well. After spending one long Night in the place, she now knew why there was no path to lead Travelers through its eerie wilderness. Because noCreature dared to enter it.

Most people, er, Creatures, that is, probably prefer to go around the Forest. Nelson has no choice but to lead us through it – we cannot waste any time in getting him to the Sparkline Mountain to claim the Throne,

"I raeh taht leurc secrof fo live era gnirehtag ni eht Lauteprep Sniatnuom ydaerla," Rockwicha told Serena as he joined her. "Yeht era gniraperp ot eka-trevo eht Enorht of Reverof."

Serena shook her head in amazement when she had decoded the language.

"Hopefully, er, I mean, yllufepoh, ti lliw ton tceffa ruo … ytefas elihw … gnilevart ni eht … Sniatnuom." The Girl spoke slowly, attempting to picture the words of her reply backwards in her head. She looked, somewhat envi-ously, over at her friend Nelson, who was talking so fast in the backwards language that even the Sky Warrior he was speaking to seemed to have to decipher the message before replying.

How does he speak so ... so fluently? she wondered to herself in thought. And, as if on cue, an answering thought fluttered up to her like a white Dove with an olive branch in its mouth. *Because he was taught the language by his scholars as a Prince, no doubt.*

Serena plodded ever onward, listening to the echoing of their crunching footsteps, the Birds trilling, and the buzzing of small, annoying Insects. She began to think of home, of Jerry, of the Goblins they had tied up. She thought of her friends at Bendar – Lilac, Mosslyn, and even that scratchy, pesky Prince Errenon.

How terrible at romancing that Boy is! she thought, and wondered sadly if he would ever find a Princess to marry. *I am not even a Princess, and yet he considers me a suitress. Hah, and I probably never will have a royal title in front of my name unless I marry a Prince.*

A fleeting picture of Nelson's face swept across Serena's mind and then disappeared into the Mists of her dreams. She felt her cheeks flush hot.

No, she did not have any other feelings toward Nelson except friendship. Serena shook her head with her eyes closed sheepishly.

That is not true, she realized. For over the past few Days she had noticed herself growing fonder and fonder of the Boy – to the point where she now questioned herself as to whether she felt the two were more than just friends. After all, he too had blushed when their hands touched.

The very thought rose a blush to her cheeks again, and she glanced over at the Halfbreed Boy.

I mustn't let him know until I am ready to, she thought, playing with her swishing blue skirt. *Though I cannot help but wonder if he is better at romancing than that dolt, Prince Errenon.*

She glanced up at him again to find him this time gazing at her as well. She smiled shyly and looked at the ground.

And I cannot also help but wonder whether he feels the same.

That evening the small group found the Boulder Tribe Camp. Serena was indeed very glad to find some sort of settlement with more than just a few Creatures. And, in truth, there were a lot more than a few Creatures in the Boulder

Tribe Camp. There were, perhaps, hundreds of the blue-skinned Humans in the camp, which was a great comfort to Serena for more than one reason. She always had felt much safer in a group of larger numbers - and never more so than now in the Forest of Many Eyes. She was also enormously tired from her long travels that Day – as they had not stopped once save to partake lunch. Her feet and legs ached, her shoulders, too, from the weight of her knapsack on them, and she felt quite ready to accept a warm meal and a long nap. Yet as she walked through the Sun-dappled loam that Day, she felt the horrible eyes watching her every move. Even though the monstrous Beasts were invisible and therefore unable to harm her in any way, Serena still knew that those green, orange, yellow, red, and all other eerie-colored eyes were closely observing her. They were watching her, staring firmly at her, boring nails of dread deep down into her very soul.

The Sky Human Camp seemed a place of great calm, security, and protection to Serena. The huts of the camp had been hardly visible at first, but the telltale streams of smoke, drifting up through a few of the large reed pipes in climbing tendrils, had warned her of the inhabitance. The huts were like nothing Serena had ever seen: they were about as big as little haystacks, and their coverings of leaves, twigs, seeds, and even small Trees and Weedy Plants melted them evenly into the disguise of the Forest floor, making them very hard to spot.

Another factor that told Serena that they were rapidly approaching the camp was the tall line of torches that stood out in the distance. At the moment, they were not lit, for it was broad Daylight and there was no fear of the Prowlers stealing anything from them. They were also very well disguised with the background, looking like tiny Tree trunks grown straight in a row. Only did Serena spot these torches when Theo pointed them out to everyCreature.

And the last and final sign that Serena received that they were coming upon the Sky Humans' Campground was that the Sky Human Warriors rushed forward and yelled and whooped loudly. Serena knew that they were very glad to be home; apparently they had been away from their previous camp for quite some time, and could not wait to relieve their homesickness.

"Ew era emoh ta tsal!" declared Rockwicha joyously, both arms upraised and his staff held high in one hand. This only sent the Warriors galloping quicker, panting heavier, their hearts swelling with pride as they grew closer to their home.

Serena smiled.

Oh, how fast Bertha might see me come running, if only I could find my way home, she thought sadly. She watched the Sky Humans racing ahead of each other, eager to be home and in safe arms. They leaped one by one over the tall torches.

And then Serena noticed something very odd, very quaint. Something she had not noticed at all before. Where were the doors to those little hutch-houses of the Sky Humans? She could see tiny windows – with tiny blue faces peeking out of their circular shapes warily. But there were no doors.

How does somebody get into those little hutches? They can't climb in the windows: they're too small...

The first Sky Human poked his head up out of the ground.

The ground!

Serena, puzzled, grabbed Nelson's arm as he strode over to her.

"The ground, Nelson!" she howled, testing the Boy's circulation. "His head – his head just poked up out of the ground!"

"I know," Nelson chuckled calmly. "That is the way they enter and exit their hutches – by tunnels dug in the ground."

Serena relaxed a little as, all over the campground, circular disks of clay topped with loam, dirt and twigs popped off of holes in the ground, much like Man holes in the City. It was out of these tunnels that the Boulder Tribe of Sky Humans appeared, quickly finding loved ones and welcoming them back.

Serena and the remaining discovery team did not have any one certain hutch to report to, and so they simply wandered into the center of the camp, where an ever-burning fire was kept, Day and Night, watched and fed by a Man known as the Fire Tender.

This they learned from Nelson as he hurried to join up with them by the fire.

"Rockwicha has granted us permission to sleep in his hutch toNight," he broadcasted. "He is a very generous Man, and told us that he did not want us outside in the Night time in the Forest of Many Eyes."

"Sounds like he knows these parts very well," Bob noted, his thankful dark blue eyes alit by the fire.

"He does," admitted Nelson. He squatted on the ground next to where Serena sat. "He says that his people use the term 'campground' as a title for a temporary settlement."

"And if this is a temporary settlement, that probably means they've been here for awhile," Lindsey figured, stretching her legs out in front of her.

Indeed, Serena thought. She tucked her legs under her skirt ruffles. *It must have taken them long enough just to dig out their hutches and disguise them to deceive the eyes.*

"They also said that they are going to have a great ceremony toNight to welcome home their Warriors," Nelson continued, flicking a small piece of bark into the fire. All around them, torches were being lit – next to the small holes leading into the hutches, inside the hutches to give them light, and especially around the torches that gated the small settlement away from the wild horrors that roamed the Woods. Slowly, like the Stars emerging in the Night Sky, the blinking, evil eyes of all colors and shapes appeared once more. The hair on the back of Serena's neck pricked and stood up again, and, instinctively, she scooted closer to Nelson.

Before long, a group of Sky Humans including the Warriors who had traveled with Nelson and Serena, emerged from the well-lit hutches. Or rather, from the small holes in the ground which led to them. They came dressed in strange, oddly-stitched clothing and dangling beads and bones which clacked in their hair, from around their necks, wrists, ankles, waists and clothing. All were colored blue and blue-green, and a few even blue-violet. Symbols in blue paint were written on their bodies and arms, and a scent hung on them that reminded Serena of the Ocean.

Serena watched them make a circle around the fire, join hands, and bow their heads in silence. A single drum pounded softly from behind a hutch somewhere, and slowly the Sky Humans lifted their heads to gaze into the blazing flames of the fire. Rockwicha nodded his head and pulled some sort of blue dust from his pocket. He took a step back; the others followed his example. He threw the blue powder into the fire. Instantly, the flames roared and flared up in solid blue, tiny white-blue sparks shooting, cracking, whistling and popping in the air.

All at once, more blue people emerged from the blue-lit village, and joined the first in a wild dancing spree. Singing, chanting and laughing tinged the air along with flutes, drums and many other sounds Serena had never heard.

The seven newcomers sat with their backs to the hutches, staring shamelessly. None of them, save for perhaps Nelson and Theo, had ever seen such a grand show. Mike and Bob laughed, Theo clapped his hands, Lindsey and Serena got up to go see what fun there was to be had, Kate drew up a nostril in disgust, and Nelson simply smiled and leaped up to greet the dancers.

~*~*~*~*~

That Night, Serena had to admit, was probably one of the greatest Nights of her life. Lindsey and she (and sometimes also Nelson) danced around, sang some odd, yet somehow melodious songs, and ate many delicious foods cooked by the Sky Human wives. They also found new friends with the Sky Human Children, Warriors and mothers. A specific group of adolescent Boys followed Serena and Lindsey around for a long time, hooting and whistling ignorantly until their mother found them and dragged them away by the cartilage of their ears.

Serena was in the middle of talking to a new friend (who was also a Warrior and an expert cook), named Karnilia, when Nelson suddenly found her and beckoned her to follow him. The look on his face was urgent.

"What? What is it?" she breathed, searching for some sign in his wide green eyes. He led her away from the celebration to a dimly lit corner. Serena was very uncomfortable with all of the blinking, forever-watching eyes peering out at her from the darkness in all directions. She felt her face lose color and go white with fear; she did not much like being away from the festivity in a dark corner.

"I – I have to tell you something." he said finally.

"Yes?" Serena replied, cautiously glancing over her shoulder at the narrowing eyes. She gulped, knowing that they were listening. She pawed the ground impatiently

But then she straightened like a board.

She was alone.

With Nelson.

Is this the time to tell him? she wondered in thought. She glanced at the eyes. *No, the eyes are listening to us ... and I am too frightened.*

"Something ... very important," Nelson continued.

"Yes?" Serena whinnied, sounding a touch cross. Seeing his confused expression, however, she softened and then blurted, "I'm sorry, Nelson, I just don't like all these eyes watching us ... it's making me anxious and uncomfortable,"

Nelson shifted his feet and Serena could see that he, too, was not exactly delighted with the presence of the ever-watching eyes.

"I know," he murmured, glancing at them in ware. "Listen, I've kind of been noticing something-"

"Serena! Serena!" cried Theo, bursting into the clearing and grabbing

251

Serena's arm. "Come dance with me! Come on!"

Serena's face broke into a grin and she looked at Nelson.

"Only if Nelson can dance with us." she laughed.

Nelson's face turned beet red, and he took a couple of steps back.

"Oh, no … you two go on, now. I, uh … I don't know how to dance,"

"Well, neither do I!" Serena exclaimed, her heart beating with the sound of the drums. "We can teach each other!"

"Yeah, we'll all dance!" cheered Theo, dragging the two off to the center fire. Serena hoped that Nelson missed the blush that arose to her cheeks.

Serena's muscles ached.

But she was warm and very comfortable.

She was lying on her stomach, limbs sprawled.

Something sweet that reminded her of honey, hung on the air.

And, to her surprise, something warm was covering her hand.

She swung her head over to see-

- Nelson's hand on top of hers!

The worst flush the Girl had ever experienced rose to her cheeks. She knew that Nelson was only being comforting and friendly because he knew of her dislike for the Prowlers' eyes, but now that she had discovered her true admiration of the Boy, to her it meant something entirely different.

I must not let him know until the time is right. she reminded herself again, withdrawing her hand slowly. Feeling the drowsy effects of sleep still lingering in her eyes, she rested her head on the ground, chin on hands, and stared at the sleeping Boy.

She remembered, vaguely, the Night before. Serena had been so exhausted after the ceremony that she even fell asleep outside next to the fire while watching the Warriors and dancers close up the celebration. Nelson or one of the other Boys must have picked her up and taken her into this hutch. Probably Nelson, or so she wished.

Look at him … she sighed in thought. *He is so humble, so ordinary. Who could even suspect him of being the true Heir to the Throne of Forever? And yet, he is anything but ordinary! He is his own person, and so unique in all of his inimitable little ways. He speaks smoothly in a backwards language, he uses his secret Powers to save us from danger, and he flies … oh, he flies … something I could never do if I tried.*

Slowly, Serena reached out and stroked the uneven bangs that hung over Nelson's brow handsomely. Oh, how she admired him!

"Aneres?" came a soft voice from the tunnel-like door.

It was Karnilia.

The long, dark-blue-haired Sky Human scuttled into the room and sat beside Serena. And only then did Serena notice the shape of the room: dome-like, the floor (carpeted in a clean, soft Animal fur) being the only flat surface. Two tiny circular windows poured the first pink rays of light into the large hutch, or at least the upper portion.

This must be like their attic … she thought, and questioned her new friend on it.

"Siht si tros fo ekil eht citta. Eht mottob roolf si hcum regral naht siht; dna yb eht yaw, tsafkaerb si pu dna gnimoc yltrohs – taht si yhw I emac pu ereh. Uoy yam emoc nwod fi uoy tnaw – I kniht eht tser fo ruoy maet si pu."

Serena nodded in reply, noticing that the rest of the team must be downstairs, because she and Nelson were alone in the small, warm room. The only other feature from the inside that she felt was interesting was the large, fat pipe made from little bundles of hollow reeds tied together that ran from the floor to the clay-smoothed ceiling. This, she surmised, was their chimney.

"I lliw emoc nwod htiw uoy won," she stuttered, stopping to make sure she had constructed the words correctly.

Nelson stirred beside her, and she sat up and quickly added,

"Sa noos sa Noslen snekawa,"

Serena and Nelson quickly found that the bottom floor was quite commodious and spacious with strange, home-made furniture and rugs. There was no light in the downstairs, save for the light that streamed down from the dome-like attic and in through the tunnel with a ladder that was the door. Instead of torches, which would burn away the oxygen, the Sky Humans carried around little lanterns that held within them a particularly bright species of Firefly. It was not at all uncommon to see a Sky Human "feeding" his or her lantern.

The ground on the lower floor of the hutch was much like the upstairs in that it had Animal fur for carpeting. It was quite unique because there was not only one Animal skin, but many, with all of their varying colors, textures, designs and thicknesses gracing the bare feet of the blue-skinned people. The walls and ceiling were coated with rock-hard clay, which also varied in sheen, and from such hung woven tapestries, Firefly lanterns and other such decorative items. Blue-tinted Humans buzzed about officiously, constantly crawling in and out of the little narrow tunnels that connected one hutch to all the others; Serena felt like an Ant when she followed Nelson and Karnilia through one of the wider passageways. This led them into a warm, well-lit kitchen and dining area.

There Serena met up with the others from her crew, and together they partook of a splendid - and very filling - breakfast of blue eggs, rice and juice that tasted very tart. Serena thought it had a twinge of blueberry in it as well.

"Ahciwkcor sah dediced ot dael uoy dna ruoy werc ot eht Eulb Hsram, rof ruoy cioreh stroffe ni gnieerf ruo Labirt Sroirraw morf regnad. I llahs ynapmocca uoy sa llew. Ew lliw evael nehw uoy evah dehsinif gnikaerb ruoy tsaf." Karnilia announced to the dining team of explorers. She caught Serena's gaze and smiled happily, obviously thrilled about getting to accompany the discoverers on their trip to the Blue Marsh. Serena smiled, too. The Girl would be good company for her.

Lindsey and Mike sat across from them, Mike's befeathered cap swaying in the Breeze of a blue Human as he walked past. Bob and Kate were sitting behind them with Theo, talking animatedly with a blue Human that had caught Kate's eye.

"Wow, I don't even think we could have gotten service this good even in the bigger cities on Earth," Lindsey said, cutting up her egg. She salted it and prepared to eat it. "Mmm, these people are so hospitable – and all we did was arrive."

"I agree," added Mike, buttering a piece of toast that looked to be studded with blueberries. "Even at Bendar – I would never have guessed that they would be so humble and generous. They treated us like royalty!"

"We did save some of them from slavery, though," Nelson reminded them. "That is, Serena did."

"We worked together on that effort!" she argued, smiling at him from the corner of her eye. "And so we worked together to save ourselves, and the Sky Humans unknowingly, from the purple Monkey Prowlers. I'd just say we were lucky on that – and I'm really glad we found some Creatures who know how to camp in this Forest better than we do."

"I'm starting to think these Sky Humans are overly generous in their reward for us," Nelson muttered to Serena as Karnilia left to tend to clearing another table in the kitchen that a group of Sky Humans had recently departed with.

"Me too." Serena agreed. She watched a group of young Boys staring wide-eyed at them. Obviously, it was not often (or even likely in their lives) that they got to see a Sun Human. Theo found them and taught them his personal stance of staring, and before long, his two huge green eyes had joined the Sea of blue ones that stared shamelessly at Serena and Nelson.

"I'm starting to think that a certain Boy has become rather obnoxious lately," Serena brought up.

Nelson looked up in surprise, and Serena directed his gaze to Theo, who, upon hearing these words, was also smiling fiendishly.

"Me too," growled Nelson, and he stood up, eyeing his younger brother warningly. He straightened his back, flexed his arms, and pursed his lips closed determinedly. His chest was pushed forward in a show of strength, his cheeks grew red and his eyebrows lowered. His flaming eyes narrowed at the group.

Serena wanted to laugh at his act – for she did know, or at least she thought she knew, that the Boy was acting. He did look so stern! Yet, after awhile, he actually took on a menacing appearance with a battle light in his green eyes that Serena had never seen before. She nearly gulped and felt herself cowering under his haughty glare, even though it was not directed at her.

Nelson drew in a breath, his nostrils flaring, his jaw grim, and his eyes burning. He did not need to wait for an expected result. Theo's eyes grew larger, as did his peers' (if that was even possible) and before Nelson could open his mouth, the Boys had scampered off, striving to put as much distance as was possible between them and Nelson.

And as soon as the last blue-haired head had vanished, Nelson slumped back into his seat, releasing a long sigh. He smiled at Serena.

"About scared them wet, did I not?" he chuckled, digging into a bowl of grainy, hot cereal.

Serena laughed, sitting up at once. She did not say so, but she felt that the Boy had nearly scared her wet, too. She had never seen him in such a dreadfully frightening stance before. It was like seeing a different person in him – a hidden personality that was seldom revealed.

It was then that Serena had a thought.

A horrible, terrible thought.

Could he be going back for revenge?

"Heeheehee!" the Boy snickered suddenly, slapping a napkin over his mouth as Mike dug into his own bowl of cereal. Lindsey shook her head as Mike discovered a small blue newt poking its head up at him from the middle of his bowl.

"So that's what they were up to," Mike sniveled sarcastically. He straightened his polished spectacles and stood, the feather on his hat wobbling in a

256

wisp of air. "I'll show them… check your food, friends, I'll take care of the problem."

Nelson was red in the face as Mike ambled off, pulling up his hoes imperiously.

Serena and Lindsey rounded on Nelson.

"Nelson, you didn't-" Lindsey gasped, putting her spoon down.

Nelson pushed a hand through his hair, chuckling.

"No, I didn't," he replied, and Serena narrowed her eyes at him.

"Then who did?"

"Theo. I was laughing because that is what he used to do to the poor, old cook in the kitchen. He used to say that he was too big to be eating third helpings. Hahaha – poor old Tinger would chase him round and round that kitchen for hours, just dying to swat him and teach him a lesson. Oh … sometimes I do wish I could go home,"

Lindsey made to inquire of his origin, but Nelson, suddenly standing, looked at Serena nervously.

"Well that was a superb breakfast. I think … I think I'll go help Karnilia now. Can I take your dishes for you?"

Serena sighed, obligingly helping him clear the table.

If only he knew that I knew … then there would be no more secrets between us, she thought longingly.

The group of 12 set out from the Sky Human campground directly after breakfast. Rockwicha wished them well, because he was unable to accompany them on their quest under the fear that his people would suffer attack, and when they would have needed him, he would be elsewhere. He was, after all, their Leader and had been away from his Tribe for longer than he had wished in the first place.

"Yam kcul levart htiw uoy sa uoy yenruoj ot eht Eulb Hsram!" the Tribal Chief had called after them as they marched off, guided - and Guarded - by five of the Sky Warriors. "Dna od hctaw tuo rof eht Thgin Srelworp!"

Even that simplified, polite term for the Monsters, said backwards, sent chills up Serena's spine. Night Prowlers indeed!

With their heads – and hopes – held high, the journeyers set off in the Forest of Many Eyes. They traveled until noon, talking excitedly about their

257

quest. They stopped at a small clearing surrounded by bountiful Banyans, their branches drooping, laden with Jeweled fruit. Of these Banyans the Travelers partook, saving rations for the journey ahead. Serena soon learned the names of the other four warriors, other than Karnilia.

There was Achel, tall and lanky with her dark blue hair pulled up in a braided bun, Jedin who was stocky and had piercing light blue eyes, Bameis with his deadly spear and strong limbs and looks, and Sealth, who was by far the smallest but was exceedingly agile in her speed and acrobatics.

Introductions had been made before they took off from the camp, and in their excited chatter as they moved ever Eastward (and a touch South) the four had come to be warmly accepted and well-loved by the time lunch rolled around.

Serena was conversing with Karnilia, Lindsey and Sealth when the whole team heard a muffled shout pierce the air. Their conversation shattered like broken glass shards and died immediately.

Finally, Jedin spoke.

"Tahw saw taht?" he enthused.

Silence stung the air.

"Ydobemos si ni elbuort!" Sealth exclaimed, leaping up with her spear at the ready.

"ON!" shouted Bameis, putting a hand to steady the crew. "Ew tonnac droffa ot og ot s'erutaerCyreve eucser ta ruo nwo esnepxe lla eht emit," he reasoned.

"Ew evah ruo nwo tseuq ot wollof," Achel added, shaking her head in agreement.

Serena had heard the outburst too. It was high-pitched and murderous, a very unpleasant, scratchy sound to meet anyCreature's ears. Yet Serena had already looked past the physical sound of the voice – and seen the ferocious message it carried with it - distress. Some poor Creature was in great distress. And Serena suddenly felt determined to release the Creature of its peril. Why she was drawn to it, she didn't know.

"We have to help it!" she said loudly, just as the call sounded again through the Forest.

Nelson's eyes snapped over to her.

"But you heard what Bameis said! We can't – SERENA! NO!"

But the Boy was too late.

Serena, her heart thundering, was already sprinting to the scene, skirts flashing wildly as she was drawn ever closer by some odd feeling of defense. She could hear, as she blundered along, the sounds of the others crashing through the undergrowth in her pursuit. Mike had almost caught up to her, his long strides being two of hers.

"What are you doing?" he hissed, making to grab her. She dodged him and kept running.

"We may be that poor Creature's only hope!"

She burst into another little clearing just in time to see a winged Human with the legs of a Bird look sharply in her direction. At the same time he released an arrow at a cornered, wailing Creature that resembled an overgrown Snake with hefty front limbs and the back legs of a Bird.

"No!" she shrieked, rushing to shield the howling Creature. Nelson, who bumped into her from behind, caught her wrist and pulled her back into the Trees.

"No, Serena!" he hissed into her ear. Serena had an offensive feeling from the tone of his voice; he sounded like a mother scolding her young Child. And by no means was Serena a young Child! Mike took her other arm and tried to pull her back into the branches.

"No, do not interfere! Both Harpies and Sirrushes can be dangerous!" Nelson told her.

Jedin, Achel, Sealth, Karnilia and Bameis arrived behind them. Bameis had a panting Theo on his back.

"Tahw si ehs gniod? Ll'ehs llik su lla!" Sealth huffed.

Serena had no idea which Creature was the Harpie and which was the Sirrush, but she did know that the Snake-like Creature was injured badly from the arrow that had pierced its front paw. It whined and moaned in its raspy little voice and thrashed about on the ground, blood being turned and folded into the Sand.

"But you guys, the Creature is wounded! Can't you see-"

"HALT!" growled the Human, flexing his great feathered wings. Nelson's grip on her tightened. The wings were rustic orange-yellow color, the very same color as the Man's hair. His thin, storky legs were bent backwards, and though they could not see the actual legs (because the Man was wearing thin leggings), they knew that they were the legs of a great Bird from the sharp-looking talons that stood rooted into the ground in place of Human feet. The dark eyes of the Creature studied them; those that were visible to him stared back. Kate drew in a sharp breath while still trying to catch her breath.

"Who are you?" shouted the Human-like Creature, pushing back his cloak with his bow in one hand. "Why have you interfered?"

Serena did not feel the least bit sorry or embarrassed, looking now to the blue and green scaled Creature, blood gushing out of its open, dirty wound. It laid heaving and panting on the ground, moaning softly and blinking its large, beady black eyes, which now had warm, clear liquid running freely from it - tears.

An extreme feeling of pity welled up inside Serena until she felt her heart was near to bursting. Freeing herself from Nelson's sweaty grip, she stood from her place behind a Tree and walked straight out into the clearing.

Alone.

Unshielded.

And afraid.

Behind her, she could hear the group whispering quietly. She hoped they weren't planning anything.

Ignoring the look of shock that masked the Human-like Creature's face, the Girl kneeled before the moaning Snake Beast, and ripped a ruffle from her petticoat. Lying a comforting hand on the Animal's brow, she plucked the arrow from its tender wound, snapped it in half, and threw it to the feet of the winged Human.

She began to bandage the wound with the strip of cloth without saying a single word. The Man's dark eyes blinked and he seemed to overcome his shock. His eyes were now filled with anger and hatred. Serena saw that his knuckles were white, fisting around his bow.

"Why have you done this?" he demanded. "EveryCreature knows that Sirrushes are dangerous, flesh-eating Creatures!"

"Not always!" said a calm voice from the Woods. Nelson stepped out, hand on hilt. "They are near extinct nowaDays, too. Certainly a good Harpie such as yourself would know this."

The Human-like Creature, or rather, the Harpie, stood tall with his chin protruding boldly.

"I did," he replied, staking his bow into the ground.

Serena stood now, holding the unconscious Creature like a babe. And as she studied its sleeping features, she found that it was a Child. The fangs in its open mouth were not fully developed, and Serena could feel something of a fontanel on the back of its tiny head as she ran a hand over it. A single glance from Mike confirmed her beliefs.

"It's a Child," Serena half-whispered, stroking the baby Sirrush's brow. Her eyes met those of the Harpie. "Why would you do such a thing? To a Child? Haven't you got any Children of your own?"

"As a matter of fact," growled the Harpie, turning to face Serena, "I do. And they are very hungry Children right now, having nothing to nourish their growing bodies. Their mother is sick and I am left to care for them - and I must hunt in order to do this."

Serena looked back at the limp figure of the baby Sirrush. To think that a person would attempt to eat it sent nauseous pangs to her stomach. An idea struck her, and carefully, she laid the sleeping babe into Lindsey's outstretched arms. She removed her knapsack, checking to be sure that Teresa's diary and the money within it was safely hidden in a pocket in her skirts. She held the haversack, bulging with provisions, out to the Harpie, whose expression had changed from frustration to surprised hopefulness.

"Take this as a replacement," she said swiftly, handing the knapsack to him. "Inside is dried meat, fruit, and other tarts and cakes that will nourish your Children."

Serena did not care whether the Harpie Man was lying or telling the truth about his Children - the only thing she cared about at the moment was getting the baby Sirrush away from him and its wound cleaned and more efficiently bandaged. She turned and followed Nelson back into the shadows of the Forest, and only stopped when she heard a squeak behind her.

"Fank yoo!" chirped a small Harpie Boy who had suddenly appeared at the Man's ankles. A tiny Girl, presumably his sister, leafed through the haversack next to him. The Harpie Man smiled, awestruck.

"You're welcome." Serena replied, and hurriedly scampered off after Nelson.

"What were you thinking?" screeched Kate, safely out of hearing range of the Harpies. Something within Serena kept her attitude calm, as though all her anger had left her long ago.

"I was thinking of how I, as a mother, would feel if my Child was eaten by Harpies out of hunger," she responded softly as though she were speaking to herself. She shifted the sleeping baby Sirrush in her arms to allow Lindsey more space to bandage and clean the terrible wounds.

It was nearly evening now, and the group had stopped temporarily to restock on fruit from some close-growing Banyan Trees. Bameis and Jedin talked excitedly to Nelson as they watched Kate, Theo, Karnilia, Sealth and Achel gather fruit from the Banyan Trees. Mike and Bob were doing their best to speak to Nelson, who had been leaning against a Tree, obviously disheartened. Serena wished she could speak to him, but she was busy with the baby Sirrush.

They had traveled all Day, not quite as excited as when they had started out. Lindsey took the opportunity to rebandage the infectious wound on the Sirrush's little forepaw, which seemed to be very deep. They had not had the chance to rebandage the injury earlier because they had set off again straight after the close incident with the Harpy, determined to put as much distance as was possible in between the two. Nelson had had a harsh word or two with Serena earlier, but she repelled his blame with fact and guilt, and he soon settled down to agree. Serena knew that his anger was only his fear in failing to protect her.

Serena's arms were indeed very sore and tired from carrying the sleeping babe (who was about as big as Theo) just as her feet were aching from prolonged traveling. Yet her shoulders felt pleasantly light without the added weight of her knapsack, and she was thankful for that.

"Taht saw yrev evarb fo uoy ot eucser eht Hsurris, uoy wonk." Achel commented to her as they pressed off to find a suitable camping spot for the Night. "Ti saw ton gnihtemos neve I dluow evah eht egaruoc ot od."

Serena smiled at the compliment and shifted the baby higher on her chest so that both of its little paws rested over her shoulder. She watched the limp, scaly tail, complete with a cluster of rattles perched on the end, swinging back and forth as she walked.

"I dluoc ton dnats ot ees ti reffus," was all she said. Jedin, with his burning bright blue eyes, caught up with her.

"Sey, Sehsurris neve ta siht gnuoy ega era semitemos suoregnad. Ti si a doog gniht taht siht eno saw oot kaew ot etib uoy." he added, plunging his thick spear into the soil. Serena leaped over a fallen limb, careful not to jostle the resting Sirrush.

Little did she know that her efforts were in vain.

"I t'nod kniht ti saw gniog ot etib em," she said calmly, patting the bony, scaly back.

This was a wrong move.

"Errrrrraaaaaaaagh," grumbled the Sirrush in a low tone, and both Achel and Jedin leaped back as though Serena were on fire. Serena herself stopped in her tracks, eyes wide with fear. She gulped as she felt the Sirrush's back talons clawing at her skirt.

"Put it down," advised Mike in a loud whisper. "And nobody move. Judging from its eyes, it seems to hunt whatever moves."

Serena was the target of every eye. She would have to move in order to put it down.

But I cannot put it down, she reasoned with herself, *I cannot simply let the Creature go along its own way when it is injured – then it would only make itself into an easier prey.*

She let out a silent sigh, and calmly began stroking the growling babe's back.

Perhaps if I soothe it, it will stop its fussing.

The babe stopped growling, not certain what to make of this. Nelson came up and laid a hand on the Sirrush's large, flat, Snake-like head, and its tensed little body slumped against Serena again.

And, just when the baby had been soothed and cooed almost back to sleep, a dark shadow appeared from out of the Trees.

A very tall, very long shadow.

With gleaming blue-green scales and beady black eyes.

And it spoke.

"*Mine*!" the mother Sirrush rasped, the colossal head held high. She was enormous - five times as large as any crocodile Serena had never seen, and five thousand times as scary. Her black eyes studied the group critically, her throat pulsing, tongue flickering, teeth gleaming, and sharp front claws and back talons raking deep graves in the soil.

"That Child isssss mine," wheezed the mother, advancing menacingly. "Give him back to me!"

Serena felt sweat trickling down the back of her neck already. Obediently, she held her stature calm and lowered the baby to the ground slowly. As the mother spotted the injured front paw which made the juvenile hop, skip and limp, she let out a low roar.

"Rrrrrrr!" she growled, teeth gnashing. "What have you done to him?! He isssss injured!"

"We saved him," Serena said boldly, sounding much more calm and confident than she felt.

"Sssssaved him? From what, pray?" hissed the mother Sirrush, eyeing each and every one of them warily.

"A Harpie," answered Nelson, courageously striding forward a pace. "A Harpie who was in great need of food for his own Children."

"Ssssss, bah! Did he not know that Ssssirushessss are nearly exsssssstinct?" the mother demanded.

"Well, if he didn't," Serena put in, catching a sidelong glance from Nelson, "he does now. I do believe he won't be hunting Sirrushes for awhile."

A smile spread on Nelson's face as he saw the double meaning in the Girl's quote.

The baby Sirrush finally managed to scramble over to his mother, who shielded the Child with her hefty front paws.

"I ssssssssshall exchange the life of my Child for your own livesssssss, for if I had not known you had, ah, sssssaved him, I would most likely have taken you home to feed him and the resssst of hisss ssssiblingssss."

Serena felt a burst of adrenaline in her system. That meant plainly that if she and Nelson had not spoken out when they did and she had not released the baby Sirrush, they would all be dinner to this overgrown Snake and her brood.

"Well," she started, kicking the dust with her shoe nervously, "at least he is safe now. W-we were starting to wonder what we would do with him,"

"You would give him to me, that'ssssss what you would do with him,"

"But, see, we did not know where you were … we are lucky you found us," Lindsey noted.

"True, true," hissed the mother Sirrush, stroking her baby's back with her paw as she looked up at the darkening Sky. Already the Woods were growing shadowy, and smaller eyes were beginning to appear. Serena shivered.

Those eyes are going to be the death of me, she thought, feeling her skin prickle uncomfortably. *No wonder there are none but the bravest souls living in this horrific place,*

"Ti si llew emit ew detrap; eht Srelworp llahs eb tuo noos," Bameis stated, pawing the ground impatiently. Or nervously.

"What did he-" grumbled a confused mother Sirrush.

"He says that it is well time that we parted, that the Prowlers will be out soon," translated Bob. He, too, pawed the ground, sending a sidelong glance at Serena.

"Ew deen ot tes pu eht sehcrot!" Achel realized, jumping to life. "Ew tsum tup meht pu erofeb-"

"Siht lliw eb ruo etispmac, neht," Nelson decided.

"Tub-"

"Sssssssstop!" hissed the mother Sirrush angrily, stomping her front claw to get their attention. And it certainly did, for the ground shook as she did. She cleared her throat and began to speak in a calm, perhaps even kind tone.

"I do not even know what you are ssssssquabbling about, but my name isssss Trumple, and I ssssssshall housssssse you for the Night ssssssinccce you have brought my baby back to me," Trumple, the mother Sirrush, seemed to smile. "I have noticcced that your lot issss not well pleassssed with the many Eyesssss. You ssssshall be well sssssshielded in my den from the Prowlersssss,"

Something, Serena felt, *about her Child being safe and close to her has calmed this mother.*

Jedin straightened his back and answered in a jumble of words that he spat out so fast that Serena could not catch them. Kate, however, did. Her face burned with either the fear of oncoming Prowlers or embarrassment.

"Jedin said, 'What kind of fools do you take us for?'." she narrowed her hollow, dark brown eyes at Trumple in warning. "We may be 'not well pleased' with the Many Eyes, but if we follow you, how do we know we will not be bringing ourselves into greater danger? How do we know that you and your brood will not just-"

"Because she is our only hope," said Mike suddenly, face upturned to the Heavens. He squinted through his tiny spectacles. "If we set up the torches, they will only be extinguished in the Rain."

"What Rain?" squawked Kate, thrusting her head back to observe the blue Sky. Her black hair, nearly as dark as the Night Sky itself, swung back in its purple bow and smacked Sealth on the nose. The Sky Human sneezed. "I don't see any Clouds!"

"Yessss, but you do not ssseee any Sssstarsssss either, do you?"

"No."

"Sssssso the Raincloudsss are thick enough to sssssswath out the Sssstarsss." Trumple pointed out. She looked straight at Serena. "I believe your friend there issss correct. It issss to Rain thisssss Night, and the Prowl-erssss will be out thick."

Nelson, in one fluid movement, had appeared beside Serena.

"What do you think?" he whispered into her ear. "Should we trust her?"

Serena smiled uncomfortably, and moved closer to the Boy.

"You tell me," she breathed. "You know more about these Creatures than I do."

"Emos Sehsurris era doog-derutan, I reah," Karnilia put in, watching Trumple caress her injured juvenile. "Dna I t'nod wonk tuoba uoy, tub I ev-eileb siht eno si efas. Ees eht yaw ehs si htiw reh Dlihc? Tahw erom foorp od uoy deen?"

"Hcum," Nelson replied. "Esuaceb I evah draeh taht yeht era yrev ykaens sa llew, hguoht emos fo meht yam ton eb live yltcaxe."

"Dna siht dluoc osla eb a part," Serena pointed out, talking very slowly indeed. She was still becoming accustomed to this strange backward language of the Sky Humans. "Ehs dluoc ylno eb gnitca taht yaw ot eveiced su,"

"Yan, ees woh eht Dlihc si gnitcaer yletanoitceffa oot? I kniht ew lliw eb enif," Karnillia put in. She tossed her head of long blue hair back over her shoulder.

Nelson nodded.

"Neht ti si delttes," announced Bameis, who had been listening closely to the conversation behind them. "Thginot ew lliw dneps ni eht S'hsurris ned."

~*~*~*~*~

266

In Trumple's den, Serena looked outside to see the Rain pouring down in thick white sheets. It pelted the ground all over, streaming in very small Rivulets in the Forest. A merry fire, which Nelson had lit to the delight of Gomper (the baby Sirrush they had saved) and his two sisters, Treklin and Hantor, now crackled brightly in the center of the place.

Trumple's den was actually no more than a tiny Cavern, smoothed out by some unknown source. Three even walls, ceiling, and floor reminded Serena of when she was a tiny Girl in a Sand box – she used to take a spoon and scoop little holes out of the Sand. Days later she would come back to check on her miniscule den, and would find a fat Frog or Toad roosting in it to hide from the hot Summer Sun. This brought much delight to Serena at her young age.

Regardless of the Cavern's symbolism to the Girl's past memories, the very first thing Serena had checked for when they had first approached it was the signs of a CaveLore. And, to her relief, she found that the place had a couple of stalagmites at the entrance, and no stench of rotting death clinging to the air. It was true that the place carried its own specific odor, not exactly a pleasant one, but one that was much more tolerable than the distinctive smell of the CaveLore, which seemed to have burned itself into the Girl's nostrils.

There was a back to the Cave, which rose Serena to her conclusion that were was no environmental danger here. There were a few scattered Rocks and Boulders covered with Moss in the back, and the ceiling and floor was Sanded smooth by wear, and over all, Serena felt the place was very homely. That is, homely compared to the perilous Prowlers that lurked in the shadows of the Forest, staring in at them from the entranceway, like a living Sea of eyes.

It was over this crackling little fire that Nelson offered to cook a Deer that Trumple managed to drag in. Serena was appalled at watching Nelson skin and cook the poor, dead Creature. The sounds of ripping flesh and dripping blood echoed in the Girl's ear, and even when she turned away, the shadows cast upon the smooth walls by the fire were magnified to a monstrous size. Serena had simply to sit back in the corner by some Rocks and wait until he was fin-ished while Nelson impressed his audience with his knowledge of cooking.

Theo sat with her at the back of the Cave for awhile, watching the two Sirrush sisters, Treklin and Hantor, playing with each other while poor Gomper crawled up and set his head on Serena's knees and fell asleep. Sneakily, Serena questioned Theo as to where he had come from, but the little Boy only looked at her, shrugged, and told her that Nelson forbade him to tell her. Disappointed, she moved on to the subject of Sirrushes and what he had learned about them while he was still a Prince.

Given the circumstances and with her knapsack being gone, Serena forced herself to eat a portion of the roasted venison. She found it to be quite good, and even helped herself to another piece after finding that she was very hungry.

After supper the group huddled down in the back with full stomachs and droopy eyelids to catch some slumber. Trurmple laid at the entrance to her Cave like a Dog at a Man's feet, guarding her three Children and her newfound friends. After commenting earlier that she was the scariest thing they would probably find in the Forest, Serena felt somewhat secure and believed that she may be able to sleep that Night.

But, just as she was leaning over on a Moss-encrusted Rock to fall asleep, a hand found hers in the dark. A big hand.

"Serena." whispered Nelson, sliding around in front of her. "Are you alright? Where were you when I was fixing supper?"

"I," Serena sighed, searching for his green eyes in the dark. "I wasn't really … fond of of the sounds of ripping skin and … and blood … and …"

"Ohhh, I see." Nelson sounded sarcastic. "You're just jealous of my cooking. What did you think of it?"

Serena erupted into a long, Cavernous yawn.

"Actually, I thought it was very good. And don't tease me about gore – it's just one of those things some people never get used to seeing."

She heard Nelson's tenor chuckle and found his twinkling almond-shaped eyes in the dark. He was sitting straight in front of her.

"So, ah … do you … remember …"

"Remember? Remember what?" Serena said sleepily. "What haven't I remem-"

"Shhhh …" Nelson's finger somehow found its place over her lips. "I meant, Serena … about … well, you know … when I tried to tell you something last Night?"

Serena's memory flashed before her, and she remembered when Nelson had pulled her aside at the Boulder Tribe Campgrounds.

"Yes?" she said, suddenly eager. Slowly, with the waning embers of the fire glowing behind him, Nelson reached up and grasped her hand. He nervously rubbed the back of his neck and sighed.

"Serena, I …I have … I have this cramp in my shoulders … I was wondering if you would relieve me of such pain," he blurted.

268

Serena tried not to giggle. She knew that this was not what the Boy had intended on telling her at all, but, nonetheless, she smiled and accepted. She was too tired to milk any more information out of him, at least for toNight. Gently she massaged the Boy's shoulders until she was so exhausted that she could barely keep her eyes open, and so she laid her head down in her arms on the Mossy Rock and fell asleep.

~*~*~*~*~

When Serena awoke, it was not yet dawn. But it was coming – she could smell it in the air. The Cave was heavily scented with burnt wood, smoke, cooked meat, and a rather muffled fragrance that was somehow similar to fresh Rain. Nelson laid softly snoring in her lap; apparently her skirt had provided a soft and comfortable pillow for him.

Bless his heart, Serena thought, stroking the Boy's lustrous curls. *Without him we never would have made it this far.*

She sighed, thinking of how only a couple weeks before, Jerry had been asleep beside her on a plane, just as Nelson was now. She wondered where Jerry was at that moment … in chains? Asleep? Or, a thought that gave chills of guilt to Serena through and through, dead?

Serena shook these thoughts from her head as Nelson awoke with a disgruntled snort, and sat up. She looked around and found that Bob, Theo, Achel and Bameis had already awoken and were preparing for a quick breakfast. Trumple and her three Children sat still at the entrance of the den, sleeping peacefully.

Before long the entire group had awaken and partaken of a nutritious breakfast of dried fruit. They thanked their host and Lindsey offered to check Gomper's bandages one last time before they left. Trumple agreed to let her.

The 12 travelers said a grateful good-bye and wished the family well. Afterwards they departed from the comfortable little Cave and struck out into the refreshed, blue-Skied wilderness, ready for another Day of traveling adventures.

~*~*~*~*~

All that Day the 12 companions traveled up and down the Forested Hills, through Grassy clearings with small Animals scampering about – Mice,

269

Moles, Squirrels and Chipmunks, Rabbits, Hedgehogs, Raccoons and even a small gathering of Deer. Strangely, they met no one in their questing, and, stranger yet, no perils.

The Forest of Many Eyes was so beautiful in the Daytime, very much like a luscious Garden after the Rain. Granted, there were certain mud puddles and downed limbs that they needed to watch out for, but for the most part Serena thought the place was just gorgeous. The colorful fruits of the Banyan Trees sparkled in their Rain-washed branches, dew collected and dripped lazily from every Flower and every blade and leaf, and iridescent Butterflies fluttered and flipped in the air everywhere, alighting on Flowers and chasing one another in the Golden Sunlight. The fragrant smells of Rain, upturned soil and loam, blooming Flowers, oozing honey and nectar, and every other delightful aroma of wild herbs and spices and fruit mingled in the air and wafted under their noses.

Another example of how looks can deceive, Serena thought with a sigh. *This place is a regular paradise in the Daytime, but as soon as the Sun goes down, it's a Nightmare!*

Serena did not want to think about those terrible, ever-glowering eyes at all that Day, having had about enough of them for the last three Nights. So she pushed the matter to the back of her mind and focused on another thought: how the Mother of Forever was faring.

She hadn't a doubt that the Princess had tried several times to claim the Throne since Serena had last heard. And, with a pit of hopelessness settling in her stomach, Serena knew the Princess probably hadn't prevailed.

If she had, word would have been around to us already, the Girl thought as she leaped over a small puddle. *But there is no one here in the Forest who is worthy of passing on important information without a will to eat us ... except for the Sirrush - and she probably would have told us –* Serena sighed again. *If the Princess really would have claimed that miserable Throne …*

Ah, but you see, if the Princess is not the true Heir, then how can she claim the so-called 'miserable' Throne? whispered a small voice in Serena's head.

True, Serena told the voice, *she cannot.*

She swung her head in Nelson's direction. He was watching her protectively, as always, and quickly grew red and looked at the ground. Serena shyly followed his example.

Nelson. Only Nelson can claim the Throne. But it's so strange ... He has hardly spoken to me at all toDay. I wonder if he is feeling well.

"Yesdnil sah dlot em ruoy noitanitsed." Karnilia whipered suddenly, shattering the Girl's thoughts. Serena looked into the blue-tinged face of her friend.

"Ho, sah ehs?" she replied in surprise, looking over at the team's pink-cladden nurse. "Did uoy lesaew ti tuo fo reh?"

Karnilia smiled and laughed at this.

"On, on! Ehs did nethgilne em no reh nwo. Os uoy era gniog ot eht Enilkraps Niatnuom?"

With her third sigh, Serena hesitantly nodded, and she began to explain her thoughts to Karnilia before she even knew what she was saying.

"Esaelp od ton llet erutaerCyna siht – on eno ta lla." Quickly she stole a glance over her shoulder to make sure nobody was eavesdropping.

"Ew … ew evah eht eurt Rieh ot eht Enorht fo Reverof htiw su!"

Karnilia's blue eyes grew like Serena had never seen them grow before. She, too, looked around the group, eyeing Mike, Bob, Lindsey, Kate, Theo, and finally Nelson, each in turn. Then she leaned close to her friend, eyes still clinging to Nelson, and hissed,

"Ohw? Hcihw eno si ti?" out of the corner of her mouth and into Serena's ear. Serena's face grew hot – from either the way Karnilia was looking at Nelson, or the haunting decision of whether to tell the Girl this private piece of information or not. She arrived at the safest of the two choices seconds later.

"I … I t'nac llet uoy. M'I yrros, tub taht dluow eb oot hcum ot evig yawa,"

Karnilia smiled understandingly.

"Taht si enif. I eveileb I evah a doog aedi ydaerla."

"T'nod llet enoyna! Esimorp em, Ailinrak, esimorp em uoy lliw llet on eno!"

Serena gripped her friend's arm, and glared her straight in the eye to get her point across. Karnilia smiled and shook her off almost moodily. Then, seeing the blue-eyed Girl's expression of tearful deception, she put an arm around her.

"I esimorp, Aneres, I lliw llet on eno."

But, Serena thought (as well as felt), *in a way, she already has...*

Chapter Thirty-Two: Secrets

Bameis halted the group for camp in early evening; they had covered good ground that Day by setting out early, so they could afford the time to stop.

The team of Sky Humans had chosen a nice, little clearing next to a small Pond as a campsite. Jedin had announced earlier that what Moonlight that made it through the net of the canopy in the Trees would shine off of the Pond and provide a minimal amount of light to their camp.

"Srelworp t'nod yllausu dnab dnuora Retaw ta Thgin," Sealth informed Serena as they lined up the torches. It was still very bright and Sunny out – without a single Cloud in the Sky. Dark would roll in and envelop the Heavens eventually – but not until later on.

Serena quickly found a spot to call her bed for the Night and lined it with soft loam, picking out any stubborn-looking stick she saw. She helped the others as they established their own beds all around her. Standing, she watched as the group dispersed. The Sky Humans were holding some sort of conference by the Forest fringe across the clearing, Bob was amusing Theo with making silly Faun faces, and Lindsey, Mike and Kate were laying in their beds staring at the Sky, still attempting the backwards language, although now their skills were much better. Serena wanted to go join them, but her stomach growled, and then she spotted a little Bush with bright orange berries on it. She wandered over to where it fringed the Pond and stood next to a tall, straight Oak Tree to harvest a skirt full of them.

But something stopped her just as she reached to pick her third handful. It was a voice.

No, two voices.

And one of them Serena knew only too well.

"What bothers your young soul, Boy?" whispered a soft, Watery voice. Serena heard a small splash and the sound of moving Water.

"Who are you?" Nelson hissed.

As slowly as she could manage, Serena crouched and turned to face the Oak Tree on her left. She peered her face around the fat trunk and saw Nelson staring awkwardly into the deep blue Waters of the Pond. Serena's eyes moved to the spot, and what she saw there made her drop the berries she had collected, eyes wide and mouth agape.

A SeaLore.

True to her eyes, there, floating softly on the surface of the Pond was the outlined image of the face of a female Elf, very pretty indeed. Serena knew how Nelson had inherited his handsome looks, for one of his own parents had been one of the Elven species. The face of the Elf Girl in the Water was stunningly beautiful, with long, pointed ears, almond-shaped eyes and long eyelashes, full cheeks and lips, and a tiny nose and chin. Silvery-blue strands of Water-hair framed her pretty little face, as straight and shiny as though it were real. Serena, if she had still possessed the notebook that Dr. Birkwood had given her, would eagerly have written that the SeaLore looked just as though a person had carved a face into the Water.

The SeaLore swam around in a circle, her colorless, Watery eyes observing the Boy.

"You may call me BlueWater," hummed the whistling, echoing voice, "and who may I have the pleasure of addressing?"

"My name is Nelson," Nelson greeted cautiously, taking a step back from the bank of the Pond.

"Nelson," chirped BlueWater in her lovely little voice, swirling to face the Boy on the bank. "What troubles you?"

Nelson's green eyes gleamed suspiciously. He moved closer to BlueWater and kneeled at the side of the Pond.

"How do you know that I am troubled?"

"I am a Spirit," BlueWater boasted, smiling widely. "I can feel your emotions as though they were my own."

Nelson sighed and sat back cross-legged, as though giving up on the matter.

"I don't suppose they are the greatest feelings in Forever, are they?"

"Most certainly not!" sang the SeaLore, shaking her blue face in the Water. "I should like to know what troubles you."

The Halfbreed Boy stared solemnly at the tranquil Waters. He hesitated to the point where BlueWater opened her mouth to speak again but quickly closed it when she saw his reply coming.

"A Girl," Nelson said finally, blinking at a Butterfly that fluttered past his face.

Serena's cheeks warmed.

"A Girl that knows a secret," Nelson continued.

"A secret?" bleated BlueWater, her almond-shaped eyes growing. "Oh, my! What kind of a secret?"

"A secret secret," Nelson replied promptly. Behind the Trees, Serena's cheeks grew hotter by the moment. BlueWater drew closer to the Boy, narrowing her blank eyes, as though probing deeper into his soul.

"Ah, but that is not the only emotion that troubles you."

It was Nelson's turn to flush.

"No," he admitted with a sigh. He stared almost longingly into the Waters behind the SeaLore. "It's not."

Serena's clear blue eyes grew and her heart Thundered in her ears. Busily, she began to collect her spilled berries. She had to get out of there before-

"And what's this? Another soul I feel!"

Too late.

Serena closed her eyes as she heard the sound of swishing Water. For the second time that evening, the berries dropped from the Girl's hands.

"Another troubled soul. Arise, Child, for there is no one to hide from."

Obediently, Serena rose from the Bushes slowly, a few stray berries still clutched in her white hands.

"I wasn't hiding," she stated innocently. "I was picking some berries." She looked at Nelson, who was sitting sprawled on the Grass looking very surprised. And embarrassed.

"Hey, Nelson! There's a whole Bush of them over here!" Serena added with a white smile.

Nelson looked imploringly at the SeaLore, who grinned fiendishly at him. He leaped up and bounded over to Serena.

"Serena, I have to give you something," he blurted. He took her hand and pulled her out next to the Pond.

BlueWater smiled, seeing she was no longer needed, and swirled herself into a tiny typhoon and vanished.

Serena looked back at Nelson, ready to ask him about BlueWater's odd disappearance. His eyes, full of excitement, hushed her before she could even draw a breath. Something was about to happen.

Nelson locked on her ice-blue gaze and came very close. He reached slowly into his pocket and pulled out a tiny vile filled with twinkling powder of every color, and held it up in front of her.

"What-"

"Shhh," Nelson hushed her. "This is Pixie Powder," he whispered.

Serena's eyes grew.

"Oh, Fairy Dust?" she smiled. Nelson shook his head.

"No, Fairy Dust is too light to give you flight."

"Give me … - ?"

Serena could not finish her sentence, because her mouth twisted upward into the biggest, prettiest smile. Her heart thumped inside her chest, so loud that Serena was afraid that it was going to burst out of her.

This little handful of – of Pixie Powder is going to let me fly? But how?

Nelson, seeing her obvious excitement, smiled and handed her the vile.

"Do you want to try it out?" he smirked.

Serena's blue eyes told him the answer; she was utterly speechless.

Nelson quickly patted her cheek like a treated Child and moved around in back of her. He began to unbutton the back of her dress.

Serena suddenly found her voice and withdrew, her smile fading rapidly.

"What are you doing?" she exclaimed, holding the Pixie Powder in one hand and the unbuttoned back of her dress in the other. Luckily, he had left the top button fastened.

"Well, the wings have to sprout somewhere," he reasoned, wringing his fingers nervously. He looked up at her with a red face. "And surely you don't want to rip your nice dress. Believe me, cramped wings aren't very comfortable."

Wings?

Serena apologized, brightened by the very word. She allowed the Boy to unbutton the rest of the back of her dress to the middle of her back. He did so extremely slowly, making Serena nearly impatient to be in the air. She looked up at the azure blue Sky, clear of everything but the happy Sunshine. With a grin, she thought of how in only a few moments she would be up in all of its splendor and beauty, soaring like a Bird.

Then she looked at the vial of Pixie Power, shimmering and glittering in the low-floating Sun. Dusk would not be long in waiting.

"Alright, let me see that vial," Nelson said, brushing shoulders with her as he strode around in front of her. Serena handed him the little bottle, staring up at him through long Golden lashes as she straightened the shoulder of her dress.

Nelson coughed in sincerest apology and popped the tiny cork out of the bottle. It landed soundlessly on the Grass.

Serena smiled and closed her eyes. When she opened them again, multi-color glitter was swirling and floating around her, tickling her skin as it Rained down upon her. Nelson watched, smiling, as she spun around in it and giggled. He stared shamelessly.

Serena stopped suddenly, feeling a small twitch between her shoulder blades. Her eyes grew as she felt her skin bubble and prickle on her back – and then, very suddenly, something sprouted behind her, sounding like a parachute opening. Her skin stopped prickling, and she then felt something that didn't exactly tickle – her face cringed in mild pain as new muscles grew and attached themselves to her.

And then Serena looked over her shoulder, flexed her new muscles, and saw the flash of a glowing tip of a narrow, leaf-shaped wing - a Pixie wing.

"Nelson, look!" she gawked, brushing sparkling powder from the tip of the multicolored wing delicately with her fingers. She rubbed the powder between her fingers and looked straight at the vial.

"Can we use-"

"No," he answered, tucking the empty vial away. "The only Pixie Powder that has the Magic to give you flight comes from true Pixies."

Serena nodded, opening and closing her wings like a Butterfly. She looked at the Sky with a smirk.

"Shall we?" Nelson inquired, holding out his hand. Serena needed no second bidding.

"We shall," she chortled happily.

And so they took to the air.

~*~*~*~*~

Serena was living her dream.

Up and up through the clear blue Sky she sailed, hair and dress fluttering, wings pumping, wind whistling, and Nelon's hand in hers. They soared together up over the Forest of Many Eyes, so far up that Serena could feel the air pressure. Nelson pointed out the Blue Marsh to the near SouthEast about half a Day's travel from the spot they were now. The Marsh truly did look blue, and Serena wondered why it was so.

He also showed her the hardly visible quilted patches of FarmLand to the SouthWest. To the direct North he showed her the MeadowLands where they had escaped from the slave-driving Goblins, a very long distance from where they were. A small gray spot brandished the existence of the Castle Barrift and the City of Dooditan, their second destination, with a River snaking close to it, the Thistleglade River, or so Nelson said.

Across the Basstooth River far to the NorthWest, a smudge of Gold appeared on the horizon: the Golden Plains, which they seemed to have passed ages ago. And lastly, far, far to the West over the vastness of the Forest of Many Eyes, lay a Coastline and the Ceaseless Ocean.

After learning the surrounding geography, Serena and Nelson spun about in the Skies, weaving over and under one another as they skimmed the tops of the Trees. The view was absolutely gorgeous from above the lower, shorter Trees, and even more beautiful above the tall-rising Redwood Trees. Serena felt a bit like being in a Forest above a Forest as she twirled among the Redwoods, which poked way up over the tops of the Banyans, littered with fruits of all colors. They flew with the Birds, dropped and soared upward again, the wind rushing past their faces and their hearts one with the Sky.

When, finally, Nelson insisted they land, Serena objected. It wasn't every Day that she got the miraculous privilege to fly. But the Sun was already dipping into its descent over the horizon, the Skies growing slightly darker, and she knew that she hadn't much choice but to obey.

They landed side by side on the bank of the Pond, laughing merrily from their splendid flight. Excitement wound down as the Trees darkened, and Serena knew that those atrocious eyes would be out before long. She sighed and turned to Nelson, who was staring critically at his reflection.

"Why did you do this for me, Nelson?" she wondered in a soft voice. Nelson looked back at her, eyes shining, and he pulled another vial from his pocket, this time a larger one. Its corked neck was fastened to a short, strong-looking chain. This he clasped around Serena's neck, pushing her Gold hair aside gently. She marveled at the sparkling powder held within the clear glass as Nelson answered softly,

"Because I know you have always wished you could fly," he snatched up her hand and admired her long, slender fingers. "And now you can. Anytime you wish to escape your troubles, sprinkle a pinch of Pixie Powder over yourself and you will fly."

Serena's heart skipped a beat just at the very word.

It is time, she thought, staring shamelessly at the Boy's flawless features.

"Thank you, Nelson," she breathed, and, squeezing his hand gently, continued in a very soft voice, "But I do want you to know …"

And her voice failed her, trailing off. Nelson's green eyes seemed so big, his hair gleaming so handsomely, and his expectant was expression so … expectant.

"To know ..." he repeated in a whisper, waiting. Serena looked at the ground, humiliated. "To know what?"

When Serena looked up, her eyes stung with unshed tears. She fought the urge to let them spill over her pink cheeks.

"Nelson, I know your secret!" she blurted without thinking, and covered her mouth quickly in realization of what she had just said.

"My secret?" Nelson gasped, growing red as the Sunset. He released her hand and backed up. "But Serena ...Don't you ... How did you-"

"No, I know it, Nelson! I'm sorry – I didn't mean to find out, I really didn't! I'm so sorry, I-"

Hot tears sprang to her eyes, despite her efforts to hold them back.

"Shhh ... settle down," Nelson crooned, wiping away one of her escaping tears. He cupped her cheek in his hand comfortingly. "At least I know that there is nothing to hide from you any longer. Do not cry."

Serena dried her tears and felt her temporary Pixie wings shrivel up and disappear behind her, leaving her back bare and cold. She began to button up the back of her dress, but Nelson insisted on helping her, and so she allowed him to finish the job. Meanwhile, she stared into the Moonlit Pond at her reflection.

Three Days ago this Girl discovered her true love, she told herself, and narrowed her eyes. *And now she has only to prove it.*

Nelson wrapped his cloak around the Girl's shoulders tenderly.

"It will be a cool Night." he explained, nuzzling his face into her hair. "I should lend you my cloak for the Night."

"I'm afraid it isn't your cloak that I want." Serena said, hardly believing what she was saying. Carefully, she turned around and faced the Boy, coming very close to his glowing, pale-skinned face. He looked somewhat surprised, and placed his hands on her shoulder in preparation to say something.

But Serena hushed him.

"Nelson, I know your secret. It's true. But, do you know mine?" she breathed.

The Boy seemed as though he were testing her as he answered,
"No ..."

Serena smiled slyly.

And then she leaned forward to kiss him, but he smiled and kissed her before she could.

"Serena, I know your secret," he whispered.

Chapter Thirty-Three: Eht Eulb Hsram

For the first time in the Forest of Many Eyes, Serena did not feel frightened of the Prowlers' blinking eyes. Although she was sleeping outside on the cold, hard ground surrounded by torches, that Night she felt that she needn't fear anything. For Nelson was sleeping close behind her, his hand entangled with hers, his warm cloak draped over them both.

Serena awoke to bright Sunshine; perfect traveling weather, and a tasty breakfast that Jedin and Sealth had prepared.

The group set off in late morning, purposefully lingering on their former campsite to stash away the torches and collect fruits, nuts and berries from surrounding Bushes and Trees. Also, Bameis took the opportunity before they began to travel to widely proclaim that as soon as they reached the Blue Marsh, the Sky Humans would wish them well and leave.

"Tub woh lliw yeht tcetorp sevlesmeht tsniaga eht Srelworp?" Achel argued, stamping her long-legged foot. "Tuohtiw sehcrot, ylrus eht Sretsnom lliw kcatta meht."

"Yeht era wef ni rebmun - lla yeht lliw deen si a doog erif dna a tuokool. Sediseb, eht Srelworp od ton yllausu etagergnoc dnuora eht egnirf fo eht Tserof esuaceb fo eht retaerg sregnad gnikrul ni eht Hsram," Bameis reassured her.

It was late afternoon by the time they reached the Eastern border of the Forest. Bameis, Jedin, Sealth, Achel, and Karnilia prepared to say their farewells. Their travel to the bubbling Marsh was neither a tiring nor a long one, very contrary to their journey the Day before.

Jedin and Karnilia began the Warriors' departure with warning.

"Ot levart hguorht eht Hsram tuohtiw gnisu eht htap, uoy lliw deen Hsram Seohs ot tcetorp ruoy teef."

Karnilia stepped forward and unfastened her large traveling basket. In front of her she laid seven heavy-looking boots with long necks that reached up to about the knee and rope-like bootlaces that snaked around.

"Sa a nekot fo ruo edutitarg ew evah dedivorp eseht rof uoy. Esu meht ylesiw." Jedin said, eyeing each of them with his cool blue eyes.

Karnilia spoke next as she straightened the basket on her back.

"Eno erom gniht. Rebmemer won taht uoy evah neeb denraw fo eht sregnad taht lwarc ni taht Hsram. Od ton tel sti evisserped edutitta gnirb uoy nwod,

279

esuaceb ylrus fi uoy llaf otni sti desruca part, ti lliw nword uoy. Erweb, sdneirf! Yam doog enutrof yrrac uoy ssorca taht lufdaerd ecalp!"

And with that, the Sky Humans departed, waving and calling their backwards farewells to the seven journeyers. Serena, despite her slight distrust for Karnilia, called a farewell to her so that they would part as friends, not enemies.

"Goodbye, Serena! Farewell! Take your time in moving into the Blue Marsh!" Karnilia shouted back.

Serena froze, as did the team.

"So they can speak our language!" hissed Kate, her dark eyes twinkling with unsatisfied revenge.

"Of course they can!" chuckled Nelson. He laid his hands on Serena's shoulders, seeing her disappointment. "They only use that language in the Forest of Many Eyes because of the Prowlers – who can understand the English language. There have been times when secrets have been lost in this Forest and then spread to the passerby by the Monsters. The best way to keep a secret in the Forest is to use another language to send it. That way they cannot understand you."

Serena shook her head. She still did not understand.

"Why haven't they picked up on it yet? Over a period of time, certain words will start to sound familiar, won't they?"

"They may," Nelson replied as the last of the Sky Humans vanished into the shadows of the Forest. "They still do not understand their language. I believe it may be a part of the Curse, but who knows?"

Serena closed her eyes and shook her head, hiding a smile, and then turned to face the Marsh, gurgling and oozing behind her.

From a distance, it really does look blue, she sighed in thought. She studied the Mist-shrouded landscape in its Watery existence – gooey blue-green bubbles rising and popping from its scummy surface, which also collected a certain type of blue-green mold, algae or fungus. This, Serena guessed, was the reason the Swamp was named the Blue Marsh. Mounds of peat, tall-rising groups of Boulders and Rocks, a few dead Tree skeletons and scattered Brambles littered the place among sprouting Reeds, Cat Tails, and other Marsh-growing Weeds and Plants. Serena could see from where she stood the light and dark patches over the vast blue Bog – clearly signifying which spots were thick and dense with matter and which were less in volume and more Watery. Dragonflies and Water Bugs of every color buzzed about in every which way, descending on dead Vines and Reeds to lay their eggs and expand their brood. Overall, the Blue Marsh did not quite look like a paradise. Parasitic, yes. Paradise, no.

The blonde-haired Girl turned away from the horrible sight, her curls flashing in the waning Sunlight. Kate was crying after one glance at the Marsh, Theo was laughing at her, and Lindsey and Bob were trying to restore the peace. Mike was sitting on the edge of the Forest fringe, poking a stick into the goop and trying to pop any bubbles that strayed too close to him. Serena was disgusted at the nasty-looking Land.

"We won't have to move into the Marsh toNight, will we Nelson?" she consulted the Halfbreed Boy.

"Well, would you rather sleep under the Trees toNight, or the Stars?" he replied, batting around one of her locks distractedly.

Serena gulped.

"I have a bad feeling that there will be more out there than Stars toNight," she lamented, glancing fearfully behind her at the SwampLands.

"Then, we'll stay in the Forest," murmured Nelson, playing with her hair. "We're more accustomed to them than the Marsh."

"It sounds like we'll be safer here," Serena sighed, satisfied with the tone of conclusion in her voice. Exhaustedly, she leaned back against her new sweetheart and caressed his tough hands affectionately.

In Days to come, she would soon find why she had felt such a bad vibe from simply looking at the Blue Marsh in all its repulsive Nature.

In the morning, Serena pulled on her Marsh Shoes and surveyed the surviving team as she laced up the thick bootlaces tightly, wrapping them several times around the circumference of her shin and calf.

All of them, save for the runaway Jerry, had seen plenty of adventure in this short amount of time. They had trimmed up from their frequent motion in traveling and running, had all become a bit darker in skin tone from their exposure to the Sun, and had now begun to develop a very slight British accent. Serena studied her traveling companions.

There was Mike, who was now a bit thinner from their adventures with his tiny, thick glasses that hid his eyes from sight and his waving feathered cap. Bob had also become stronger physically (as Serena was sure they all had) and become more involved in conversation, not near as shy and reserved as he had been before. Kate's attitude had changed dramatically – yet not so much for her to seem a completely different person; she was still slightly whiney and snappy in some aspects. Lindsey's characteristics had hardly changed. She had slimmed down like the rest of them - but Serena felt that over the time she had known the Girl their friendship had grown.

Serena knew the nurse Maid did not mean to give away their destination – Karnilia had probably sneaked the information out of her. And even then, Lindsey would have thought that Serena would only tell her why they were going – and in a way she did, but she felt that she had opened her mouth too wide and told Karnilia something entirely different. Serena accepted this as her fault and scolded herself on the lines that not every so-called friend was to be trusted in this new World.

But it really doesn't matter if she goes and blabs it to her entire little Village, Serena thought with a smirk. *The Prowlers cannot understand her language, and who is there to tell in the Forest of Many Eyes? Travelers prefer to go around the place these Days anyway.* She recalled the facts she had learned from Nelson Days before when they had entered the Forest. Eventually, her thoughts turned back to her evaluation of their little group.

Theo, tiny, quiet little Theo. The small Boy had been so silent over the past five Days that Serena had hardly noticed he was there. Probably because the Forest itself, either Daytime or Night, frightened the little Lad, and continued to frighten him for as long as he walked among its Trees. Ever since he had heard his brother speak of the invisible Prowlers that stalked the place and haunted its inhabitants, he had not been the same.

The poor Child, Serena thought, shaking her head. *I hope he brightens up once we leave this dreadful place.*

And, finally, there was Nelson, the Boy she knew and loved from the tips of his moccasined (but not booted) feet to the top of his Sandy blonde head. Her best friend and true love. A Prince. And the one and only Heir to the Throne of Forever.

Late afternoon came and the group stopped for lunch. They were, to say the least, very tired from their ventures in the Blue Marsh.

Serena's legs hurt from lifting them so terribly high only to plunge them back into the vile-smelling Bog again. The whole place was humid and foul, smelling like something so rotten that Serena had never smelled anything like it before. The air was suffocating, thick and hot. Their feet made squishy sucking sounds as they forced them up to take another step. The team had also constructed a small raft to carry their knapsacks and other possessions, which they took turns tugging behind them on a short rope.

Overall, Serena was taken aback at the state of the Bog Land. It seemed so … depressing, so lost and unwanted. Tempted though she was to match its mood with her own, she remembered Karnilia's warning and strived to heed it.

In the afternoon, as they stopped to make lunch, the Mists became thin and departed, and the Sun shone hot and bright in their faces. Being in the Forest for so long and no longer needing her bonnet to shield her eyes from the Sun, Serena had tucked away her ruffled bonnet with Teresa's diary in her skirts. But there were no tall or fruit-laden Trees to provide shade in the Blue Marsh. So, as Mike and Lindsey laid out a variety of Banyan cakes and scones to feast upon, Serena retrieved her crinkled blue bonnet from the pocket she had made in her skirt and tied it under her chin. Immediately, she felt relief from the burning rays of the Sun, and so, satisfied, she indulged on the matter of lunch.

"So, tell me, almighty navigator, just what is so scary about this Marsh?" Kate inquired to Nelson, who sat on a soft mound of peat, scoffing a tart. He hesitated before replying.

"I think … I think it is better that you not know," he murmured, and stuffed his half-tart into his mouth before Kate could protest.

"Does it have a Curse on it like the M-Monsters from the Forest of Many Eyes?" Theo squeaked, sitting between Mike and Bob on a neighboring peat pile where they had landed the raft. Serena moved to sit in between Nelson and Lindsey, having collected two honey-soaked Banyan cakes.

"Not quite," the Halfbreed Boy replied. He tore into a scone ravenously.

"Is it haunted by a Spirit or something?" Bob wanted to know.

Nelson paused to think and chew.

"Well … sort of. I guesss you could say that."

Serena bit into her Banyan cake; it was sweet and exquisite in flavor. She could taste the many different flavors of the Banyan fruits in the cake: blue tomato-like fruits, spiral green fruits with red polka dots, white apples that tasted like orange and tangerine mixed, and ripe, pink little berries that reminded Serena faintly of bubble gum. There was a certain taste in it that made the cake somewhat addictive, however, and the very aroma of its sweetness reminded her of Bendar and of all the strange and beautiful things she had seen there.

But the Blue Marsh was just about anything but beautiful.

Serena savored the taste of the Banyan cake before swallowing and saying,

"What's the next Town we'll be visiting?"

"Middleton, I believe. The Town is an odd but a pleasant one from what I hear. It lies along the West side of the path leading NorthEast."

"Sounds good to me." Mike shrugged, reaching for another Banyan cake.

"Anything sounds good compared to this place!" Lindsey giggled, shaking her head of brown curls, concealed by a pink bonnet. A hearty chorus of agreement followed, and then Kate asked,

"So, just what did you mean when you said this place might be haunted by a Spirit?"

Nelson, his bright green eyes gleaming in the Sunlight, leaned back and gazed up at the Sky.

"Well … I guess it's sort of difficult to explain," he muttered, sounding very much like he was talking to no one in particular. He drew a breath and nearly coughed on the humid, reeking air. Serena slid behind him and played with his hair, her lunch being finished.

"But then, I suppose it really isn't. You see, the Blue Marsh, before it ever was a Swamp, was once a great battlefield – FlatLand, like a Meadow, that is. It is a story told by old house wives to pacify their Children and scare them into behaving,"

He stopped, eyes wide, seeing that every soul in the group was hanging on his every word. He looked around at them, unsure of whether he should tell them now or wait until later.

"Oh, just tell us, Nelson!" Serena urged him.

He looked at her dolefully and sighed.

"Oh, alright," he said, repositioning himself. He cleared his throat and closed his eyes, and began his dreadful tale.

"Long ago the Blue Marsh was a battlefield – this we know. On a battlefield, naturally, you find bodies – corpses. Well, what happened with the Blue Marsh was this: After the battle had been fought, a great Rain swept over the FlatLand, as though Forever itself was endeavoring to conceal this malicious act. The Rain did not stop until the place was BogLand, and so it remains to this Day. The corpses, however, because of their unseemly deaths, began to

284

rot in the bottom of the Marsh. Some were preserved, others were not, but all I know is that whenever there is a full Moon, something happens to them and they rise to the surface to torment any Travelers. I do not really remember the complete story – do you, Theo?"

The 7-year-old shook his Sandy blonde head.

"No, I did not reach my studies of the Blue Marsh before we … well … you know … we … left …"

Silence hung on the air.

And before they could question him on his origin, Nelson exclaimed,

"So, yes! Let us begin our trek once more and see how far we can get toDay!" He slapped his knees and stood, then turned and helped Serena up.

"Nelson," she said in a soft voice, still puzzled about the awkward sounding story. "I still do not see where the haunting Spirit comes in. Are you sure that the-"

"That's it!" Nelson said, snapping his fingers. All stopped and watched him. "I remember clearly now. The Spirits of the dead were trapped under the Swamp, and still are, as a matter of fact. It is only on a Night of a full Moon that they arise to seek revenge on any of the living that happen to be crossing their Swamp. They cannot leave the Swamp – they are still chained to their bodies. I do believe it is the Moon that lengthens these chains and allows them to haunt the surface. When we begin to hear howling and moaning, we will know that the Spirits are readying themselves to visit the surface of the Marsh – like a warning."

What a bone-chilling story, Serena thought with a shiver. She followed Nelson back into the hot, steaming Swamp, the goop rising to the middle of her shins and begging her to stay that she might sink further into the mess. Nelson had told the entire party earlier that Day that if they stayed in one non-solid spot for too long that they would sink.

And I haven't a care to join those troublesome Spirits, at least not toDay. It must be the sadness of their deaths that haunts this place.

The Girl caught up with her sweetheart, who was now tugging the raft along of his own accord. It skimmed over the slimy surface somewhat smoothly.

"There is just one thing that I still do not understand, Nelson," Serena told him, her feet sucking and oozing in the mush as she kept up. "If the Spirits of the dead are only Ghosts, then are they able to kill a mortal being?"

"That I cannot tell you, love," Nelson mused, tugging sharply on the rope. His gaze met her blue eyes. "But brace yourself to find out, because I have recently found that by tomorrow Night, the Moon will be full."

Serena stifled a shudder.

"We will be in Middleton by then, right?" she asked. The Halfbreed Prince eased a long sigh, seeming to ponder one thing or another as he watched her.

"No."

Chapter Thirty-Four: Marsh Troubles

Later that Day, the Travelers moved into a more Watery part of the Swamp, the oozing mush rising to three-quarters of the way up their Marsh shoes. Small, dark Pools similar to tiny Ponds, filled with clean, clear Water occurred occasionally. Serena wondered as they passed on the first ones just how the Water managed to stay clean in such a place.

"Whew! Can we just stop to get some Water, Nelson?" Kate wheezed, making her way over to one of the Water pools. "My Water bottle is dry and I'm thirsty."

Without waiting for an answer, Kate plunged into the shallows of the Pool and cupped a handful of Water. She brought this to her mouth and quaffed it.

"Alright, but only for a-" Nelson started, halting the group.

"Ah! I'm sinking!" the navigator shrieked suddenly. Her black hair swished about her face as she tore off her pale purple bonnet and flailed helplessly.

"Get me out! Get me out! Oh, hurry! I can't move!" she cried.

"Tar pits!" Nelson muttered contemptuously under his breath. He looked at Serena sadly. "I should have known!" Serena almost smiled, for she quickly detected the hint of sarcasm in the Boy's voice.

"Stop moving!" yelled Mike. "The more you move, the faster you will sink! Stand perfectly still!"

Kate obeyed, standing in a frozen, stiff position. Serena could see the sticky black goo clinging to Kate's ankles and shins and shining maliciously under the Sun.

An idea popped into Serena's head. There was a Tree – an old, dead Tree, - leaning crookedly over the pit Kate was in. Immediately Serena took action – wading over to the raft and pulling a rope out of Nelson's knapsack.

"Grab hold of this if you can, Kate!" Serena shouted, and squeezed in between Lindsey and Mike, who were crowded around the pool with the others. They threw anything they could get their hands on at her rapidly sinking feet to loosen the tar while Nelson had the Girl's arms and pulled with all his might to release her from her captivity.

Serena took one end of the rope and threw the coil over the trunk of the bent old Tree. Nelson caught it on the other side and hastily wrapped it around

Kate's waist. Now the Girl was sobbing piteously.

"Just go on without me!" she wailed, her tears mingling with the sparkling water. She was now shin-deep in the tar. "You never needed me anyway – and now you have Nelson to show you which direction to go!"

"No!" barked Serena, surprised at the volume of her own voice. "We will not leave you here. We will get you out, Kate, just watch and see!"

Mike, Bob, Lindsey and Theo joined Serena at her end of the long rope. Nelson gripped Kate's waist and prepared to haul her upward with the rope. The wildly bawling Girl stared straight at Serena, her hair as black as the tar that threatened to overtake her. She was now knee-deep.

"On the count of three!" Serena shouted, gripping the rope and hoping for the best. Her heart pumped madly inside of her chest as she stood her ground, bracing to pull.

"One, two…"

The four questors behind her gripped the rope and drew in sharp breaths.

"Three!"

"Nnnnnnnngh!"

Sssssshhhhhhlupp!

And then Kate was dangling, dripping, from the branch of the Tree, staring open-mouthed and wide-eyed at her rescuers.

It wasn't until later that evening that Kate finally spoke to them. And then she apologized for all of the mean things she had done and the rude remarks she had made – something had definitely changed in her over the amount of time it took her to be pulled out of the tar Pool. Everyone could tell.

Serena's first Night in the Blue Marsh was a spooky one to say the least. The group of Travelers had mounted a Bramble that grew on a more solid part of Land, and crawled inside the protection of its Vines and branches for the Night. Nelson believed it would be an ideal spot to sleep hidden safely away from unwanted Night predators and Marsh Goblins. And if Nelson believed, then so did Serena.

Though the air outside the Bramble swam with howls and eerie wails, Serena slept snug inside their hideout wrapped warmly in Nelson's cloak and curled beside the Boy himself.

And, in her great comfort, Serena lapsed into the dream that she had had at Bendar. Yet now, now the feeling of flying and falling was not at all a pleasant, satisfying one. Something dark and empty sat on her heart as she felt the thrill of flying being ripped away from her as a toy from a disobedient Child.

So she fell through the pale-colored Clouds, turning in the air to face Jerry and Prince Errenon once more. She fell past each one of them in turn, each of their faces worn and white. The third figure loomed in the distance – much further down than either of the two before it.

This figure must catch me, or surely I will die. she thought, twisting closer to the shadow-shrouded form. Her hair and skirt fluttered behind her; the Wind rushed past her cheeks. And the figure loomed ever closer, the Mist parting.

Nelson.

Serena gasped, and her heart leaped.

But her eyes were playing no tricks. The figure was unmistakable. It could be no one other than Nelson.

Surely he will catch me.

The Boy's face was pale; his green eyes glazed over uncharacteristically – he was as stoic and frozen as the other two.

Catch me, Nelson! Catch me! Serena wanted to shout. But her voice had left her too. She swirled lower and lower, fully expecting her sweetheart to catch her.

But, to her dismay, he did not.

Nelson stepped back at the last moment, just like all the others, and put his outstretched hands to his sides.

No! No! This isn't happening! Serena felt like crying as she sailed past, clawing for the support of warm hands that would not come. *This isn't happening! This isn't happening! THIS ISN'T-*

"NO!" Serena screamed, kicking and awakening in a cold sweat. Her chest heaved, her heart was pounding, echoing in her ears, and she opened her eyes to a spinning Bramble.

Nelson jerked awake beside her. Serena's eyes focused and she placed a hand over her mouth, suddenly realizing the meaning of the dream.

Jerry left my life when I dreamt about falling past him, and Prince Errenon, too. This could be a sign that Nelson is going to-

"No!" she said in a loud whisper, shaking her head in disbelief. Her Sun blonde curls lapped at her face. Tears rolled down her face and she looked at Nelson, who sat up rubbing his eyes. The rest of the team was still asleep.

He grasped her shoulder.

"Are you alright, Serena?" he asked in a hazy, sleepy voice.

"Please don't leave me, Nelson!" Serena sobbed, throwing herself into his arms. "Please don't ever leave me!"

"Why would I even think of doing something like that?" he whispered. Serena gazed deeply into his spring green eyes as he stroked her Golden curls comfortingly.

Serena buried her face in his herbal-smelling tunic and shook her head.

"I had a dream telling me that you would leave me soon," she squeaked, looking up into the shadow of the Boy's face. His two starry green eyes shone out like beacons in the darkness.

"Oh, my poor Serena. Sounds more like a Nightmare to me," he chuckled. "But you do know that not all dreams come true."

"I have a feeling this one will," Serena said shakily, and promptly reached out and grabbed his hand. In a low voice, so as not to wake the others, she reiterated her terrifying dream to Nelson. When she had finished, he drew her close and stared her straight in the eye.

"This dream is purely coincidental. I have no intentions of leaving you and the group stranded out in the middle of the Blue Marsh. Not now. Not ever," he told her slowly. Serena's eyes wandered off and she bit her lip. She could feel more tears brimming in her eyes, and did not like to let the Boy see her cry.

"Darling, look at me," Nelson urged, cupping her cheek in his hand. He turned her face and caught her gaze. He leaned very close to her.

"I will never, ever leave you of my own will, do you understand? Never. I promised you this."

He sealed his vow with a kiss.

The Girl's chest felt full to bursting as she embraced Nelson and laid down next to him to try her luck at sleeping again. She draped Nelson's cloak over them both and snuggled close under his chin.

"Nelson?" she whispered after a short time.

His chest rumbled deeply in reply.

"Yes?"

Serena nuzzled deep into his soft, warm chest.

"I love you."

A hand slithered around her and caressed her back affectionately.

"I love you too, Serena."

290

~*~*~*~*~

The next Day was a slow, long and laborious one. The Travelers awoke at dawn, ate a small yet filling breakfast of Marsh Berries (small, tart yellow fruits that grew in the bramble) and set to their quest once more.

The Day passed slowly and proved to be considerably uneventful. Although the Sun shone down upon Serena's crinkled blue bonnet, it did nothing to cheer her Spirits. The SwampLand was still putrid and wet, with those despicable little bubbles rising and popping out of the goo and smelling up the air with their nauseating odors. The Fog was heavy and volumous in the morning but cleared up well by midafternoon and allowed the bright Sun (and the darkening ThunderClouds that now followed them) to show through.

Serena also found another meaning to the name of the Marsh. Although she was quite sure that the person that had dubbed the place the Blue Marsh did not know this, Serena felt that the mood of the atmosphere and Landscape tended to make a traveler "blue." When Nelson asked her what this meant, she explained that on her planet, it meant that a person felt sad, depressed and generally low-spirited. And that was just the way she felt after her horrific Nightmare the Night before.

Serena hardly let go of Nelson's hand or let him out of her sight that Day, fearing the worst. Save for once when it was time for her to take in lunch, the Girl practically guarded her sweetheart, watching him with eyes as sharp and keen as a Hawk's.

Only when evening rolled around did Serena wind down some and become less tense. Nelson picked out a large mound of peat to stop and make dinner on. The raft was pulled up and latched onto a protruding stump that at one time must have been a Tree. Before long, a lukewarm stew of dried meat and sliced vegetables was served; the eight ate hungrily and settled down for the Night on the steaming lump of peat.

"I'm wondering," Nelson murmured thoughtfully, stroking his fair-skinned chin. He rounded the top of the slightly flattened peat Hill just as a soft sprinkle of precipitation began to fall. Serena, who was sitting between Lindsey and Kate, looked up at the Boy.

"Wondering what?" Lindsey asked, buckling her haversack shut and slinging it down on the peat to serve as a pillow for the Night.

"Well," Nelson tore off his cloak and shielded the three Girls with it, "it looks like there's another Bramble over there hidden behind a soft little Sandy patch of Land with some Trees sheltering it. It looks like it might be a good hiding place, yet I sort of feel that it might still be too exposed."

Kate laughed, shaking her black-haired head.

"Oh, come on, Nelson! What could possibly be more exposed than us sleeping on top of a Hill like this? I mean, look at this!"

She spread her arms wide to emphasize her point. Theo bounded over from where Mike and Bob were observing the StormClouds and the Marsh and plunked down comfortably in Serena's lap.

"That's true, but I wasn't planning on spending the Night up here where all of creation can see us," Nelson mumbled after the pause, and draped his cloak over the three Girls again, as it had begun to slide off. He slung his knapsack next to Serena. "I'm going to go check it out. Watch my things for me, will you?"

Serena nodded and dragged the haversack closer to her.

"I will. And make sure you take yo-"

"My bow, yes, and loaded, mind you," Nelson unslung his bow from his shoulder, where he normally kept it, and pulled a feathered arrow from the full quiver that was slung over his other shoulder.

Serena smiled, satisfied, and watched him notch the arrow into his bow and lean to look along the shaft. The Boy suddenly looked at her, a mischievous smirk playing with his fair face.

"Am I free to go now … Madam?" he said smoothly, his voice dripping with sarcasm. He loosened his arrow.

Serena shot him his own mischievous smile back, and replied,

"Yes, and do come right back, Sir!"

Nelson shook his head, laughing. Serena watched him lean close to her, kiss her forehead gently, then shouldered his bow.

"I will be right back, Princess," he declared. Serena felt the sharp point of the arrow as he tapped it against her nose.

And then he marched happily off, his arrow held over his shoulder like a soldier with a rifle.

It was not long until Serena heard him let out a bloodcurdling scream.

292

"Nelson!" she shrieked, leaping up just as Theo lifted off of her lap. Her hands flew to her burning cheeks. The group immediately flew off in the direction of the scream, but something similar to petrifaction solidified her body to the spot. Shock ran down her spine. She watched in horror as Theo bounded down from the Hill and, with a great leap, took to floating rapidly over the ground by two feet. Indeed he had been practicing his flying, and prevailed grandly, but that was the least of Serena's attention at the moment.

Her love had screamed.

She had never heard the Boy scream in such a way before.

Something had happened.

Or was happening.

Without another thought, she regained mobilization and dashed off after Theo and the others, hauling Nelson's knapsack up onto her back with his cloak and hiking up her skirt to gain speed.

The sight that met her eyes when she reached Nelson made a surprised and terrified gasp leap from her mouth. Tears gathered in her eyes.

No, he was not dead.

He was still very much alive.

But he was being eaten.

Eaten alive.

Nelson was being eaten alive by a bubbling, gritty QuickSand Pit.

"QuickSand," he growled, staring at them from under furrowed brows. He crossed his arms and looked at his knees, to which the Watery, silky Sand was rapidly rising. Serena could see from the looks on the others' faces that he had spoken to them briefly before Serena arrived at the scene. They watched her sadly and curiously, then looked back at Nelson.

"That's easy." chirped Kate nervously, reaching for her knapsack. "We will simply use a rope to make a pulley with one of the Trees, like Serena did when you rescued me."

Nelson sighed unhappily, wincing as the dreadful mush trickled up his knee.

"It is not easy. It cannot be undone," the Boy mumbled, looking fearfully at Serena. "Marlan QuickSand Pits cannot be undone. They are irreversible."

He stretched his hand to her (for he was but a foot and a half from the shoreline of solid Land) and she took it. Serena was mortified, tears already pouring down her cheeks, leaving small Rivulets and Streams that stained her smooth complexion.

"My Nightmare is coming true," she realized. "I should have seen this coming – it's all my fault."

"It is not your fault," Nelson assured her, squeezing her hand comfortingly. He looked around at the shocked faces of the other five onlookers. "It is noCreature's fault that this happened – none but my own. I should have known to check if the surface was solid. I should have known that Marlan QuickSand Pits are especially common in the Blue Marsh. Only now do I wish I would have paid more attention to my schooling Mistress," Sadly he looked around at the group. Kate and Lindsey were crying, and he signaled for them to come closer. He hugged each of them.

"Girls – we've had some good times and some bad times. I want you to remember me, now – and remember what I've told you. Don't let the fear of losing something keep you from playing the game."

Sniffing, Lindsey kissed his forehead and Kate stroked his hair.

Mike and Bob came forward, looking Thunderstruck, and Nelson turned to them.

"The same goes for you, friends. Protect yourselves, take care of each other. Mike, Bob – I can't believe this is it."

"I can't either," choked the wildlife expert, wiping his nose. Bob leaned on Mike, his dark blue eyes Watery and forlorn. He shook Nelson's hand and pursed his lips.

"We will not easily forget you." he sobbed, a hand in front of his trembling mouth. Kate sat down in the mush, suddenly weak at the knees, and Lindsey trudged over to poor Theo, who laid face-down on the ground, crying hysterically.

Silence gripped the still air until Serena dropped to her knees to come face-to-face with Nelson. The Boy was now mid-thigh deep in the mush, and looked very sorry for himself indeed.

"Nelson … Oh, Nelson … please look at me." she said. He obeyed reluctantly. His cheeks were wet now not from the gradually increasing precipitation, but from something else. His face was red.

"Nelson, if you must … go, then who will-"

"I told you I would never leave you, Serena," he croaked, shaking his

294

Sandy blonde head and ignoring her request. "I promised you that I would never leave you, and now-"

"The dream has proven itself correct," Serena finished for him. She sighed and looked at the forlorn crew, but especially Theo, who had fallen face down on the ground and was sobbing uncontrollably. Lindsey and Bob could hardly help him.

"Nelson, we need to know where we should go now, and what we should do-"

Whoooooooooo, echoed a hollow moan.

"What was that?" Kate whimpered.

"The Spirits!" Nelson hissed. Serena saw a glint in his eyes that she had never seen before – a glint of fear. "The haunted Spirits of the deceased Knights of old are coming!"

Wiping Rain from her dew-clung eyelashes, Serena looked up at the luminous Earth Moon, which was slowly revealing itself from behind a dark Cloud. It was full – she could tell – but at the moment it was only partially visible. In a few short minutes, it would brandish its full body to the darkening World below. She turned back to Nelson just as another skin-peeling howl pierced the still Night air.

"What will we-"

"Shhhh!" ordered Nelson. He turned his head toward Theo, who was still on the ground, sobbing. Bloating his chest as best he could given his condition, Nelson turned his pale face to a stern expression.

"Theodore Bosephus!" roared the sinking Boy, now hip-deep in the QuickSand.

Theo looked up, Sand clinging to the wet tears of his face.

"I demand you stand to attention this instant, young Prince! I will not bear to see a brother of mine weep like a Maiden – no offense, Ladies – at my passing!" Nelson issued sternly. With a grim look of importance on his face, he undid his belt and threw it and its contents to the dirty, booted feet of his tall-standing brother. He removed his bow and quiver and handed them over too.

Theo gasped, unsheathing the beautiful, Emerald-hilted sword.

"All possessions that lie at your feet are now yours. Take care of them for me," Nelson said.

Theo admired the sword further, the Emerald on its elegant hilt sparkling as green as his large, round eyes. He held up the sword and pointed to it.

"Even-"

"My sword is now yours, Theo. My herbs, my money and my bow and quiver – all are yours. And," he cleared his throat, as though finding the very words was hard, "and now you must also lead this group to Sparkline Mountain. If you need help or have lost your way, do not hesitate to ask for directions."

"But," Theo began, tears gathering in his eyes. His bottom lip trembled heartbrokenly. "But I am only-"

"No buts," argued Nelson.

Whooooooooooooooooooooooooooo!

The team's eyes widened and shudders passed down every spine.

"All of you! Take care of Theo for me! Should he need advice or council, you shall be the ones in charge. Do this for me, please – at least until he is grown! And one more thing – you all must promise me that you will keep traveling to Diamondia. Promise me!" hailed Nelson in attempt to gain their attention.

"I promise!" Serena shouted.

"I promise!" cried Lindsey and Kate.

"I promise!" added Mike and Bob.

"I promise!" Theo sobbed.

Serena looked at the Earth. It was half exposed now.

Whining, moaning growls, wails, and howls suddenly sprang up and filled the ears of the seven Travelers. The most horrible, bone-chilling screams, teeth-chattering shrieks and knee-knocking screeches could be heard rising to the air and reverberating through the unprotected, living souls. Eerie howls pierced the air – none with specific words, but obvious intentional meaning through the echoing, bouncing tones. Serena shivered and longed to be back in the comfort of Nelson's arms, but found quickly that she could not. After he was gone, she realized, she would have no one. She could help no more than to burst into tears; Kate and Lindsey, and eventually Theo followed. Mike and Bob looked as though they were trying to be strictly stoic and solemn. But even they, in time, showed some sparkle of sentiment in their eyes.

"Remember what I have told you!" Nelson cried.

The Rain grew. The howls persisted. And Nelson sunk chest-deep in the Watery Sand. He tossed Raindrops from his blonde hair, as Sandy as the pit engulfing him slowly.

"Do not stand and wait for them to come!" he shouted over the roaring Wind, Rain, and wails. "Seek shelter immediately! You must hurry! If you do not, you will surly perish! Go, now! Go, for me and for Forever!"

Serena considered his warning, then stood and looked at the frozen, pale-faced group. Mike, his glasses fogged and his nose red; Bob, Rain dripping from the bangs of his brown-black hair; Lindsey, her brown eyes wide as a Deer's; Kate, tears mingling with the Raindrops that ran down her cheeks; and tiny Theo, gripping the belt in one hand, the large quiver slung over his shoulder, and the bow in the other. She pursed her lips in determination.

"Well, we heard what he said!" she barked, tightening her bonnet strings "Let's find some shelter – and quickly! Look for a Bramble or a Briar or something!

Whooooooooooooooooooooooooooooooooooooooooooooooooooooo!

With half-suppressed shudders, the six needed no second orders. Like a cluster of frightened puppies, they high-tailed off. Serena, taking a moment to regain her composure, began to follow in pursuit. Nelson's voice pierced through the moaning voices and the gale.

"Serena!"

The Girl followed his voice back to the Marlan QuickSand Pit. Her eyes leaked involuntarily as she spotted the progress of the terrible QuickSand. The Rain had softened it – only the Boy's arms, shoulders and head remained.

"My love – my one, my only … love … give me … your hand …" he wheezed uncomfortably. He spoke slowly, only as fast as strength and limited respiration would allow.

Glancing hesitantly in the direction the group had run off in, Serena knelt by the side of the pit. She held out her hand to Nelson.

With what remaining strength he could muster, he took her hand and kissed the palm. Serena brushed the side of his face softly with her fingers, but he took them and curled them around the kiss he had placed in her palm.

"When all else … fails," he rasped, locking on her tearful gaze, "remember this … and never … ever … forget me …"

Serena felt as though something inside of her had been brutally ripped from her chest, just as the air from the Boy in front of her was being ripped from his lungs.

A lump rose in her throat.

"Nelson – why does this have to happen? Why are we still going to the Diamondia Castle? You know as well as I do that this quest is impossible to complete without you!" she sobbed, holding her fisted hand close to her chest – over her bleeding, screaming heart.

Nelson drew in his breath slowly and raised both hands in the air. Rain pelted down on all sides, matting his Sandy brown curls to his head. His pointed ears stuck out stubbornly, and he winced as the QuickSand enveloped him up to his neck. Howls and wails of excruciating volume shattered the sound of the Rain and Wind.

"If there is … one thing … that you learn … toDay … Serena ..." gasped Nelson as the Girl stood, cradling her hands like a newborn Child to her bosom, "It is … tha t…" he stopped short of breath as the Sand engulfed him up to his chin.

"That … that?" Serena urged him nervously, crestfallen. She watched one of her own tears slide to the ground and failed to notice the tiny Flower that sprouted where it fell. She stared deeply into the spring green eyes for the last time, knowing that she would miss them sorely when they had finally closed.

"That nothing …" Nelson stopped to draw a wheezing breath. "Nothing … is impossible … in Forever."

And then, with the ease of a leaf falling from a Tree in Autumn, the Boy's head disappeared underneath the boiling, swirling Marlan QuickSand Pit.

Mike found Serena moments later, a small bushel of Flowers growing where her tears fell to the ground.

"Come on, Serena! We found a place to stay!" he told her, and took her arm to help her up. She glanced briefly at the one hand that protruded from the pit. It stood as limp and dead as a Tree of the Marsh itself.

Slowly, Serena kneeled by the Pit and drew the hand to her. It was cold and white, but one of the fingers twitched, which only coaxed more tears to the Girl's face. Reverently, she kissed the palm of the hand, wishing with all her might that Nelson could have survived the Sandy pit, and curled the fingers around it. Then she stood.

His Prince of Forever Powers must only go so far, she thought with a melancholy shudder. *Now Forever is truly leaderless. What will happen to us all now*?

Mike led her to a large Hill of peat not far away. And though she fought grief like she never had before, she still felt her conscience's nagging presence.

"Why are we camping on a Hill? The Spirits will surly see us if we-"

"We aren't camping on it," Mike explained, shaking Rain from his hair as he glanced up at the nearly exposed Earth. He wrung the Water out of his hat and flopped it back onto his head. Then he took her hand and put on a burst of speed. "We are camping in it."

At first, Serena was flabbergasted. How were they going to camp inside a massive Hill of peat?

Surly he isn't thinking of burrowing into the side of it? Serena thought. She blinked Rain from her eyes. Droplets clung to her eyelashes as she hitched up her skirts and drew Nelson's cloak (which she now wore) around her.

Serena's question was soon answered. Mike strode around the front of the round Hill in a hurry and encountered a flatter backside with a large white Rock placed in the middle of it.

It looks something like a tomb… Serena thought with a shudder.

Mike rapped the Stone sharply twice and shouted,

"Lonvirc!"

Minutes passed, silent minutes, save for the menacing shrieks and piercing howls of the ever-present Spirits.

"Who's Lonvirc?" Serena had to ask at last. The suspense was killing her – and the bright blue Moon was rapidly revealing its luminous smooth surface. In 10 seconds, it would show completely.

Serena shuddered and grabbed Mike's arm. She saw the fear blaze up in his face as he turned to speak to her.

"I don't understand why he isn't answering," he said, looking at the Moon.

Eight seconds, … seven …

"Knock again!" Serena urged him.

Five … four …

Knock, knock, knock!

Three …

BAM! BAM! BAM!

Two … one …

Whooooooooooooooooooooooosssssssssssssssssssshhhhhhhhhhhhhhhh!

All of a sudden, the Wind picked up immensely, throwing itself willy-nilly in all directions. Rain spattered in every which way, showing the twirling, wild dance of the Wind. Whistles and howls screamed even louder than ever now – Serena felt her ears pop, the wails grew so loud, so quick.

Serena slammed her back against the white Stone door so hard that she almost knocked the air out of her lungs.

"They're here!" she hissed. Mike's red-rimmed brown eyes were larger than she had ever seen them before.

"I know," he whispered quickly, turning to the door. He began to beat on it ruthlessly.

Serena was shivering now. Shivering uncontrollably. She could not help it. Fear gripped its icy hand over her heart, squeezing it mercilessly.

Forms, no, Ghosts began to rise from the ground as though rising from the grave. They were short, fat Dwarves and little, skinny Gnomes. Fauns and Elf-like Nymphs accompanied them. Their faces were hideous, ugly and scarred. Toothless mouths fell agape to bring forth the toe-curling wails, and white, transparent hands reached out with long claws to rake the throats of the living and reap them down, like a farmer harvests a crop of wheat. Eyeless sockets glowered at the two helpless, trapped souls, and the Apparitions advanced on them.

Now Serena was nothing less than mortified. Mike had long since stopped his ceaseless beating to gasp in terror at the thousands upon thousands of ragged Wraiths that rattled up from out of the ground to sing their blood-chilling songs of death.

Slowly, dragging their torn, pale bodies along, the armies of the deceased Warriors proceeded to take their revenge on the two petrified companions.

"We're going to die," Serena informed in a terrified voice. She recoiled in horror as the Wraiths drew ever nearer.

"Oh no ... don't say that," Mike sighed, the blue rays of the Moon gleaming spectrally off of his dark bangs and his fogged glasses. The feather on his hat was bent double, dripping little spits of Water on the cap. He placed one arm protectively in front of Serena, as though he wished to push her behind him in the absence of a door.

"Think positive, Serena, not negative. Negative thinking is the last thing we need right now."

"Alright then, I'm positive!" Serena shrieked as a Dwarf Warrior came within about four feet of her. She straightened her back and leaned her head back against the door. "Positive that we're going to die!"

"Ha ha!" Mike mused sarcastically. "We'll get out of this, just wait and see."

She could feel Mike tensing his body next to her.

She closed her eyes. Serena could feel the ice cold fingers of the Spirits touching her unshielded skin already, and she failed to suppress a horrified shudder. Her skin prickled. Her heart Thundered in her ears. The reeking stench of rotting death hung on the air. The Rain pelted her skin, nearly as cold as the chilling presence of the Wraiths.

When Serena opened her eyes again, the ugly, toothless Dwarf Warrior was only inches from her face. With a triumphant grin, he reached out his pearly white hand to touch the Girl's cheek.

Serena was frozen.

Speechless.

She wanted to close her eyes, but couldn't.

She wanted to run away, but couldn't.

She longed to scream aloud, but was unable.

And so she thought,

I really wish Nelson was here.

Emotion welled up within her, but it was chased off like a hound from a Man's supper by the white fingers of the Apparition.

Gently, almost affectionately, the white fingers brushed across the Girl's bare arm.

Serena screeched in pain – the fingers were cold – so cold that they were hot. Serena looked, wide-eyed and panting, at the burn. Steam was rising from her skin, from three long, freshly burnt new scabs. She looked back at the Spirit. He grinned all the wider, and reached to caress her with his flesh-burning fingers again.

"Don't you dare touch me again!"

Serena had suddenly found her voice.

Mike, who she had heard screaming beside her, must have been touched as well by a Faun Warrior. Looking at her, he finally pushed her in back of him and glared at the two grinning Ghosts.

"Leave her alone, you bodiless brutes!"

The Dwarf recoiled with wide, empty sockets, and then, with another toothless grin, he drew his gleaming sword.

Serena and Mike watched the glittering weapon shine under the luminous blue light of the Earth. They saw the Moon almost smirking at them, rising up behind the Dwarf Warrior and the snickering Faun Warrior as the Dwarf prepared to strike, slaying them both at once. He opened his hollow mouth and issued forth the loudest, most ear crackling scream ever imagined – his Warrior call. Then he smiled again.

This was the last thing Serena and Mike saw of the Dwarf Spirit.

Faster than a hummingbird can flap its wings, the door behind Serena and Mike opened. Serena felt herself fall backward into darkness, the screaming, cursing Spirit dancing and growing smaller before her.

And then the white door closed into darkness.

"Mike?" she squeaked, scrambling and crawling in the darkness. She felt a hard, cold Stone floor beneath her hands, but nothing more. Everything was dark, darker than the deep Night Sky itself.

Serena could hear nothing as well – the screams, moans, and howls of the Ghosts were mute to her ears inside this place. Fearing Mike may have been knocked unconscious, she decided to test her voice again.

"Mike? Mike, are you okay?"

Her voice echoed as though she were in a Cave. She could tell from the length of her echo that she was in a well-sized room. Then she heard footsteps - the sound of bare feet slapping on Stone.

"Ohhhh, my head…. Serena! Serena, where are you? Are you okay?"

"Yes! Are you?"

"Yes, I'm fine. Hey Lonvirc, how about some light?"

Serena's ears perked as a new voice, a hesitant, gravelly older voice floated through the room.

"Hold your Unicorns, young one! I am working on it!"

Serena could not stand in the darkness for fear of losing her balance, so she crawled around on the floor, tripping over her skirts and searching for Mike. She found him quickly and sat down beside him, hugging him and thanking him for his protection.

The sound of tinder striking flint awoke their ears from the mysterious silence.

"Who is Lonvirc?" Serena whispered again to Mike, leaning back against the hard Stone wall that he had found. She smelled something unpleasant drifting down from somewhere, and endeavored to block it out of her nose.

"You will find out soon," Mike promised her.

Not far away from the two, red and yellow sparks flashed before their eyes. They bounced off of the momentarily illuminated white floor before extinguishing. Then, as Lonvirc, whoever he was, had predicted, one of the sparks fell onto a torch that he had set on the floor. Immediately, it flamed up into a bright fire, and brought out of the darkness the few things that had before puzzled Serena in appearance.

Under the torch stood a hunched old Man, dressed in rags with a tangled silver beard that grew to his knees. He had beady, little brown eyes, and was more than balding on the top of his round, skinny head.

Serena was right about the room – it was a well-sized place with white Stone walls, floor, and ceiling. Strangely, there were no creases or cracks to signify specific blocks or bricks – all was smooth and pure (also, awkwardly, without any discolorations or spots) as though it were carved out of a perfect white Stone.

The floor was bare from what the torch showed, save for some expensive-looking rugs that Serena spotted under the torch light, and also some wicker chairs, short tables and couches. A fireplace was fashioned out of the wall that the old Man stood next to with half-burned logs laying in wait for a hungry flame.

The hungry flame soon came, carried by the old Man with the slapping feet that, having lit his torch, stripped off his ragged disguise and stood up straight, instantly transformed. A fine, silver-trimmed robe of shimmering pale green graced his impressive appearance. His skin was nearly white; his ears sharp and pointed handsomely, and his tiny brown eyes grew and changed to a flawless green.

An Elf.

His home was most remarkable, or so Serena thought when Lonvirc waved his hand almost carelessly, and more than a dozen pieces of furniture, rugs, vases, mirrors, and other expensive-looking items appeared and graced the once-poor-looking room.

That a person could live such a rich, luxurious life in the middle of a despicable Marsh came as much of a surprise to Serena.

And indeed her thoughts were true, for the old Elf did live a life of luxury.

From the few small rugs and chairs, tables and couches were transformed into elegant furniture, brightly colored and treasure to the eyes. Potted house Plants grew from the floor, tapestries, pictures, and torch sconces from the walls, and highly priced vases and crystal dishes of Flowers and fruit from the wooden furniture. In seconds, the bare-looking room had blossomed into an eloquent, polished chamber fit for a King. A Bird cage of many odd and lovely-looking - and lovely sounding - Birds hung on one wall, while in another cor-

303

ner was thrown an absolute slew of poofy pillows and blankets.

Serena was positively awestruck. In an instant, she forgot her stinging new wound. She looked with wide eyes at Mike, who was studying the room with limited interest.

"It is not the same as when you took us in for the first time," he noted, standing and brushing off his red leggings.

"Ah, yes, but I do like to have some, hm, shall we say, variety in the décor of my humble abode," explained the Elven Man in the same deep, wise voice. He stared critically at a bare spot against a wall and, with a small jab of his fingers, there appeared a cedar chest in the place.

"Where are my friends?" Mike wanted to know. He stooped to help Serena up.

"Oh, yes," mumbled Lonvirc, stroking his long, shiny, smooth beard ponderously. "Nearly had I forgotten them."

He whirled and faced an enormous bookshelf. In a flash, he had the thing scrunched over, and in its place he created a white-walled Stone hut with a pointed circular roof. Out of the only door walked Bob, Theo, Lindsey and Kate, blinking and staggering.

"What did he do to us?" Theo whinnied, shaking his head.

"I made you immortal, young Halfbreed, but only momentarily to deliver you from the claws of danger." Lonvirc replied, his brow creasing as he studied the small Boy.

Theo smiled up at the old Man curiously.

"Really? Wow, that was neat! Can we do it again?"

The Boy's request met a solid chorus of "NO!" from Bob, Lindsey and Kate. Lonvirc ignored the sulking Child with a faint, fluttery smile and moved on to more important matters.

"Now, my friends, how about a nice, long bath and some hot food?" he suggested with a heart-warming smile and a clap of his hands. "And, after that, a bedtime story and a good long rest."

"It sounds wonderful!" Serena said, studying the surrounding beauty. "But… and I do hope you don't mind my asking, but how are we sure we can trust you?"

"Simple!" chuckled the old Elf. A staff popped up beside him and he took it, folding both hands over it patiently. His twinkling green eyes watched her Owlishly for a moment, as though waiting for her to speak.

That smell – that rotten, rancid stench - drifted up to her nose again, seemingly from behind her. Serena felt it was time to find the odor's source. In one fluid movement she turned -

- and came nearly nose-to-nose with a grinning black corpse!

Serena's excitable nerves prickled and she leaped back with a small scream. A cold, white hand with long yellow fingernails grasped her shoulder.

"The answer, my jumpy, young Damsel, is because I am the only one you can trust in these parts."

Serena gulped and tore her eyes from the gruesome corpse. It was con-joined to the wall by a glass case, and was held in a standing upright position by an iron pole that was strapped around its decomposing remains. The body was dressed in metal armor from tip to toe, and the only part of it that could be seen was the face, as Serena had recently found. A handsome Gold helmet was placed on its head, with a long iridescent feather plume poked from the top. Glass eyes made the mummified corpse even scarier to look at – for wherever in the room a person stood, those unpredictable-looking eyes seemed to be watching them, although they never once moved.

"His name was Lord Volcrin, rest his soul," Lonvirc rumbled behind Serena. He sniffed airily. "What a tragic, dramatic end his life came to be. I see you have a small, hm, wound there, my pretty Maiden."

"Yes, and so does my friend Mike." Serena accepted, looking over at Mike's bleeding arm, which a floating pair of hands was already cleaning, treating and bandaging. She looked down at her burnt skin. The three long marks were gradually turning a brownish-black, and becoming very tender.

"Allow me, Child, to mend this flaw."

With this, the old Elf Man placed his hand over the sizzling wound. Mumbling something similar to a Spell under his breath, a tiny flash of white appeared in between his fingers, and when he pulled his hand away, Serena's skin was as tan and unbroken as it had been before the incident with the Dwarf. She looked at the grinning old Man. But he spoke again before she could thank him for his kindness.

"Ah, yes, poor Lord Volcrin. I was unable to save him. Alas, I shall say no more until after supper. Ladies first into the bathing rooms, friends, there should be some Maids in there to tend to you. Gentlemen, I shall entertain you in the meantime. I have many games we may play that have been sitting

305

useless to me for quite some time. You see, it is not often that I have visitors."

Serena had no energy left in her to protest Lonvirc on anything. She quietly followed Lindsey and Kate into the white Stone hut. Inside, they encountered three Servant Girls (Elves), who promptly stripped them and bathed them in the three small bubbling Pools built into the floor like round bath tubs.

Multicolor, fragrant bubbles floated and popped around Serena as she stretched luxuriously in her steaming hot bath. Out of nowhere, three more Elven Maidens appeared and whisked away the Girls' dresses, no doubt to clean, mend, and iron them. Serena removed Teresa's diary beforehand and laid it where it was easily in her sight.

Serena had indeed had a very tiring Day, to say the least. Her muscles ached from traveling, her head throbbed from the sudden brightness of Lonvirc's chamber, and her heart was scattered all over the place in thousands of tiny pieces; she could see now that it would take her months, possibly even years to pick them all up and put her heart together again.

Silent tears mingled with the frothy, foaming bath water. Lindsey and Kate were sniffling as well, and sat next to her in the big Pool-bath. The three Girls mourned together, wiping each other's tears and stroking one another's hair. It felt nice to Serena to have support; it seemed to her that she and the team members had grown somewhat apart while they traveled in the large groups, each having different friends. Now the team was more united than ever – even the Boys, Serena noticed, were still red-nosed and sniffing when they had left them – especially Theo.

Never before had Serena suffered such a close loss. Of course, she had dealt with the knowledge of her parents' deaths, but she didn't even know them, and had still shed a few tears when she learned that she may never return again to her home on Earth. But the more she thought about it, the more she felt as though there was little life for her to be had back on her home planet.

I wonder if Nelson ... oh, Nelson.

Serena's mind was even disrupted.

So she settled back to relax in her bath and release her troublesome thoughts.

~*~*~*~*~

After a very soothing bubble bath, Serena, Lindsey, and Kate (all of whom had settled down some) were oiled and perfumed and dressed in soft, silken white Nightgowns. Serena smiled a mild smile as she spun around in it, admiring the pretty ruffles that decorated the bottom hems. The long, wide-sleeved Nightgown was form-fitting in the chest, abdomen, and hips, but flared out in a cluster of soft, lacey ruffles at the bottom near her ankles. The long sleeves were styled in a likewise position, being tight around the shoulders to about the elbow, and then flaring out precisely at that point. Serena allowed her hair to fall down around her shoulders and dry in its natural position; her scalp ached from having it pulled up for more than a week in its showy, silky blue bow.

The Girls were led back out into the single, one-room chamber by the Maids. Serena snatched up the diary protectively before exiting and, as she had done before, she made a pouch on the inside of her ruffled white skirt and kept the diary there.

Lonvirc entertained them with his Elven Powers whilst the three Boys received washings. He changed the chamber's décor around several times, moving full wardrobes from one side of the room to the other in the air, adding a vase of Flowers here and deducting a small wooden table from their sight there. Serena was nothing less than amazed as the pale-skinned Man made the three Girls weightless with a snap of his fingers, allowing them to float around the room as though on wings.

Serena smiled and looked down at the tiny glass bottle of sparkling iridescent powder. Not long ago, in fact, she had wings. Pixie wings. And on them she had soared through the setting Skies, free as a Bird and 10 times as happy, holding the hand of the one and only Prince of Forever, Nel-

No! Serena thought suddenly, landing on a pile of feather pillows and velvet cushions in one corner. She tried to make herself seem only tired and unnoticeable as she bent forward to thrust her face into one of the pillows. She closed her eyes and shook her head, wanting so to erase the newly burned memory of Nelson's cold, white hand standing limp from the ravenous Sands. Tears leaked down her clean cheeks and stained the pillow. She did not want to spoil the fun of staying in luxury. She could not think about that horrid disaster, not now, not here. She absolutely did not choose to trouble herself and the others with the dramatic, tragic thought of their loss, especially since such behavior could lead to Lonvirc asking her what happened, which would cause her to have to explain the story to him through even more tears.

"Ah, young Flower," whispered a gravelly voice.

Too late.

"What troubles you?"

Lonvirc stood behind Serena and laid a sympathetic, wrinkled white hand on the Girl's back.

Serena could have sworn she had seen this coming; the very feeling of another presence close to her had popped into her senses just as she stood to take flight once again.

"I …I do not want to speak of it," she replied softly, wiping a tear away distractedly.

Loncirv seemed to ignore her comment and promptly strode around to face her. His twinkling green eyes reminded Serena of a similar pair that were now closed forever, and never to shine with the vigor they once possessed.

Flowers awoke from the ground as a wave of fresh tears sprung to Serena's eyes.

Kate and Lindsey, both looking tearful, landed on either side of her. And the three Girls cried, holding each other.

"It is the loss of one who was, shall we say, essential to you, was he not?"

Serena's heart nearly stopped.

"How did you know that?" Kate demanded, staring the wise elder figure close in his bewhiskered face. He tucked his hands into the long sleeves of his shimmering pale green robe.

"Elven Lords can sense another's feelings if that person is closely observed," he answered smoothly, peering at them through slitted green eyes. Lindsey changed the subject and Serena was glad.

"You are an Elven Lord? Isn't that something similar to a King?" Lindsey sniffed. Serena's eyes opened wide in sincere curiosity.

"Was, dear Girls, I was an Elven Lord. And yes, it is something similar to a King. An unmarried King, in Forever, is a Lord."

Serena forgot her own emotional perils for the moment, seeking to push the thoughts to the back of her mind and learn more about the tall, thin Elven Lord (or, as he had promptly pointed out, former Elven Lord.) who stood before her, Lindsey and Kate.

"Why … I mean, how come you are no longer in that position?" she wondered, stepping forward a bit.

"I was once the subject of a great King …" he began after a ponderous pause, "I was his loyal Servant, so shall we say … Yet one Day that great old

King died, and his young daughter stepped up to take the throne. However, when the time for the crowning ceremony came, instead of the Princess taking the throne, another subject of the King pulled me forward. I was crowned King, and found that for safety purposes, the supposed Princess and I had been switched at birth. My mother, whom I had been living with, was not my own, but hers, you see. I learned this and settled down to rule as the Lord of that Kingdom."

Lonvirc blinked Owlishly and made his way over to a circle of couches and chairs set squarely in the middle of the room. Like three eager young puppies, the Girls followed him and seated themselves on one of the poofy couches.

Serena felt the almost-too-soft cushions swallowing her up. Lindsey and Kate bounced on either side of her, trying to cheer her and themselves up. They watched Lonvirc light up a fire surrounded by decorative Stones right in the center of the couches. For further entertainment, he pulled a vial of multicolor glitter from his robe and threw it unscrupulously into the fire. The fire, in return, flared up into their faces in various colors - red, blue, purple, orange, yellow, green, silver and white shone brilliantly from the floor.

Serena marveled at the Magical fire, then suddenly remembered the reason Lonvirc had led them over to the social circle. She looked at the old Elf, who was seated in an elegant, high-backed armchair directly across from them over the fire. His complexion flickered with the shadows cast by the colorful flames.

"You said that you settled down to be the Lord of your territory, but you have not yet told us of how you came to live in the Blue Marsh," she tested him softly.

Lonvirc leaned forward in his chair, his hands on his knees, and his pale, strangely wrinkle-less complexion dancing under the Rainbow firelight. He stared each one of the three Girls in the eye; Serena felt shivers as his gaze passed hers, remembering the almost identical pair of eyes that she had once known and loved dearly. Her heart collapsed within her chest and she felt tears leaking to her eyes again, but she hastily shook the emotion away and forced herself to focus her attention on the pointy-eared Elf that sat ready to reiterate a long story to them.

Lonvirc stroked his long, silver-white beard and opened his mouth to answer.

Just then, Mike, Bob and Theo appeared, looking somewhat comical in their long, white Night shirts and fuzzy white Night caps. Still digging Water out of their ears, they seated themselves silently on another couch.

"When do we get our clothes back?" Theo required glumly.

"In the morning." Lonvirc returned, staring somehow longingly into the iridescent fire. He looked up at the group of six.

"And now, my friends, since we are gathered together, I shall allow you to eat while I relate to you the Legend of the Blue Marsh."

With a soft crackling sound, long coffee tables appeared before the discovery team, filled from edge to edge with tantalizing dishes. Meat platters, soups, stews, fruits, puddings, cakes, skewered vegetables, and all other manner of delectable food danced persuasion before their eyes, their mouth-watering aromas caressing the explorers' noses. Without missing a beat, Serena followed the others' example as they hungrily devoured the food. She didn't doubt that they were all glad to feel a warm meal in their stomachs again.

Lonvirc's slow, rhythmic voice hummed in her ears in soothing tones as he began his long tale.

"Handed down from father to son, grandfather to grandson, and Storyteller to Traveler, this is the long-told saga of the Legend of the Blue Marsh."

Chapter Thirty-Seven: The Legend of the Blue Marsh

Once upon a time, the Blue Marsh as we now know it was neither blue, nor Marshy. Nay, the very place was a Land of Meadows – part of the Windy Meadows to be exact. The Land was beautiful and prosperous, so it was told, filled with soft Grasses, luscious Banyan Trees here and there, and Fields, Hills, and Valleys scattered with an array of colorful singing Flowers. Upon feeling the warmth of the Sun, the Flowers would open their delicate petals and bring forth a song, each one different from the next. Birds chattered and nested in the Trees, Fish swam in the Edgewood River that bordered the Meadow's Southernmost reaches, and Animals and Travelers alike roamed the Land in peace.

Meanwhile, a union between the Fortress of Dekksor, that bordered the Edgewood River to the South, and the Castle of Raunette far to the NorthEast in the Forests, was taking place. Lord Volcrin, an ambitious young Nymph of Dekksor had recently taken Lady Jasmine of Raunette as his bride. Now, Jasmine the Nymph Princess was a beautiful Damsel – a Maiden that several young Lords at that time had taken note of. She also was the type of bride that was not particularly easy to win over. But somehow, Lord Volcrin convinced the good Lady to marry him, and so the marriage was held out in the magnificent Meadows.

Now, there also lived at this time a terrible Nymph Warlock by the name of Lord Falbitrex, who, upon hearing the happy marriage proclamations of Lord Volcrin and Lady Jasmine, was enraged farther than anger itself - for he also felt personal feelings for the fair Damsel. Every Day while the young Mistress was still unmarried, she would walk along in her Gardens, and every Day the evil, ugly Warlock Lord Falbitrex would meet her there, and plead for her hand in marriage. And of course, every Day, Lady Jasmine would order him out of her beautiful Gardens, and turn down his desperate beseech for her to marry him.

And so, when Lord Falbitrex discovered that Lady Jasmine had chosen another to be her husband, he was a very furious fellow indeed. He gathered for himself an army and ordered the death of Lady Jasmine in his rage.

So, Lord Falbitrex's orders were carried out, and one of his sneakiest, most wicked and most sly Creatures was brought forward to hunt down and

311

assassinate the good Lady Jasmine. In less than a few weeks the dirty deed was done, and Lady Jasmine was murdered in her own bed. It was said that the killer, under Lord Falbitrex's orders, was so quick and so smooth that Lady Jasmine was dead before she was even halfway to fully conscious, and so she never knew why, how, or even that she had died at all. The killer had stabbed Lady Jasmine in her back, and through her heart, so that her death was easy and painless.

Now Lord Volcrin, when he found that his beloved had been condemned to death because of the evil Warlock's jealousy, was overcome with a mixture of grief and anger. When the good Lady Jasmine had been put to rest in her beautiful Gardens, where she had walked every Day while she still breathed life, Lord Volcrin pledged revenge for the death of his betrothed, and vowed that should he even die in battle himself, he would avenge the death of Lady Jasmine.

Lord Falbitrex had risen for himself a mighty army of Dwarves and Above Ground Gnomes, while Lord Volcrin had called upon aid from Castle Raunette, which was comprised mostly of Fauns. They came together with his own forces at Dekksor. After learning of each other's solid vows, they agreed to meet one another in battle – not war (for there is no such thing as war in Forever) – but for a one-time battle that would settle the rivals' feuds for good.

For months, the two sides built up their arms, strengthened their troops and exchanged venomous threats. Lord Falbitrex was not the least bit sorry for what he had done (that is, what he had ordered to be done), and was willing to defend his case in any manner.

But Lord Volcrin was not a Creature who was ignorant in the ways of battle – he was taught many wise battle techniques by his father and schoolmasters - and therefore he knew many tricky moves to make should the occasion arise. And although the young Lord Volcrin was being provoked and goaded by the eager Lord Falbitrex, he took his time in agreeing to come to battle. For you see, Lord Volcrin was not an eager type of Creature. No, Lord Volcrin was a wise ruler in the ways of battle, and planned his actions thoroughly before setting to the Meadows.

And when that fateful Day did come, Lord Volcrin was cautious in leading his forces onto the field. "As many as the blades of Grass," or so it had been said, was the forces of his mighty ambush that lay in wait through that cool, Rainy Night.

Morning opened with a Sunrise that was the color of a grapefruit - red, orange and pink. Being also taught in the ways of sailing, Lord Volcrin knew that a blood red Sunrise meant Rain. He smiled to himself. A good Rain was all he needed to hide his position from the oncoming opponent.

And Rain it did, only moments after the Sun rose over the Hills of the horizon. The fat drops pelted the faces of the many soldiers, each one silent and steady, waiting, waiting for the forces of Lord Falbitrex to encounter them, and each one knowing his role in the play; and what he must do.

Around midDay, when Lord Falbitrex's troops arrived at the Meadows, they found an empty battlefield.

Or, almost empty.

For there, standing very plainly out in the middle of the raging Rains, was Lord Volcrin, wearing his best battle armor and waiting patiently for the large army to stop before him. Deep behind them, a voice ordered them to halt. And Lord Fabitrex flew up from the middle of his massive troops, and conversed with the single Warlord before him in loud, bass-voiced barks.

"Where is your army, almighty Lord Volcrin?" sneered Lord Falbitrex.

Lord Volcrin remained silent, his long, elegant cloak fluttering in the Wind.

"And your weapons, almighty Lord? Where are they?" sniveled Lord Falbitrex. For it was true; the Warlord had not hide nor hair of a sword or scabbard on him.

Yet, still Lord Volcrin remained silent.

Lord Falbitrex took several steps forward in the air, and drew his long, sharp sword. He strode straight up to the lone figure and placed his sword at the Lord's throat.

"And your dear wife, MiLord, where is she? No, do not answer me, for I alone can tell you. Or, rather, I can send you …"

And he beheaded the Nymph Lord with a single, strong swipe.

" … so that you may unite with her in death!" Lord Falbitrex seethed. He executed a sly smile. Finally, after all this time, his revenge had been quenched, his anger satisfied. Lord Volcrin was dead.

But Lord Falbitrex was wrong.

Terribly wrong.

For it was then that he noticed not blood gushing from the neck of the figure, but cotton.

"Tis a fraud!" Lord Falbitrex howled.

And then an arrow flew from out of the Skies.

And it planted itself in Lord Falbitrex's back, through his heart.

It is said that the Warlock was dead before he even hit the ground. This may very well have been true, for so fast and well-aimed was the arrow that Lord Volcrin had shot that it hit its target straight on and pierced him through his heart, or what small emotional organ the Warlock may have possessed at that time.

Before Lord Falbitrex's army could react, heavily armored Nymphs came dropping out of the air carrying Faun Warriors on their backs. From every side and direction they came, hurtling their strength at the leaderless, unprotected ranks of Gnomes and Dwarves.

The Rain persisted and the battle raged on, and for the rest of that long Day and into the Night the two sides fought, triumphing and falling each in turn until, nearly five Days later, not a single soul was left living on that battle-field.

Except for Lord Volcrin.

The devastation in the Meadows was great; corpses and bodies lay strewn over every Flower for miles around, so that they could no longer sing when the Sun greeted them at dawn. Blood flowed through the Land in thick Streams, drowning the Meadows, burying the bodies, and mingling with the tears of the Sky. It Rained and Rained and Rained, and the Land flooded and drowned, and turned into a red Lake.

Yet there was something special, something Magical, about the full Moon shining on the mixings of blood and the tears of the earth, for that red Lake was wrought the corpses of both armies, searching for more living souls to kill. They could not and did not fight one another any longer, being joined in death, and sought to destroy any living Creatures that happened to inhabit or even pass by their Lands. They sought revenge for their untimely deaths.

Lord Volcrin knew he was not safe out in the Lake. He could not return to either Raunette or Dekksor, for if he returned alone with not even one survivor of the army, surly his empire would overthrow him and sentence him to prison. So, he found for himself an abandoned temple of ivory, and found that this warded the Spirits away, because ivory was bone, and bone was already dead. It was here that Lord Volcrin sought refuge after that terrible five-Day battle, and it was here that he died of hunger and thirst, for there was no food or clean Water to be had in the red Lake, and no Trees to make for himself a raft to flee its devastation. And so it was here that the great Lord of Dekksor fell, wept, and died, satisfied that he had both avenged his beloved's death and brought

314

about his own that he may see her again in his life after death.

Years later, the Lake drained, leaving a rotting Swamp in its wake. The blood that was shed so many years before still lingers here in that very same Swamp, dying its waters and its features blue because of its extreme age and amazing preservation. And the Creatures who fought in the battle still seek, upon the rising of a full Moon, to destroy any living being and to spill their fresh blood upon their own reeking remains. The Bog Lands' haunting inhabitants prowl its Waters during the Night, seeking fresh prey. It is in this way that the Blue Marsh is attempting to expand.

The Ghouls' hunger for revenge is seldom satisfied, for most wise Travelers have learned of the perils of the Swamp and when to stay well away from it because of these perils. However, every once in a while there will come along a foolish young Traveler who wanders away from the path and finds himself transformed into one of these wicked souls seeking fresh blood. And, because of the Rivers of blood that still run in the veins of this Land, these Swamp Lands have appropriately been named the Blue Marsh.

Serena awoke to the appealing melodies of SongBirds trilling in her ears. Something smelling faintly of brown sugar wafted in the air and caressed her nose.

Drowsily, she remembered the Night before. Theo had crawled into her lap and fallen asleep during the story. Serena had felt her own eyelids drooping after gorging herself on the tasty platters that Magically vanished once they had finished with them. She clung to the very last word of Lonvirc's story, and vaguely remembered finding six beds lined up behind her. She had carried the slumbering Halfbreed Child to one of the middle ones and they had all tucked him in. She kissed him goodNight on the forehead like any good mother would do to her own Child.

She felt, as she had climbed into her own soft, white bed, that it was now her responsibility along with the guidance of the other explorers to care for the young Lad, since his only caregiver, his brother, had miserably perished.

Serena hardly slept that Night, despite her grogginess after the bedtime tale. For one thing, Lindsey and Kate were still sniffling; Kate was moaning. Mike and Bob stifled a few stoic sniffs and whispered to the Girls comforting things. Serena thought she may have been the worst. Although she did not moan, she still sobbed openly, her own tears mingling with those of the others. In the end, they pushed all their beds together as one and whispered softly to each other until they dropped off to sleep one by one. Around midNight Theo awoke crying up a Storm from a Nightmare, crying more when he realized that the Nightmare was true, that his brother truly was dead. Sniffling, he deserted his own bed in the midst of them all and sought out Serena in her bed. He snuggled next to her, wanting to feel warmth and comfort, which she offered even in her own sorrow and grief. Serena was the last to fall asleep. The nagging thought of Nelson, her best friend, her love, and the one and only Father of Forever, had prolonged her grief and barred her away from the path of peaceful rest. Her eyes never stopped leaking from dusk until dawn, though she kept herself quiet so that Theo would fall asleep (which he eventually did). She had to set aside her dripping pillow and sleep on the flat but soft mattress of her bed because of it. Fewer than three hours before dawn, her emotions settled and she was allowed to sleep.

For a moment, Serena laid with her eyes closed and her senses alert. She began to think that the past weeks, now almost a month, was all just a silly dream.

Yes, that's it, she thought, nuzzling into the security and comfort of her bed. *This is all just a silly dream – I am still sleeping in my attic, it is summer, and there are songbirds outside my window. Bertha is downstairs whipping up a batch of microwavable French Toast. There is no Dr. Birkwood, no Teresa's diary, no team, and ... and no Nelson.*

Of course, Serena knew that she was wrong except for her last assumption, and opened her sore, red eyes, which, almost involuntarily now, were still leaking with hot, stinging tears. Her cheeks burned also, and her nose was congested and hard to breathe through. Her throat was sore from breathing through her mouth.

Life goes on , she told herself as she sat up weakly. She somehow felt much better now that she had accomplished this new, optimistic motto. She spotted Mike, Bob and Kate already up and assisting Lonvirc (who had somehow disappeared overNight and reappeared again in the morning) with arranging dishes of delicious-smelling sausage, eggs, biscuits, fruit and pastries. All three were fully dressed in their former clothes, the knapsacks being revived and hung on some hooks nearby. Their weapons lay at the base of these hooks.

Life goes on ... Life goes on. Serena chanted in her mind. She slowly sat up, looking down at a stretching Theo. She hugged him warmly and helped him get up.

"Serena! You're awake!" exclaimed Lindsey, leaping up from the corner filled with cushions and pillows. Her brown locks bounced up beside her face and Serena noticed that she, too, was fully dressed in her clean, pink dress once more.

"Yes," Serena croaked, and studied a thick cloth wall for changing behind to one side.

"Oh goodness, Serena, you look terrible! Here, let's get you back into your dress."

Serena had little energy to object as Lindsey bustled about herding her behind the curtain and fussing over getting her back into that uncomfortable corset and frilly, ruffled blue dress. However, when she was done, Lindsey wrapped her arms around Serena and asked her how she was feeling. Serena replied honestly – she knew that Lindsey could not have been feeling much better, judging from her sleepy pink eyes and pink cheeks. At that time Serena

317

realized just how much like sisters the two Girls were. They shared all of their feelings with each other.

Tucking Teresa's diary away, Serena found that all rips in her dress had been mended, and the dress itself cleaned, ironed and starched for looks. She hated to rip apart the neat stitches that had been sewn across the gap where she had kept Teresa's diary, but, muttering her new motto, she undid them and slipped in the diary along with her hair ribbon and bonnet. She washed her face and hands, and followed Lindsey to the breakfast table.

"I'm still full from last Night," Kate announced, picking at her food.

On either side of her, Bob and Mike were tucking in with a will, and little Theo, now awake, not dressed, but very hungry, was attempting to mimic their heroic feats. He soon was dressed, not feeling a bit better, and got sick behind the curtain.

Lonvirc ordered his trusty Elf Maids to come out of their white Stone hut and clean the young Halfbreed up, all the while casting Charms to settle his stomach and his heart. He appeared from the curtain clean, dressed, and feeling quite a bit better, but he still would not smile at anything.

Serena did not admit that her appetite was lousy, but nonetheless proceeded to feed herself.

Just because fate has taken a hand at my destiny does not mean that I will forget to care for myself, she told herself. *If Nelson where here right now, he would not want me starving because of grief.*

And so the Girl downed a pastry and two eggs.

Life goes on.

After breakfast, Serena retreated to her bed, which she found made up with a new haversack sitting on its quilts. Smiling weakly, she accepted it, and hitched it up onto her back. She felt the familiar weight of its contents in return.

"We will set off now," she heard Mike telling Lonvirc. "We are eternally grateful for your kindness in having us at your humble abode."

Lonvirc's smile could not have been any wider. His Elven green eyes shone at the group as they banded at the wall that was supposedly the wall which held the door.

"Nay, thank you, young Travelers, for staying with me. I do so very much enjoy company, so whenever you may be passing through these parts again, do stop by to visit me. For it does, after a time, become somewhat quiet and lonely about this old white temple, just poor Lord Volcrin and I."

"Certainly we will, should we chance by these ways again," Bob promised, and nodded his head politely with his hand over his heart.

Serena wordlessly joined the group, nodding her own blonde head to the Elf Man in respect as she passed.

With a smile and a wave of his hand, Lonvirc had opened the square little door –

- which, embarrassing enough for the team, just so happened to be positioned on the exact opposite side of the room.

Stifling humiliated, nervous chuckles, the group of six plodded across the room to the open door. Serena felt a hand lay on her shoulder as she passed the old Man, and she stopped and turned to face him.

"I do believe, young Serena, that you have forgotten something," noted Lonvirc with another of his wide, Elven smirks.

Serena admired the aged creases in the Man's forehead. How very much like a father he had been to them in their short stay with him!

"What have I forgotten?" she asked.

Wordlessly, Lonvirc held up a necklace, to the end of which was attached a tiny bottle with silvery glittering powder inside. Serena felt her mouth drop open in surprise. She reached for it, and Lonvirc gently clasped the keepsake around her neck.

"I … thank you!" she finally gasped, grasping the Pixie Powder. Without that necklace, she would have nothing to remind her of Nelson, save for the dark-colored cloak that she now wore upon her shoulders, regardless of its contrast to the bright color of her dress.

"You are very welcome, Madame," Lonvirc returned, smiling all the wider. Serena turned, yet she felt hesitant to go. Still one thought bothered her about this strange, kind old Man.

"How did you come to live in this place? You never quite finished your own story," she inquired. She turned back in the doorway to face him –

- and gasped.

The Man was no longer mortal, standing under the rays of Sunlight, but transparent and Ghostly. She glanced back at the group, which was stooping at a nearby peat mound to wait for her and to tighten their Marsh Shoes for traveling.

"L-Lonvirc … you're," Serena stuttered.

319

The Elf, or rather, now, the Nymph, pulled out of the Sunlight and back into the shadows of his home. The group gathered around Serena, wondering if what they had just seen was real. Lonvirc's voice seemed to change tones as he explained.

"Immortal, yes. For you see, young Travelers, that I already have told you my story. Know you now that the name Lonvirc and Volcrin are the same – save for the order of the letters. Volcrin and I, dear Children, are forever to be the same, for we are but one. I, Lonvirc, am the Spirit, whereas Volcrin is the body. Together we are one and the same, and forever shall remain so."

Slowly, Serena understood. The group was silent in awe and smiled at one another. Volcrin was Lonvirc, and Lonvirc was Volcrin. Both names carried the same letters, both meant only one Creature. Serena smiled. Why had she not seen before?

"Well, Lonvirc-Volcrin, we bid you farewell, for we must leave now. Thank you for your hospitality. If it had not been for you, none of us would be standing here right now. But stay well, for if we should pass these regions again someDay, you should expect my visit. I pray you keep well!"

And Serena, in a flourish of Golden curls and ruffled blue skirts, turned and followed the others, who had backed off at the sight of the ghostly Man and started talking among themselves. Lonvirc-Volcrin stood in the doorway, smiling and waving them goodbye while being painstakingly careful not to step into the Sunlight.

Serena shivered as soon as the little place melted back into the distance. She now knew that the ivory chamber was neither Lonvirc's chamber, nor Volcrin's temple, but for both an eternal tomb.

~*~*~*~*~

Shortly before noon the explorers stopped to make lunch and to rest their weary limbs. Serena again felt the familiar pain in her legs from doing complete knee-highs every time she took a step. She could see that Kate, Lindsey, Mike and Bob all had similar aches. Theo was exempt from the pain because from time to time he would build up his strength and hover a short distance to save him the trouble of walking. He kept up with the group well, despite his sudden illness that morning.

Serena studied a green fruit chained together by a single stem – five perfectly round spheres of fruit, one on top of the other, hanging from what looked similar to a grape stem, but what clearly was not. One by one she plucked the ping-pong sized fruits from their stem and ate them, enjoying the burst of peppermint flavor the fruit embellished. Then she set to a small, hard, flat cake that carried cream in its center. This, she knew without a doubt, was a cake that she had tasted before in Bendar.

Bendar. Oh, how long it has been since we departed from the Fortress. she thought, watching Bob's tall, skinny figure bend to pick a particular good out of his haversack. She bit again into the cake, savoring the rich creamy center. *I wonder when we will reach Middleton... and what it will be like there.*

"HEY!" she heard Lindsey shriek behind her.

In a heartbeat, Serena turned-

-and found a dark green Goblin advancing on Lindsey with a cutlass.

Theo suddenly leaped in back of the Goblin and tripped him at the ankles with Nelson's sword. With a howl of pain, the Goblin fell forward and nearly slew Lindsey, but Mike grabbed her at the waist and leaped away with her.

Before the Goblin could get to his weakened feet again, Theo had roared his own battle cry (which Serena did not understand at all), and ran the sword through the back of the Goblin, slaying him instantly.

Panting, Theo withdrew the sword and wiped it clean on the peat mound.

The explorers stood speechless, frozen and stunned.

Then Mike and Bob rushed forward and lifted the Boy shoulder-high and congratulated him.

"I did it! I killed the Goblin! I slew my first foe!" Theo laughed, and sheathed the sword.

"You killed it," shivered Serena, looking away from the unpleasant sight.

"You saved my life!" Lindsey gasped.

"First Kill!"

"Got a good one, Theo!"

Serena smiled some to reassure the Boy that she had indeed seen his heroic deed, and was proud of him for accomplishing such a feat, but deep inside she felt pity for the Goblin.

Of course, the Creature had every intention of slaying poor Lindsey, and if Theo had not stepped in, the Girl easily could have been killed. But Serena felt that there was really no need to murder the assailant – she felt that just as soon as Theo had him down on the ground, he had already won the fight.

Perhaps I am too skeptical on the subject of killing, Serena thought to herself. She spotted a Tree not far away and made her way over to it to hang her haversack up off the ground to prevent it from getting wet. *Killing here in Forever is just a matter of self-defense, and I will need to grow accustomed to such an act ... and life must go on.*

She stopped to think about her new motto. Faintly, she heard the other five explorers still yelling and celebrating Theo's first victory. This she blocked out with a fresh thought.

And yet how can life go on when life is being destroyed?

Serena sighed and shook the thought away. She turned to look at her five celebrating companions – but - found herself nose-to-nose with a dark green Goblin.

She gasped, realizing her state. She was unarmed with her back to the Tree, and she could see over the Goblin's shoulder that more of its kind had surrounded the rest of the group. All over, Goblins were popping up from the Marsh, dressed in baggy rags, carrying sabers, cutlasses and swords, and all uglier than the Night was black.

Serena winced as the Goblin almost reverently placed his saber at the Girl's throat and smiled a wicked, crooked, and mirthless smile. Serena held her breath to escape the Goblin's foul breath. She scowled at the sweaty green face of her attacker. And, for some reason, found herself unafraid of the death that was threatening her.

That soon changed as the saber was raised to slay her.

Life goes on, she thought as she closed her eyes

Serena braced herself for pain.

Excruciating pain.

Excruciating pain that did not come.

Serena heard a whoosh and a thump, then a splat.

She opened her eyes.

And found a Pixie.

But this was no ordinary Pixie.

"Jerry!" she gasped, overwhelmed. She looked at the lifeless figure of the near-murderer lying face-down in the Marsh muck.

"Serena!" laughed Jerry, flexing his iridescent, temporary wings. He propped his hands up on his hips. "Don't look so surprised. I've been follow-ing you all morning."

"You ... but what about,"

She looked over at the group of explorers, who had formerly been belea-guered by Marsh Goblins, and found that all of them had suddenly sprouted Pixie wings, and were hovering high over the heads of the raging Goblins. Theo was even pulling faces at the miscreants as he dodged the globs of Marsh mud they threw at him.

Black, colorless eyes turned to the only wingless intruder – Serena – and began to advance on her.

Grabbing her haversack from the Tree, Jerry lifted Serena away from the oncoming danger just in time, and followed the group in the air to a stur-dy-looking Tree. There he perched and quickly sprinkled Serena with Pixie Powder from a satchel he wore around his chest. As soon as she realized he had done this, she removed Nelson's cloak, as not to damage it, and stuffed it carefully into her knapsack. And, finding that her back was no longer vacant to carry the knapsack, she pulled each strap over one arm and wore the thing backwards as all the others seemed to be doing. The group paused to rip larger holes in the backs of tunics and to further unbutton the backs of dresses on the females. Then they all took off after Jerry.

Wordlessly the explorers fled the scene and flew up over the thick morn-ing mists. Once they had gained some altitude and caught their breath, the team praised Jerry for his unexpected return and his clever escape. Serena was glad to see that he was safe and well, after worrying about him for so long. It was plain that he had stopped at Bendar; he was finely dressed in a red tunic with leggings and a cape with a long slit for his wings, and he now carried a large satchel and a sword.

"Middleton is this direction," he stated, guiding them in a SouthEasterly direction. "Er, that is where you are going, isn't it?"

"Yes." Bob replied, tossing his black-brown bangs from his face. His hair ribbon must have been lost in the scuffle. "That is our next destination."

"Good. Then that is where I shall lead you." Jerry told them. Serena took note of the slight British accent in his voice. Apparently, he was beginning to develop the accent just as they were.

"We should make the town by Nightfall tomorrow if we travel fast. I used the last of my Pixie Powder on our escape from the Goblins. So, most likely, we will be walking the last part of the way there."

Serena stretched her wing muscles and cherished her flight over the Marsh. Bob, Mike, Kate and Lindsey enjoyed their own wings as well, as this was a new experience for them. Freely they looped and zigzagged, soaring and falling and gliding gracefully on the Misty breath of the Marsh. Theo followed in close pursuit, flapping his own pair of small Pixie wings.

Serena listened intently as Jerry told them of his adventures after he had parted with them. Apparently, after his argument with Kate, Jerry had traveled South and a touch West until he ran into the Village of Tenbarrum. There he stayed for a number of Days, and then he made a beeline for Bendar and Fifftor. Serena learned that he had missed them by one Day, arriving the morning after the Day they had first set off. He learned of their plans of traveling through the Forest, and immediately set off after them on wing and with enough Pixie Powder to last him a full trip to Middleton.

"That was originally where I planned on meeting you guys," he continued, dodging a small Cloud. "In Middleton, because I knew that you would have to cut across the path in order to reach the Windy Meadow, and I figured that since you probably wouldn't have been at any Towns or Cities since Bendar, Middleton would be an ideal spot to stop and reload. Am I wrong?"

Serena had only to shake her head. Of course, Jerry was not wrong at all, but there was a second reason Serena was shaking her head. There was a question that had been left unanswered, and probably because, up until now, it had been left unasked.

"Why did you come after us, Jerry?" Serena asked tentatively. She looked

324

over at him and tossed her tousled curls away from her face. Jerry beat his Pixie wings almost ponderously.

Silence passed, all six of the airborne crew listened intently for an answer, hanging on the Boy's words when he did respond.

"I ..." Jerry sighed, looking each of them over with sad, truthful blue-gray eyes. "I couldn't make it out there all on my own. I only had so much knowledge of the place, only so much money to get me by and so much instinct on what to do."

Kate looked perfectly satisfied with a big grin on her face.

"So, in other words, you needed us?" she interrogated, eyeing him with her deep brown eyes.

More silence passed.

Then,

"I guess you could say that, Kate. I knew I would be discarding my post as captain if I just left you guys leaderless. I thought about what you said, Kate, and really, you were correct when you stated that you guys didn't need me – I mean, I don't know this Continent any better than you do, and you really would be no better off here with me-"

"Jerry!" Serena exclaimed softly. Studying his blue-grey eyes, as mystic and wondrous as the Mists that swirled around them, the Girl reached out and took Jerry's hand.

"Jerry, I was wrong when I said that."Kate apologized in a shaky voice. She wiped away a tear, hugged him and took his hand. "There is no excuse for what I told you. I was just plain and simply wrong to threaten your position as the captain. I'm only a minor member of this team, and I had no say whatsoever in firing you. I was wrong, Jerry, and I'm sorry for it. Can you ever forgive me?"

Jerry's ears were red, and for a moment Serena thought he might have been crying. But when he lifted his face to forgive Kate, he only looked tired and relieved.

"No." Jerry said.

Serena's chest froze.

"No, I," he added quickly, "should be the one asking for forgiveness, Ladies. I was ignorant not to forgive you – I knew that something was building up inside of you." He wet his lips nervously. "But at the time, I didn't see that. At the time, it just seemed a better idea to leave you guys on your own … you know, to see if anything would improve, and make you realize that you did

325

need me … which, after awhile, you did."

Serena smiled and nodded knowingly.

"I just … I just figured you wouldn't need me because that Nelson kid was… well, taking matters into his own hands. He seems so much more of a leader than I do."

Serena's smile faded and she felt a lump rise in her throat at the mere mention of the perished Boy's name, and, regardless of the voice screaming "Life goes on!" in her head, she corrected Jerry as Lindsey and Kate flew ahead to join up with Mike and Bob, who were scouting the area and batting around the Mist.

"He … he seemed," she corrected him, feeling like there were bricks in her lungs.

Jerry looked at her.

Serena could feel the tears rising already.

"Seemed? Surly you mean he seems. Excuse me, but I believe I have another apology to make," Jerry stretched his neck forward, looking around the faces of the airborne team. For the first time, he seemed to notice that Nelson was not around. He scratched his brown-haired head. "Where is that kid anyway?"

"He's not a kid!" Serena sobbed. "He wasn't a kid. Jerry, Nelson is … Nelson is …d-d-"

Serena felt the lump in her throat squeeze hot tears onto her face. She turned away, hands over mouth, embarrassed with both her stuttering speech and her failure to accept the truth.

"He's dead?" Jerry whispered, shocked.

Serena shook her head in her hands, urging her wings on to greater speed.

"Y-yes …" she stammered finally, making a diligent endeavor to regain her shaken composure. She dried her eyes delicately, staring up at the Heavens as though begging for support. A single sigh escaped her constricted throat.

"Yes, Jerry, Nelson died. Last Night. He accidentally stepped into something called a Marlan QuickSand Pit. That is why Theo now carries his sword."

Feeling confident that the worst part was over, Serena went on to explain some of the minor details, and, much to her surprise, felt somewhat refreshed afterwards, as though the past had left her as she explained the story to Jerry.

She also filled him in, with the occasional input of Mike, Bob, Kate, Lindsey and Theo, on their ventures since they had last parted. Jerry seemed full to bursting with questions about their journey, and the team instantly obliged to answer these.

Time flew by just as the seven explorers flew over the Marsh, heading ever Easterly with a tiny touch South. Before Serena knew it, dusk was setting, and the Skies were tucked in with their sparkling, Diamond-studded blanket called Night, its two crescent Moons poking their heads out of the covers to peer down on the World below.

Jerry stopped the team just after dusk when the light was so dim that they could not see where they were flying. This forced them to land, much to the protest of Mike, Bob, Kate and Lindsey, this being their first experience with flight.

Serena felt somewhat relieved to be in the air and to feel herself flying up in the azure blue as free as a Bird. It was as though all of her troubles had left her behind when she took to the Skies. Even more so was this theory believed correct when she landed to make camp – and felt the swirling problems return to her head. Her wings crumpled and vanished soon after she landed, stranding her on the wet, Swampy Land and barring her from the clear Night Sky above.

Solemnly, Serena ate her supper – a lukewarm stew that the Boys had attempted to cook over a strangled little fire. She noticed that they had great trouble in even starting the fire; the ground was wet after the Rains and was not the fastest to absorb collecting RainWater.

Afterwards she fell asleep under the tiny cloth roof that they constructed with their cloaks. Her slumber was dreamless, yet satisfying.

The next Day was a quiet one to say the least; every person seemed to be submerged in his or her own thoughts, and that was perfectly fine for Serena. She, too, had much thinking to do herself.

Traveling was harsh that Day, since all of their Pixie Powder had run out and their pointed wings had shriveled and vanished the Night before. The Travelers were further burdened with the weight of their knapsacks on their backs. Their little raft had been forgotten and abandoned in the chaos of Nelson's eternal departure and the oncoming of the Spirits of the deceased. Their knapsacks had been stocked full with provisions by the kindness of Lonvirc-Volcrin, for which they were grateful and yet still a little shaken with the thought of having spent the Night with an immortal Creature. Nonetheless, the questors plodded ever onward in the stinking muck, determined to reach the town called Middleton by evening.

Serena was lost in her own thoughts. She was debating whether their mission to install the Heir of the Throne was still attainable, or whether the whole Continent was doomed to endure the rule of tyranny.

Nelson is lost ... gone ... out of the picture. So then, does that automatically make his sister, the Princess, the true Heir? Or even ... even Theo?

Serena looked at the young Halfbreed Boy as he lifted into the air briefly and flew a short distance, then dropped, exhausted, back to the mush and continued on his way.

He is strengthening his flying skills, Serena thought with a fond smile. *But could he be the one and only true Heir to the Throne? Perhaps, because he has seemed awful quiet lately, and yet perhaps not, because he is so dreadfully young, and may not even know how to possess such Powers.*

Yet what if ... what if Nelson was not the real Heir? What then? What if he, or she, is still out there, hiding from the Throne because he is afraid to accept the responsibility of inheriting the Throne? Because he feels he is too young, too inexperienced, or too unstable to take on such an important position? Could there possibly be another Heir to the Throne out there?

But nonsense – Nelson even told me plainly that he had nothing left to hide. That meant that I am correct – he was the only Heir! How else could he have broken the chains on the Centaurs, or made the log in the Forest move? He was the second most powerful Creature in Forever – what now will we do without him?

But, even worse, what if there isn't another Heir to the Throne? What if Nelson was the only Creature who had the Power to claim the Throne? Forever's last chance to bring itself up out of its leaderless state, sunken together in the Marlan QuickSand Pit with the hopes of Forever being capable of redeeming itself. Then what is to become of Forever if her one and only Heir has perished? Will the Mother suddenly revive, or won't she? I do hope she lives after all – if she doesn't then who will rule Forever? Perhaps my first thoughts were correct. Maybe... maybe Forever really is doomed to fall once and for all.

Chapter Forty: Melabon of Middleton

Although the traveling was not exactly as pleasant as the experience of flying, the party of seven plodded doggedly onward at a quickened pace. To their great relief, their efforts paid off, and shortly before Nightfall, they came upon a Town.

Yet at first, all that Serena and the rest of them saw was a clustered bunch of Trees, live Trees, with very thick branches and limbs, and tall, sturdy trunks. Something that looked like a green rope (but was clearly a path of some sort) snaked behind the Trees, looking like a twisted thread strung through the place.

As they ventured closer, however, Serena began to notice small tendrils of smoke climbing higher in the air from directly over the leafy green Trees. The muck around their ankles grew more Watery and deeper, so that it oozed into the tops of their boots, which were tied tightly just beneath their knees. Blue-gray water sloshed around their shins as they increased their speed.

Now Serena could see lights, bright lights glowing from between the thick-grown leaves. Also, Vines hung from the Trees, in long loops and strands, giving a tropical appearance. A hard-looking, rough green road paved the space between the trunks of the Trees, while certain figures bustled about on that road in little groups, some carrying bright lanterns to guide their way.

It was near dark when the seven tired explorers reached the outskirts of the Town. With full hearts and aching limbs, they traipsed onto the strangely paved road, and looked about in awe and wonder.

This place is stranger than Bendar and the Boulder-Tribe Campgrounds! Serena marveled in thought.

Indeed the place was certainly an odd, yet welcoming sight. Wooden Houses with up to three levels and twisting decks lined up neatly in the Trees. They were built there complete with glass windows and front porches, on which old grandmothers sat in their rocking chairs, knitting or entertaining young grandChildren. Pixies with their iridescent wings, Gnomes with their long beards and pointy hats, Dwarves with their short, stocky figures, Nymphs with their power of flight and unrealistically colored hair, Animals that acted just as Humans did, and all other Mythical beings swung from one house to another on the Vines, dropped rope ladders from the houses for friends to climb, and waved at the newcomers merrily from their large, open windows. A couple

329

Stores, a Bank, a Restaurant, a little Chapel, and a tall, large Hotel perched in the Trees also.

"The Hotel," Mike yawned, gesturing to the place. "There, I hope, we can rest. Let's see if they-"

"Wait," Jerry said, squinting up at the square, lighted windows. He gestured to a sign that was hung up stubbornly on the front door: *No Vacancy.*

Its message was brandished clearly.

Kate huffed.

"We don't have any money anyways," Bob put in helpfully, turning out his pockets.

"Where are we going to stay, then?" Theo asked, gripping the hilt of his brother's Emerald-topped sword.

Silence.

Serena studied the faces of the explorers. They were all mud-flecked, Sunburned and worn out. They looked in desperate need of rest. Serena knew her own face portrayed need of slumber as well. She stared up at the residential TreeHouses on the other side of the broad Street they were on through Golden eyelashes.

"Perhaps we could ask one of the inhabitants if we could stay with them," Lindsey suggested.

"Lindsey, we don't have any money!" Bob reminded her in a singsong tone.

"I know, but ... maybe we could give them something else." she returned.

Mike tossed his brown-haired head. His tiny glasses glinted under the light.

"Like what?"

"Like ... oh, I don't know ... food. These haversacks have been too heavy for us anyway – they're slowing us down, and we don't need that right now," Jerry sighed.

"Look!" Kate suddenly exclaimed, pointing at a two-story House across the rough-textured street.

On a wooden deck stood a kindly-looking old WoMan in a plain-looking green dress with a stained white apron, waving at them. Yet something was odd about this WoMan. Serena could not quite put a finger on it. Her knees were bent backwards and she had dainty black hoofs. A Faun?

No, a Satyr, Serena thought as she looked closer, remembering how Nelson had once described the inhabitants of Forever to her. The WoMan had the legs of a Goat, the torso of a Human WoMan, and two pointed ears on either side of her black-haired head, which was also streaked with some gray. Her face was wrinkled yet kindly, her eyes dark and mysterious, and her smile honest and wise.

"Is she waving at us?" Theo wanted to know.

Serena looked behind them.

Nobody there.

And the streets were beginning to clear as the Sun set over the fiery horizon.

"She must be." Jerry answered finally, bringing himself forward. He pointed at himself and the crew and hailed the WoMan.

"Do you need our help, good WoMan?" he called.

The WoMan smiled and stopped her vigorous waving. She bent and picked up a rope ladder. The wooden planks clattered together as she released it from her deck.

"Nay, good Sir, but are ye in need of mine? I understand you need a place to stay for the Night."

Serena caught Jerry's surprised gaze.

"How did she know that?" Kate hissed to Lindsey.

"I am a Fortune Teller, my dears, that is how I know! Come now, into my abode, before it becomes too dark to see!"

Serena did not release Jerry's gaze. She could tell that they were both thinking along the same lines.

Is this WoMan to be trusted?

"Come hither, Children! The Sun sinks lower on the horizon as we speak!" the WoMan persuaded them.

Then, much to the team's surprise, three new voices sounded.

"Yes, come!" trilled one. A tiny black-haired head appeared from behind the WoMan's apron; a little Satyr Girl in a lively pink dress.

"Granny Melabon is fixing her special Marsh Berry Pie after supper!" chirped another. Then, another black-haired head appeared from behind the Satyr Fortune Teller, this one dressed in the same yellow dress.

"She says that the sooner we eat our supper, the sooner she will prepare the dessert for us!" sang the last. And finally a third little Satyr Girl poked her pretty little head out of an open window on the bottom floor of the house, wearing an identical dress to the other two, only this one was blue.

This settled Jerry's decision. Heaving his haversack up onto his back,

331

he signaled the team to follow him to the homey-looking wooden TreeHouse.

Serena soon found herself in a sweet-smelling kitchen, sitting at the large square table with a steaming platter of food in front of her. The heavenly aroma penetrated her nose and caused her mouth to Water.

"Eat, eat, eat!" urged Melabon, the old Satyr Fortune Teller. Her three identical triplets, her grandChildren, also sat at the table in their color-coded dresses (probably so Melabon could tell them apart). They bowed their heads for grace, and then fell to the food with an appetite.

Maci in pink, Laci in yellow, and Daci in blue, Serena thought, remembering their brief introductions. The three young Satyr Girls were only six years of age, living with their grandmother whilst their parents were off on a grand quest. Serena yearned to know more of this magnificent quest that the Girls' parents were on, but Melabon refused to speak any further of it. Apparently, it was quite private. Serena respected that.

She watched as Mike, Bob and Jerry dug into the food before them with vigor. Lindsey conversed with Theo about his progress on learning to fly, and Kate picked at her food, obviously still feeling sorry for herself. Jerry winked at her and she allowed a small smile to brighten her dull features. Serena grinned warmly at Jerry and the other Boys – they were all very happy to be a full team once more.

Melabon was indeed a Fortune Teller – this Serena could see just as she walked in the door, for on a small table and resting in a decorative holder was a crystallized eye about as big as a bowling ball. The thing seemed to draw all of their attention.

A Cyclops's eye… Serena marveled to herself. The thing gleamed and sparkled under the dim kitchen lights, sending radiant specks of color up to dance on the ceiling.

Melabon had seen her shameless gawking as she had entered.

"You have never seen a Cyclops's eye, dear Girl?"

Serena shook her head slowly, still admiring the wondrous object. What would have been the white of the eye was clear, and the iris sparkled with every color of the Rainbow, flecked like iridescent little threads all woven the same direction, away from the pupil. The pupil itself was black – and very wide indeed – so black that Serena felt the equivalence to its color would be all of the Night Skies crammed together to make one single large circle of darkness.

"Ah, then you shall discover its Magic – it will be my treat. I shall demonstrate after supper."

And so it was that after the companions had finished their supper (and what a delicious one it was, thanks to the Magic of Melabon) that they all seated themselves around the little table after helping themselves to a piece of the kind WoMan's pie. Maci, Laci, and Daci had seen their grandmother's workings before, and scampered off upstairs to play a game. With an "ahem," Theo proclaimed that as a token of his gratitude to Melabon for taking them in, he was to supervise their play. At a nod from the Fortune Teller, he scuttled off up the stairs to join them.

"So, you wish to see how a Cyclops's eye works?" Melabon began, polishing the crystallized ball by spraying a waxy substance on it and buffing it up with a hand towel.

"Yes," Jerry said, watching her in wonder.

"Alright, then. It shall be so," the Fortune Teller declared. She took a black cloak that was hanging up on the wall. After donning the cloak, she drew a curtain around the table, so that all light was blocked out.

Serena felt like she was blind. She felt Jerry's hand slip into hers, and Lindsey's hand slip into the other. After a moment their eyes adjusted to the darkness, and they could make out the hazy figure of Melabon. Pulling the hood of her cloak up over her black-haired head, the Satyr WoMan seated herself and massaged the surface of the crystallized eye with her deft little fingertips.

The whole eye began to shine with a magnificent radiance. The light met an astonished and pleased group of explorers. Serena stared amazed at the brilliantly glowing thing. The black pupil dilated further, allowing the onlookers a glimpse at what it showed.

Like the view of a fast-flying Bird, a scene that zoomed over the Dragons' Lairs, the Golden Plains, MeadowLands, Bendar, the Forest of Many Eyes, the Blue Marsh, and Nelson's single, cold, dead hand flashed before their eyes, each scene somehow melting into the next with an air of marvelous wonder.

Serena failed miserably to restrain the urge to let her jaw drop. This Cyclops's eye was not showing them the future – but the past!

"You have come a long way," stated Melabon, clenching her eyes closed tight in concentration as she leaned over the eye like a mother protecting her

Child. Her delicate, frail fingers tenderly massaged the polished Cyclops's eye, gliding easily over the smooth, glassy surface.

"Many troubles you have had, but many more are yet to come. You are searching for … your home,"

The Cyclops's eye glowed brilliantly, and then the pupil showed the scientists' institution, a highway, a plane and the Bird's eye view of a City.

Melabon opened her eyes.

"What's this?" she said in surprise as she looked at the objects as they flew across the screen. She stared for a long time, then inquired, "This I have never seen before. What is the place that you call home?"

Serena studied the Satyr's wrinkled old face from under the glowing orb beneath her fingers. Other Earthly figures continued to show in the pupil.

"Earth," Jerry answered calmly, his own face aglow in the rays of Magical light.

"Earth!" gasped Melabon, looking back at the eye. "This is your home Land? Surly you come from Forever, in a dress such as that!"

She nodded at the companions' clothing.

"No, we changed our clothes," Mike said, squinting through his tiny glasses, "to Foreveran dress, so as not to seem suspicious."

"But we do come from Earth, all of us here, except for Theo," Serena put in. Melabon did not look like she believed them and laughed good heartedly to show so. Kate sighed.

"Here, I will prove it."

Kate leaned onto the table and pointed out certain figures as they floated across the screen. "That, there – that is a car, an automobile. That is a building, a bank, that is an airplane, which takes us from place to place by air, and that is a television set. Telephone, elevator, refrigerator – see, all of these things come from Earth."

It was Melabon's turn to look Thunderstruck. She stared wide-eyed at moving, colorful figures floating in the dilated pupil of the Cyclops's eye.

"So you do come from Earth." she admitted at last. She smiled up at their glowing faces. "Whoever could have thought that the people of Earth could dwell without Magic?"

"We do not have Magic," Lindsey explained, tossing her brown curls out of her face, "but we do have electricity. That is how we have modernized into a world of science, computers, and robotics."

"Electricity. Science. Computers. Robotics." Melabon repeated meticulously, "None of these strange words have I heard before. And that is amazing, for look how old I have become!" She laughed. "You simply must tell me of your home planet sometime, young Travelers!"

Bob yawned.

"Well, I don't know about the rest of you, but I am ready to turn in," he said.

"Are we to sleep upstairs?" Lindsey said, playing with her brown curls.

"Yes, dear one. One of the triplets should show you to a guest room, in which I have cots laid out, for I often find myself housing other Travelers when the Hotel is full. There should be two rooms – one for your Gentlemen, and the other for your Ladies. Feel free to clean yourself up, but do let me know if I must bring up some heated Water for a bath. Up you go, now, young ones! Breakfast will be served shortly after dawn."

Serena watched the others get up and leave with grumbles of thanks. Yet she stayed, for she had just found a way to pay Melabon back for her kindness.

"Aren't you going to join them, young Miss? You must be dreadfully tired," Melabon offered kindly. The old Satyr Woman stifled her own yawn.

Serena shook her head. She knew she would have trouble sleeping anyway because of her recent loss.

"I will be fine, Melabon, but thank you. I will join them later after I tell you more of my planet."

"Oh, that would be wonderful!" Melabon crooned, hugging the now blank Cyclops's eye to her chest. The pupil displayed little sparks of excited color as Serena began to reiterate her knowledge of the scientific world.

After nearly an hour of planting the principles of modern Earth science into Melabon's absorbent mind, Serena began to grow weary. Her head and eyelids drooped, both weighing a thousand pounds. Serena's heavy breathing and her slowing heartbeat echoed in her ears as she leaned forward half-consciously, and fell fast asleep on the little table.

Serena found herself flying once more, enjoying the Winds and the Mists that swirled and played around her, tugging at her curls and her skirts. She flew and flew, then felt herself falling, and falling.

She fell past Jerry, and Prince Errenon, and finally Nelson, each of their faces pale, expressionless, and stoic. Each staring straight forward and not moving except to put down their outstretched arms and step back on their fluffy Clouds of Mist, allowing her to fall past.

And fall Serena did. She fell and fell, past the three statue-like Boys and ever downwards. Through the sheets and columns of Mist of all colors she fell.

And then, miraculously, a new kind of hope arose in her chest. She could fly again!

And fly Serena did. Like an arrow out of a Warrior's bow she rocketed herself straight upwards. She propelled herself forward to Nelson, hoping with all her young heart that she could just reach him and awaken him from his statue-like slumber.

Serena was very close to reaching her love. She could already see the bottom of his Cloud of Mist – growing larger and larger.

I may not be able to save you in real life, Nelson, this we already know! But in my dreams, anything can happen, and I can always find you here and save you … she thought determinedly. She pursed her lips. Now she was very close to the Cloud, and she felt her heart warming to the presence of her deceased sweetheart.

We will be together again, Nelson, watch and see.

Serena gave a final burst of energy and shot upward –

- but then her flying Powers left her again.

Chapter Forty-One: Magic

There was Serena in her own dream, clinging for dear life onto the edge of a white Cloud. The texture was somehow Watery yet soft, like cotton. But the texture of the Misty Cloud was the last thing on Serena's mind at that particular moment.

For there, standing on that very Cloud was her true love – Nelson. Even in his stale, frozen position, the Warrior Halfbreed looked charming. Serena sighed and stared up at him dreamily.

She tried to speak his name, but her voice had left her also.

Touch him, said a small voice in her head. Serena smiled; she had not yet given up hope.

That must be it… I must touch him – awaken him from his stoic slumber…

Stirring her strength, the young Girl lifted herself onto the Cloud, and reached up, gently touching the very tip of Nelson's moccasin. She slipped as the Wind and the Mists suddenly picked up speed and gusted against her. She dug her hands into the soft Cloud and clung to it as a Child would cling to its mother. She closed her eyes, feeling her arms trembling, her strength waning.

And then her chest was filled with a new light, for from out of the swirling Mists a face appeared – Nelson's face. He blinked Owlishly as though awakening from a long slumber, and smiled at her.

Serena smiled back.

Then the Mists on the Wind, flurrying about with multicolor Flower petals, glitter, and scraps of soft silk, grew a little too strong and the Cloud that Serena clung to, a little too weak.

I am falling! Was the Girl's next thought, and before she could reach to pull herself up, a final gust of Wind blew her off of the Cloud. So she sailed amongst the winding, soaring Mists, her hair and ruffle-hemmed skirt billowing out behind her, her arms held out on either side of her, with their long wispy sleeves flapping.

But now Serena did not feel morbid or crestfallen – for she now carried with her a new light that rested on her bosom like a furry baby Animal, and warmed her pounding heart. Two large hands appeared from above her and clasped themselves to her middle. Attached to those hands were strong arms, and to those arms a healthy-looking, laughing Nelson.

Serena laughed too. She was glad to have Nelson back.

Then Serena awoke, panting, and sweating, but smiling.

"Nelson?" she breathed hopefully, finding herself facing a figure. Her eyes adjusted. Was it Nelson?

No.

It was Melabon.

Serena sat up, suddenly remembering how the Boy had perished. She was still at the table; apparently she had only been asleep for a few moments.

Those few moments were not long enough, Serena thought with a sad sigh, her smile vanishing.

"There, there, my dear, I knew you were tired," Melabon chattered. She bustled about drawing back her black curtains. "Marsh traveling is a tiring task, I'll have you know. Should have waited to find out about your World until morning, when you were all rested up. Ah, well, up to bed with ye now, young Miss! You must rest!"

Serena stood, eyes wide, and stopped Melabon from drawing back the curtains any further.

"Melabon, can you interpret dreams?" she had to know.

Melabon pondered the Girl's urgent request, slowly closing the curtains again.

"Why … yes, Serena … why do you ask?"

"I … I have been having these dreams,"

Serena told the Satyr Fortune Teller about her dreams and how they had seemingly predicted the disappearance of certain people in her life. Then, she told her of her most recent dream.

"Is this a sign?" she finished. She watched eagerly for a response, and Melabon, who had absorbed every drop of information that Serena produced, hunched over her glowing orb and stared almost menacingly into the black pupil of the Cyclops's eye.

Spots of light danced on the walls, ceiling, and in Serena's own face in their many bright colors. Like a thousand glittering Jewels, the dots were cast about, some slowly drifting whereas others hastily zoomed around.

Serena watched them in awe and wonder as Melabon muttered something she couldn't quite distinguish (but which sounded suspiciously close to some type of Charm) to the shining Cyclops's eye.

Then, much to her astonishment, the black pupil of the Fortune-Telling crystal orb melted into a scene of multicolored Mists and Clouds.

338

It was Serena's dream!

Melabon studied the swirling image ponderously and stroked her pointy chin in thought.

"Ah, so you have Seeing Powers?" she croaked at last.

Serena was taken aback.

"Seeing Powers?!" she gasped, "No … n-no … well, not that I know of, anyway."

Melabon chuckled, massaging the glassy surface of the Cyclops eye with her diligent little finger tips.

"Now, don't you be trying to fool me, young Miss! That dream is dripping with Seeing Powers if I've ever seen them – and take a gander, 'tis all right here!"

"But what does it mean?" Serena interrupted, pushing the diagnosis aside. "What is going to happen because I have 'Seen' this dream?"

Melabon observed the information Serena had given her, then interpreted to the Girl the significance of the dream in Serena's future life.

"This boy – Nelson, you say – he is coming back," she smiled simply.

Despite the limited amount of sleep Serena caught that Night, she awoke refreshed and ready to start a new Day. She looked out her window to hear songBirds chirping, wagons scuttling along on the rough green streets (which, she had learned, was comprised of the textured skin from a Crocodile's back), Children playing, and rope ladders clacking as they unwound from the decks and porches of the TreeHouses. She saw the inhabitants of Middleton skipping about to their morning tasks, singing, dancing little jigs, and welcoming the dawn of a beautiful new Day in the Lands of Forever with a Cloudless azure Sky above their heads. She smelled fresh Rain, wet bark, dense Mists, and something so tantalizing that it nearly made her mouth Water – breakfast.

After a splendid breakfast, Melabon caught Serena as she made her cot up and reorganized her knapsack, shifting the more volumous provisions to the bottom of the sack so that it would seem less heavy.

"Do you remember telling me of the objects you call … telly-phones?" she asked, opening the curtains and the shutters to another second-story window.

"Yes," Serena answered. She tightened the silken blue sash on her dress and made to tie her hair up and put on her blue bonnet. "Why?"

"Well," Melabon confronted the Girl, pulling a red velvet bag out of her apron. She gave this to Serena. "We in Forever have our own method of communication. This is one of them. Take a peek," she beckoned.

Serena carefully pulled out the drawstring to the little red bag. Inside were circular, flat, palm-sized clear Stones, about eight of them in all. Trying not to gawk, Serena took one out and held it in her hand. It was as smooth and shiny as glass and so clear that Serena could see every wrinkle in the inside of her palm as she held the transparent item.

"What are these?" she wondered, stroking the surface to see if it would do anything.

"These, my darling Girl, are not telephones, but TeleStones." Melabon explained, fetching one for herself. She held the Stone in her palm, as Serena did, and rubbed the top of it until it was warm. Then she leaned close to the Stone and said, "Serena Gordon of Middleton!" very clearly, and Serena showed in the Stone.

How the Satyr WoMan had come to know her last name was obvious, she being a Fortune Teller. Serena smiled as her eyes snapped back to her own Stone to face the elderly complexion of Melabon looking up at her.

"So, you see," said the figure of Melabon, just as loudly as though Serena was standing next to her (which she was). "You rub the Stone to activate its communication Magic. Stroke it once," she stopped to demonstrate, "TO MAKE THE VOLUME LOUDER, OR STROKE IT TWICE," again she stroked the Stone, twice, "to make the volume softer. When you are finished, you simply tap the Stone twice," she tapped the clear Stone with her long nails, "and it will store away its communication Power until it is summoned again."

"Wow!" Serena marveled, turning the plain-looking object over and over in her hand. "How does it … do that?"

"It is Enchanted," Melabon said simply, and dropped her Stone back into the velvet sack that Serena held in her hands.

"That is very interesting," Serena mumbled, closing the drawstring pouch. She held it out for Melabon. "This is a wonderful device that I am sure is very helpful to many Foreverans."

"It is," Melabon replied with a warm smile, "especially for Travelers." She stopped to eye the Girl for a moment with her dark, wide eyes, then continued, "And do not speak of yourself as though you are not Foreveran – because believe it or not, Serena, you are. I want you to take these with you, and

340

if you ever need to get ahold of me, whisper, 'Melabon of Middleton' into the Stone. It should reach me."

Serena, flattered, slowly smiled and packed the velvet bag into her knapsack, thanking Melabon for her courteous generosity.

"Magic is a wonderful thing," Serena couldn't help but notice as she packed the bag away. Melabon clasped her hands with the Girl, a fondness twinkling in her creased brown eyes.

"And so is friendship," she said.

Jerry appeared at the staircase to report that the team was in the process of lightening their knapsacks and sharing a small portion of their food with Melabon to thank her for her kindness.

Travel for the team that Day was somewhat slow, yet productive. The Mists that shrouded the Bog in the morning lifted away into the Cloudless blue Skies later in the afternoon, revealing a thick green line just ahead of them.

But the seven didn't have to dirty their feet as they traveled, because they were not journeying their last Day in the Blue Marsh on foot. Their Marsh Shoes had long since been abandoned at Middleton, their state being less than what the Travelers required them to be in order to move on. So Melabon had led them to a nearby shop and rented them some Turtles.

The Turtles she had rented them, however, were not small in any way. Each one was large enough to carry two full-grown Men. Their shells were fitted with comfortable little saddles and reins just as a Creature would ride a Unicorn. Apparently, Turtle traveling was a very popular means of transportation in the Blue Marsh; any and every Creature that Serena saw entering or exiting the Town had been on Turtleback.

And now she had the once-in-a-lifetime experience to ride the green and brown reptiles, who clacked their beak-like mouths around their bits, blinked their large black eyes, and hummed in their deep, rocky bass voices, which vibrated their speckled shells. The sound itself seemed to echo inside the Creature as it stretched its large muscles and reached out its pointed, flat, and ichthyic flippers to scoot themselves along smoothly over the top of the bubbling Blue Marsh. The Bog Waters licked up at the sides of the great Creatures, making to reach the unsoiled feet of the seven questors, but failing because of their determination.

Serena thought the progress was slow, bumpy, and jerky, for the style of this particular transportation was a short spurt forward through the sloshing murk, a jerk to stop, then another spurt of strength, then another lurch back as the Turtle moved its flippers. It was in this way that Serena developed a little pain in the back of her neck and on her lower back. Yet she was grateful not to be traveling on foot.

Flying was so much easier, she thought as they jerked along, *and so much more free.*

"Hey, Serena," whispered Jerry from behind her. They were sharing one Turtle while Kate and Bob shared another, and Mike and Lindsey the third.

Melabon had suggested they place one Boy with each of the Girls in case the Turtle expedition was attacked. Theo flew around from Turtle to Turtle, riding on each one in turn.

"Yes?" she replied, lurching forward as the Turtle stopped, and then backwards as it jerked forward again. Jerry reached around in front of her and placed his own large hands over hers on the reins.

"Do you really think we have a good chance of getting back to Earth?"

Serena did not take long to formulate a reply; the same question had crossed her mind countless times on her journey.

"No," she said sadly, closing her eyes and savoring the hollow rumble of the big Turtle beneath her. How she loved that sound! To her, it sounded very much like a mild Thunder rolling in the distance.

"Why?" was Jerry's next question. Serena opened her eyes and looked at the thickening line of Meadows just ahead of them. They would reach the place easily by dark.

Should I tell him about Nelson's secret? It probably wouldn't matter if I did – Nelson is already ... gone, she thought with a heartbroken sigh. And then a new thought struck her: *But Melabon had predicted he would return ... but he hasn't ....and how could he return if he had perished ...as a Ghost?*

Serena did not like that thought at all and promptly pushed it to the back of her mind.

Should I tell him? Or should I not?

She arrived at the safest of the two decisions, believing that if Nelson did return, he would not be happy to hear that another soul knew his secret.

"Because," she sighed, closing her eyes again. "Because we cannot go back."

"Why?"

Serena took one of his hands and squeezed it.

"Don't you remember what Nelson said? We would have to wait at least a hundred years to go back, unless we saved the Mother from dying. We haven't found the Heir to the Throne, and noCreature knows where he is. If we went back to Earth, Jerry ... we would be treated like aliens."

Jerry snorted.

"Oh, come on, Serena-"

"No, really! Think about it! The way we're dressed now, on Earth, a hundred years from now – who knows what we'll find? They'll cage us up like wild Beasts and study us – isn't that what the Earth now would do to

343

someCreature that Magically appeared from the Stars? We'll never have our old lives back again – all the people we once knew will be dead."

"You're painting a rather morbid picture, Serena," Mike chuckled.

Lindsey nudged him irritably.

"Oh, stop it, Mike."

Kate sighed from Serena's right.

"You know, she's right."

The Turtle beneath her groaned happily as it jerked forward with a slurp.

Silence, sad and slow, hung on the dank air.

The rest of that Day was particularly uneventful. It was already dusk when the group reached the Windy Meadows. They were terribly exhausted from their travels, and immediately set up a campsite. The Meadows, with a faint Breeze, surrounded them in darkening beauty as the Sun sunk low into a colorful horizon in the West.

"These are very highly trained Turtles …" Serena remembered Melabon telling them at the shop as she watched Jerry tie the reins of the Turtles to the Shore of the Meadow. "When you have reached your destination, feed them and tie their reins together, then send them back in the direction they came. They will automatically return to Middleton."

Serena huddled in Nelson's warm, Forest-smelling cloak as she warmed herself next to the small fire Bob had made. They were a Stone's throw away from the Marsh when they stopped to make camp. Jerry stayed back with the Turtles to feed them the fruits and grain that the storekeeper had given the group. She smiled as the big Creatures groaned and rumbled in pleasure, gulping down their condensed feed and clacking their hard little mouths for more. After they had finished and taken in some Water that Jerry held out for them in a wooden bowl, he replaced their bits and tied their reins together. He didn't even need to guide them back in the direction they were to return; the massive hard-shelled Turtles instantly turned and started their way back all on their own.

Serena could still hear the Creatures' hollow singing in the distance as Jerry came and sat by the fire.

"Long Day," he sighed, rubbing his temples.

"Uneventful, long Day," Lindsey moaned on the other side of Serena. She dug in her haversack and pulled out a fruit that resembled a purple pineapple, minus the hard shell. The nurse bit into it, revealing a white-seeded, dark blue interior.

"That's for sure." Serena said with a mirthless laugh. She poked a stick into the fire, stoking the little logs. "But 'uneventful' is a good thing right now. I mean, after all that happened in the Blue Marsh ..." Her voice trailed off, and she fell silent.

Serena was persuaded that the team's minds were all lingering over the recent loss of Nelson. She pursed her lips tight, thinking her own thoughts on the matter.

But then she remembered, as she played with her skirt, how she had passed out the TeleStones that Melabon had given them and felt for her own, buried deep in her skirts next to Teresa's diary. She remembered Melabon telling them that they also came in a variety of colors and textures, but a plain, clear one was the cheapest. Being a Fortune Teller, Melabon had had plenty of these lying around from her travels when she was younger, and told Serena that she may as well put them to a good use, since it was unlikely she would be needing them again.

Serena thought for a moment about using her TeleStone to talk to Melabon, but decided to wait to contact her – as it was evening, and she figured that at that time Melabon would be busily tucking Maci, Laci, and Daci into their warm, little beds.

Lindsey's voice shattered Serena's thoughts and broke the silence that gripped the air around the crackling campfire.

"How long will it take us to reach Diamondia Castle?"

Jerry looked up at the twinkling stars with a ponderous expression. Finally, he spoke.

"I'm not sure," he replied. His blue-grey eyes searched the Night Sky carefully, as though looking for guidance and counsel. "Seems to me that it shouldn't be too long."

Theo crawled over and sat next to Serena, burying his weary face into the material of his brother's cloak.

"What will we do when we get there?" Serena had to know, placing an arm around the sleepy Child. "We cannot provide a cure for the Mother's sickness unless ..."

She bit her lip, trying to disguise her nervousness with a look of expectance.

345

"Unless we find the Heir the Throne and bring him forward to claim the Throne," Mike finished. He held up a flat Rock with steaming biscuits on it from the fire.

"And, of course, we have no way of doing that, since we aren't from this World, and we wouldn't know what to look for if we decided to anyways," Kate put in, accepting one of the biscuits.

Bob stood from where he had been searching for something in his knapsack.

"And even if we did, we would have to go to Diamondia anyway to make the government aware of our activities. That's if they would even allow us to."

Jerry looked at them.

"Dragon-feathers! The lot of you sound more down than those Ghosts in the Marsh! You'll listen to me! We cannot give up now – we can't be that far from the Perpetual Mountains now, and I'm not going to let you forget it! Yes, Nelson may be gone, we may be tired and sore and disheartened, but let me tell you something – we did not venture here to piddle around and argue. We're going to find that Heir if it's the last thing we ever do!"

Serena looked at Theo beside her, who had his knees drawn to his chest and was presently hunched over them as he stared solemnly into the fire.

And when she looked close enough, she thought she saw the small glint of a tear gathering in one corner of his eye; her belief was confirmed correct as something with the equivalence of a liquid Diamond ran down the Boy's cheek, suppressed by the flickering firelight.

After supper, Serena found for herself a shallow dugout in the Mossy Grasses around the fire. She wrapped Nelson's cloak around herself warmly and stared almost reverently into the crackling flame. She was half scared to fall asleep for fear of her dream returning – the very same dream which she could not imagine coming true.

Nelson won't come back, she had persuaded herself earlier that Day. *There's no way he could! He said the Marlan QuickSand Pits are irreversible – how can he escape and live after being swallowed by one? He's nowhere from there to go except ... down.*

Her heart sank as his crumpled body once had.

Then Serena's thoughts scattered like Mice in a barn as a large hand

346

found hers.

"Nel-" she began hopefully, but stopped when she realized who the hand belonged to. It was smooth and soft, not rough and hardened like those of her late beloved. It was not Nelson's.

"Jerry," Serena corrected herself in a small, disappointed whisper. Jerry helped Serena up and stared at her. "What is it?"

"I need to tell you something important," he replied in a low tone. He led her away from the camp for privacy.

Serena gazed over the Moonlit Meadows sleepily, observing the blue-bathed Trees and Flowers. As she looked to the East, further into the Meadows, a soft Gust breezed past her and danced with her curls and ruffles. She closed her eyes and inhaled; she smelt Rain coming. Then she exhaled and allowed her breath to be borne aloft on the whimsical Wind. When she opened her eyes, she noticed something she had not before – the scattered, shadow-shrouded Trees, from her position, were very oddly shaped.

For the second time that Night, Jerry interrupted her thoughts.

"Serena, I have to know something."

The Boy turned her face to look at his blue-grey eyes, as dark as the StormClouds that were rolling in overhead from the SouthEast.

Serena studied Jerry's white, Moon-bathed complexion. She drew Nelson's cloak around her as she felt another draft.

"What is it?" she repeated in a low whisper.

I hope he didn't hear about my dream … she worried in thought.

"You," Jerry began, wetting his lips nervously. "You and Nelson … you two were friends, right?"

Or maybe he already knows Nelson's secret! she thought with a jolt. Her heart began to thump loudly in her chest and she looked at the ground as she felt the blood rise to her cheeks.

I will not lie to him, she decided finally, looking up.

"Yes, Jerry, we were … friends," Serena sighed hesitantly. She wrung her hands uncomfortably. "Very good friends, in fact,"

Jerry's eyes bored holes into Serena's Starlit features. She stared at the Flowers at her feet.

"Were you … in love?"

Serena's heart stopped.

"Why?" she inquired, thinking it had nothing to do with Nelson's high place in Forever or the possibility of his return.

347

Jerry took her hands and stared at her.

And then Serena understood.

"Because ... because I wanted to know the chances of our-"

"Being together?" Serena realized, feeling a Boulder of solid Stone sitting on her chest.

Even though the Night was dark (and darker still with the inky black Clouds that blotted out the Stars), Serena could just see his face growing red.

And she could feel her own face growing red also. For she now had two paths to take from the fork in the trail where she now stood: the first to follow her instincts and accept a new relationship with Jerry; the second was the path that followed her heart, to not open a new relationship, but to stay faithful to a former one, and to solemnly believe that Nelson would return to her.

Serena bit her lip as her heart and her instincts battled one another.

I walked myself into this one, she thought nervously, scuffing at the soft Grass with her feet. *Maybe if I don't give him a direct answer, he will not pursue me.*

"I ... have to tell you something," she whispered finally, looking back up into his waiting eyes. They stared her through, straight down to the depths of her soul. Hesitantly, she told the Boy of her dreams.

Jerry sighed and looked at the ground after she had finished. Lazily he snatched up her hands again.

"So then ... your relationship with Nelson is not dead ... but still alive?"

She gently removed her hands from his. She felt proud and courageous to have followed her heart.

But then Jerry looked up at her with a wild fire burning in his eyes. He looked ready to cry, his face now shadowed, not Moonlit, by the Clouds above. With trembling lips he leaned very close to her, and hovered for several moments, staring sadly at her. Then he came alarmingly close.

Serena turned her head, petrified, and the Boy kissed her gently on the cheek.

"No!" she hissed. She felt familiar tears stinging her eyes as she pushed him back. "Do not tempt me!"

Serena stepped away from Jerry, pulling Nelson's cloak to her face to dry the tears and to inhale its inimitable, comforting aroma.

"We are better off being friends."

And then Serena turned and ran back to the campfire.

348

Morning dawned as a symphony of beauteous creation, the works of Mother Nature gleaming upon every dew-bathed petal.

Serena awoke at the crack of dawn, and allowed her eyes to grow at the sight that greeted her. The Meadows flourished under the happy Sunshine, multi-color Butterflies swooped about the singing Flowers, the gnarled Banyans lifted their glittering Jewels of fruit up to the Cloudless blue Skies, and shimmering droplets of dew clung to every leaf, blade, and petal just as a Child would cling to its mother. The fiery orb of a Sun was just peeking her glowing head up over the hilly horizon, her shining Golden rays of hair trickling slowly over the long Meadows, awakening Plant and Creature alike for another glorious Day of paradise in this luscious Garden of Meadow.

Whoosh!

Serena was blown backwards from her sitting position by a great, whistling gust of Wind. Regaining her balance, she stood to get a better look around. Her dress and knapsack were mildly damp with dew, and Nelson's cloak was sparkling like a frosted Hillside with it. She admired the cloak fondly where it was positioned on the ground, wrapped snugly about little Theo, who was still snoring softly.

With a sad smile, Serena recalled how she had discovered the Boy weeping some time after the rest of them had fallen asleep.

"Come here," she had crooned, and drew the sniffling Child into her arms. "Do not cry."

"I miss Nelson," he had sobbed in a high-pitched whimper. Serena remembered him burying his face against her shoulder and Nelson's cloak. "Why'd he have to die now? There's so much that I never got to do with him … so much I never told him …so much-"

But he stopped in midsentence, gushing forth another wave of warm tears. His grief over his brother's loss was burning solid inside him.

Serena felt absolutely heartbroken and almost on the brink of tears. But one flickering little flame of hope had awoken inside her, and she remembered her dream.

She did not care anymore if the whole team knew about her foreshadowing dream – they would probably find out in the end anyway. Although hesitant to do so, she finally cradled the Boy in her arms and told him the dream she'd had of Nelson's coming. She told of how Melabon translated it, how she had not believed, and how that one tiny flame of hope was still burning within her. She told Theo that he should have the same hope, to truly believe that Nelson would somehow return to them. And when she had finished her tale, she found the young Halfbreed staring wide-eyed up at her. He kneeled and bid she bend her ear to him. He told her that he believed he would return, then kissed her on the cheek and dozed off in her lap. So she gently covered him with Nelson's large cloak and looked up at the rest of the team. Each face had been turned to her, every eye open and smiling. She sighed and nodded that the dream was true, and after bidding them all a good Night, she went to sleep.

Serena's thoughts were brought back to the present as a second draft of Wind blew at her face from its origin in the East.

"The Windy Meadow," she whispered to herself, bracing her body against the draft.

"That's what they call it," said a voice behind her. Serena didn't need to turn to know that it was Jerry. Another cold gust of Wind attempted to make Serena lose her balance, but she stood firm and offered resistance.

"And very appropriately so," she sighed. Jerry strode around behind her and came to stand next to her. He mimicked her sigh.

"I think," he began, then stopped to take her hand. "I think you should reconsider, Serena."

Serena turned and looked at Jerry's pleading blue-grey eyes. She did not miss a beat, having had plenty of time to think the matter over.

"Jerry … no. We are eight years apart, and besides that, I'm still getting over Nelson's-" she stopped short, the familiar lump rising in her throat. Shaking her head, she took her hand from Jerry's and stepped away from him, staring forsakenly off in the distance.

Jerry sighed again and pursed his lips in determination.

"Serena," he reasoned, his eyes growing soft. "Age has nothing to do with it, and Nelson … I mean, just give it up, he's not coming back."

Something moving in the distant Meadows caught Serena's eye. She saw a shadowy form, then a certain figure emerging from the light Mist. Realizing this, Serena instinctively stepped forward and squinted. Jerry watched her every move.

Finally, after minutes of frozen, Breezy silence, Serena spoke, not once moving her eyes from the figure straight ahead of her.

"Speak for yourself," she hissed bitterly, and then took off in a dead sprint ahead, yelling at Theo over her shoulder.

As she ran, she saw the muddy figure collapse and try to stand again. Heart pumping wildly, Serena quickened her pace.

When she reached the figure, she nearly bowled it over in excitement.

"Nelson!" Serena cried, kneeling and throwing her arms around the filthy Boy.

"Serena!" the miracle himself coughed, leaning on her heavily in seemingly both relief and weariness. "I thought I'd never find you,"

"Oh, Nelson!" Serena laughed, holding him at an arm's-length to get a good look at him. Kneeling, he was filthy from top to bottom – a sure sign that he hadn't stopped in Middleton to clean up. She smiled winningly at the way the rising Sun formed a sort of halo around his head, and the colorful, reawakened Banyans, Flowers, and berry Bushes twinkled with cool dew about him.

Suddenly, a great gust of Wind blew at the weak Boy's back, causing him to topple forward onto Serena. His Sandy hair hung over his face as he stared down at her face in relief, taking her all in.

She giggled, playfully tickling his sides so that he finally collapsed, exhausted, onto her chest. Serena picked mud clods from his hair, studying the Springy green eyes that she thought she would never see again now shining brighter than ever before.

"I knew you would come back," she said finally, sitting herself back up again as Nelson shakily lifted himself off of her. He seemed to stifle a chuckle.

"How so?" he replied, lifting a rough hand to stroke her dancing curls. Serena drew very close to him and faced him nose-to-nose.

"I had a dream," she said.

"You're quite the dreamy Creature, aren't you?" he coughed, his light tan locks showering Serena with grains of Sand. "A dream, you say?"

"Yes, a dream. Telling me that you would return." Serena told him.

Nelson shook his head in wonder, then cupped her cheek in his hand and kissed her tenderly on the lips.

Jerry emerged, puffing, behind Serena. He stared contemptuously at the couple and hitched his knapsack up.

"Ahem," he coughed.

Serena and Nelson ignored him. Nelson stared Serena deeply in the eyes.

"I am so glad I found you." he whispered, a twinkle in his eye. "Because I forgot to tell you how much I lov-"

But he got no further, because Theo rocketed out of the Mist and bulleted him over.

"Nelson! You're alive! Gosh, you stink! I thought I'd never see you … oh, Nelson!"

Nelson was close to tears as he hugged his little brother. Soon Lindsey, Kate, Mike and Bob came trotting out of the Mist, pooling around him and peppering him with tears and hugs and stories and questions. Nelson was moved to tears. It was the only time Serena had ever seen him cry in front of so many people. It did not much matter to them then anyway, since she and Theo and all of them were crying alongside him - except for Jerry, who stood stoic as a shadow behind them, and would do no more than nod at the returned Boy.

But later, Jerry apologized to him, in the quiet and calm of the Meadow.

The group of eight covered good ground that Day, rejuvenated by the unexpected return of Nelson. Serena walked hand-in-hand with him all Day, more than overjoyed to be reunited with her sweetheart. Nelson did not protest and spent every breathing moment by her side, making kisses and promises that he would never leave her again.

Nelson explained, several times, his tactic with which he had escaped, much to the delight of his ecstatic younger brother, who yearned to know every detail so that he might some Day perform such a heroic feat. Theo was altogether too happy to see his brother alive, and instantly occupied the Boy's other hand, having returned his bow, quiver, and sword. Serena also gave Nelson his cloak back, which he accepted gratefully as the only clean article of clothing he owned.

"Just how did you escape that Sand pit again, Nelson?" Theo inquired for the zillionth time that Day.

Nelson coughed and flattened his tan-blonde locks to his head.

"Well," he began in his dry, rough voice, also for the zillionth time that Day, "there I was, completely submerged by a Marlan QuickSand Pit, with the breath ripped away from my lungs and the howls of the deceased pouring into my ears."

Serena's grip tightened around that of the Halfbreed's although she had already heard the story several times.

"I was ready to die," he continued, looking at her. "My blood ran cold and my heart slowed. But then, from out of the dank murkiness, I heard the sound of the Sands shifting, and I knew that the Spirits were rising from their eternal graves to haunt the Marsh. I remember how I worried about you all, whether you had found a safe shelter from the Spirits or not. And then I thought of something else – of a possible means of escape. Because you see, whenever a Spirit of old arose from beneath the Marsh, the Sands parted away from it, Magically. And so I thought, if I could just grab hold of one of those Spirits, perhaps I could lift myself with him and pull my body up out of the QuickSand. I tried my theory, holding my breath and still in my fatal position. I waited like this for what seemed like minutes. Surprisingly, just when I felt my plan had failed and my life was ebbing away from me, some Spirit or another seemed not to notice my decomposing existence, and swept right past me. With what strength I had left, I grasped his ankle just as he drifted upward. Miraculously, the Sands leapt away from me, making a hollow tunnel through which I was hauled by the ascending Spirit. He lifted me clear of the Sands and threw me onto the hard peat, believing me to be dead. I kept my composure lifeless, although my lungs were near to bursting. When the danger had passed, I allowed air to fill my chest once more and scrambled under cover to a Bramble. There I spent the Night, due to my excessive weakness, the next Day and all the next Night. After that, I managed to drag myself out and eat something. I figured by then all of you would be reaching the Meadows and so I cut straight to the chase."

Like the rest of his reiterations, a long breathtaking pause followed, like the lull after a Storm.

Serena shivered – she always got the jitters after hearing of the Boy's narrow escape. She always loved hearing his warm tenor voice beside her, like a distant roll of Thunder, reverberating in her ears. It always brought about a certain calm in her - a warm, smooth feeling in her chest. It amazed her even more how much she knew she would have missed that voice if Nelson would not have come back. This was another reason she now clung to every little word the Boy had to say.

Evening blossomed upon the Magical Windy Meadows with a purpling Sky and heavy, rich blue Clouds. The Sunset was a most majestic scene to witness, or so Serena thought as she stood looking Westward. The whistling Winds whipped about at her back, singing and dancing with her liquid Golden locks and her ruffled, bell-shaped skirt.

Serena leaned against the slanted trunk of a nearby Banyan Tree, watch-

353

ing the glowing Sun ease into its bed of horizon and summon forth the Moon and Earth to watch over its domain whilst it sought dreamless slumber. Serena sighed wearily, and protested to strengthen her aching muscles once more against the gale.

Despite his unexpected escape and eagerly accepted return, Nelson had prevailed to inform his renewed companions of the Land they now treaded upon.

"See the Trees?" he had pointed out, gesturing to the twisted Banyans. Their trunks were all leaning out of the ground at an odd angle, all towards the West. The small Plants and Flowers – and even the Grass – were all leaning in that direction.

"It is because of the persistent Winds," Nelson explained. Serena remembered watching his wind-chafed face as his hair was swept away from it. "The Winds are always blowing, and so the Trees and the Flowers of the Meadow have been bent and shaped to its whim."

"Is it always this fast-" Mike stopped to dampen a finger and lift it in the air. He pursed his lips and squinted through his teeny spectacles. "About 30 miles an hour?"

Nelson nodded casually, stepping over a little trench.

"Always at a constant speed, save for during a Storm, and always running West – that is, in this part of the Meadow. In other parts, it runs North or South or East."

"They say that the Winds of the Meadow come from the Perpetual Mountains at the base of Sparkline Mountain," Theo declared, skipping over the same shallow trench.

Serena restrained herself from gasping aloud – were they really that close to the heart of Forever (or so Nelson called the Perpetual Mountains, Sparkline Mountain and the Diamondia Castle together) already? And yet, the more she thought about it, the more it made sense. Now, as she stood alone looking over the darkening Meadows, she reminded herself that they had been traveling for approximately 19 Days, nearly three whole weeks, so close to a month that it didn't even seem believable. Serena could have sworn that they had traveled for much longer.

Soon we will reach the Perpetual Mountains, and ride on the backs of the Pegasus to the Diamondia Castle, she thought as she turned to look back at the camp that Jerry and the rest were arranging just then. She hid a smile, seeing her Halfbreed sweetheart making his way over to her. *Perhaps this mission is not hopeless after all.*

354

Dawn in the Meadows grew into another glorious, warm, Breezy Day. The dew that had gradually formed on the leaves and petals and fruits overNight glittered lusciously in the morning light and faded away into the Winds during the afternoon. Serena and her companions were up and off at the first streak of Sunlight in the morning Sky.

They traveled restlessly until noon, when they entered some sort of natural-grown Orchard with patch upon patch of colorful, fragrant Flowers. Roses, Daffodils, Irises, Marigolds, Tulips, Primrose, Carnations, Morning Glory and other namelessly gorgeous Blossoms littered the place. The melodious song which projected from those iridescent Flowers seemed louder under the fruit-laden Banyans, for the small, safe haven was somewhat sheltered against the swirling Winds. Usually, the dainty music was carried off by one thieving gust or another, robbing it from the ears of the Wind-burned Travelers.

For indeed, Serena's face, as well as most of the others' was red and dry, chafed from the rushing Winds. To relieve herself of this, Serena took her bonnet and tied it around her nose and cheeks; Kate and Lindsey followed her clever example. Nelson instructed the Boys to use the cloaks as temporary masks, which relieved them of the same burden.

It was in the natural-grown Orchard that the explorers stopped to make themselves some lunch and to gain some strength to move on afterwards. Serena seated herself against a leaning, twisted, drooping Banyan, with the colorful, healthily budding Blossoms growing at chest-height all around her.

She opened her knapsack and extracted a sheet of dried, cooked venison. The texture was rough and salty, but Serena did not care; she was starving.

As she ate, Serena observed the fat little buds of multicolored Flowers all about her. The buds seemed to sparkle with the little specks of dew that the Trees had saved from being blown away. And, Serena noticed, they were also shimmering daintily with some glittering substance that she could not quite identify. The tender budding shoots swayed lightly on the breath of the Breeze that rustled through the small Orchard. Soft, whispering hums danced about on that gentle Breeze, reaching the ears of Serena, who felt positive that the glorious melody had been echoed from the unopened throats of those fat little buds.

Then, something beyond amazing happened.

A ray of ginger Golden Sunlight streaked down from between the boughs of the fruit-beJeweled Banyans, splashing the fat little buds like precious gems themselves with its warm, delicious magnificence.

And the Flower buds trembled, each exerting a tiny puff of iridescent glitter that lingered for a very long moment on the air, and was then swept away by the gentle gust of Wind.

Serena, not knowing what to make of this, dropped her venison jerky and backed up a little bit. Her eyes grew. There was no Flower that she knew of that spurted sparkles upon the touch of Sunlight. She called on Nelson –

– who, after glancing only once at the glitter-purging buds, called upon the others to congregate silently in back of Serena to see what was happening.

For, indubitably, something was happening. Something very beautiful and wondrous - something very special. And something, Nelson was prompt to inform them in a low whisper, that was not normally a privilege for ordinary Travelers to witness every Day.

Serena stared shamelessly in awestruck wonder.

What was this special event that was to happen?

She and her curious companions soon found out as the warm, sleepy Sunlight continued to Rain down onto the drowsy, dewed, and glitter-breathing buds. In a flurry of Magical skin-tickling dust, the delicate petals of the tightly-wrapped Flowers gently yawned open. Lying in the soft, downy mouth of each brightly-hued bud, suckling tenderly on the nectar of the Flower, was something that until now, Serena had only seen in Fairytale storybooks.

Baby Fairies.

With varying skin shades, hair colors, and bright, eye colors, each baby Fairy was aged a little over a year at best, and all wearing according to gender either tiny multicolor dresses or tunics and hoes, seemingly woven by the maternal Flowers themselves from the same silky material as that of their glittering petals. Serena thought that the Children looked very much like little Angels.

Fairy Dust glowed and drifted all over the place, tickling the noses of the curious onlookers. The dust wisped about the glowing Fairy Children in colors, mainly blue and green, with an odd scattering of yellow here and there. It did not take Serena long to realize that the colors of the dust depended on the moods of the tiny Fairies – as she had learned that blue meant happy, green meant excited, and yellow meant curious.

But what was more marvelous than anything else to Serena was the baby

Fairies themselves. Each tiny infant had its own plump little body, none of them much longer than a Human pinky finger. Their faces were fair and flawless with youth; their tiny, chubby cheeks and noses pink with flush; their lips cherry-red; their large, almond-shaped eyes twinkling in the Sunlight and the glow of their own miraculous existences. Pointed ears with no ear lobes stuck out stubbornly, yet attractively, from between short mops of Human-colored locks that topped their round little heads. Their skin, tinted pale, tan and dark brown shimmered with the dust produced by their thin, delicate wings that fluttered about behind them. The wings were narrow and pointed slenderly at the tips, making them appear leaf-like in both the large top lobes and the smaller bottom lobes. They were each slightly transparent and elegantly decorated in their own colorful, natural designs, extending the startling beauty of a first glance at them.

Serena failed miserably to restrain an awed sigh. Her eyes grew along with the eyes of her astonished companions. She leaned closer to get a better look.

The sight was perfectly awe-inspiring, breath-taking, and even shocking. The yawning Flowers seemed to smile through their coats of dewdrops as they peeled back their delicate petals to brandish the arrival of youthful, new life. Fairy Dust floated everywhere, lodging itself on the garments of the Travelers, mingling with the fresh fragrance of dew, aromatic Flowers, and blossoming greens. The juvenile Fairies stretched their tiny little bodies and their perfect wings and yawned widely as though awakening from particularly pleasant dreams. The long, nectar-filled calyxes of the interior of the blooming Flowers dripped with their sweet, rich nutrition as the mouths of the baby Fairies departed from them at last. Assuming these calyxes to be similar to umbilical cords, Serena watched in fascination as the new arrivals flapped their little wings and Magically lifted themselves into the air, showering the travelers with their sparkling Dust.

And up they flew, rising gently on the soft Breeze, all the while giggling, sneezing, yawning and performing other adorable Child-like acts. A little hiccupping Girl in an Iris dress with lively red curls, freckles and bright blue eyes approached Serena, her glittering dust changing to a liquid Gold hue. She came very close, her pale, freckled skin glittering with Fairy dust, and her tiny cheeks flushing each time she hiccupped. She came to stare Serena straight in the eye.

Startled, Serena released a silent gasp and blinked.

The tiny Fairy giggled, although not a sound audible to the Human ears escaped her cherry-colored lips.

Then, as though summoned, another infant Fairy, this one a Boy with black hair and skin, large brown eyes, and cladden in a delicate tunic with hoes and a diaper woven from a Daffodil's petals, flew around Serena's head, covering her in illuminatory green dust. He landed on the Girl's outstretched palm, no bigger than her own pinky. Serena chuckled and tickled the miniature Fairy under the chin, making the Child bubble with unheard laughter.

As Serena looked around, the other baby Fairies were rocketing around the explorers' heads, discovering their new sense of flight and meanwhile sprinkling the awed onlookers with the multi-colored dust. A baby Fairy with Watery brown eyes was attempting to crawl on Kate's nose, another with a vivid green smock was bungee-jumping from Lindsey's curls. Two Boy Fairies were playing hide and seek around Bob's head, and five little blue-dusted Girls were admiring themselves in Mike's glasses. Theo chased them around, Jerry snorted at an impish Boy who made a face at him, and Nelson laughed as several Fairies picked what dirt clods they could still find from his tunic and his hair. In spirals and loops, the Children zigzagged about in the air, curiously touching and dancing around the team. As the infant Fairies capered about in the air, the gap in the Trees seemed to widen to bathe the travelers and their newfound, silent friends in delicious, Golden Sunlight.

Serena drank it all in - the Fairy Dust, the Flowers singing, dew-gowned Flowers, the shimmering rays of Sun, the dancing, glittering Child Fairies and the laughing face of her beloved Halfbreed sweetheart, coming to dance with her among their glowing new friends. Surely she could not be happier!

Serena was crushed.

It was the next Day, late afternoon, and the Winds were blowing hard. Nevertheless, the team proceeded to travel through the bountiful Land of never-ending Flowers, Grasses, Ferns, Bushes, and fruit-sparkling Banyan Trees.

But this was not the reason that Serena felt the miserable way she did.

Not long after the infant Fairies had been born, their parents arrived to claim their miniscule Children. The parents were friendly with the Travelers, rounding their new broods up to take them back to the Fairy village where they lived. They more or less spoke by using expressions and gestures, aided

358

by their mood-colored Magic Dust, or else traveled to the ears of the explorers and whispered in their soft, bell-like voices.

All but one of the birthing flowers blossomed into tiny Fairy Children. One Fairy parent told Serena that the little white Rose bud held the offspring of two perished questor Fairies, instantly dubbing the babe an orphan.

'You may pick the Flower and take the Child with you if she has not also perished,' offered a kindly mother Fairy with bright red hair. She picked up the hiccupping Girl in the Iris dress.

'Yes, we will have no place for her in the village,' noted another mother with brown hair.

'Her parents were traitors to our kind,' mumbled a third indifferently. She turned at Serena's nod to chase down her galloping, dusty blue Child.

Serena was heart-broken for the unborn baby.

At a nod from Nelson, Serena hastily accepted the offer and picked the stem of the white Rose bud as close to the base of its stem as she could. Then, in a flurry of glittering Fairy Dust, the great crowd of Fairies, young and old, dispersed into the Orchard, vanishing under the Golden Sunlight.

Serena had no idea how to care for a baby Fairy, and it seemed most fitting to her to turn upon Nelson for instructions. So that Night he explained to her the physical traditions of Fairy reproduction and some of their culture so that she might understand a bit more of the unborn Fairy Child's origin.

"A Fairy mother will lay an egg," he told her, his face dark (for they could light no fire because of the excessive Wind), "no bigger than the nail of your pinky finger. She will then plant this egg into a forming Flowerbud, and when the Flower blooms, the Child is born. The egg hatches, and for the last few weeks of a Fairy's gestation, it will feed off of the nectar in the Flower."

Nelson went on to tell her some of the customs of the Fairy folk. Fairies lived in Nature, usually in Forests and Meadows, and in other places rich with Natural beauty. They had their own little Houses, their own little Schooling systems, and sometimes even a few tiny Castles for their little Kings and Queens. Serena listened intently, but after awhile, both grew tired and turned in.

In the morning the white Rose bloomed, producing a tiny Fairy Girl with white-blonde hair, pale skin, a ruffled white dress, and the largest, most adorable green eyes Serena had ever seen (save for Nelson's). Serena had slept on her stomach facing the East with the Flower planted in the ground before her, so the first thing she saw that morning was the birth of the Rosy Child with the

Sun rising in a halo behind her. Promptly, and with fond memories of having temporarily adopted the title before, Serena named the infant Fairy 'Dawn'.

Now Serena shielded the tiny babe close to her chest with her bonnet to protect the Child from the Wind. She wondered if the Mists that had lingered with the Meadow since early that morning would ever disappear when suddenly, as though beckoned, they lifted.

What the explorers saw then stopped them dead in their tracks and erased all memories of the beauty of newly born Fairies.

The Perpetual Mountains.

And behind them, shrouded in a distant, light Mist, lay a glittering Sparkline Mountain.

With a shock Serena realized that the great Mountain was much closer than it seemed. And now that she had seen the colossal place for herself, she suddenly knew why the Mountain had been named 'Sparkline Mountain' - for once the Mists parted and the Sun came out, the Mountain seemed to sparkle with its colorful beauty. The clear Waters only magnified this radiant glimmer, setting the Sun bouncing off of the Water and the Jewels in such a manner that Serena felt her eyes were never again to behold such a brilliant sight, even from her distance. Instantly, she fell in love with the Mountain.

The Perpetual Mountains, not one third the size of Sparkline, were wrapped at their peaks in cold white Snow despite the fact that it was Mid-Summer. They showed not a thread of shimmering iridescent glory that the great Mountain behind them possessed. In fact, they looked much more like some type of wall that reached from the very corners of their vision to Heaven. Their sides were grayish black and Rocky with a slight tinge of Sandy brown here and there to brandish the spiral upward-leading path that curled around each Mountain as a Snake will often coil around its prey. A dark brown blotch showed very faintly in the distant Snow-covered peak of each Mountain. Serena watched in awed wonder as a Pegasus – a white one with what looked to be a Golden mane and tail and the shining white wings of an Eagle - flew down from out of the Clouds shrouding the top half of Sparkline Mountain and landed behind one of the dark brown blotches.

"Pegasus!" breathed Lindsey beside her.

"Flying Unicorns!" Serena exclaimed, shuddering in wonder.

"Our transportation to Castle Diamondia," Nelson pointed out.

"We should reach them by toNight," Mike said, shielding his squinty eyes from the Sun. He stepped forward and eyed the distance between them and the Mountains. "The base of them, anyway. But we'll need to move quickly."

"Then what are we waiting for?" Jerry agreed. He hiked his haversack up and eyed each one of them. His gaze lingered on Serena. "Let's go!"

~*~*~*~*~

And go they did, protesting the quick-paced Winds that tugged and pulled at their clothes and hair. Serena shielded the tiny Fairy Girl, Dawn, in her bonnet, and plunged head first into the warm Summer Wind. The drafts scorched their faces and howled in their ears urging them to turn around, to go back, seemingly warning them of the dangers that lurked in the Perpetual Mountains.

Yet the determined Travelers did not listen to the Winds and persisted. They pursued their goal to reach the base of the Mountains by dusk, and, in good time, they accomplished it.

But not before their first taste of the dangers in the Mountains had encountered them. Halfway to their destination for the Day, a scuffle arose between a traveling family of some type of Two-Leggers (which Serena had learned were Animals with Human characteristics) and a Mountain Troll. And, since they were mistakenly out in the open, they had little choice in the matter but to join their fellow questors in the fight.

The Wind, they found, as they approached the scene, was now blowing as hard as it had ever blown on them before, as though it were trying to protect the journeyers from danger. Nonetheless, and ignoring it for a second time, the team proceeded to join the scuff.

Nelson's heroic Warrior instincts immediately took over as soon as the Troll looked in their direction. Serena could not help but gasp for three reasons: the ugliness and size of the Troll; the ferocity and stern determination in Nelson's face; and the mortified family of "CatFoxes" (as Theo had informed them) as they huddled around one another under the menacing shadow of the Troll.

The Boys drew their weapons and prevailed to join the father of the family, who stood stubbornly in front of his wife and two Children. The Cat whiskers of his feline top half lifted back in a hiss that sounded more like a growl as it escaped his gritted teeth. His Foxy tail swayed warningly behind him, curving and shaking like a very angry Rattlesnake. His rusty, reddish-brown coat shone in the late afternoon Sun and was spotted with yellow markings, seemingly even menacing in itself at the moment.

The Troll, who had the family cornered with their backs against a tall Rock, was much bigger, probably as tall as a Banyan Tree, as Serena estimated, with gruesome blue-green skin covered in warts, scars and blisters. He had a flat face with a bulbous, fat nose, beady brown-black eyes, a wrinkled forehead, and few sparse strands of greasy, limp black hair hanging from his otherwise bald head. Drool came in large sticky columns as he opened a mouth, littered with pearly-white, razor-sharp fangs and he raised his trunk-sized club (which was studded with sharp pieces of Rock) to smote down the poor family of CatFoxes.

And, at the last moment, the mother CatFox seemed to lose her grip on her youngest, a Boy, who ran out in front of the giant Troll just as he prepared to strike.

"NO!" Serena and the Child wailed in unison. The Mountain Troll grunted piggishly, and then smirked its ugly smirk, brandishing its shining, slobbery white daggers of teeth.

Serena felt an overwhelming sensation pool up within her heart and she knew at once that she must save the poor Child, even if it meant placing her own life in danger.

Quicker than lightning, she shed her knapsack, handed little Dawn to a shocked Lindsey, and leaped out to push the Child out of the way just before the monstrous Troll swung its club.

Many things then happened simultaneously. The mother CatFox fainted, the female Child screamed, the Troll roared and rose his club to strike again, and Serena curled herself around the whimpering Boy protectively.

And then Nelson was there, standing tall in front of Serena, teeth gritted, eyebrows lowered, and both hands gripping the handsome sword tightly.

"If you want her, you will have to pass through me first!" he roared at the top of his lungs.

Mike joined him, then Bob, their eyes dark.

"And me!"

"Me too!"

Finally, Lindsey, Kate and Theo hurried onto the scene, forming a wall in front of Serena and the Child.

"You'll have to go through me, too, snot-brains!"

"And me, flap-belly!"

"I might not be much, but my brother taught me an awful lot!" snarled Theo.

Shaking his head at last, Jerry stepped between Nelson and Lindsey, placing his arms around them.

"Just try and go through all of us at once, you great Ocean of warts! No Creature can mess with this team when we're together! Right, guys?"

"RIGHT!"

The great Monster tossed back its ugly head and released a loud howl, beating his bare muscular chest, then it turned its gaze upon that of Serena's who was curled up on the ground. Under her chin, a Kitten-like face appeared, peering out at his heart-chilling assailant between the legs of the team.

"Tell him what for, Nelson!" Serena muttered, more to herself than to the Monster. "Tell him to go home and leave us all alone! You know how to, my Prince!"

Nelson growled. The Troll's facial expression changed and its beady black eyes widened. This group meant business!

"I order you out of my sight THIS INSTANT!" the Halfbreed Warrior hollered, pointing his shining sword straight at the Monster's heart. "Or else we shall all spear you through the heart with-"

The Troll needed no second bidding. With a thunderous cry of outrage, it dropped its club and high-tailed itself back to the Mountains, with Nelson pursuing him a good way before coming back.

"Is everyone alright?" Serena checked, standing to dust off the tiny Cat-Fox Boy. After all, she had been face-down in the dust while the team faced the Troll, and as a consequence did not see anything the Troll may have done. The team was hugging the poor CatFox family lovingly and openly. Kate and Lindsey rushed to the unconscious mother, Mike, Bob, and Jerry comforted the grateful father. Even little Theo was hugging the crying little Girl while a purple-dust-cladden Dawn aided him in the effort, and Serena herself picked up the wailing Boy to offer him some comfort while his mother was being revived.

"NoCreature was injured," Theo reported to his brother as soon as he had returned. "And Mrs. CatFox is coming around nicely."

"Good," Nelson panted, wiping his sweating forehead on the back of his arm. He removed his cloak and placed it over the trembling Boy Serena was presenting to him. She accepted the bundled babe back into her arms word-lessly.

"Thank you, good Creatures," started the father CatFox, striding over to them. He bowed his head in thanks first to Nelson, and then to Serena, his hand over his heart in the Foreveran tradition. "We are truly blessed to have encountered such luck on our quest."

"You are very welcome, friend. We had only to assume that the miscreant was as much our trouble as it was yours," Nelson greeted, and then, one by one, he introduced himself and the other Travelers in their group. The father CatFox nodded in acceptance and sheathed his dirk.

"Beruga is the name," he introduced himself, greeting them again in the Foreveran tradition. "My wife's name is Tarsena, our son, Veldon, and our daughter, Pinniose. We are destined to visit the Diamondia Castle and the Fountain of Youth before it is all gone." Beruga's whiskers twitched as he spoke, a trait that Serena soon came to admire in the CatFox culture.

"Gone?" Kate asked in surprise. She hobbled over to them with Lindsey. Tarsena, the mother CatFox, was supported between them. Theo, Pinniose, and Dawn trailed behind them.

Nelson and Serena exchanged a sidelong glance.

"Yes, gone … Kate, is it? The Mother has not much longer to live, and evil forces are already gathering in the Mountains to overthrow the Throne. We are lucky to have discovered this Mountain – the small one – has very few evil souls lurking within its shadows. I hear that the evil ones are planning to set up a tyrant Forever, ruled under-"

"Enough!" Nelson cried, then quickly added, "friend Beruga, I sincerely apologize for interrupting, but all of that still has a chance to change."

Beruga's furry features rippled in the Wind and turned over to a confused expression.

"Change? But, friend Nelson, how is it possible for a situation such as this to be changed? Are you telling us that there is still hope left in Forever for a future?"

"Yes," Nelson began, but Beruga cut him off.

"But the entire Continent has been searched, under every Stone and behind every Tree – there is no Heir to the Throne! This is the end of Forever as we know it! To believe, now, so close to the Mother's death, that there is hope left somewhere in Forever is … unconceivable! Unthinkable! It's … impossible!"

A lonesome silence followed the outburst, filled with the solemn wisping of the Wind about the group.

And then Serena stepped forward, holding the bundled Veldon to her chest for warmth. With a long look at Sparkline Mountain, she said,

"A wise Creature once told me, nothing is impossible in Forever…"

Chapter Forty-Six: The Perpetual Mountains

By Nightfall, the group had reached the base of the great Perpetual Mountains. Ironically, after the scuffle with the Troll, the Wind reduced itself dramatically to a gentle, warm Summer Breeze, if it could even be called that. The baby fairy, Dawn, who was still learning her language, took to the air and had a tendency to hover over Serena's right shoulder and to chase her ponytail of curls as they walked.

The questors camped separately that Night and around their own campfires. And although opinionated on the matter of what was to become of Forever, their new CatFox friends remained grateful for the team's heroic deeds in rescuing them from the Troll.

Morning dawned as the brought-to-life purity of a dream as the 13 adventurers left the Windy Meadow behind and began their long upwards trek in the Perpetual Mountains.

Serena's feet kicked up dust as they pounded along the Sandy trail. Many times little Dawn sneezed because of it, sprinkling Serena with her mood-colored Fairy Dust which was quite often blue or green. Serena, in turn, would sneeze because of the excess Fairy Dust, and so it was that the two companions exchanged sneezes throughout the Day as a result of one another.

Serena did not have a very hard time taking care of her baby Dawn. Because of her Natural motherly instincts for the Creature and the guidance and council she received from Nelson she successfully taught the tiny Girl the basic English language, fed her nectar from Flowers she had picked back in the Meadows, and also gave her certain soft fruits and berries to nibble on from time to time (as the blooming youth was teething). Serena bathed the darling Child in a cup-like leaf filled with Water, played with her, sang her songs, and at Night tucked the babe into her bonnet and kept her close to her chest so that she might hear her drowsing heartbeat and lull off to sleep with it still drumming in her tiny, pointy ears.

Serena was in the process of teaching the miniature Fairy how to say "Rock," "Tree," and "path," when early evening came on, and Beruga and Nelson began to look for someplace to make camp. The Children – Theo, Veldon, and Pinniose – played on the trail, scouting ahead and making imaginary adventures as the rest of them followed behind. Tarsena and Kate became almost attached at the hip from the start, and talked so fast and so much about their differences and similarities that Serena thought there was not to be a moment of silence between them. Beruga, Jerry and Bob traveled in a group and talked while Mike and Nelson followed on likewise.

However, all conversations suddenly went dead as the group rounded the next bend.

~*~*~*~*~

"Do … not … move …" Nelson breathed in warning, standing stock-still. Everyone, even the babies, Dawn and Veldon, followed his example.

For there, sitting grandly in front of them was a miniature Mountain, as big as a Hill.

But something was very strange about this miniscule Mountain -

- it had eyes!

Two eyes.

Just below the snow-capped peak that would be its hair and above an upside-down cliff serving as a nose and the long, horizontal crack that marked the presence of a mouth sat two unmistakable, brown eyes.

The eyes stared hard at them and blinked.

Serena, hardly believing her own eyes, blinked.

And then the ground began to tremble.

It did not take much reverberation in the ground before all 13 Travelers had lost their balance - after all, the path they stood on was not exactly level. Dawn, who had stoically been flying over Serena's right shoulder, released a silent squeak and dove under Serena's bonnet on her head. Shivering orange fairy dust, the pointy-eared, green-eyed Child peered her tiny head from under the blue bonnet and shuddered, nestling deep into Serena's mass of bundled blonde curls.

From her position on the ground, Serena caught her breath and stared in startled astonishment as the Mountain transformed – shifting its Rocks – into a life-sized Giant, formed entirely from the dark gray Stone. Serena estimated that its height was close to a hundred feet tall. Lindsey found Serena's hand and the two Girls huddled together, astonished.

With an earth-shattering, disgruntled bass rumble, the great Creature swung its monstrous head and stared at the group of petrified Travelers.

For several painstakingly long moments the gigantic monstrosity stared

367

at them all, uttering hollow, deep, gravelly hums which echoed in the Valleys and in the ears of the frightened questors. The sounds had a specific ring to them – if the emotion evoked by the sound could have been put into words, Serena would best have described it as legendary, wondrous, adventurous, and heart-etching.

Then, with a cavernous yawn that howled in their ears and shook the earth, the great Creature lunged forward and took a Thunderous step, making its way down the Mountain path.

"To the Mountain side!" Nelson hissed in between the volumous foot-steps. "Get out of its way!"

Instantly the group obeyed, flocking to hug the tall Mountainside and escape from being crushed underfoot. The ground rumbled and shook as the Mountainous Rock Giant moved further down the trail to pose as another tall peak. As soon as the loud footsteps and Thundering sounds had subsided, Jerry began to move back onto the path.

"What was that thing?" he gasped, studying an impression in the hard-packed road that the Mountain Creature had left.

"No!" Nelson warned him, gesturing for him to come back, "It is not safe yet! Where you will see one MountLore, most likely, you will see another!"

No sooner had the Halfbreed Warrior spoken these words than another series of Thunderous footsteps was heard further up the path, coming from around the bend. The color drained from Jerry's face and he scampered back to the Mountainside like a Rat running from a goodwife's broom.

BOOM! BOOM! came the footsteps.

Zoom! went Theo as he clutched Serena's skirt and Nelson's hand.

"No … no Sauropods …" the wide-eyed Child demanded.

"No," Nelson assured him with a comforting pat, "no Sauropods this time. Sauropods do not come into the Mountains. What you are hearing are MountLores."

"MountLores…" Theo repeated in awe, his grasp on Serena's skirts loos-ening considerably. He looked up at his Halfbreed brother questionably. Be-fore he could open his mouth, Nelson answered his foreseen question.

"MountLores. 'Mount' means Mountain and 'Lore' means Legend. They are invincible Spirits created in the dawn of time-"

BOOM! came another footstep, nearly causing the Travelers to lose their balance again.

"-that have taken the shape of a proportionate chunk of Mountain Rock-"

BOOM! The footsteps were growing closer by the moment, making the ground quake violently. Serena was now wondering how they did not break the path or the Rock of the Mountain because of their powerful steps.

"-and are presently headed in our direction! Keep your back as flat against the Mountain as you can, and-"

BOOM! pounded a particularly earth-moving footstep.

"-slowly move up the path – hold hands, now, just in case!"

Just in case? Serena's mind screamed, *Just in case what? I don't even want to-*

BOOM!

Lindsey and Theo's grasp simultaneously tightened on her white hands, and she felt the tiny Fairy toddler burrowing into her nest of curls beneath her bonnet, gripping her hair and quivering like a leaf in an Autumn Wind.

Serena felt a bit blind as she blundered along, for the Mountain wall that she hugged close to on her left hand side was so tall and immensely round that she could not see what was up ahead, only the backs of their traveling band.

Suddenly, Theo turned to look at Serena with wide, hopeful eyes and he breathed to her,

"Mike spotted a Cave up ahead, hold tight, watch your step, and quicken your pace. Pass it on!"

BOOM!

Serena hardly had time to turn and whisper the message to Lindsey before the ancient MountLores peeked their Stony heads around the corner and rumbled into view.

Despite Theo's order to quicken her pace, Serena could barely manage more than a petrified shuffle along the Mountainside. She gulped and gawked at the enormous Mountain Spirits that thundered by, leaving in their wakes six inch deep footprints that could have served as miniature Pools.

Solemnly the Stone Giants thundered past the line of Travelers, somberly they glanced at them out of the corners of their eyes, and stoically they lumbered past after the first MountLore with their terrifying footsteps - BOOM! BOOM! BOOM!

Serena kept her stumbling feet moving, finding her strength suddenly as she darted forward, ever upward until finally she was pulled onto a Cliff-like landing, where a Cave rested in the Mountain side.

Fear wound down as the footsteps became softer and less frequent. Serena released her breath slowly in a long sigh after the last BOOM!, staring up at the sparkling, Misten Mountain that stood in front of them like a great wall, reaching up to kiss the cotton Clouds. She stopped and released her tightened grip on her friends' hands, and stared speechlessly at Sparkline Mountain and its crown of Mist as it sat, larger than life itself, surrounded by its smaller sibling Mountains.

But the Mountains that cradled the famous glittering Mountain were also beautiful in their own specific features. The Perpetual Mountains grew in clumps like Flowers, their Valleys wide, deep, and luscious with Streams and Creeks that branched off of the Rivers running to the greatest Mountain of them all. The Mountainsides were Rocky and gray with several small Caverns and Cliffs jutting here and there in the shadows.

As she came to sit on the edge of the Cliff and marvel at the Valleys and the Perpetual Mountains, she noticed that the temperature had lowered also, creating a chilly Breeze that wafted past them more and more often with its cold breath and icy fingers. Serena wondered, as she sat, why it was that the Water running up the enormous sides of the great sparkling Mountain did not freeze or even slow at the cool temperature they now encountered.

Later, in the Cave campsite, Nelson explained to her that the atmospheres surrounding the Jeweled Mountain, regardless of the Season elsewhere, was always warm and youthful as in the Springtime.

"This is just another part of Forever's ancient Magic." the Halfbreed Warrior told them as he roasted a Mountain Rabbit over a smoky, dry fire. "And it is another reason for why we are not spending the Night up at the Inns on the top of the Mountains. I know from experience-" he glanced at Serena and caught her eyes with a fond smile, "that it gets dreadfully cold up here during the Night – especially in the Winter. Mountain traveling is never easy – even in the Summertime because of all the frigid temperatures and the scarcity in food, and those every-prowling predators."

"Predators!" gulped tiny Pinniose, crowding closer to her mother, Tarsena. "I don't like predators!"

"There, there, now, you're scaring the Children." Beruga snapped at him, glaring unkindly at Nelson across the fire.

"Theo isn't scared." Nelson chuckled, drawing back the roasted, steaming meat. He blew on it tenderly and revolved it slowly in the flames while his younger sibling blew out his chest proudly, cheeks flushed.

"And besides, we're much safer where we are now, in a Cave, and since we're climbing one of the smaller Mountains. Predators may be out thick during the Summer, but they are more likely to attack smaller groups. We have safety in numbers."

This seemed to settle the dispute of being hunted while they journeyed, and quickly satisfied Pinniose and Veldon's want of affirmation of safety.

Thus, the 13 journeyers settled down - and bundled up - for their first Night in the Mountains.

Soaring like an Eagle upon multicolor Mists, Serena twirled and spun, weaving herself around the Clouds and Nelson, who flew laughing and playful, beside her in her dreams. Through many pale, creamy Mists they flew, hearts singing, eyes shining, and Spirits soaring.

Serena savored every last moment of flight until it was ripped away from them both. And so they were condemned to fall, but together, which for both of them made the fate lighter on the heart, and comforted them in the knowledge that they were not to be separated. On a great white pillow that absorbed the couple's fall easily, Serena landed. She was dizzy, not having any more Mists or Clouds spinning and rushing past her face. She laid back to relieve herself of a throbbing motion sickness, which quickly subsided as Nelson stood and helped the Girl to stand.

They were in a square little room, perfectly stainless, with no furniture save for the huge white pillow they had landed on and a raised white platform with little white steps leading up to a white Stone alter on which was placed a tasseled white cushion. And on that cushion, Serena could not be sure, but she thought she could see a tiny glint of white, like a Diamond.

Nelson silently led her across the windowless, spotless white room to the raised platform and took her gingerly up the steps. He stopped before the white Stone altar, and stared with glowing eyes down at the object on the pillow. He released her hand, seemingly in awe, still gazing almost reverently at the pretty item.

Serena, curious, lowered her head to look at the object, too, and found the item to be a necklace on a Golden chain. The pendant, which was glowing, was too bright for Serena to see the actual pendant. Serena had no idea what this gorgeous object was, or what it was called, but she certainly did know that if she had not known it was a dream, she would had presumed the glittering Jewelry to be as real as she was.

She looked at Nelson and found him staring fondly at her with those two large green eyes that were the equivalence of real Emeralds. With the warmest smile ever issued he nodded, and with careful hands picked up the necklace and held it up in front of her face for her to see.

As soon as he touched it, the glow dimmed enough for Serena to see what it was.

It was the symbol for infinity, a sideways, stretched out figure eight. The Golden chain came together and attached where the two lines met in the middle. The necklace, though looking simple, was far from it. The material the symbol was made from was pure Diamond, smooth as glass. It was shining with the Power which radiated from its plain being. The light glowed almost too brightly.

Serena gazed deeply into the precious treasure, and smiled as she felt a particular warmth flare up inside her chest – the same feeling which she had felt several times before – that unmistakable emotion that could be placed somewhere between love, hominess, humbleness and mystery at the same time. It was an inimitable, Magical feeling of unknown Power and adventure such that Serena had grown to prize.

Blinking still at the glow, she looked happily at Nelson.

He held the chain up between them both. But just as he prepared to place his head through the chain to wear the symbol and kiss her, Serena's dreams were shattered into wakefulness. Reality dawned on her as a shadow-shrouded, Rocky, smoky-smelling Mountain Cave, with a tiny baby Fairy pulling on her Golden locks to wake up and feed her.

The questor's second Day of Mountain traveling pushed off with both a good and a bad start.

The good start was Beruga's confession of judging Nelson and the others before he truly knew them – and after they had been so kind as to save him and his family from that perilous Mountain Troll, he felt as though he had been negative, uncompassionate and even a touch rude at having assumed that Forever was to fall into the merciless claws of tyrants. He quickly apologized and was warmly accepted of being an honorably trustworthy CatFox.

However, there was one bad aspect that led some of them into dull moods. Earlier on, as the Sun began to rise and shine as a halo over the great Sparkline Mountain, the Clouds that had once formed Mist the Day before shrouded the Mountain and gathered over their heads, all the while blowing very cold air on them as though wishing to push them back down the Mountain with its frigid efforts.

Chilling as it was, the Travelers flexed their healthy muscles and proceeded to climb the narrow, dusty, upward-leading path, hoping to reach the Pegasus stalls and the Inns by dusk. Serena wished they could move faster, and so did Nelson, who was determined not to spend another bone-chilling, frost-bitten Night in the Mountains. He hastily proclaimed that they would board the Pegasus as soon as they reached the top, be it Day or dusk, to endure a Night trip to the Castle of Diamondia.

Serena was half scared of falling asleep on the back of her Pegasus and falling off to plunge to her death. She merely pushed the thought aside with a reassurance that they would have at least some form of ensuring a safe trip through the long Night.

Now, Serena knew that Night traveling was extremely tiring, and felt that this particular trip would be even more so since she had been deprived of some sleep the Night before due to the cold, howling Mountain Winds that passed through the shallow Cave. The Cave itself had looked used and questionable to them as they had first arrived, but Nelson reassured them that the footprints and burnt logs were only the remnants of other Travelers before them. He judged that since the little Cavern was positioned directly to the side of the path, it was an ideal campsite and therefore frequently in use. It was not the best shelter against the wild Mountain Winds, but it was somewhat comfortable.

Serena trudged alongside Nelson, lost in her own thoughts as she stared wonderingly down at the Springy-looking Valleys in between the range of Mountains.

Suddenly, Dawn fluttered up in front of Serena's face, using what gestures she knew to tell Serena that he could see the Clouds clearing from the top of the Perpetual Mountains. Serena nodded and turned her face upward to the blue Sky. It was a beautiful Summer Day, regardless of the temperature and the drafty gusts that blew them around on the Mountain.

The Girl sighed longingly, wishing so that she could be up in that lovely blue Sky already, free-wheeling and climbing ever higher to dance and caper about with the Clouds. As it was early morning the Birds were already flittering about in the Sky, trilling their melodious tunes to the cool World below. Oh, how she wished she could fly!

Serena nearly stopped in her tracks, having found a solution to both her fear of having to travel during the Night and her yearning to fly. Grasping the tiny bottle of Pixie Powder at her chest, she suddenly felt that that tiny bottle was not so tiny anymore.

"Nelson! Nelson!" she cried, lifting her prize high for all to see. She

374

hiked up her skirts and lumbered after her Halfbreed sweetheart, who was half walking and half flying in the front lines of the wayfaring team. "Nelson!"

"What is it?" he returned urgently, eyes wide. "What's wrong?"

"Pixie Powder!" Serena panted, hugging him with the Powder grasped tightly in one hand. "We can fly to the Pegasus stables – we don't need to waste our time walking.."

Nelson smiled and patted her cheek admirably.

"Clever!" he exclaimed, then looked at the sparkling bottle of Magic glitter. "But are you sure that that tiny little bottle is going to be enough for…" he stopped to count, "12 Creatures?"

Serena smiled at him slyly.

"If you don't count yourself – because you can fly – or Theo or the two Catfox Children, that only makes eight Creatures, and I am more than sure that this bottle can accommodate that many."

"What about the Children?" wondered Tarsena, who was traipsing behind them in her full-length faded red dress, a little paw in each of her hands. Her soft, kitten-like fur gleamed under the Sunlight with its gray, white, and orange mottled coat swaying gently with the Breeze. Her brown eyes studied them.

"They can be carried and switched off from Creature to Creature when the first carrier becomes tired," Serena explained, admiring the natural beauty of the CatFox Woman. She loved the simplicity and wonder in the Creature herself, who seemed to be just as interested in Serena as she was in her.

"A splendid idea!" Beruga agreed, scooping up tiny Veldon from behind.

"Indeed!" piped up little Pinniose.

The group stopped in the middle of the path and allowed Dawn to soar over them all, sprinkling them with the glittering Powder from Serena's glass bottle. In no time at all the happy journeyers had sprouted for themselves their own marvelous wings and were in the air on the way to the top of the Mountain.

The very first thing Serena did once she reached the Inn just before midDay was to order herself some hot Water brought up for a warm bubble bath. Nelson had since proclaimed that they were to take some time to clean up, rest, and restock at the Inn before continuing on to Sparkline Mountain. He also unanimously decided to teach tiny Dawn the essentials of Forever – the very presence of Sparkline Mountain and how its Magic worked. Thus Serena took the opportunity to clean herself up, seeing as how she had not had a warm bath in a while.

She had enjoyed her short flight immensely, loving the extended bouts of twisting and weaving through the Misten Skies as she had in her dream. But, consequently, her wings and the rest of the troops' wings shriveled and vanished almost as soon as they had reached the Inn, so now the group was left flightless.

Serena thought about her most recent dream as she bathed herself in a porcelain white tub in a tiled little room reserved for just that purpose. The others were presently off serving similar tasks. She wondered what it meant, what it was trying to tell her this time, and even if it was meant to be some form of a warning. Her thoughts were disrupted by a voice just outside the wooden door.

"Serena!"

Tap, tap … rapped a hand on the door.

"Serena, are you in there?"

Hastily, Serena snatched a large towel and wrapped herself tightly in it.

"Yes, Nelson." she replied calmly, admiring a decorative potted miniature palm Tree as she strode to the door. "Why?"

"Well I thought you ought to know , it appears that the Innkeeper also owns a small store of basic necessities, and I've found some elegant gowns that will be a lot warmer and less of a hassle for you and the other Girls. The only stipulation is that you must exchange your old dress for the new gown. I thought it was a good deal,"

"Sounds fabulous!" Serena admitted. She secretly had longed for a change in attire for some time. She quickly scooped up her old, worn blue dress and unlocked the door.

Smiling, Nelson accepted the dress. Dawn popped up from behind his shoulder in a Cloud of green Fairy Dust.

"I thought you might want some new clothes – I know that I am in great longing for some cleaner garments myself."

"With a smile like that, I'm sure the Inn Maids will have no problem lending you some cleaner clothing," Serena giggled, patting his cheek. She began to close the door. "Thank you!"

"Oh, wait, don't you want to take the d-"

"The diary!" Serena gasped, swinging the door open again. Gently she rustled through the skirts of her old dress and detected her ancestor's diary. She wasn't quite sure whether she could feel an air of suspicion as she retrieved the diary; she didn't remember telling Nelson anything about it other than that it belonged to one of her ancestors. She was actually ready to do battle over the matter in her mind when another, more intense thought dropped into her head.

She looked up into the shining green eyes of Nelson.

"How did you … know that I hid it in my skirt? Or even that I still had it?" she inquired. The Halfbreed's cheeks grew mildly pink.

"Oh, I … I've seen you … concealing it, often," he said, "But does that truly mean that much to you that I know? I mean, I haven't told anyCreature of where you hide the-"

"Did you read it? At Bendar?" Serena needed to know, advancing on him as she hugged the precious thing to her chest. She was determined to know if the Boy was keeping anything from her – he had been acting suspiciously nervous lately.

Nelson looked at the diary, and his eyes widened slightly.

"I – no … it isn't mine, so I really shouldn't – I mean, I didn't,"

Serena smiled out of the corner of her mouth and came nose-to-nose with the Boy. Now she was getting somewhere.

"And I'll just bet you know exactly who wrote it, don't you?"

Nelson sighed and stared truthfully into her bright blue eyes.

"Your ancestor," he sighed. "That's all I know."

Serena knew that this was not all that the Boy had been keeping from her, but decided not to provoke him any farther, as her legs were becoming cold and she was yearning to be back into her nice, warm bath.

"Correct," she smiled, blowing on his uneven bangs so that they flipped ridiculously about on his brow.

"Well … I'll … I'll just get a Maid, then … that is, to come up and fit you with a gown … and I … I'll talk to you later …"

Now Serena definitely knew that something was up. She secretly promised herself that she would look into the matter later as she smiled all the same and kissed him on the cheek.

"And I will talk to you later, too, sweetheart." she vowed with a smirk.

Nelson shook his head to himself, his face red in humiliation, and with a baby Dawn following close behind him, he turned with Serena's old blue dress and strode down the hallway, his cloak billowing out behind him like a MerMaid's hair underWater.

After her luxurious, warm bath - one of the most pleasurable she had had in awhile, she had to admit - Serena was fitted with several long-sleeved velvet gowns, and chose a comfortable pale bluish-white one. The gown was V-slit-ted and minimally low-cut in the front with long, soft sleeves that were tight in the arms to the elbow where they flared out with a soft, transparent silk dyed the hue of a Robin's egg. Tiny silver-white sparkles infused in the dainty fabric twinkled out at Serena. The sleeves were wide, but not so wide as to droop to the floor and drag with the short train that was trimmed with the same silken fabric. The chest and waist of the light blue gown were tight, but only until it billowed out precisely at the waist.

But more than anything, Serena admired the soft material of the gown itself. It must have been a special type of fabric that the gown was made out of, because Serena was delighted with the comfortable appeal and the soft touch. Later she questioned Nelson as to whether the gown was an expensive one, but he waved his hand airily and told her it was nothing compared to what the Lady-Creatures wore in royalty. Then his face suddenly grew red and he turned away.

Serena had noticed that the Boy was becoming more and more nervous that early afternoon, and she felt that he had every right to be so, given the circumstances.

He is the Heir to the Throne, she thought, allowing her hair to be con-ditioned, styled, and admired by the two Nymph Maids that had dressed her in the gown. *And so he will soon be crowned the Father of Forever. I would probably be nervous too, if I were in his position ...*

The Nymph Maids fussed about her hair distractedly, disturbing her thoughts. Serena did not mind answering their curious questions as they styled her hair elegantly. She learned much about the pretty Nymph Maids them-selves as she spoke to them. She found that Nymphs were really just Pixies without Wings, and with unrealistic-colored hair and eyes. The Maidens in turn questioned Serena about her culture and she patiently quenched their cu-riosity as best she could.

After being doused in lotions and perfumes, Serena decided that she could not stand the suspense any longer, and stole away from the Inn to the very Cliff that was hung perfectly in front of the great Sparkline Mountain.

Surprisingly, she was only mildly cool standing in the wet Snow, and all alone on the overhang of the Cliff. Her dress accounted for much of her warmth. She could not yet see the Diamondia Castle, however, for a thick shade of Mist had mysteriously collected just above the peak of the beautiful place. And although the glittering, light-bathed Mountain looked to be a good distance from them, Serena had a feeling that it would not take them very long to reach it.

Sighing with the gentle Breeze, Serena looked down over the side of the Snowy Cliff, and could not help but smile as she saw two particular Rivers - the Basstooth and the Edgewood Rivers - melting together far, far below her around the Mountains' bases. Their dark Waters joined together to defy gravity and trickle their way up the mystical Mountain. Serena also noticed that the higher the Water climbed, the purer and clearer it seemed; by the time the Water had reached the top (or as close to the top as Serena could see) it was the clearest, purest Water the young Girl had ever seen. All in all, Serena felt that the breath-taking view could be poetically described as an upward-running Waterfall.

Then Serena turned and looked behind her. The path on which her troop had traveled came up from the right side of the Mountain and melted into the Stone front steps of the Inn that they were resting at. The Inn itself was roughly three stories tall, built thickly with wood, and was somehow warmed on the inside by some unknown Magical Spell. The Pegasus stalls were located just beside the Inn, also wooden, and strewn with oats, fruit and hay. There was only one doorway with no door in and out of the stable, where one Pegasus at a time would file out on its own. The Creatures were not domestic enough to be tied up. Serena marveled at one Pegasus as it flew low to land, and she smiled at its gleaming white coat and wings, its Magical alicorn which protruded from its forehead and its long, flowing mane and tail of green and Golden hue. Serena saw that the Pegasus was no different from a Unicorn aside from the feature of its white, feathered wings, that stretched much longer than any wing span Serena had ever witnessed in her life time.

Gently the Pegasus touched down beside her, and with a yawn and a nod of its lovely head, it trotted off grandly to enjoy a coupe of grains. The tireless Creature had not even broken a sweat or a single pant during its journey.

Soon we will visit the Mountain, Serena reminded herself. *But, for right now, I have other situations worth my concern.*

With this, Serena remembered just what she had come up here to do. She had been suspicious of Nelson's strange behavior, and even more of her wild dream that she had encountered the Night before. She wondered if the two could somehow be connected, and knew that there was only one Creature who could tell her what she wished to know.

Smiling, she pulled Teresa's diary from a purse-like satchel that she wore strapped over her chest to match her liquid-blue dress. Carefully she retrieved the small, clear TeleStone from the inside front pocket and gazed into its transparent center.

Remembering a now happy memory of Middleton, Serena gently rubbed the glassy surface of the Stone. It seemed to warm slightly in her hand as she bent and whispered to it,

"Melabon of Middleton."

Immediately the center of the Stone turned black, studded with Diamonds (looking similar to the Night Sky), and something similar to a muffled giggle was heard.

"Hello?" Serena spoke, trying to get the giggler's attention. "Is anyCreature there?"

A playful shriek was heard.

"Did you hear something, Laci?"

"Yes …" was the reply, and the screen of Serena's TeleStone suddenly burst into Sunlight, with three pretty little faces shining down at her.

"It's the Serena Girl!" Maci exclaimed, giggling.

"Hello Serena!" Laci smiled.

"Do you want Gramma Melabon?" asked Daci, her blue bow falling limp on top of her little head.

"Yes, if you could fetch her, I would appreciate it," smiled Serena.

Quickly, little Maci scampered downstairs and led Melabon up to the velvet sack that her TeleStone was in. Greeting almost as old friends, Serena told Melabon of their great adventures, how Nelson had indeed returned, and where they were now. She even turned the TeleStone's face to the Mountain so that Melabon could see the beautiful view. She found that when she looked at the back of the Stone that it was as clear as though nothing was there. Quickly she turned it back and told Melabon of her last dream.

Melabon seemed perfectly ponderous after hearing Serena's dream, and suspiciously silent when she heard the details of the necklace described in the Girl's dream. After many long moments of silence, Serena decided that she could not restrain her suspense any longer and spoke.

"So … what does it mean, Melabon? Do you know? What is it trying to tell me? What-"

"It is a very peculiar dream … most unlike any dream I have ever heard of," the tiny head of Melabon shook, as though she were ready to give up.

"Is it a foreshadowing dream?" Serena had to know, bracing her body and her warm, velvety gown against the Wind. She told Melabon of how strange Nelson had been acting lately.

"I know what it means," Melabon chuckled finally. She brought her withered, wise old face very close to the glass.

"It means that Nelson-"

Suddenly Serena was pushed playfully from behind, and the TeleStone was swept out of her hand, over the Cliff, and onto the wings of the Wind, forever to plunge down the Mountainside into the upward-climbing Waterfall.

"Hey, Serena!" Jerry laughed. "What are you doing out here all alone? Trying to fly like the Pegasus?"

With that seemingly hilarious remark, Jerry erected an arm on either side of him and flapped them around ridiculously in imitation of a flight-able Creature.

Serena remained silent, half shocked, half frustrated, staring blankly at the Misten, many-faced Mountain that the TeleStone had rushed to join.

"What's wrong? Are you alright?" Jerry asked finally, abandoning his playful mood. He came to stand next to the stoic Girl.

Serena sighed.

"Oh, I am fine." she breathed, and looked at him with eyes as blue as the Water climbing the Jewel-adorned Mountain before them. "I was only just about to find out the interpretation of my last dream."

"Another one?" Jerry laughed, his gaze fixed on her, "I thought you only had one of them,"

"Well … I didn't," Serena returned, looking back down the Mountain below her feet. Silent moments passed. Then Jerry cleared his throat.

"Ah, Serena … there's kind of something I've been meaning to tell you," he began, pacing nervously. Serena lifted her head and stared at him, waiting for him to continue. He wrung his hands. "Er, you see, I am not … realistically 24 years old,"

His eyes found widened, sparkling blue Jewels.

"You're not?" Serena said softly. She was confused. "Then … then how did you-"

"I lied, okay?" Jerry grumbled, crossing his arms and staring at the light Snow on the ground. "I'm a fraud, I cheated to get that job, just because I wanted a good adventure in life. I stole the identity of someone else, took his name, just to romp off and get myself lost, and make a horrible mess out of everything,"

Now Serena was not only confused, but also scared. She clutched her new, wildly Wind-dancing skirt and stepped back, shaking her head in disbelief. Her Sun-Golden curls caressed her cheeks.

"Who are you?" she half demanded, half gasped.

The Boy's newly-ironed cloak billowed out behind him.

"My real name is Kevin," he admitted with a tremendous sigh. "Kevin Smithson, gas station attendant," His voice lowered to a pathetic wheedle, "18 years old,"

"No!" Serena exclaimed. "All that you told me about your life, your background, your age ... even your own name ... they were all lies?" she hissed incredulously.

Kevin stared at the ground silently, his face red in embarrassment.

"I ... I had no idea it was going to turn out like this ... and then I met you ... and ... Serena," Kevin drew very close to her, voice trembling, face flaming, and eyes glassy under the Sunlight, "if I would have known that it would have ended up this way, I never would have said or did any of the things I did! I ... Serena ... if I hurt you ... in any way ... I want you to know that I am so sorry-"

"No," Serena said softly, shrugging his hands from her shoulders and placing a finger over his lips. He stared deeply at her, his Watery soul gathering in his eyes. And Serena stared back, probing this new soul, listening to the Wind and the sound of copious amounts of running Water.

"No, Je- ... Kevin," she breathed, catching herself. She removed her finger. "It is not me that you should be apologizing to." She stepped back, her gown skirt fluttering and flaring out prettily. "It is not the team nor any of the kind acquaintances we met on our journey here."

Serena stopped purposefully, seeing a shadow of nagging suspicion cross the Boy's face.

"Who is it, then?" he asked at last, his voice near to cracking.

Silent moments, filled with the smell of fresh precipitation flying through the air, passed.

"It is you," Serena stated in a low whisper, laying a hand on his shoulder comfortingly. "You must first apologize to yourself."

And then, like a breath of Wind herself, Serena fled back to the Inn.

"There you are!" Nelson sighed in relief as Serena entered the Inn lobby. He held out a half-filled knapsack. "What shall we do with this?"

"Why?" Serena wondered, looking at the worn thing thoroughly. "Aren't we taking our knapsacks with us?"

From nowhere in particular, Dawn emerged and landed on Serena's right shoulder.

Nelson looked at the knapsack.

"Well ... no, actually," he replied, scratching the top of his shiny-haired head which, indubitably and like the rest of him, had been scrubbed clean and conditioned to a glowing luster. It was evident that he had taken on his old garb of a sleeveless green tunic with dark brown leggings and tall moccasins. "Usually we do not need to bring such supplies with us; the Diamondia Castle should already have them."

"It must be a lovely place," Serena smiled, taking the knapsack from him to leaf through it. "And very large, too, to be able to shelter, entertain and feed so many earnest Travelers."

"Oh, it is!" Nelson admitted. His cheeks grew pink and he waved at Mike and Beruga as they passed on their way upstairs. "It is the largest and most beautiful thing in the whole of Forever! The Castle is made completely of Diamond, and it is so large that it could probably hold all of Forever's inhabitants and still have room for more!" He smiled as Serena's eyes widened. "Oh, yes, it is that big!"

"You speak as though you have lived there!" Serena jested, handing him the knapsack. Giggling, she kissed the flush Boy on the cheek. "Donate my knapsack to the Inn – perhaps some Traveler coming back from the great Mountain will need it for his travels home."

He gave her hand a nervous squeeze and strode off with Dawn close in tow.

Lindsey, Kate and Bob found her on her way up to her room.

"Hey, Serena!" Lindsey called. Serena smiled as she noted that Lindsey's British accent was nearly perfect.

"Yeah?"

"We're going to say good-bye to the CatFoxes before they leave for Diamondia. Won't you come with us?"

Bob had himself another hairtie, and took this opportunity to tighten it.

"Yes, actually."

She joined them on their trek down the stairs.

"So, can you believe that we're truly going to see this Diamondia place?" Kate asked. She pulled the skirt of her vibrant green velvet gown up so she did not trip on the long hem.

"It sounds fantastic." Lindsey said. "I heard little Theo talking about it earlier – the Child could hardly be more excited! Pinniose told me that this is their first time to Diamondia, and Theo was filling them all in."

"He's been to Diamondia before?" Serena said suspiciously, turning to her curly-haired friend.

"Oh yes, lots of times, he said."

"I rather think he was boasting," Bob huffed.

But Serena smiled and pulled a piece of lint from Lindsey's Sunshine-yellow velvet dress.

"Somehow, I don't," she giggled.

Late afternoon was setting in before the team made their way out to the Pegasus stables. The Pegasus, in their rare and mythical beauty, were waiting for them patiently and emerged from their little barn in single file. The winged Creatures must have somehow known that they were coming. Each Traveler (minus the CatFoxes, who had left around noon) was then chosen by a Pegasus as the lovely Creatures kneeled on their forelegs before them. A cluster of six or seven Pegasus chose Serena all at once, and feeling a bit guilty for not choosing any of the others, she closed her eyes and laid her hand on the closest one. Thus she boarded the bare back of a pure white-maned Pegasus.

"We do not have saddles?" Serena asked, somewhat nervously, as her white Pegasus stood and pranced over to the other mounted Pegasus. The Child Fairy, Dawn, saw that Serena was making to take off and dove into her satchel playfully, ready for an adventure.

"No," Nelson replied, patting the neck of his green and blue-haired Pegasus. Its pale, pretty colors gleamed as it tossed its head back for more attention. "Pegasus never ride with saddles; they feel too restrained. They feel that flight should be carefree and comfortable to the ridden as well as the rider." He shielded his eyes from the glowing Sun.

When Serena looked again, the Clouds and Mist that had hung over their heads and the twinkling Mountain was moving off to the SouthEast, brandishing the legendary Sparkline Mountain, and majestically perched as though floating over the inward pouring Waterfalls (which Serena had recently learned were called the Neverending Falls), was the most marvelous, enormous, fantastic Castle ever imagined. Even from their great distance and true to Nelson's word, the Castle looked fit to house the whole population of Forever and still have room left over. The design was intricate and delicately carved towers, keeps, windows, balconies, turrets, stairs and ramps littered the grand place; great, long halls, gigantic chambers, beautiful rooms and Gardens all filled to the brim with colorful decorations which a Creature could see plainly through the smooth, glassy walls.

Remembering the rich description that Mosslyn had once made to her of the Fountain of Youth, Serena looked for the fabled Spring from her distance. Since she was still on the Perpetual Mountains, even though she was on the very peak, she could still only see a select few top towers of the Diamondia Castle. She did, however, observe a rounding, glowing something on the very top of the tallest tower, sitting inside the bloomed petals of a great Diamond Rose, growing up out of a great, railed platform. The glow from the something was tantamount to the gleam of the necklace from her dream – almost so lovely to look at that it hurt her eyes.

Yet as she looked, she thought she detected movement of the Castle itself. Was the structure truly spinning as slowly and as swiftly as her eyes were telling her it was?

We're too far away, she thought at last, disappointed. *And I'll just bet my eyes are playing tricks on me – we have been a long way just toDay!*

She scratched her Pegasus behind the ears affectionately, waiting for Nelson to give orders to push off. Suddenly, she found herself sliding off of the Pegasus's back, because she was sitting in a side-saddle position in order to preserve her dress and herself.

But, strangely, something happened to catch Serena as she slipped, like a Magical Breeze, and lifted her back onto the Pegasus's back. She smiled as Nelson told them all about the Pegasus.

"NoCreature knows how or when the Pegasus came to the Perpetual Mountains. All we know is that every Pegasus that is born up here is automatically Enchanted and lives on these Mountains and around the Castle all of its life. In its lifetime it will transfer Creatures to and from the Diamondia Castle. They are Magical Beasts, I warrant you – noCreature has ever fallen into the Misty Lake after falling off the back of a Pegasus on their way to or from the Mountain. It's their Enchanted Magic that holds the Traveler secure, like another pair of arms."

Another pair of arms was certainly the correct description of the Breezy, sweet Magic that had swept Serena up and returned her to the Pegasus she had chosen (or rather, the Pegasus that had chosen her). The wondrous Creature nodded its head, white mane flashing, uttering a melodious whiney. It stamped its hoofed foreleg, impatient to be off.

"Shh, shh," Serena calmed the Creature, petting its wide brow. Curious, she leaned forward and rubbed the tender spot just around the spiral alicorn, and in return the Creature's eyes turned to a comfortable, peaceful white with a tinge of blue. She smiled.

"I've told them," said a proud voice behind her. Serena turned. It was Kevin, mounted tall on top of an Orchid-maned Pegasus with streaks of dark indigo in its hair. Serena ran her fingers through the fine, shiny mane of her own white-maned Pegasus and began to braid it distractedly.

"So you have," she replied, admiring the silky softness and the complete absence of disorder and imperfection in the hair. She looked up at Kevin with a mild smile. "You did the right thing." She patted his shoulder proudly with a long gaze, then turned to look at Nelson.

The Halfbreed, despite his own abilities in flight, had mounted a Pegasus whose mane was such a pale blue and green that it was hard to tell it even had color to it. The pretty Creature nodded its head and snorted softly, eyes an energetic green and ready to go.

"When we get there, we will go straight to the Fountain Chamber." Nelson told them as his Pegasus turned to face Sparkline Mountain. "We will go from there."

And without another word, the Boy leaned forward and his Pegasus began to lunge into a trot.

Feeling nothing more than a tiny lurch, Serena was pressed down against the back of her own Pegasus by the "invisible arms" that held her in place. Fearing the worst, her arms clasped to the Animal's neck, then slid back to grasp the muscular wings as they spread open. Serena was frightened at first, her body bumping up and down somewhat insecurely as the Pegasus graduated to a healthy, strong gallop. She could see the edge of the Cliff growing closer and closer each time the sleek Creature lowered its head. All around her, Serena could hear the stampeding hooves of the other Pegasus, could smell the muddy Snow churned up from those same hooves, and could see – very clearly, in fact – the rapidly growing wall of upward-running Water that symbolized the breath-taking presence of the colossal Jewel-adorned Mountain.

Dawn, her tiny eyes in slits and her pointed ears sticking out stubbornly, peeked her little head up out of Serena's satchel momentarily. Her green eyes widened, her already pale skin whitened, and her glowing Fairy Dust turned to a mortified orange. She opened her mouth to utter a little shriek that was inaudible to Human - and Halfbreed - ears. In a flash of white-blonde hair, the Fairy burrowed deep into the satchel and trembled, petrified.

Serena looked around at the others - Mike was laughing; Bob was holding on for dear life; Lindsey was screaming; Kate was burrowing her head in the Animal's Sunshine-yellow mane and crying; Kevin was dawning a look of horror; Theo was shivering and giggling; and Nelson was expressionless. He looked very much like he had done this same thing several times before. With a smile, Serena knew that he had.

Turning back to her own situation, Serena became scared speechless – at least until the Pegasus took a final leap off the Cliff, spread its wings, and dove toward the Valley, spiraling towards the Water.

Something must be wrong... Serena thought at first, clutching the Pegasus's wings. She closed her eyes to stop the spinning Water and Rock. She fought herself to stop trembling. *Why aren't we flying? We are supposed to be-*
Whoosh!

And Serena was left speechless again. The entire team's screams rang in her ears as the Pegasus stretched out their mighty white wings and caught a thick draft of Wind which lifted them all as though they were weightless up into the air and closer to the Mountain which was covered in running Water and Jewels.

Serena could feel the Sun coaxing her already sweating skin to perspire ever more as she and her team was carried upward to the great Mountain.

Then the Pegasus split apart on their own little routes of playful flight, their wings pumping as they galloped on the air, chased one another, twisted, turned, zigzagged and looped, taking their riders on one of the greatest rides of their lives. Serena's Pegasus wheeled about and flew so close to the Mountain that one of its wingtips touched the pure, saintly Water. Its white tail suddenly lashed out from behind as Serena, all fears forgotten permanently, reached out with her own hand to touch the cool, refreshing Water.

Splish!

The tail slapped at the Water and sprayed Serena playfully. She laughed and in turn took a handful of the Water and sprinkled the excited, strong Creature with a bit of its own medicine. It chortled in its melodious, hollow voice and jerked into another plunge, only to soar upward again and begin looping and twisting with Mike's olive-green-maned Pegasus.

Moreover, the ride with the Pegasus was enough to get Serena's heart pumping, and even more so when the Pegasus smoothly landed onto an extremely narrow perch, marking the two-thirds point of their journey, on the very ridge of the great hollow Mountain. There the Rivers all poured over the inside into the great, mystic, endless Waterfalls that persisted around the circumference of the mouth of the Mountain.

The Neverending Falls.

Serena could help no more but to stare in disbelief, mouth agape, eyes wide, and cheeks pink. The lightest Breeze rustled her curls as she took it all in.

The hollow ridge around the Mountain was gargantuan – larger, Serena estimated, than 10 well-sized Mountain Valleys put together. The Castle seemed like nothing more than a fancy little dollhouse compared to the mystic pit's enormous size.

But obviously, the Diamondia Castle was not a fancy little dollhouse. Elegant and finely-crafted though the delicate structure was, Serena thought it was nowhere near little. Instead, the Castle was possibly even larger than the Mountain they had climbed on Sparkline's outskirts, or so Serena thought. Its build was rich with tall towers, crystalline bridges, and glassy, spotless ramps and stairs. Serena could see into every room and distinguished kitchens, living rooms, hallways and more. Even little Waterfalls protruded right from the eternal walls, trickling down the pure, stainless sides of the structure to drip off of the platform in its tiny Rivers. But the loveliest aspect of the Castle, by far, was a great chamber in the very front, which seemed alight with Jewels and Water. The Water must have been leaking out of the chamber, Serena thought, because tiny Streams of Water and Jewels poured delicately over the platform to rejoin the glittering Mists. And, as Serena had predicted before, the magnificent Castle was, indeed, spinning.

Backed by a ring of Neverending Waterfalls, a long, graceful stem grew up out of the thick, multicolored Mist and flattened into a circular platform on the top. The platform was wide but not thick, and was so great that it could accommodate the wondrous Castle Diamondia in its center and still have room for some rather big lawns and Gardens, which mysteriously grew right up off the platform without a speck of dirt in sight. The Grass of pure green was shining, as after a Spring Rain. The Flowers and Ferns were all vibrant and intermixed with hues and the sparsely planted Tree here and there hung with Jewels of fruit that glistened with the Mist and dew set up from the Misty Neverending Falls. Multicolor Birds chirped and trilled their blissful melodies and played under the tiny Streams that poured like tiny Waterfalls over the Lawns and Gardens.

The Diamondia Castle itself glowed with a radiance so vivid and so lovely as it turned under the Sunlight that Serena nearly had to shield her eyes. Colored manes and tails flew like ribbons from the hordes of Pegasus that swarmed around the Castle in great numbers, weaving in and out of its many towers, landing on its balconies, Lawns and Gardens, splashing through its Waterfalls and Rainbows, and generally playing and chasing one another within the Mist and the Waterfalls, neighing their happy songs to the Castle and all other souls within it. Serena watched as their sleek, graceful bodies, wet with Mist and dew, darted through the air like knives through butter, their alicorns gleaming under the brisk, delicious Sunlight. The temperature of the place was extremely comfortable, as in the Spring - not too cool, yet not too warm - it was perfect. Rainbows, pale and bright, swathed the blue, Cloudless Skies over the Diamondia Castle thickly, making the scene appear as some sort of tropical paradise of Heaven.

The Breeze rustled Serena's curls again as she studied the scene before her. She could hear the Water of the Neverending Falls splashing over the hooves of their Pegasus, and felt the cool, soft spray of the Water as it fell into the hollow ring in the Mountain, taking its many-faced Jewels with it. She watched a group of Pegasus bearing other Travelers perch on the ridge of the falls off to their distant right, and then swoop about to the spinning Castle.

Like pollen pollinates a Flower, Serena thought, watching them in fascination, the Pegasus bring their travelers to their fertile Castle. *If the Mountains were stamen, the Pegasus were pollen, and the spinning Diamondia Castle the pistol, then the Fountain of Youth would be the seeding fruit of this fantastic Land.*

Serena was proud of her poetic assumption, and tapped her satchel so that Dawn might peek her pale little head out of her purse and see the fascinating sight that she was seeing. Eventually she did, and issued a gasp nearly loud enough to be heard by Human ears. Her Elfish little face turned up to Serena with a happy, bright smile as bright as the shimmering Rainbows overhead. And then the Pegasus beneath them both lurched into flight and heaved upwards, its silky white hair falling into Serena's face, and she laughed joyously at the same time that the Pegasus chortled again. It leaped upwards and spun backwards, then looped and twisted all about in a merry dance with the Magical Breeze. At one point the Creature was flying so steady that Serena forgot to hold on, and lifted her arms on either side of her so that she felt as though she had wings and could fly.

Just then a laughing Kate flew by, and pushed Serena hard from behind. Losing her balance, she tumbled off the Pegasus's back. Only when she had turned onto her stomach to face the Mist did she realize the significance of this action. Serena was living her dream, flying in the Mist. Her fears at that point seemed to leave her – and she could almost feel them leaving. They could no longer follow her where she chose to go. She no longer feared death or danger, and screamed with joy as she spun in the Mists. Unfortunately, the Pegasus knew the moment she had been taken from its back, and it swiftly spiraled down to catch her neatly.

Serena's eyes grew and grew as they flew closer and closer, and already the beauteous Castle seemed to look more homey to her, like a mother with open arms. Already Serena knew that she never, ever wanted to leave this glorious, wondrous place.

Chapter Fifty: Forever Forever

The Travelers' landing was very smooth and almost flawless. Serena leaped at once from the back of her new Pegasus friend and hugged her around the neck, thankful for the blithe and thrilling ride. Bare feet touched the soft, Sun-warmed Grass on the Lawns, as many of the wayfarers, including Serena, had lost their footwear during the trip. Serena secretly admitted as she reached to pluck a fruit from a nearby Tree and present it to the strong, graceful Creature, that she had never had so much fun flying in her life. Her fears of height over Water were now gone – vanished, without a trace – as though the minor phobia had never once visited her in her lifetime. Serena was content and refreshed as Dawn flew out of her satchel in a flurry of green sparkles which drifted up to Serena's nose and made her sneeze. Dawn laughed and nuzzled into the hair on top of Serena's head. The white Pegasus, gulping down some of the sweet, fresh Water that trickled through the Grass in small rivulets, spread her wings and nodded her head to Serena in farewell, her shining ivory-hued alicorn touching Serena lightly on the shoulder. Serena, feeling honored and dignified by this symbol of affection, picked a white Flower that grew at her feet and wove it into the mane of the blue-eyed Creature, then stood back and bowed her head with a hand over her heart.

In a flash of white mane fur and blue eyes, the merciful winged Unicorn lifted herself into the air and neighed as she sailed off to go soar with the other Pegasus in the Rainbows. Serena stretched and turned to see Nelson striding over to her. Some of the others were still dismounting behind him.

"You never told me the Castle spun," she teased him, tweaking his nose. "Or that the water leaks off of it like so many more miniature Waterfalls."

"Minor details," Nelson shrugged, taking her hand. He led her over to the group as they detached themselves from their new Pegasus friends.

Serena noted the short, glass-like railing that lined the very edge of the platform, no doubt to keep pesky Children from wandering over the side, despite the safety of the Pegasus's constant lingering. A heavenly, alluring sound suddenly burst out of the Castle like a choir of Angels singing. Serena savored the melodious harmony as she watched the ring of beJeweled Waterfalls slowly turning around her. She had never been on such a magnificently spinning Castle before, and if she had not known it was spinning, she probably would not have noticed. For the great Diamondia Castle was spinning so silently, so steadily, so smoothly, and so slowly that it was hardly even noticeable.

"As long as the Rivers of Forever run up the sides of this great Sparkline Mountain," Nelson told them as they all seemed to be noting the movement at the same time, "the Diamondia Castle will always spin."

He led them over to the biggest pair of doors Serena had ever seen.

Kevin looked around at the faces of the exhilarated team members.

"This is it, guys. We made it!"

A warm Breeze brushed past them as Nelson took the glassy handles of the tall doors and flung them open for all to see.

Serena, when she opened her eyes, nearly fainted.

So staggeringly beautiful was the sight that met the Travelers' eyes that it actually left them without words. Standing before them was an extravagant, beautiful Fountain, composed purely of genuine Diamond. The Fountain was tall, glassy, and shining with the sweet-looking Water that ran down from spouts. The design of the Spring was eloquent and graceful, with spirals, loops, and other delicate symbols and pictures embellished perfectly into its Jewel-adorned surface.

The Fountain Chamber was cavernous and commodious, with murals painted here and there of historical heroes, tapestries depicting ancient stories, and figures and symbols carved straight into the wall. The floor was trickling with Water that overflowed in the smaller Pools that were associated with the biggest pool – nearly as big as a small Lake – around the base of the great Fountain. Channels ran around the exterior of the room to collect the endless overflow of Water that coated the floor ankle-deep. Jewels of all colors, shapes, and sizes were strewn majestically across the Water-flowing floor, and flattened then popped back into shape Magically when a Creature stepped on them.

There were several Creatures visiting the Fountain when Serena's troop came to call. Nymphs - with their Rainbow-colored hair, Pixies - with their narrow, leaf-shaped wings, Gnomes - with their pointed caps, Dwarves - with their burly, stout figures, Elves - with their pale, lovely complexions, Humans - of any spectral-colored skin, Animals - in their Human-like forms, Satyrs, Fauns, and Sileni - with their half-Human, half-Beast characteristics, Minotaurs - with the heads of Cows, and even a Creature that Nelson identified as Anixies – Animals with Pixie wings - all crowded around the Fountain. They were barefoot, as was a reverent custom to remove any footwear before stepping into the chamber. The walls held shelves here and there, filled with shoes, cloaks, and knapsacks. To ensure them of the safety of these strewn items, Nelson promptly stated that all Creatures that entered the Fountain Chamber were removed of any and every evil they may have possessed as they came in, therefore securing the items of the visitors.

The Creatures sloshed happily about in the ankle-deep Water, discovering all of the wondrous Magic of the Fountain of Youth and its Spring Water. Children picked dirt clods from their clothes and dipped them into the Pools, turning the dirt into different colors of Jewels. All around, little Creatures were giggling, "I got a Ruby!"and, "I got a Sapphire!" and "I got an Emerald!" The adults, too, were enjoying their visit to the legendary Fountain. Full grown adults were known to pretend to slide and fall on the floor only to feel the pleasure of being bounced back up to a standing position as though the floor was made of some elastic-type of element.

All over Serena saw the Magical Water work its power. An ugly Pixie washed her face in the Spring Water and was transformed immediately. She emerged looking most lovely. A stout Gnome sprinkled the Spring Water over his head, and became slim. An old Nymph Woman sipped the Spring Water from her cupped hands, and was a young adult again. A sickly-looking, pale Dwarf took in the Spring Water, and was healthy. A skinny, lanky Raccoon Two-Legger rubbed the Spring Water on his arms and legs and was made strong. Miraculously, the Water improved the lives of every visitor, young and old according to the Creatures' wishes. Creatures could be seen picking up the small Jewels and stashing them in their pockets. Serena wondered how they could take them without being caught for thievery. She consulted Nelson on the subject.

"Oh, don't worry about it – the Jewels always crumble back into dust once they leave the Mountain anyway," he replied, reaching down to remove his moccasins. The few explorers who had not lost their shoes on the Pegasus quickly followed his example.

"We can look around for awhile if you like," Nelson told them as the stunned team started, barefoot, into the magnificent room. "But soon we will need to find the Mother. Try not to stray too far away."

Serena could hardly suppress a Childish squeak of glee as she stepped into the Water-flowing room. Her feet and train were immediately drenched in the Water, but she didn't care. The cool, refreshing feeling of innocence and purity felt good to her skin as it worked up from her feet to her legs, her legs to her stomach, and her stomach to her heart. It continued throughout her arms and her head, and dwelt within her heart as though becoming a part of her blood, to pump the deliciously wonderful feeling throughout her entire body. Serena sighed as a peculiar calm stole over her and she watched in awe as the same feeling worked into the souls of the other Travelers. Theo performed a cartwheel and capered off to go play with some of the other Children, Dawn tagging along behind him in a flash of blue Fairy Dust. Lindsey and Kate bent to pick up the Jewels and admire them. Mike, Bob and Kevin made straight to the Fountain of Youth. And Nelson, with a nervous smile, took the blue-eyed Girl's hand and led her over to one of the Pools.

"This … this is the Pool of the Future," he informed her. Serena smiled faithfully and turned to look in the clear, pure-Watered Pool.

She saw herself first, though looking older, perhaps in her twenties with the same starry blue eyes and Golden curls, grown very long. She was wearing a very pretty pale green gown with long, wide sleeves and a slim skirt that flared out into ruffles at the bottom. She was wearing a necklace, but she could not see the pendant, for it was hidden behind the ruffles on the collar of her dress. And then she saw Nelson beside her, also looking much older and dressed in a very fine tunic with his sword and scabbard at his side. And, of course, he was wearing the necklace from her dream – she was sure of it, although his pendant was also hidden. But the chain was Golden, as Golden as the necklace appeared in her dream.

And, finally, a third figure trickled into view.

It was an Angel!

No!

It was a little Girl, the most beautiful little Girl Serena had ever seen, that popped up between them. She was unmistakabley an Elf, with pale, delicate skin, and long, white-blonde curls, even longer and lighter blonde than Serena's. She had a white circle of light floating gently over her little head. Her eyes looked like pure crystal Diamond with long, adorable eyelashes. She was about three years old, cladden in a perfect little white dress, her hair woven and intertwined with white Flowers. Serena opened her mouth as she saw what the Child did next. She opened her long white wings, and her pointed ears lifted underneath her crown of curls (and also a delicate Diamond tiara that depicted a white Rose) as she executed a heart-warming, lovely little smile, her cheeks flush with youth and her tiny lips bright pink.

"What do you see?" Nelson whispered softly, coming behind her.

"A little Girl," Serena replied after a lengthy pause, filled with laughter and the sound of splashing Water. She watched the heavenly Child draw a harp out from behind her skirt, begin to strum it, and sing a wordless melody as she took flight and hovered between Serena and Nelson. The real Serena in front of the Pool gasped. "She is an Angel!"

"Is that so?" Nelson went on, wrapping his arms around her warmly. "What kind of Angel?"

Serena did not take her eyes from the Pool and the bewitching Diamond eyes of the beautiful Child. She closed her eyes with a drawn out note, and when she opened them, the flash of vibrant green in her eyes was so alive and shocking that Serena almost stopped breathing as the green slipped away and the Diamond color returned.

"A Child Angel with a tiara of Diamond, like a Princess, with soft, pale, fair skin. An Angel with Emeralds for eyes, who looks as much a heavenly Flower as the white Diamond Rose on her head." Serena turned around and looked at Nelson. "A beautiful little Angel, that is what I see."

"Just like you?" Nelson mused, lifting her chin. His eyes smiled at her. "Serena, I want to ask you something very important. And I do need you to listen to me, very closely."

This is what has been making him so nervous and so suspicious – I just know it! Serena thought. Her ears perked and she instantly shut out the sounds of Water splashing, Jewels ringing on Diamond, Creatures laughing, and the choir of lovely singing so that she could only hear Nelson.

The handsome Halfbreed drew close to her, almost nose-to-nose, and stared straight into her blue eyes, as blue as the rippling, Jewel-studded Spring Water.

"Serena, I think we both know some things are going to happen very soon here," he began. Serena knew exactly what he was talking about, and hung on his every word.

"We may not be seeing each other so frequently after … after it happens. So I need to know now,"

Serena searched his eyes. Was he going to break up with her? She could feel her own eyes beginning to Water already.

"Serena … now don't do this to me," he added, seeing her eyes reddening, "I only wanted to know … do you want to go back to Earth?"

That's right! When he is Father, he will have the Power to send us all back! Oh, I should have told Kevin ... then again, that would have caused such a commotion.

Nelson wants to send me back! she thought dismally, then brightened, *but, no, he is giving us a choice to go back. I wonder what the others think.*

One look at the Pool of the Future confirmed Serena's personal decision.

"Well … I mean you'll have to ask the others too, but me …"

She glanced in the Pool again, and at the Golden chain around Nelson's neck. When he became Father, he would be the most Powerful being in Forever.

"No … No, I want to stay here with you … forever."

Without warning she felt herself hug the Boy. "I never want to go back …never … I want to stay here …. in Forever," she paused to looked back up at him. "Forever."

"Then," Nelson said, pulling a tiny velvet bag from his tunic. He opened it and brandished a ring made of pure Diamond, the most envious, bewitching object in the World. "Then, if you choose to stay here forever,"

He dropped one knee into the thin water.

Serena didn't see Kate grab Lindsey's arm and Kevin gasp as Mike's and Bob's mouths dropped open.

She didn't hear when someCreature shouted very loudly, "HEY EVERY-CREATURE! LOOKA DIS!" and several hundred faces snapped to look at the pair.

She saw nothing in that still moment except for Nelson, her true love. A lump rose in her throat. But this was so soon! Did he really want her to make a decision right then and there? If she said no, would they stay together? Then what would happen if she said yes? Could it be that the Child in the Pond could be her own?

Adrenaline pumping, she looked back at Nelson, who still had her hand. His green eyes were sparkling at her. Everything was silent but the trickle of the Fountain. "Serena Gordon, will you marry me?"

Serena felt her knees try to give out, and for the second time that Day she felt like she was going to faint. This was unexpected! She figured that he had been up to something completely different! But she was only 16!

What if I am destined to marry young? She stared helplessly into Nelson's bright green almond-shaped eyes. She could see perspiration gathering on his brow already, although the temperature of the Castle was very warm and comfortable. The only thing she could think to do at that moment was to place a hand over her open mouth.

I am not too young! According to the customs here in Forever, Girls marry as soon as 13 years old! Oh, but what of Bertha and my home on Earth? Should I really return?

"Nelson ... I," she began, but then stopped as tears gathered at the corners of her eyes.

Then Nelson showed some emotion – his cheeks grew pink and his eyes became glassy. "I don't know what to say ... I mean ... to not go back ... ever again ... now that I can,"

Nelson looked at the ring and turned it over in his hand. She thought she heard him sniff.

"I understand," he said, and he began to put the ring away, but she took his hand away from the bag. Her heart was thumping. He looked up at her, crestfallen, and she lifted his chin.

"You see ... I have nothing to go back to. That is why I choose to stay here forever. I have a future here, I saw it in that Pool! Nelson ... I-"

She stopped. Her heart was overwhelmed. She was not too young. She had a future here. Would she choose her future in Forever?

She flung her arms around him and fell to her knees, weeping with joy and happiness. Her heart soared within her as she exclaimed her final decision to the world.

"Yes! Yes, Nelson, I will marry you! And I will stay here with you in Forever ... forever!"

Chapter Fifty-One: The Heir to the Throne

It was in the tallest crystalline tower, in the highest room of that tower that the gracious and merciful Mother of Forever resided. Her quarters were flawless – gorgeous to say the least, filled with expensive vases, Flowers growing straight from the walls, more paintings and murals and tapestries and grandly carved furniture with cushions. A great closet was fashioned out of one corner, composed of all the latest Foreveran fashion – only the most pale and lovely colors, and the softest and prettiest velvet and lace adorning her pretty gowns and dresses. Some of them even had Jewels sewn right into them, all the more magnificent for the great and wonderful Mother of Forever.

A textured glass dressing room with all types of pretty patterns in its curtains of Diamond sat to the side of the wardrobe, with shelves of hair tonic, brushes, ribbons, and all other manner of hair items. And, of course, in another glass-curtained room, there was fashioned a beautiful bath tub and her own personal stock of lotions, oils and shampoos, conditioners, soaps, and perfumes.

Her bed was made from the sturdiest Crystal with the finest silks, with a canopy and several colorful transparent curtains drawn around it. She had a Diamond table with chairs and a white lace table cloth with a basket of fruit placed upon it. She had a Diamond piano, a Crystal harp, Diamond bookshelves of her own personal library books, and, of course, a lovely little Fountain of Angels right in the middle of it all. Windows with lacey, dainty curtains fluttered in the warm Summer Breeze while two Diamond double doors sat on either side of the room. These elegantly decorated doors led to a circular balcony that one could walk all around the perimeter of the tower on. The balcony floor was as Grassy as a lawn, pumped to bursting with Flowers, Ferns, fruit, and herbal Grasses. It was more or less a luscious little Garden, with a total of three beautiful Fountains (in which iridescent little goldFish with transparent fins swam and played) interspersed among the Day beds, the Roses, Tulips, Daffodils and Violets, and many, many more Flowers and fruit Trees not named. Birds sung in the Trees, Frogs croaked by the Fountains and Crickets chirped in the Fern Bushes.

Clearly, the Mother had the best of everything, and made the Diamondia Castle look like nothing compared to that simple, large chamber.

Serena felt that by the time they reached the tallest tower that they had indeed seen the whole Castle - of course they had not, as Nelson hastily informed them. Their journey from the Fountain Chamber to the Mother's Quarters was only about seeing one thousandth of the whole Castle. And that one thousandth, Serena felt, was splendid enough! Nelson led them through a strange network of hallways, corridors, chambers and rooms and dens, up ramp-like slants and Diamond stairs, and around corners, and occasionally stepping across bridges and balconies. Inside, the walls were decorated with more murals and Flowers, potted Trees, torch sconces, and even, at intervals, tiny Waterfalls spouting right out of the wall into little Pools, presumably for washing hands and drinking. The stunned group passed libraries, with Forests of books, kitchens, lingering with heavenly aromas, Servants' quarters, flooded with beauty as was the whole Castle, Schoolrooms, swarmed with Children of all shapes and ages, Garden rooms, grown with the best care, and the Great Council's quarters, which were rooms where the Great Council of Forever's members resided.

Serena questioned Nelson as to why he had not told them of the Great Council, and he replied directly that, at the time, the Great Council was weak without the Mother, and yet they were trying their very best to ward off the threats of the rising evil forces. He told her, as a side note, that it would not be easy for an evil Creature to get into the Diamondia Castle, since the Fountain Chamber was the only entrance save for the heavily guarded windows (guarded by the Pegasus) and since the Fountain Chamber's ancient Enchantment drained all wickedness and evil from that Creature's body before he got any further than the front door. He also told her that the Great Council consisted of two delegates from every civilized species in Forever, one male and one female, with the Mother to preside over them all. The Giants' quarters were monstrous - for the Merfolk were Water-filled Pool-like rooms, and each member was housed in his or her own environmental traditions in a likewise fashion. Serena loved the Castle already.

Yet one humorous aspect Serena found of the Castle was the curious way that the ceilings were always textured with design, either for a pleasing decoration, or to keep mischievous young Lads from looking up the skirts of young Maidens. Or, as Serena thought, for both. She could see the colors from the top floors very vividly, but there was no certain form or detail that the colors took, preserving the privacy of the upstairs World. Certain walls, also, such as the Great Council Room, and bathing rooms, were also textured and sometimes painted also to accent the features of the delicate carving.

Serena did not know how Nelson managed to navigate them all the way from the Fountain Chamber to the Mother's Quarters without becoming lost at least once. He ordered a small squad of Diamond hovering platforms, called Discs, which they stood upon as the flying things glided over the ground at a rapid speed. Once they were going so fast that Serena was certain she was to lose her balance, but something like a Magical wall stabilized her. Nelson told them that if they had not taken the Discs, it would have taken the Travelers a whole week to reach the top.

They did stop for the Night in a guest room when they were half the way there, but they traveled on in the morning after a short breakfast and traveled all Day, ascending up ramps and hallways and mazes of Diamond beauty. At last, in the early evening, they came to a large pair of lovely Diamond double-doors. Two Guard Servants, one a Minotaur and the other a Goose Two-Legger, stood before the door with spears and helmets. Nelson stepped off of his Disc. It vanished with a pop. The others followed him.

"This is it!" he said. "We all must be upon our best behavior for the Mother! Stand up straight, do not interrupt, and be sympathetic to the family. And, need I remind you, we are here for a reason!" he winked at them, especially at Serena. "We need to support that reason firmly."

"Yes, Father!" Serena snickered before she could stop herself. Nelson flushed in the face, his gaze catching hers, and a tiny smile flickered across his face. *Literally,* she thought with a giggle, *he's going to be Forever's Father toDay!*

Swiftly he turned to face the Guards.

"We should like to enter," he stated, hands clasped behind his back.

The Minotaur Guard snorted and laughed, his ugly bull's head tossed back. The Goose stood up to full height and hissed at them,

"It is not a matter of what you should like to do, young Travelers. It is only with a matter of safety that we require to know the reason for your entry. Indubitably, you all know our Mother's delicate condition."

"Certainly," Nelson returned, putting on his bravest expression. "We … well …" he leaned forward and whispered in the Goose's ear.

"The Heir to the Throne!" honked the Goose.

The Minotaur gasped. Serena watched the group's expressions as they exchanged glances that clearly said, "what is he talking about?"

"Do you know what he's doing?" Kate whispered to Serena.

"No … but he's got some sort of plan, I just know he has!"

In reality, Serena knew exactly what the Prince of Forever was doing. She smiled proudly.

"T-the Heir to the Throne? Well, step right in, your High-" the Minotaur began, pushing the doors open.

"JUST a minute there," the Goose corrected him, his orange beak clacking. He used his spear to herd his fellow Guard back to his post "How do we know you aren't feeding us a fib? We require proof!" he snapped.

"Proof, he wants!" laughed Nelson. The two Guards looked at each other with uneasy eyes. Obligingly, Nelson put an arm around each of them, facing their backs to the group (who whispered and 'shh'ed excitedly, straining to hear what was said) and spoke with them for a long time. At last, they nodded their heads, and he patted their backs. When all three turned around, Nelson's face was beaming red, and the Guards were both crying.

"The Heir! The Heir is here at last! Oh, we're saved! Go in, friends!"

And the large double doors were opened.

It was with great pride and dignity that Serena walked the upwards spiraling ramp, her feet being tickled by the cool, smooth Diamond floor beneath them. There were windows with small balconies every now and again, and the walls were studded with Jewels, pictures, and all other manner of lovely decoration. The first chamber they passed, according to Nelson, was a massive library filled with hundreds upon thousands of books, old and new. The next was a sewing room with Maids scattered all over the place, sewing, embroidering, ironing, and trimming new garments and patching up older ones. The third room, which was very much like the Mother's Quarters, was the Princess's Quarters, with one large balcony jutting out like a patio from one side. And, finally, the group came to halt before yet another pair of textured Diamond doors and the corridor came to a dead end.

Nelson knocked on the door. From within, a sickly-sounding Lady's voice issued - a young Lady, or so it sounded. A Man with black hair and brown eyes, wearing a crown and a very handsome outfit answered the door and let them in. A Girl about Serena's age was kneeling beside the Mother's bed.

"Forget it, Juliana … cough, cough … you are not …"

The voice stopped suddenly as the doors closed.

Then, trembling, it returned.

"THE HEIR ," it wheezed with an outrageous amount of enthusiasm, then coughed, "is in … this room,"

This was how the Travelers came to the Mother's Quarters.

Inside the Mother's Quarters seemed to linger upon the air a sort of Magic – Serena felt it wave across her face and burrow into her chest as soon as she entered.

"The Heir … is here … at last …" rasped the voice. Apparently, it had issued from the curtained, pastel silk-swathed crystal bed that sat with the head of the furniture against the Diamond wall. The man who had let them in was obviously the current Father of Forever, and looked the group up and down before allowing them to crowd around the foot of the bed. Serena knew that this Man was a Human, and so settled upon the decision that the sick and dying Mother had to be of the Elven species.

The Princess, a dark-haired Human Girl with shining hazel eyes, stooped from her kneeling position beside the bed and stood. Her skin was a tannish white, which contrasted well with the curvy, fashionable light pink silk gown trimmed with white lace that she wore. Her wavy black hair was left down, very long indeed and nearly reaching the back of her knees, and was woven with pink and white ribbons and Flowers. Strangely, she looked nothing at all like Nelson did, but Serena surpassed that assumption with a fact - not all brothers and sisters are destined to look exactly alike. The Princess was also a pretty Girl, and Serena noticed that Kevin had made it a point not to miss.

"Juliana," said the Man, taking a goblet of Water from the crystal bedside dresser and handing it to the Girl, "Try and give this to your Mother, will you please?"

Juliana, with one last, long stare at Kevin, obediently did so.

"So," the Father started, rubbing his clean-shaven chin. "You come to claim the Throne at last, have you, Heir? Well, it has been long enough! For how long have you been in hiding? Did you care not for your own Mother? Well? Speak up!" he demanded, eyeing Nelson in particular among all of them.

Each of the Traveler's skin pricked as the dark-haired Father searched their eyes. Finally, Nelson spoke up, holding Serena's hand

"The Heir has not been hidden but lost!" he stated. He looked at Serena nervously. "Lost and now found."

A small squeak issued from across the room without warning.

"Father!" the Girl cried, the glass goblet falling and shattering on the floor. Magically it melted into nothing. "Look!"

The Father of Forever quickly rushed over to the bed and bent over the crumpled form that lay maimed in the shadows of the half-transparent silk curtains of the bed. Serena saw a burst of yellow dust, similar to Fairy Dust, like the yellow Fairy that stood rigid and solid as Stone on her right shoulder. Then, over the Princess's shoulder, she saw a withered, shaking white hand of a young WoMan reaching up and pulling out the top drawer to her bedside dresser. Out of this, with a tired and sad sigh, the hand pulled a diary – a very fluorescent diary, spangling with hand-made beads, glitter, realistic-looking Flowers, ribbons, painted glass and silk glue to the front cover.

"The last ... entry ... holds the rhymes ... from my most ... recent dream ... Cough, cough! ... It holds ... the description ... of the Heir ... to the Throne," panted the Woman's voice, sounding very much in pain. A long, cold sigh escaped the same throat that the voice had projected from, and the withered hand dropped in exhaustion.

The Father caught the diary at the same time the Princess caught the hand. The Father strode over to them, leafing though the diary, and stopped before them. He looked up at them with wide eyes, his gaze fixed on Nelson.

I knew it! Serena's mind sang. *Nelson is the Heir to the Throne!*

"Juliana," beckoned the young Father, not taking his eyes from the Boy. "Come here."

Nelson squeezed Serena's hand nervously.

Hesitantly, the Girl obeyed.

"What is it, Father?" she inquired in the crisp British accent.

"Stand here, next to this Girl," he gestured to Serena. The Princess obeyed. Serena was about to step back, leaving Nelson and the Girl standing together, for she knew it was not in her place to be standing at the choosing of the next ruler, but Nelson gripped her hand and looked at her, eyes pleading for support. Of course he was scared, and he wanted her to stay, so she did. She could hear Kevin, Mike, Bob, Lindsey, Kate, and Theo whispering very quietly behind her. She felt guilty for not telling them what she knew, for they were just now understanding Nelson's true self.

The Father cleared his throat and read the first rhyme, enunciating clearly.

"Mother of Forever, you never led us wrong, but

403

On the Throne of Forever you have lingered too long.

Therefore you must go in search of another,

Heir to the Throne and Flower of Forever.

Eternally serene this Flower shall be.

Replacing you, Mother, yet giving life to thee."

"Mother! It spells Mother!" Nelson interrupted, "The first word of each line-"

"Well that's because that's what she is! She's our Mother!" Juliana pointed out, and, at a stern glance from her Father, she folded her hands neatly in front of her and looked at the floor.

The Father continued with the second verse:

"I am the code of Forever.

I am the completion of the Mother.

Though should I be changed for the Flower,

Switch two letters,

And I shall be whole again."

"Switch two letters ..." Nelson thought aloud, and then, "Aha! Now it all makes sense!"

The Father, ignoring this comment, closed the diary carefully, staring each of the three before him in the eyes: Princess Juliana, Serena, and a smirking Nelson.

"Now," he rumbled, stepping back and standing tall, "Will the true Heir to the Throne please step forward?"

A very long, tense silence passed. The sounds of Birds and Pegasus, Crickets, soft Breezes, and Waterfalls were dampered in Serena's ears. The smells of fresh, sweet Water, nectar dripping from the Flowers, Herbs, and Grasses, and the dainty smells of mixed Castle perfumes shied away from her nose. The sights of the Neverending Falls and the soaring Pegasus through the walls, the Rainbows and Cloudless blue Skies above their heads, and the lovely, attractive décor of the Mother's Quarters all blocked away from her vision so that the only thing she could see was the Father of Forever standing right in front of her.

She was so excited and happy for Nelson that she almost jumped back, but his grip tightened again, and then she knew something must have been wrong. Was he going to run away from his responsibility? Was he going to make some odd excuse and dodge the Throne? Or would he openly accept it?

What is Nelson waiting for? her mind shrieked nervously.

Finally, from out of the corner of her eye, Serena detected a movement. Juliana stepped back.

Go on, Nelson! You can do this!

Now it was only her and Nelson.

Nelson, you are forcing me to do this. She prepared to step back and copy the Princess's wise move, but before she could, she detected another movement from the corner of her eye.

Finally! she thought.

Nelson lifted his foot.

And took a step back.

Serena felt her knees going weak again. What was going on? She turned around and looked straight at Nelson.

"What are you doing? Get up there!" she whispered.

She could heard the Father behind her,

"Is there a problem?"

"But I'm not the Heir!" Nelson told her.

Serena froze, mouth open, eyes wide.

"No," she began with a small, nervous giggle. With eyes bluer than the Heavens above, she stared at Nelson and her friends behind him. "No, seriously …Nelson … please tell me you're joking,"

"Not at all," Nelson replied, grabbing up her hand again. He kissed the back of it with a fawning smile. She looked at Lindsey, who had tears rolling down her cheeks, at Kate, who was hugging Lindsey and looking encouragingly at Serena, at Bob, who stood with his arms crossed and a smirk on his face, at Mike, who peeked over his tiny glasses at her with a smile, at Kevin, who had his hands on his hips and nodded at her grinning, and at Theo, who was beaming up at her.

"You all knew, didn't you?" she asked. "You all knew and you didn't tell me!"

"But doesn't it all make sense?" Theo piped up, popping out beside his brother.

"Look at your feet, Serena," Lindsey whispered into her ear.

She did, and saw the brightly blooming, flamboyant Moss Flowers blossoming richly at her feet in a bed of vivid green Moss.

"The Flower of Forever." They all whispered in unison, crowding around her. Even Juliana put her arms around Lindsey and Theo.

"No … no, it can't be …" Serena babbled, her mind spinning.

How could this be? All of the signs I was given… how could Nelson not be the Heir?

Mentally, she went through each sign she had seen that led her to her wrongful conclusion.

"The harnesses … on the Centaurs – wasn't that you?"

"No, Serena," said Nelson.

"And the Unicorns – you were the one that drew them in."

"No, it was you, Serena."

"But … but the log in the Forest of Many Eyes … and the … the secret!" she clasped his shoulders. "Nelson, you said there was nothing to hide!"

"And there wasn't. I thought that you knew."

"And the Troll ... So … so all of those things that happened … they happened because … but how did I do it?" Serena could hardly believe what was happening.

"Some part of you willed it to happen, and it did. You are the Heir, Serena. The Heir to the Throne of Forever," Nelson told her.

"Think about it, Serena. You acted just like a mother any time some Child was in danger! First Theo, then the Sirrush baby, then little Dawn, and finally the Catfox Boy on the Mountain! You were like a mother to all of them!" Lindsey explained.

"But," Serena gasped, "I came from Earth! How can it be that I am the next ruler of Forever when I was born and raised on Earth?"

"There's a very good reason for why Forever decided to accept us all, Serena," Kate said, "Because the Creator of Forever and Forever itself needed you. They are what has called you here, with all of us."

Serena looked at her friends, who stared at her proudly.

"And you knew – all of you! You thought I knew what I was, didn't you?"

"Nelson told us," Kate beamed. "And we told Je- or, that is, Kevin."

Serena looked at Kevin, who shrugged and smiled.

"And besides, the rhymes all fit!" Lindsey said.

Nelson rubbed her hands.

"Eternally serene this Flower shall be."

"Serene means kind, forgiving," Kevin spoke up.

"Calm, collected," said Kate.

"Trustworthy, honest," Lindsey continued.

"Courteous, generous," said Bob.

"Patient, valued," Mike added.

"Warm, soothing," Theo sniffed.

"Never leaves someCreature ahinds," whispered Dawn.

"Loving, and understanding," Nelson said, squeezing her hand. "And if I've ever heard such a rare description of a person in my life, Serena, I would say it is you."

Serena was pushed to tears. She hugged each one of her friends in length, thanking them for their extreme kindness, and came to stand before the Father, drying her tears and heart burning.

"I ...I apologize, sir ...I did not know," Serena trembled. What would happen now?

The Father laid a hand on her shoulder.

"Father ... I am ready to claim ... the Throne ..." she stuttered, shifting from foot to foot nervously. Her velvety Sky blue gown swayed at her feet. She could hardly believe what she had just said. Inside, her heart was pumping with adrenaline as it never had before. It drummed loudly in her ears, giving her goosebumps despite the warmth and security of the Breeze wafting through the open windows.

The Father smiled a gentle, fatherly smile, and laid another hand on her other shoulder.

"Come to the bed, my Flower. You must first receive recognition from the Mother," he told her.

"Recognition?" she repeated curiously, and stopped before the bed.

How is it that I am related to this Woman?

Immediately sympathy overtook her as she looked upon the withered, white form of a young Woman, probably in her twenties or thirties, curled up in pain under its light silky sheets. The Woman had dark hair, grown very long, with large brown eyes, which were hollow with disease, and soft, smooth, fair skin in spite of her deathly position.

"Yes ...it is her ...at last!" she wheezed, then shielded a painful cough. "Father Jacob ... have the entire Castle ... meet in the Fountain Chamber ... at the great central Thrones ... It is time ... for a ... cough, cough! ... a Crowning Ceremony!"

Hurriedly, Serena was rushed into the Princess's Quarters, no doubt to be cleaned and redressed by a squad of Palace Maids, varying in species. Nelson stayed behind to help transfer the Mother into something the Father had called a palanquin. The odd contraption was merely the body of a fine, curtained bed set upon two thick poles, which only the strongest Palace Guards borne upon their shoulders.

Serena had not had much time to study the Mother of Forever before she was whisked away by Princess Juliana and the Castle Maids, but she kept getting an odd feeling of semblance when she thought of the poor Woman. She was certain she had never seen this Woman before - perhaps only in her dreams.

Time passed in a blur. In what felt like a moment, Serena had been scrubbed clean, oiled with lotions, drowned in perfume, rubbed down and polished up and readied for the biggest moment of her young life. A silken white gown was chosen for her, in a similar, attractive form as the Princess's gown, if not prettier for her special occasion.

In less than an hour she was finished, and felt stiff to the bones with all the makeup the Maidens had applied, and the sweet-smelling shampoos and conditioners, and her starched, silken white gown, and her expensive Diamond earrings, bracelets, anklets and berets. Her chest was kept bare for the acceptance of the pennant that she saw in her dream – that outstandingly beautiful Jewel of a Diamond, fashioned in the smooth shape of a stretched sideways figure eight - The Everlasting Diamond.

Serena did not see her friends again until the Maidens had hurried her down to the Fountain Chamber (with a Castle Portal, of course), which was filled with any and every type of Creature, realistic or mythic, and a healthy slew of Flowers, Jewels, ribbons, bows and all other colorful commodities.

A single aisle was left bare in between two large rows of pew-like seats. Tall stained glass windows stood at intervals, decorated richly. At the head of the room was an elevated platform with its Diamond ramp leading up to it, upon which the Thrones sat with their tall, beautifully carved backs, adorned in wreaths of Flowers and Jewels. The Fountain of Youth splashed and twinkled and bubbled behind them, for the Chamber had seemingly grown to twice its own size for the ceremony. The floor no longer was strewn with ankle-deep Water and Jewels, but had been dried, swept clean and buffed to shine.

Seeing the Thrones, Serena became nervous. She stood alone in back of the loudly conversing Creatures, right in front of the Fountain but not yet graduated to the aisle. She could pick out the Giants – great burly Creatures, standing near her in the back - the MerMaids, in their glass boxes of Water, moved by wheels. She also saw Centaurs, Fauns, Satyrs, Sileni, Minotaurs, Two-Leggers, CatFoxes, Nymphs, Pixies, Elves, Brownies, Dwarves, Gnomes - and it would have been useless for her to name all of the great and wondrous Creatures she saw gathered as one in peace in that single chamber.

More important to Serena at that moment was the happy faces of her traveling companions. Each one of them had been redressed and washed head to toe, each looking only their best for Serena's honorable ceremony. She laughed nervously, remembering how even tiny Dawn had found herself up to her armpits in bubbles in Serena's bath just for following the new Flower of Forever into the Princess's Quarters.

Serena beamed at her friends, reflecting on how they had changed. Kevin had changed into a faithful friend who learned the lesson of needing his team and telling the whole truth, and Kate now understood that a caring person prevails over a complaining one. Lindsey, Serena's trustworthy friend the entire adventure through, sat in the front row with Bob, who had long since shed his bashful shell and come out to show his true personality. There was Mike, also, who had learned so much of Forever that his old notebook had long ago been filled up and cast away, and little Theo, who was now a true Warrior, just like his brother. The fairy babe Dawn could not be held down and perched on Serena's shoulder. She had not been with Serena for very long, but she could tell already that the two were to be great friends. And finally, there was Nelson, Serena's best friend, her lover, and now, not the Heir to the Throne, but her soon-to-be husband.

Now the Chamber grew quiet, and trumpets began to sound, with drums joining them after a joyful first verse of catchy, musical song. Then both stopped, and a choir of flutes of all different pitches and volumes began to play, and then a choir of Child-like voices began singing softly. Wordless as their melodies may have been, the very sound of the tranquil heart-moving music seemed to seep into Serena's tight chest and loosen the knot of nervous misunderstanding that had until that point occupied the whole space.

Serena sighed and looked at her toes, at the radiantly blooming Moss Flowers, now seeming to shine under their own glory. She searched her chest for that ever-present feeling of nervous panic as she looked back up at the crowd of Creatures, all eyes now on her, but the uncomfortable emotion seemed to have vanished under that last sigh. It had gone from her, off to swim with the pleasant music and nose-tingling fragrance of aromatic Spring Flowers, to drift out of the chamber windows with the soft, warm Breeze, and then to fly around the fading Rainbows and Neverending Falls as the Sun set in a lovely bath of Heavenly hues in the West. Serena smiled at the Sunset and much to her astonishment, she saw all the Lands of Forever that she and her companions had toiled through in order to come to the Diamondia Castle in all its Magical splendor.

From her viewpoint, Serena could see the Perpetual Mountains, where the team had encountered the Pegasus stables, the MountLores, and the lovely Valleys and cool Winds. Then she saw the Windy Meadows, where they had first seen the fantastic Sparkline Mountain, they had come upon the CatFoxes and a Mountain Troll, witnessed the Magical birth of baby Fairies, discovered the ferocity of the Wind, and also where Nelson had returned to them. Her eyes roved to the lengthy splotch known as the Blue Marsh, where they had been introduced to Turtle travel, met Melabon of Middleton and her remarkable Cyclops's eye, where they had been housed by the mysterious Lonvirc-Volcrin (who was a legend of the Blue Marsh itself), where Kevin (better known as Jerry) had returned to them through ridding them of Marsh Goblins, where Nelson had been claimed by a Marlan QuickSand Pit, and where they had all worked together to save Kate from a hungry tar Pool.

Beyond that point she saw a darkening Forest that could be no other than the Forest of Many Eyes. Figuring that the Prowlers would by now be coming out to hunt, Serena remembered the place as where she had found true romance, where she had stayed in the den of Trumple the Sirrush after saving her Child from a Harpie, where she and the others had danced and sung with the Sky Humans and their backwards language at the Boulder Tribe Camp, and where they had first experienced trouble with gigantic purple Monkeys.

A small gray dot marked the wondrous fortress of Bendar, with all of its traditional Pixie splendor, and it grandiloquent Prince. Beyond the long, Snakelike Basstooth River, Serena could see the softened MeadowLands where they had escaped the captivity from the Goblins, and where they had first learned of the singing Flowers and the Magical Banyan Trees.

Serena saw a Golden smudge on the horizon after the Meadows – the Golden Plains – where they had first been captured by the Goblins, where Kevin had left them, where Serena had chased Gingel the Leprechaun straight into the mouth of a CaveLore and followed a Rainbow that changed her hair colors, where she had tamed Unicorns, Bicorns, and Tricorns easily, had all of her belongings save for her clothes and Teresa's diary ransacked by a couple of sneaky CatEagles, where she had learned of Forever from Nelson and Theo and Mosslyn, where they had met Wildder and his tribe of traveling Fauns, and had narrowly escaped a migration of Sauropods, where she and Lindsey had discovered Theo and his broken bow, and where they had all awoken to a FrogStorm one fine morning.

Beyond that she saw the thinnest line of Sandy, Rocky terrain, indubitably the Dragons' Lair. This was where she remembered meeting Nelson, who caught her after she was dropped by a Hippogryph, where they had discovered the iridescent glass-shelled Dragon eggs, and where they had first made their appearance in Forever to the juvenile Dragon, Keffle, and her short-tempered mother.

And, very, very far to the West Serena saw a tiny blue line marking the constant presence of the Ocean Ceaseless, where the team battled a Storm of blue Lightning, abandoned the Wavequeen, were battered senseless by shark-like bass Fish, and passed the bubble-like Shield that had introduced them into it all.

Now the Chamber suddenly went quiet and the Castle turned so that the Sunset was at Serena's back.

"Serena Gordon," called a dry, wispy voice.

It was the Mother.

"Yes," Serena answered into the absolute silence. Her voice cut through the still air and echoed lightly off of the Diamond-clear walls.

"Come, Child," the Mother called in a strong, yet weak voice. "Come and … claim your Throne."

Serena could tell that the Woman was in great pain and was very ready to be rid of her burdensome title as Mother of Forever. So without hesitation, Serena started down the crystal aisle.

The slow, rhythmic flutes and choir sang again, calming her step so that the Moss Flowers trailed after her. The Creatures on either side of her threw multicolor Flower petals at her from Magically floating Garden baskets placed at intervals along the seats. Serena smiled as she was showered with the soft, fragrant petals and giggled as she felt tiny Dawn catching the petals and weaving them into her hair. Serena savored the moment and stopped before the palanquin, which was set upon the shoulders of four strong, stoic Guards and stood before the two Thrones.

At a wave from a white, skeletal hand that poked out of the white silk curtains, two Maidens rushed forward and parted the curtains, tying them aside with long ribbons.

Serena restrained a surprised gasp.

Before her, lifting herself weakly up to a sit, was the pretty young Woman she had seen earlier, possibly even more painfully thin and white than before. Serena calmed herself and stood tall as the Woman came to a sit on the side of her palanquin. It was hard to tell whether the Woman was an Elf or a Human, but Serena was convinced that she must be an Elf, if she was truly Nelson's

412

mother.

But she isn't, she thought suddenly, *so Nelson must not be from this Castle at all. Where, then, is he from? This Woman is not my mother either, for my mother looked nothing like her. How then, is it that I am related to this strange, pale Woman?*

Presently, Serena readied herself to ask the question. During her bath, she had had time to think over the two rhymes the Father had recited. The longer one she understood, but the second one he had read was still nothing more than a Clouded mystery. The first two lines she had deciphered: a code was usually a name, and it was also that no Child is complete without a name. Serena was nearly positive that knowing the Mother's name would provide a clue to the last three lines of the rhyme.

And so, now, as she stared into the hollow brown eyes of the poor, sickly Woman, Serena asked her question in a low voice.

"Mother?"

The Woman coughed harshly and beckoned her closer.

"Yes, my Flower?" she replied in a quivering voice.

"I … I should like to know your name … before I claim the Throne … please,"

"I thought… you'd never ask!" smiled the Mother, lifting Serena's chin with her frail fingers. She looked straight at Serena and answered, "My name … is Teresa."

Serena's eyes grew to an alarming size.

It couldn't be!

But it was.

The Woman's hair was a curly brown, just as the Girl in the diary had described her own hair to be, and her eyes were brown for the same reason. The Father fit the description of the Boy in Teresa's diary, and to Serena's astonishment, around the Woman's neck was now hung the necklace from Serena's dream.

And Serena knew its name before anyCreature could tell her – it was called the Diamond Everlasting.

"Then," Serena said, reaching for her satchel, "if your name is Teresa Gordon, my living ancestor, then I believe that I have something that belongs to you."

A shadow of confusion crossed the Mother's face, and her eyebrows lifted nearly to the elegant Diamond crown that rested on her soft brown hair.

With a warm smile, Serena pulled the diary out of her satchel, amidst a large handful of Fairy Dust, which added to the splendor of its appearance.

Teresa gasped.

Serena blew the Fairy Dust off of the diary, taking direct aim at the playful Dawn, who sneezed silently on her own Dust and attacked Serena's curls.

"Your-"

"My-"

"Diary!" both said in unison.

Teresa began to laugh dryly as she accepted the item, which ended in a fit of coughing. Grasping the Diamond, she cracked a small smile.

"Thank you … Dear Flower … And now … I have … something … for you."

Slowly, the pale Woman splayed her hand on top of the diary and closed her eyes.

The diary began to glow brightly, showing through Teresa's fingers.

A white flash made Serena close her eyes to shield them, and she felt a Magical Wind blow her hair away from the back of her neck. When she opened her eyes again, Teresa was holding the diary out to her. Hesitantly, she took it.

"I am ... the code ... of Forever.

I am ... the completion ... of the Mother.

Though should I ... be changed ... for the Flower,

Switch ... two letters.

And I ... shall be whole ... again," recited the Mother, and she laid back slightly.

Serena, puzzled, opened the front cover.

There, written in Gold at the top of the inside cover, was the word "Teresa." A feathered quill pen popped up beside Serena as though on cue. Suddenly she understood.

Mustering up some deep Power that had been revealed to her since her first appearance in Forever, Serena placed a single finger over the letter T.

Erase! she commanded it, and it dissolved under her fingertip.

She did the same to the letter S, and the took up the quill floating beside her patiently. Scrupulously, she filled the spaces previously occupied by the letter T with an S, and the space that had been an S with an N.

Teresa. Serena.

Then, with a smile of perfect satisfaction, she looked up at the Mother, who nodded.

"You are ... a clever Girl," she admitted. When Serena next looked, the diary's pages were blank.

"But ... but where is the text?" Serena wanted to know, leafing through the empty pages.

"In ... my heart," Teresa replied, placing a hand over her chest painfully. "There ... I will always ... keep it."

Serena smiled winningly, and closed the diary, hugging it to her chest. When Teresa saw this, her descendant possessing the same trait she'd had when she was quite a bit younger, a single tear fell from her cheek, and landed on the floor with a clink!

For the tear was made of pure Diamond.

"The diary ... is now ... yours," the plagued Woman stopped to draw a breath, and coughed horribly. When she had regained her composure, she gestured for the younger blonde-haired Girl to come closer.

"And also," she wheezed, lifting the Diamond Everlasting on its chain. "so ... is this."

Serena sighed out her nervous tension and bent her head forward, biting her lip and not once taking her eyes from the deep Pools of brown in the

Mother's own face.

And so the weak Mother slipped the great Diamond Everlasting over Serena's head. It rested, glowing grandly, on her chest.

Then, carefully, the Mother of Forever removed the fascinating object of a crown from her head and turned it around, placing it tenderly atop Serena's Golden head.

At once, Serena felt a tickling sensation at her feet, and looked down in horror to find the tiny Flowers at her feet shriveling and vanishing as wings do when a person's Pixie Powder has run out. In place of the Flowers, a wide beam of the most radiant light shone on her from the ceiling, and she felt a jolt of Power as it ran through her veins. A soft shower of what looked like flakes of the Sun rained down on her, and the audience gasped and whispered in awe.

Now, she was the true Mother of Forever.

A warm tear slid down her cheek and dripped to the floor.

But no longer did her tear turn to a Flower; now, it hit the floor and bounced away as a marble-sized Diamond, identical to the one shed by Teresa.

Fighting the lump that was in her throat, Serena bent and collected both Diamonds. Dawn, giggling in great interest, confiscated the wonderful things from Serena and hid them in her satchel.

Stunned and amazed, Serena looked back up at Teresa, who now cried regular tears. The Woman nodded and then, looking mildly healthier, she pushed herself off of the palanquin and stood before Serena in her lacey white Nightgown.

Staring Serena faithfully in the eyes, she dropped to her knees, placed a hand over her heart, and bowed her head forward, eyes closed and Watering.

A gasp fell over the crowd, and then they, too, took to their knees and repeated this symbolic performance. The room was silent. The Winds were warm.

And Serena was happy. Happier, perhaps, than she had ever been in her life. Not because of her new Power, but because now, more than ever before, she actually felt as though she were at home.

When Teresa stood again, she looked much healthier than she had before.

"You are the true Mother of Forever." she said, looking up at Serena with glittering eyes.

"I am," Serena admitted. "But if I am, then who are you?"

Teresa shrugged, and without warning, the windows to the chamber burst open with racing, wild Winds that carried Flower petals and glitter on them, as if the Wind had come from nowhere. The brown-haired Woman took a few steps back and replied,

"Oh, just a little British Girl named Teresa."

The Winds began to swirl around Teresa, lifting her up above everyCreature's head in a spinning tornado of Winds. Faster and faster they spun, engulfing every last detail of her until all that they could see was a madly spinning white whirlWind. The Guards holding the palanquin and Serena were both pushed back by the Winds, and Nelson neatly caught Serena as she flew backwards from the blow.

Then the whirlWind began to glow. The light was dull, at first, but then grew brighter. The whirlWind spoke to them in a thousand whistling voices, lighting up even brighter each time a word was articulated.

"The Window Chamber is where I shall be placed," whistled the Winds.

Serena's heart was pumping nearly as madly as the Winds were blowing. She turned and clutched Nelson tightly, not once taking her eyes from the frightening scene.

Finally, the light of the whirlWind grew and lit up the chamber as bright as Day, making everyCreature turn aside his or her eyes so as not to be blinded.

Serena heard the whirlWind slowing, but did not dare open her eyes or even turn her head until the sound had all but been lost, blowing back out the open windows and slamming them shut on its way out.

Serena, standing tall now, looked over to where the whirlWind had previously been.

And there, standing straight in a puffy, little British traveling dress and holding a ruffled little diary to her chest with a quill pen, was a Diamond statue of the Girl called Teresa, every feature as perfect and plain as they had been so many years ago when she had been on her trip to America.

~*~*~*~*~

That Night, Serena made her first appearance with the Great Council of Forever, and was quickly filled in on all of its policies, and the responsibilities associated with her new position.

And also, that same Night, Serena met with the team to discuss the matter

417

that all of them dreaded to bring up - going home.

She met with them in her new Quarters, in the highest room of the tallest tower, when the full Night had descended upon the Lands of Forever, and the twinkling Stars could be seen clearly through the glass-like ceiling around the point of the roof – where Serena soon learned was perched a Magical Stone about the size of a Dragon's egg called the Eternal Diamond, which was the source of all Magic in Forever.

She met the team in her balcony Gardens.

"What an adventure we have endured," she sighed in greeting, leaning on the crystal railing. She watched gray-white figures swooping about in the distance – the Pegasus, no doubt, and filled her ears and lungs with the sounds and smells of fresh, clear running Water. The Earthlight bathed the Diamondia Castle below them in extravagant beauty.

"True," Kevin said in reply, after a pause.

Serena turned to look at him, and found his gaze attached to that of Princess Juliana, who was Watering her own Garden in her balcony below with tears, for she missed her mother very much. Serena nudged him.

"So?" she said, catching him off guard.

"So ... so what?" he blurted, looking at her with pink cheeks.

"So, are we going to go home?"

Every soul beside Serena drew in a sharp breath.

"But ... but after all this?" Kate gasped.

"Go home?" Lindsey exclaimed, her face outlined under the Earthlight.

"That would be like forgetting it all happened!" Bob pointed out.

"Why?" Mike demanded to know.

A long silence followed his quote, filled with the croaking of Tree Frogs, the chirping of Crickets, the singing of Katydids, and overall the echoing sounds of the Neverending Falls.

"Because," sighed Serena, stopping to look each of them in the eye. "because, I think we are home."

Nobody answered her statement – only smiled in agreement.

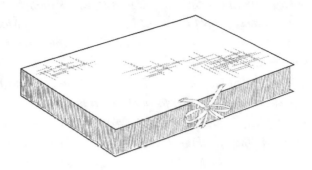

Epilogue

An extract from the writings of the Mother of Forever, 500 years after her installment to the Throne.

Dear Diary,

Twist, over, under through. Spin and pull. Spin and pull. Twist, over, under through...

My ancestor Teresa Gordon is teaching me how to crochet.

Twist, over, under, through. Spin and pull. Spin and pull.

EveryDay I am reminded of the grand adventure that Nelson, I and our other friends from the old Days encountered when we were much younger. Ah, I remember our exciting journey as though it were yesterDay!

The very Day, unbeknownst to us, that Nelson and I married (and oh! What a beautiful wedding it was, filled with Magic wonder just as Nelson's eyes were that Day!) the statue of Teresa began to move, think and see just as a living Creature would, up in her perch upon the Window Chamber, a room that has no walls, simply pillars to hold the structure up. It is there, in the very middle of this lovely, warm, and somewhat Breezy room that Teresa began to move that Sunny, happy Day, and continues to move toDay. Just as she is now, teaching me how to crochet. Though she cannot physically speak, she speaks to me and many others through her heart, while we will hear her sweet voice in our minds. She tells us now that she is immortal, and will live for as

419

long as the Diamondia Castle spins, and as long as the Rivers of Forever run up the sides of this great and beautiful Sparkline Mountain.

Kevin lives here at the Castle with his wife, the former Princess Juliana. They now have a healthy little brood of their own, including two little Girls (one of which reminds me so of Teresa, and the other who reminds me of her stubborn father) and a newborn Boy. They are very happy together, living here in this grand old Castle of ours with their Children, neither of them looking a Day older than when they married, thanks to the Spring Water that has changed and preserved all of our lives.

Lindsey found for herself a handsome young palace Guard and lives here with us at the Diamondia Castle as well. She now has four Children, all of them Boys, who are frequently seen scampering about the halls with the other Palace Children and clinging to my skirts chanting, "Auntie Serena! Auntie Serena!" Lindsey and I have become close friends, and spend much time together, remembering the old Days of our true youth.

Kate moved back to Middleton to live with Tarsena the CatFox, as she grows older every Day. Her husband, Beruga, is presently visiting the Castle, gathering more Spring Water for her to preserve her joyful existence, and also to update us that the two are now proud great-great-great-great-great grandparents (that is five greats isn't it?). Meanwhile, Kate herself is growing older and more frail. For that first 60 years, she refused to take in any Spring Water and to join the rest of us when we took it in annually. However, when she began to develop several health problems, she hesitantly came forward and drank of the Fountain of Youth and was instantly young again. Now, she has a husband and a thriving family that is forever expanding!

Mike is an old man – but a sweet, little, old man he is! He will take in some more Spring Water soon. His purpose in life now is to see all of Forever before he dies. And so he travels on foot, by wing, by ship, by Unicorn, and, every once in awhile, by Turtleback to reach his goal. He has also taken up the art of swordsmanship to protect himself in his travels, which I am not particularly fond of, but it is a necessity for him. He is the only one of us who is not married yet, but with all of the life-preserving Spring Water that I am frequently sending him, he has plenty of time.

Bob is the only one of us who had requested to go back to Earth. I made him take an oath before I sent him anywhere, however. According to the Great Council of Forever, the secret of gaining entry to Forever is to remain unknown to Earth, for fear of Man taking over the place and introducing war into the Lands. Scattered battles had been fought in the past, but since I have come into reign, there have been no wars or battles or any violence at all, other than your ordinary domestic disturbance and the necessary protection of self-defense. Anyway, Bob has just recently returned, an old Man indeed, and dressed in very strange clothing I might add, but very ready to spend the rest of his life in Forever. He won't tell anyCreature about what Earth has become, not even me. When I asked how things were going at home, he replied, "I don't know. You tell me, I was on Earth." He is now happily married and plans never to return to Earth.

Finally, there is Nelson, who is my ever-present husband. And, true to suspicions that I had when I was much younger, he is the Father of Forever, but not the Heir that I once believed him to be. He is now the supreme commander of our national defense forces, and also, lately, becoming more and more protective of me, for some reason or another which I shall explain later.

Theo, oh, dear little Theo, has run away with many jugs of Spring Water with him, many years ago. Now, he is an older man, a true Warrior, who roams Forever helping any and every Traveler who comes upon trouble.

Dawn is a lovely young Fairy, forever young (for she is very fond of taking Spring Water baths) and frisky and curious. More than usual I have been finding her hovering over one of my shoulders, sprinkling me with her blue and sometimes green Fairy Dust, making my gowns and my hair sparkle. She had been all about fixing up the Princess's Chamber below my own (which has been a free space for Children and Maids to roam for its non-vacant years), and guarding me with her cheerful presence. I suppose this is because of the new addition that our family will soon encounter.

That is correct!

Your eyes are not deceiving you!

Presently, as I sit in the Window Chamber overlooking the Lands of Forever, I am burdened with Child around my middle, and she is

421

constantly kicking at me. I know she is a Girl because I have foreseen this Elven Child before – long, long ago in the Pool of the Future. Now, when I look in the Pool, all I see is myself standing alone – sometimes it even looks like my reflection, but with something missing. And so I will wade off through the tranquil Waters, admiring the Jewels that rock gently with the small current of the shallow water.

For an extended amount of time I have pondered the title that I shall name my first (and possibly only) Child. I have assigned this gracious, little Girl the name Angeliqúe because when I first saw her in the Pool, I was with the impression she was an Angel, and the name Angeliqúe, in Forever, means "of the angels" But that is not the only name I have given her. You see, 500 years is an awfully long time to wait to conceive a Child, and so for every hundred years that I have waited, I have added another name to her title. Her second name is Nimeesha, meaning "Princess" - her third is Guenevere, meaning "soft, paleand fair" - her fourth is Esmeralda meaning "eyes of Emeralds" - and her fifth is Leilani, meaning "heavenly Flower." Put them together and her name reads Angeliqúe Nimeesha Guenevere Esmeralda Leilani. Already I know the Child's nick-name, for when her initials are written out, they spell ANGEL, and that is what my little Girl is to be called, as well as be, when she is born into the peaceful World know as Forever.

So, if you happen to be caught up with stress and strain, remember the bright North Star, and feel free to stop in to share an adventure or two, create your own story, and let your imagination fly as wild and free as the Pegasus soaring around the Diamondia Castle. We will be waiting for you. For you see, the more people that believe in Forever, the larger and more magnificent it becomes, and more rich in wonder, mystery, and adventure.

So now it is up to you. Do you believe in Forever?

-Serena Gordon, Mother of Forever

Acknowledgements

For life and love and forgiveness, I thank Our Lord and Savior Jesus Christ, who is my Rock of Ages. For their never-ending confidence, I thank my wonderful husband, David Orzechowski; my father, John Meredith; my mother, Mary Meredith - to whom this novel is lovingly dedicated; my brother, Owen Meredith; my grandfather, Roger O. Meredith; my late grandmother, Anne Meredith; my grandfather Eugene Szerletich; my grandmother, Ruth Szerletich; my sister-in-law, Amanda Orzechowski; my brother-in-law, Eric Orzechowski; my mother-in-law, Maryann Orzechowski; my father-in-law Joseph Orzechowski; and my grandmother-in-law, Helen Meteisis. You never lost hope in me, and I pray that you may know how deeply you are all loved for your faith. For offering their kind feedback, suggestions, support and help in the production of The Lands of Forever throughout the years, I thank Greg and Betsy Todd, Richard Schien, Bob and Gretchen Taylor, Lettie Crays, Father Angel Sierra, Joy Lindholm, Katelynn Worner, Zorene Worner, Jayson Howard, Diane Kurtz, Ann Reichmann, Carla Rosene, Alisa Schrader, Kristen Kichinko, Abigail Schultz, Michael Southard, Ren Draya, Naomi Crummey, Kara Trotter, Christina Mandelski, Linda Tusek, Leanne Lucas, Pastor Tom Guengerich and the members of Forest City Community Church, the Szerletich Family and my fantastic uncles, the Orzechowski and Meteisis Families, my friends and professors at Blackburn College, the class of 2015 at Gillespie Middle School, the Palsen Family, the Springfield Writers and Poets, the staff at Saints Mary and Joseph Church, my fans on Facebook and the various supporters of my website and blog, and Her Majesty (my cat), Angelique. I could never have aspired to become published without your undying support! I would like to offer special thanks to my dear friend Dian Bagent for her exquisite and radiant illustrations, and for his diligent persistence, to Neal Wooten, managing editor at Mirror Publishing, and to his hard-working staff. May joy and love and peace surround all of you, always and ... well, forever.

Eternally grateful,
Ruth Anne Meredith

How well do you know The Lands of Forever?

1.   What is the name of the ship that Teresa is traveling to America on?
2.   What is Teresa's (and Serena's) last name?
3.   How does Teresa preserve her diary?
4.   How do Teresa and Jacob escape the wreck?
5.   How old is Serena? Who is she?
6.   What does Dr. Birkwood suspect?
7.   What are the jobs of Jerry, Mike, Bob, Kate and Lindsey?
8.   What islands do they stop at before starting their mission?
9.   What three things do they escape the sinking Wavequeen with?
10.   Who does the team meet in the Cave?
11.   Where do they find the Dragons' eggs?
12.   How does Serena meet Nelson?
13.   What is a FrogStorm?
14.   Who is Theo, and what great Creatures is he afraid of?
15.   What other Creatures do they meet in the Golden Plains?
16.   Who is Mosslyn?
17.   What special characteristics do Dragons' eyes, Unicorns' eyes, and Fairy Dust have in common?
18.   What does the Rainbow do to Serena?
19.   How does Serena escape the Goblins' captivity?
20.   What fear does Nelson try to break Serena of at the Basstooth River?
21.   Who and what are Skywood and Fernwood?
22.   What is special abut the Fortress of Bendar?
23.   What is the Curse of the Forest of Many Eyes?
24.   How does Serena conceal Teresa's diary?
25.   What is the secret of the Sky Humans' language?
26.   Why does Nelson give Serena Pixie Powder?
27.   What happens to Nelson in the Blue Marsh?
28.   What was the Blue Marsh at one time?
29.   How are Lonvirc and Volcrin related?
30.   Who saves the Travelers from the Marsh Goblins?
31.   What is a Cyclops's eye used for?

32. What does Melabon give them?
33. How does the team travel to the Windy Meadows?
34. Who do they meet there?
35. What is different about the Trees of the Windy Meadow?
36. What are little Angels; who is Dawn?
37. Who are Beruga, Tarsena, Pinniose and Veldon?
38. What does the group see on their way up the Perpetual Mountains?
39. What does Jerry reveal?
40. How does the team get to Sparkline Mountain?
41. What Magical items does the Fountain of Youth carry in its Waters?
42. Of what substance is the Diamondia Castle made of?
43. What does Serena see when she looks into the Spring Water?
44. What does the Mother say when the group enters her Quarters?
45. Who is Juliana?
46. Who is the Heir to the Throne?
47. What happens to the Mother of Forever?
48. Does anybody want to go back to Earth when Serena asks them?
49. What is the full name of Serena's first daughter?
50. This is the Lands of Forever. Do you believe?

Grade yourself: How well do you know The Lands of Forever?

A= 50-45 questions correct: Let me ask you something very important. Did you originate in Forever?

B= 45-40 questions correct: Impressive! Excellent! Magnificent! Fabulous! Terrific!

C= 40-35 questions correct: Not bad at all!

D= 35-30 questions correct: Uhm … still not bad, but not good if you catch my drift.

E= (Yes, that's right. E, in a grading system. Anything is possible in Forever, you know!) 30-25 questions correct: Hrm … not so good at all.

F= 25-20 questions correct: Yikes! Try again!

1.   It is called the Cloudsail.
2.   Gordon is Teresa's and Serena's last name.
3.   To preserve her diary, Teresa ties it up with bootlaces and ribbons and puts it in an air-tight jug. Then, she screws a cork into it and throws it out to sea.
4.   To escape the wreck, Jacob makes a raft from the old floorboards of the sinking ship.
5.   Serena is 16 years old; she is an orphan who is taken in by an assigned guardian.
6.   Dr. Birkwood thinks there may be an unknown continent out there.
7.   Jerry is the team captain/body guard; Mike is the wildlife profession al; Bob is the technology specialist; Kate is the navigator and decoder; and Lindsey is the nurse.
8.   The Bahamas are the islands they stopped at.
9.   The crew members escape the Wavequeen with: 1) their scuba gear; 2) their waterproof knapsacks; and 3) their lives.
10.   They meet Keffle the Dragonling and her angry mother.
11.   They find the Dragons' eggs in a Cavern with a vicious Dragon guardian.
12.   Nelson saves Serena when she falls from fighting a Hippogryph in the air.
13.   A FrogStorm is when the Sky Rains Frogs.

14. Theo is a Halfbreed, Nelson's little brother, and he is scared of Sauro pods.
15. Other Creatures the team meets in the Plains: Unicorns, Bicorns and Tricorns, Gingel the Leprechaun, a CaveLore, a traveling colony of Fauns, a couple of CatEagles and Goblins.
16. Mosslyn is a little Faun Girl Serena's age that Serena becomes friends with.
17. Dragons' and Unicorns' eyes and Fairy Dust are all mood-dependant in color.
18. The Rainbow turns Serena's hair the colors of the Rainbow.
19. To escape the Goblins, Serena takes on a fake name, plays mute and tricks them by feeding them the Snoorbil Plant.
20. Serena is scared of heights over Water.
21. Skywood and Fernwood are friends of the escaping slaves and Serena's troop; they are Centaurs.
22. Bendar's interior décor is the outside inside.
23. The Curse of the Forest of Many Eyes is that the Monsters who live in it are invisible and harmless during the Day, but are mortal, dangerous Prowlers at Night.
24. Serena conceals Teresa's diary by making a little pocket in her skirt and hiding it there.
25. The Colored Humans speak backwards so the Prowlers don't overhear any secrets.
26. Nelson knows that Serena has always wished to fly.
27. Nelson is eaten by an irreversible Marlan QuickSand Pit.
28. Trick Question! It was once more than one thing: First, the Blue Marsh was an extension of the Windy Meadows; second, it was a battlefield; third, a great red Lake.
29. Lonvirc-Volcrin is the same Creature split in half: Lonvirc is the immortal Spirit, and Volcrin is the lifeless body.
30. Jerry saves them from the Marsh Goblins.
31. Cyclops's eyes are used for Fortune Telling.
32. Melabon gives them TeleStones.
33. To get from Middleton to the Windy Meadows, the team travels on Turtleback.
34. The team finds Nelson in the Windy Meadows.
35. The trunks of the Trees in the Windy Meadows are slanted and bent

from the persistent Winds.

36. Little Angels are baby Fairies, and Dawn is an orphaned Fairy who becomes Serena's friend.

37. Beruga, Tarsena, Pinniose and Veldon are all CatFoxes and friends of the discovery team.

38. In the Perpetual Mountains, the Travelers see MountLores, which are legendary Mountain Spirits.

39. Jerry reveals his true identity – and his name is Kevin.

40. In order to get to the Diamondia Castle from the Perpetual Mountains, the Travelers must ride on the backs of the Magical Pegasus.

41. Spring Water carries all sorts of Jewels from the Sparkline Mountain.

42. The Diamondia Castle and the stem and platform are all made of pure Diamond and nothing else.

43. When Serena looks into the Spring Water of the Pool of the Future, she sees herself, then Nelson, and then a little Angel Girl.

44. When the Travelers enter the Mother's Quarters, the Mother says, "The Heir to the Throne is in this room."

45. Juliana is the Princess of Diamondia Castle and Mother Teresa and Father Jacob's daughter.

46. Serena is the Heir to the Throne.

47. The Mother, after passing on her Power, is surrounded by a whirlWind and crystallized into a Diamond statue to be placed in the Window Chamber.

48. Nobody wants to go back to Earth at all; they believe that they are home.

49. The full name of Serena's first daughter is to be Angeliqúe Nimeesha Guenevere Esmeralda Leilani; and her initials spell ANGEL.

50. Do you believe?

CPSIA information can be obtained at www.ICGtesting.com
Printed in the USA
LVOW061146120312

272643LV00004B/3/P